MORRIS AUTOMATED INFORMATION NETWORK
0 1029 0377842 5

P9-DGX-005

Flight Lessons

Also by Patricia Gaffney

Circle of Three

The Saving Graces

Flight Lessons

A Novel

Patricia Gaffney

HarperCollins*Publishers*

HarperCollins books may be purchased for educational, business, or sales promotional use. For information, please write: Special Markets Department, HarperCollins Publishers Inc., 10 East 53rd Street, New York, NY 10022.

FIRST EDITION

Designed by Lindgren/Fuller Design

Printed on acid-free paper

Library of Congress Cataloging-in-Publication Data
Gaffney, Patricia.
Flight lessons / by Patricia Gaffney.—1st ed.
p. cm.
ISBN 0-06-018528-7 (hardcover)
1. Eastern Shore (Md. and Va.)—Fiction. 2. Family-owned business enterprises—Fiction. 3. Restaurants—Fiction. 4. Young women—Fiction. 5. Maryland—Fiction. 6. Aunts—Fiction. I. Title.

PS3557.A296 F57 2002
813'.54—dc21 2001051934

02 03 04 05 06 ❖/RRD 10 9 8 7 6 5 4 3 2 1

Always for Jon

ACKNOWLEDGMENTS

Thanks go to Sally McCarthy, Ralph Reiland, Chris the bartender, Tony the handsome server, and all the other helpful folks at Amel's Restaurant who gave me the lowdown. And to Gregory Pearson for *years* of entertainment.

Thank you to everybody who suggested names for the restaurant in this book, especially E.P., Jenny Smith, Beth Harbison, Kimberly Payne, and the readers of the *Hartford Courant.* Just because I didn't use them doesn't mean they weren't great.

All errors of fact about restaurants and restaurant kitchens are mine, and certainly not the fault of the book *Waiting* or its delightful author, Debra Ginsberg, who answered all my naïve questions kindly and tirelessly, and became a friend in the process.

I'm grateful to Mike Gaffney for, among other things, books, advice, and boating lore.

Last but not least, long overdue thanks and love to Marjorie Braman, my perfect editor, to whom I owe more than I have room here to say. Thanks for finding the best in me and knowing what to do with it.

After a good dinner, one can forgive anybody,
even one's own relations.
—Oscar Wilde

Flight Lessons

1

The problem, one of them, was that circumstances had split her life down the middle. She was always of two minds, the hopeful half versus the skeptic, optimist against pessimist. Or maybe it evened out and what she was now was a relativist, a contingency artist. Either way, it didn't help that at this late date a theme was taking shape, a motif or whatever you called it, a *pattern*, consisting of Anna walking in on trusted loved ones in bed with each other.

Then again, two times probably made a soap opera, not a pattern. She tried to lift her situation out of the excessively banal by imagining she had a connection with Sylvia Plath. Not that Anna was suicidal. Over Jay? Please. But it did help to think that she and Sylvia—she called her Sylvia; that's how bonded Anna felt—shared a context, a setting. Really, if anything, her circumstances were *worse*, because that London winter of '63 could not possibly have been any colder than Buffalo after a blizzard in early April—*early April*, for God's sake—and poor Sylvia's flat couldn't have been any icier than the windy, rattling loft Jay had left Anna to huddle in by herself while he cavorted with the voluptuous Nicole, whose apartment had a fireplace *and* central heat.

Jay's idea, the loft. They'd lived in a scruffy corner of it during the first year, the happy time, while he'd used the drafty rest for a studio. Eventually his metal sculptures outgrew it, though, went from enormous to dinosaurian, the ceiling wasn't high enough for the really monstrous ones, they needed a barn of their own. So he'd leased space in an old warehouse on the lake for a studio, and since then, almost another year, they'd had the whole basketball court of an apartment to themselves.

Except for the summer months, they'd spent most of the time in bed. Sleeping, reading, eating, having sex, etc., etc., but mostly trying to keep warm. Had ice crusted on the *insides* of Sylvia's windows? Had she huddled close to a ticking space heater with a blanket over it and her like a hot tent, and worried about setting herself on fire? If so, Anna could see why the kitchen stove had started to call to her, whisper that it was the warm answer. Lay your head flat on the metal rack, like a turkey roaster, close your eyes. Try not to mind the gas smell. Go to sleep.

Again, not that Anna was contemplating suicide. But she'd been betrayed in the cruelest way a woman could be (no, second cruelest; that life-dividing time at age twenty, that was still worse), and at least Ted Hughes had had the decency to conduct his affairs out of Sylvia's direct line of sight, with women she wasn't friends with or employed by. Some decorum had been observed. A little British restraint, missing in her case. Anna had walked in on Jay with Nicole, her boss, tangled up together in her own bed, three hours after she'd woken up from a laparoscopy for an ovarian cyst. A hospital procedure. Outpatient, yes, but still, she could've died from the anesthesia, people did. If Jay had been worried about her, he'd found a stimulating distraction.

Oh, it was such a stale, tired story, but here was another way she was trying to inject a little dignity into it—by casting herself in the role of tragic heroine. In a play by... some Greek, Sophocles, Aeschylus, she was vague on her classical playwrights this many years after freshman English. Her mother had died of ovarian cancer at the age she was now, thirty-six, and Anna had discovered Jay's infidelity on the very afternoon she was fully, fatalistically, expecting a call from the surgeon telling her she had the same disease. She didn't, her cyst was benign, nothing to worry about, would probably go away by itself—but she didn't *know* that then, and wasn't it all just too much, too full of awful significance, as if indifferent gods were playing with her life, making *literature* out of it, throwing in metaphors and parallels and corny portents—

No, it wasn't. It was just soap opera. Her life was like a Greek play only if you imagined a collaboration between Homer and Harold Robbins. And now here she was, trying to keep warm in the big, wide scene of the crime, listening to sleet peck at the frosted-over windows and wind slam them around in their uncaulked sockets, trying not to think about Jay and Nicole.

But it was hard when they'd been here so recently. Enjoyed themselves so thoroughly. They must've enjoyed themselves, otherwise they'd have heard the slow rise of the clanking elevator, at least noticed when the rickety metal doors squealed apart. The loft was wide open and wall-less, but Jay had built a two-sided partition to shield the bed from the view of—well, people like Anna. Intruders. He'd made it from tall, rusting strips of steel, like tree trunks, and painted them with bright birds and winding greenery—ah, a bower, you thought, how romantic. Until you went closer and saw that the birds had human heads with crazed eyes and mad grins, and they were doing lewd things with each other in the greenery. Then, how surreal, you thought, how sardonic and Boschian. How Jay.

She remembered very little, almost nothing of what she'd seen over the partition of the lovers in bed. Situational amnesia, no doubt, the way a car crash survivor can't remember a thing after the light turned red. Jay must've been on the bottom, because she had a vague picture in her mind's eye of his Rasputin hair crosshatching the pillow like an etching, black-on-white. But were he and Nicole visibly naked? Decently hidden under the covers? Blank. Mercifully blank: she had nothing to obsess about—this time—except the *fact* of betrayal, not the look of it.

She jumped when Jay's cat landed on the pillow and began to purr in her ear, kneading the duvet with his claws. He was only nice to her when he was cold. Chip off the old block. She lifted the covers, let him crawl down and curl up at her hip. "Miss your old man, huh?" she said, scratching him softly under the chin. "Tough."

The telephone rang. It couldn't be Jay; he'd already called, and the way they'd left things wouldn't encourage him to call back soon. Not for a couple of years. She grabbed the phone from the night table and pulled her arm back under the covers as fast as possible. On "Hello," she could see her breath.

"Hey, sweetie, me again. How're you feeling today?"

Big, huge mistake to tell Aunt Iris about Jay. But she'd caught her at a bad time last night; Anna had blurted out the truth as soon as her aunt said, "Honey, you sound *terrible*, did something happen?"

Now she forced vitality into her voice and said, "Oh, hi, Aunt I. Much better. Much stronger, really. Much."

"Good, because I've got some great news. Your Aunt Rose needs a manager for the Bella Sorella."

"What? Say that again?"

"Yeah, sweetie, she just told me. The old one quit over the weekend, apparently he wasn't any good anyway, so she's looking. Naturally I told her your situation."

Naturally. Aunt Iris was their go-between, since Anna and Rose didn't speak anymore. Well, not literally; in fact, they were excruciatingly cordial whenever Anna couldn't get out of going home—Maryland's Eastern Shore—for a wedding or a funeral; the last one had been about two years ago. They sent Christmas cards, too—"Have a wonderful holiday! Hope the New Year is your best ever!"—and Rose never forgot a birthday. Aunt Iris was the one who dispensed the lowdown on their *real* lives, though, or as much of them as they cared to share with her. Anna always weighed her words to Iris accordingly, and assumed Rose did the same. It was absurd, really, like a sit-com riff, "Tell your father to pass the salt," "Tell your mother to get it herself." Still, whatever worked.

"My situation," Anna said carefully. "So, what, you're saying Rose thinks *I*... she would like *me*..." She couldn't quite get the natural inference out in words.

"It's not just Rose, honey. Everybody thinks you should come home."

"Who's everybody?"

"The family. Me."

Anna smiled to herself, picturing seventy-year-old Aunt Iris's bony, bossy face, the total conviction in her gestures. She'd have the phone to her ear with her shoulder, because she'd need both hands to make her point. "But what did Rose *say*?" Anna asked. "About the restaurant."

"Well, she thinks the timing's perfect. You need a job, she's got a job, in fact she's in kind of a bind. Plus you've already got a house here to live in. A nice *warm* one," she threw in. "What are they having up there today, a cyclone? Typhoon? Quiet!" she called to the dogs barking in the background, the usual accompaniment to a conversation with Aunt Iris. She bred Labrador retriever–Border collie mixes for a hobby.

"Tell Rose," Anna said, "that managing a full-service restaurant would be a little different from running a forty-seat coffee house." Aunt Iris made scoffing sounds. "But I thank her for the offer. If it was one." A little explosion had gone off in her chest, though. Her skin prickled in the aftermath; she had to work to keep her voice casual. The last thing she wanted was Aunt Iris reporting back to Rose, "She sounded interested!"

"You're not saying no, are you? Come home and think about it, at least. That agent you got, the one that rents your house, he's let it go to the dogs. I'm not kidding, people are talking. You could get a citation. You need to come down here and take charge, some things you can't do by phone, not indefinitely. Now, listen, Anna, you know I would never tell you what to do."

"Never."

"When? When have I ever?"

"I said never."

"Sarcastically. You're a grown woman, far be it from me to give you advice about your life, but I have to say this for your own good. Leave that *sciocco* you live with and come home, where you've got people who love you and a job you could do with one hand tied behind your back. You're a Fiore, it's in your blood."

"Catalano, but—"

"Fiore on your mama's side, and Fiores run restaurants."

"You don't," Anna pointed out.

"I married too young, missed my calling. Honey, just come on home. It's time."

"Oh, God." Part of her wanted to. Part of her wanted to stay and make it up with Jay, part of her wanted to tear out pieces of him with her teeth, part of her wanted to leave him with no words at all, a silent, dignified exit. "I'm torn," she said.

"Be torn at home."

"Home, home—what makes you think I even—" She brought her voice down half an octave. "Okay, I'll take it under advisement, but listen, I have to go, I've got another call on this line." She didn't even try to make that sound true.

"What do you want me to tell Rose?"

"I don't know. Anything."

"I'll tell her you'll think about it."

"You can say that if you want."

Frustrated silence. Aunt Iris would never say so, it might jeopardize her role as intermediary, but Anna knew she was on Rose's side. Deep down, she thought Anna's lingering hostility was childish, she should've outgrown it by now, water under the bridge, her mother had been dead for seven years before her father and Rose had finally found some happiness together. That's what Iris thought.

Too bad it was a closed subject; otherwise Anna could have enlightened her on a couple of things. Chronologies, sequences of events. Iris thought she knew everything, but she didn't.

"Theo's not doing so well," Iris said, instead of hanging up.

"Who's Theo, again?"

She clicked her tongue. "Now, Anna. You know who Theo is."

"Oh, you mean Rose's boyfriend? That guy?" She did know who Theo was, and she wasn't sure why she always pretended she didn't. Except that the whole idea of *Theo* offended her—and that made no sense at all. As if Rose should be faithful to Anna's father's memory, all these years after she'd stolen him away from her own sister. Honor among thieves or something—Anna couldn't even follow her own reasoning.

Iris said, "Theo's still living on that old boat of his, and Rose can't make him move. She's so afraid he'll fall."

Theo had Parkinson's or something. "Sorry to hear that."

"She's spending a lot of time with him these days. It wears her out."

"That's a shame."

"Anna."

"What? You expect me to go home and run the Bella Sorella so Rose can have more time with her boyfriend?"

"Family pulls together in time of need."

"Oh—" Vulgarities piled up in the back of her throat, bitter as vinegar.

"But that's neither here nor there. This is where you should be, baby, not up there in no-man's-land. We love you and we want you to come home."

She got off the phone by swearing she had another call and hanging up.

"I used to be a decisive person," she told the hot, disgruntled cat when it crawled out from under the covers. "I could make decisions. I took chances."

Now it was too much to get out of bed and go to the bathroom. She'd have to put on socks and slippers and her woolly robe, she'd have to sit on the frigid toilet seat, wash her hands in ice water afterward. Too much.

Easier to lie here and wallow in all the grievances against her. Funny, she couldn't picture Jay and Nicole naked together in this bed only two days ago, but somebody else's nude body was as clear in her memory as a photograph: Rose's, scrambling out of bed as twenty-year-old Anna pushed open the door to her father's bedroom. Sixteen years later, she could still see the panicky blur of Rose's long arms and long white calves, her narrow back, the mad snatching up of a shirt from the floor to cover herself. She always wore her dark hair up, always in a bun, a twist, a chignon, she knew a million styles—but on that day it was down and disheveled, and somehow much more shocking than all her bare skin or even her tragic, appalled face.

The angle of her wrist as she'd pressed the collar of the shirt to her heart, that white-skinned clutch, the knuckles protruding like exposed nerves—*I've seen that before*, Anna had thought. And just then, the filmy curtain over a much older memory parted, and everything changed. That was the day disillusionment cut her life in half.

What was it Nicole had said when she'd seen Anna peering over the bower partition? Something, "Oh Christ," "Oh my God." Nothing memorable, definitely nothing mitigating.

Rose had said: "Oh, my dear, I am so sorry. This is—exactly what it looks like. But, Anna, it's never the way I wanted you to find out! We—Paul—" That's all she'd had time to say before the squeak of Anna's father's footstep sounded on the staircase.

What had Jay said when he'd seen her? Nothing at all, she didn't think. Well, he wasn't stupid; he'd understood the futility of words, but even more, the potential for sounding foolish. Jay never wanted to sound foolish. So he'd kept a dignified, actually a slightly *wounded* silence.

Her father had stopped dead in the bedroom doorway. He'd had on maroon sweats and new blue running shoes, a newspaper poking out from under his arm; he'd had an oily paper bag in his hand, coffee and croissants from the deli up the street. Under his morning beard, his face was ashen except for a smear of pink on each cheek. He said: "Annie, hey, what a great surprise! I—I'm just getting in myself, been in Newport News since Thursday. Hi, Rose." Anna said, "Daddy," horrified, but he went right on, "No—Rose stayed here last night, I knew that. How's that bat situation? Can you believe it, your aunt had a bat at her place, maybe more than one, could be a nest—" And then Rose said, "Oh, Paul. Don't," and that was the end of that.

Now Rose wanted her to come home. Just like that, pick up where they'd left off, let bygones be bygones. Why? Because she "loved" her? Anna's cynical half sneered at that, but the reluctant optimist pressed her hands together and speculated. Maybe Aunt Iris was right, maybe it was time. If not for a reconciliation, then a reckoning. How ironic—pattern or not, you had to give it that, at least it was ironic—that the same B-movie situation that had driven her out of town at age twenty was driving her back at thirty-six.

Could she really do this? It went against the grain of everything, every finely sanded principle and prejudice she had. Well, it wouldn't be permanent—that was the key. If she went, that's how she'd get through it. She'd work for Rose while she got her house fixed up and ready to sell, a matter of a couple of months, no more. Then she'd split. As long as everybody understood this was *temporary*, she could do it.

It still felt like giving in, though. She tried to think of a way to glorify going home, something to make it feel less like defeat, but no flattering, humiliation-averting comparisons came to mind. Damn. She might have to go as a grown-up. Not a mortal besieged by capricious gods, not a fierce, romantic, suicidal poet. An adult. If not capable of forgiving old sins, then at least willing to pretend, for the sake of peace, that they'd never been committed.

Clever Rose. Anna hadn't given her credit for so much cunning.

2

Iris called while Rose was drying her hair. "How are you? What are you doing?"

"I feel like I'm going on a date," Rose said. "I've tried on three outfits, and I'm going back to the first one, my old black suit. Do you think"—she laughed self-consciously—"do you think Anna's doing this, too?"

"I don't get why you're so nervous. She knows what you look like."

"Yes, but it's been two years. I just don't want her to think I'm an old lady."

Iris snorted.

"I don't want her to think I'm losing it."

"Baby doll, you haven't lost a thing."

"I don't want her to take the job because she feels sorry for me."

Iris cackled. Then, "I don't think there's too much danger of that."

"Why? What did she say?"

"Nothing, I'm just saying. If Anna takes this job, it'll be because she wants it, not because she's feeling charitable. Anyway, she's here, she didn't move back so she could tell you no."

That's what Rose was hoping, that the decision had already been made. "Iris, I'm rushing, and I still have to pick up Theo's lunch and take it to him."

"Okay, go. But call me tonight and tell me what happened."

"I will—although Vince will probably tell you first."

"I'm his mother, Vincent never tells me anything. You call tonight. And *relax*, will you? Anna's twice as nervous as you are."

"Do you think so?"

"You two, honest to God. This whole thing is ridiculous, it's always been ridiculous."

"*I'm* not the one—"

"I know, it's her, but now she's grown up and ready to act like a mature woman, maybe she'll bury the hatchet."

"It's not her fault."

"Oh, let's not get started on whose fault. I don't know why you always defend her. If you ask me, a person's entitled to one moment of self-righteousness in their life, and then they move on. They grow up and move on."

"You're right, let's not get started," Rose said, and they hung up.

She went back to drying her hair, which looked absurd and childish to her suddenly, much too short. Theo had told her not to cut it, and he'd been right. Anna would think she was a foolish old woman, trying to look young and smart. Maybe some makeup? She never wore anything but mascara and lipstick, but today, maybe some eye shadow? She was always buying it and then not using it. *This is a mistake*, she thought, even as she leaned in and daubed sparkly, taupe-colored powder in the creases of her eyelids. Better? No. Sixty years old and she couldn't put makeup on right.

Well, nobody had ever taught her. Iris was married and long gone by the time Rose turned fifteen and Mama said she could wear a little lipstick. Lily, only two years older, was the one who should've shown her, but already beautiful Lily thought of her little sister as competition. Already? Maybe she always had, even when they were children. Rose didn't know, and Lily took her secrets with her when she died.

What was wrong with this black suit? It didn't flatter her after all, it turned her skin sallow and the skirt was too long. Other than that, she looked like a million bucks. Too late now, and no point in changing anyway: this was one of those days when she wasn't going to like herself. They were coming more frequently than they used to. Inevitable at her age, but it was hard. Life didn't pace itself very gently or conveniently, or even humanely. She was losing too many things all at once.

"Four times I got up to pee last night. You know what I oughta do, Rose?"

"What?"

"Rig up a hose between my dick and the head. Save a lot of time."

"Good idea," she said, swishing Theo's dishes around in the tiny galley sink. If she worked fast, she could usually finish before the hot water ran out. He hated the low-protein, high-carb diet the neurologist had him on, but he'd eaten all the porcini polenta she'd brought him for lunch, and most of his salad. Whatever else he might be losing, he still had his appetite. "Or," she said mildly, "you could move off this boat and in with me."

"How the hell would that help? What the hell would be the point of that? What'll you do when I have to take a piss, drag the damn toilet into the bedroom?"

"No."

"Then how the hell would it help?"

She knew he wanted to yell at her. She wished he could, she'd have loved it if he could scream and shout, bellow out all his frustration. But he couldn't raise his voice above a hushed, breathy undertone anymore, and on the worst days it was only a whisper.

She watched him use both hands to pull his right knee up and brace his foot against the settee behind the cleared table, turning his back on her. His hair needed cutting. She shaved him every other day—his hands shook too much to do it himself—but she hadn't cut his thick, shaggy hair in weeks. Or trimmed the long, droopy mustache he took so much pride in. Used to, rather. Nothing about Theo's body pleased him anymore.

It still pleased her. He hadn't lost weight, so he still looked as solid and planted as he always had on his sturdy legs, his shoulders still thick, chest still wide and furry as a Chincoteague pony's. Short and brawny, he was as far from her old physical ideal—as far from Paul—as a man could be, and yet she'd liked the look of Theo from the beginning. What she regretted was all the trouble she'd given him at the start, when they were first dancing around each other, all that time she'd wasted making him wait. Caution was a virtue the middle-aged couldn't afford.

But he said his body didn't belong to him anymore, it belonged to some old, sick man, not Theophilus Xenophon Pelopidas, waterman, traveler, fisherman, boatbuilder, woodcarver, great lover of beautiful women. She loved it when he talked like that, when he was proud of himself and his old strength and vigor, his old life. But even his memory of himself was fading, and Rose didn't know what was crueler, the slow deterioration of his nerve cells or his ego.

"I brought you panna cotta for dessert," she said, unwrapping the foil around the plate. Calcium and carbohydrates, just what the doctor ordered. "Eat it while it's good and cold. Want some coffee? I'll make you a cup."

"If you'll have one with me."

"I can't, I have to get back. Anna's coming at one o'clock."

He sniffed his breath out to show her what he thought of *that*.

She set his plate on the table in front of him. "Move over," she said, wedging herself onto the narrow settee beside him. His old sailboat was called *Expatriate*. It slept two, just barely, and not with any unnecessary comfort or convenience. It had taken her four years to learn not to hit her head on bulkheads and hanging lockers, but how anyone could live full time in such cramped quarters was still beyond her. Everything on the boat was always fanatically neat and tidy, though, she had to give him that. Shipshape. Her own small apartment wasn't half as organized as Theo's minuscule cabin. And him such a scruffy, unruly man.

"How is it?" she asked, watching him scoop up the creamy dessert with the spoon held tightly in his rigid fist, swallowing with care.

"Who made it, you or Carmen?"

"Me."

"Then it's good. Best I ever ate. Melts in your mouth." He tweaked his lips in a sideways half-smile, all his facial muscles could manage these days. "You look pretty. More than usual." She thanked him by squeezing his thigh. "All dressed up for her highness."

She took her hand back. "You're going to like her, you know. You're going to be surprised."

"That I doubt."

"She's lovely."

"I know what you're trying to do, Rose, but you can't."

"What do you mean?"

"You can't put everything back the way it was."

"I know." She sighed. "But wouldn't it be nice? No, I know, but—Anna wasn't supposed to go away, that was never the plan."

"Whose plan?"

"The family plan. She was going to finish college and then come home and run the restaurant with me. I'd cook, she'd manage." Perfect, their hearts' desires; each of them doing what she did best and loved most.

Theo made a disgusted sound. "You think it's all your fault, every little thing that ever went wrong with that girl's whole life. That's bullshit."

"I know." In her head she knew it. "I love you. You're better than a priest, you know that? What would I do without you?"

"Be a lot better off." He patted her hand with his rough, gnarled one, the one with the missing little finger. She'd heard three or four different stories about how he'd lost the finger, including to a crab the size of a beach ball in the tidal swamps off Tilghman Island. She loved all his defects, all his scars and his weathered skin, his creaky old joints. But what she loved him for most was that he knew all her guilty secrets. No one else did but Anna, but Theo forgave her. No, that wasn't it—he didn't think she'd done anything that needed to be forgiven. He thought she was innocent.

"Am I too dressed up?" she asked him. "It's only a skirt. Too much? I don't want to look like I'm trying too hard."

"You look beautiful, to hell with what she thinks."

That again. "I have to go." She stood up and kept her hands to herself, didn't reach for him when he rocked back once and used the momentum to heave himself up from the bench. And she went first when he waved her toward the companionway steps, even though she'd rather have climbed the four stairs behind him. Just in case. She lived in fear that he would fall—then what? If he got dizzy and tripped, hit his head, hurt himself, and no one here to help him, what would he do? She'd asked him a hundred times to move in with her. So had Mason, his stepson. He wouldn't even discuss it. "Rather go in a nursing home," he'd say, "let strangers wipe the drool off my chin."

"What'll you do this afternoon?" She stood beside him in the cockpit, breathing in the fresh salt smell of the Chesapeake. Cork, Theo's old gray-muzzled mutt, half spaniel, half everything else, thunked his wispy tail in welcome from the patch of sun on the deck where he lay sprawled, stiff-legged. The sound of hammering echoed from a couple of boats away; reggae music drifted over from somebody else's radio. The warm spring weather was bringing out the owners who hadn't checked on their boats since last year. Sun glittered on the water, blinding. Seagulls wheeled and squawked.

"This afternoon? Maybe a round o' golf." Theo held the taffrail with one hand while he scratched Cork behind the ears with the other. "Maybe a pickup basketball game."

She usually laughed when he said things like that, but this time she slipped her arms around his waist and pressed her face against the nubby wool of his sweater. He went stiff. But presently she felt his hand on her back, patting her with a soft, helpless pressure.

Theo's eyes were a pale, bleached-out blue, as if he'd peered for too many years at the sky and the sea, stared at too many horizons. "You believe this spring?" he marveled, using his hand for a sunshade. "Smell the air, Rose. Water's warming up, starts the crabs to crawling. What I wouldn't . . ." He shook his head, trailing off.

What he wouldn't give to be chugging out into the bay on his ancient dead-rise crabber, setting out his lines before the sun came up, checking on his pots, hoping for a good catch of early-season blues. Life on the Chesapeake for all his waterman buddies started in April, and this was the first season since she'd known him that he wouldn't be in the middle of it.

"Shall I come over tonight?" she asked. "It'll have to be late, but we could go for a drive if you feel like it. Want to?"

He shrugged. "Saw a spotted sandpiper this morning. First o' the year. You can tell a spottie by the way she bobs her tail up and down." He caught her smiling at *spottie*. "Yeah, been talking to Mason," he admitted. His stepson knew everything about birds, even more than Theo now; in fact, he photographed them for a living. "They migrate by ones and twos, Mason says, not in packs. The females go around sleeping with—all the males they can find, regular swingers they are." He paused to take a few shallow breaths. "Then when they lay a nest of eggs, they make the *father* sit on 'em till they hatch."

"Smart birds. Is Mason coming over later?" Exercise was the only thing Theo could do anymore for his balance, and Mason took him on walks around the marina.

"Probably. Look." He lifted his right arm very slowly, pointing above the sway of the masts and lines of working boats and pleasure craft moored in the neighboring slips. "Yellowlegs. See 'em?" She saw three or four smallish, grayish birds swooping over the water. "I had one once. Let it go this time o' the year, join the parade."

"You had one?"

"There's greater and lesser. They're little shorebirds. Well, the greater's not so little. I found a lesser yellowlegs in the salt marsh once, had—a busted beak and fishing line tangled around one wing and a leg. Kept him all winter, let him go in the spring. They're moving up the coast now, the flocks. They go up to Canada to breed."

"Did he come back?" Sometimes they did, wouldn't fly away the first time Theo tried to release them, the injured terns and seagulls he had a habit of doctoring. Used to have—he couldn't do it now, his hands shook too much, he said, he couldn't hold them gently anymore. Now Mason was the bird doctor.

"No. Well, he come back by in the fall, like they all do. It's funny, I let 'em go and Mason captures 'em. Tries to."

"On film, you mean."

"Either way, they always come back."

"Or," Rose said, "they always leave."

"Depends on how you look at it."

Mason might look at it a little differently, she considered, having grown up with a stepfather who'd abandoned him about as regularly as some migrating bird. Who would probably still be leaving and coming back, leaving and coming back, if he hadn't gotten too sick to move on.

"I have to go," she said again, looking around for her bag. "Call me after dinner, or I'll call you. Is your phone on? Don't finish those dishes, I'll do them tonight. How did it get to be noon? Tell me the truth, Theo, do I look overdressed? It's just a *skirt*."

"You look fine, and I'll wash the goddamn dishes. I'm not a cripple yet."

She touched his cheek, and immediately the scowl between his thick gray eyebrows relaxed. "Old dog," she called him softly. "My old dog."

"Old lap dog. Got me in the palm of your hand, that's what you think."

"Oh, if only." She leaned in to brush her lips across his dry, chapped ones. "Be good till Mason comes, okay? Try?"

"My other dog walker."

"And don't fall overboard."

He smiled at that, but she didn't: it came too close for comfort. "We might go over to his place later and work on the boat," he mentioned.

"That would be nice. Perfect day for it." He and Mason were rebuilding an old sailboat together—or Mason was; Theo mostly watched. He sat in a chair in Mason's boat shed and gave orders. She kissed him quickly, then let him hold her arm as she stepped up onto the marina dock.

"I like you in a skirt," he strained his voice to say as she started off. "Nice stems for an old broad."

She made an Italian gesture he thought was dirty—a long time ago she'd told him it was obscene, but it wasn't. It always delighted him. Before she passed through the chain-link gate to the parking lot, she glanced back. He was holding on to the rail with both hands, lowering his backside slowly, cautiously, down to the sun-bleached wood of the cockpit seat, next to his old dog.

Theo's marina was about a mile from downtown, on a shallow peninsula whose north shore connected to the city by way of a two-lane drawbridge. Rarely was the bridge up, but today, of course, when Rose was running late, it was, so that an elegant, tall-masted schooner could glide out of the creek and into the river and the bay. She waited impatiently for the light to change, clicking her fingernails on the steering wheel. She tried to look at the water, the docked boats, the bridge, the pedestrians, as if she were new in town and seeing everything for the first time. Like Anna, almost. She'd grown up here, but hadn't been back except for fast dashes, in and out as quickly as possible, in almost two decades. Would she find her hometown drastically changed? It was bigger and more bustling than the city she'd grown up in, and full of tourists year-round now instead of only the summer. Would she like that? Or would she think it was spoiled? Rose could hardly decide herself.

The light changed. She crossed the bridge and drove carefully through the center square, watching for pedestrians holding maps, the ones most likely to stroll blindly into a passing car in their eagerness to ogle the pretty sailboats tied up at Town Dock. The Bella Sorella wasn't on the harbor, had no prospect of the water, not even a peek of blue. But it was on Severn Street, a one-way crescent attached at either end to the city's main tourist thoroughfare. It got foot traffic from both tourists and natives because of its midway location between dock and commercial district. Really, its situation couldn't be better. So why wasn't it thriving?

She slowed as she drove past the restaurant, straining again to see it through Anna's eyes. Carmen liked the maroon awning over the door, said it was classy, but Rose wasn't sure. Suddenly she was positive Anna would hate it. Pretentious, that's what it was, and too big for the narrow brick facade anyway. The yellow pansies in the planter by the door didn't look perky, they looked dusty and bedraggled; Louis had forgotten to water them. He'd shined the brasswork on the door, though, hallelujah, and he'd washed the bronze-tinted window. Had he swept the walk? She couldn't tell.

She turned in at the narrow, hard-to-maneuver access between the antique store and the florist's, right again at the alley, and parked in her little spot behind the garbage stockade. Twelve-twenty; Anna would be here in forty minutes. Luckily it was Wednesday, the slowest day of the week. They'd have a leisurely lunch of three-onion tart, Carmen's best appetizer, and then a lady-like crab salad, and they'd sit at the corner window table, best in the house. Lemon cake for dessert, and cappuccino—if Dwayne had managed to fix the dying machine one more time. They wouldn't talk business until after lunch, when they'd retire to Rose's office. She would make her business proposition, and Anna would...

She had no idea what Anna would do. Iris swore she was interested. She must be, otherwise she wouldn't have come home. Would she? Not just to sell her house—she could've done that long distance. Rose had spoken to her only once since she'd been back, on the telephone, and she'd sounded nice. Pleasant. Not that that meant anything. They'd been pleasant to each other for sixteen years.

She knew what was wrong even before she opened the back door. Nothing smelled like a grease fire as much as a grease fire.

"Grease fire," confirmed Jasper, the pantry cook, lounging against the laundry closet door and smoking a cigarette. She hurried past him, but she took heart from his sleepy-eyed slouch; he'd be a *little* more excited if the kitchen had burned down.

It hadn't, but the massive grill and the stainless steel wall behind it were a scorched black mess under a runny coat of sticky white flame retardant. Marco and Carla looked up from their prep work long enough to say "Hi," with pained, sympathetic faces. Dwayne called over the noise of the dishwasher, "The Sardine did it!" flashing his gold tooth when he grinned.

Carmen quit pounding chicken breasts with a wooden mallet. "It's not as bad as it looks. At least he got it put out before the smoke set off the sprinklers."

"Thank God." What a nightmare that would've been. "How did it start?"

Luca, the grill chef, "Sardine" to his mates because he was short and he came from Sardinia, straightened up from wiping greasy foam off the wall. "*E colpa mia*," he mumbled. "Too much grease, the fire went too high." His ears blazed hot pink; his shoulders slumped. "Sorry, Chef."

"All right," Rose said shortly, "okay, just get it cleaned up. My God, what a mess." Carmen would've beaten him down enough by now, no sense in taking any more whacks at him. And poor Luca was so sensitive, he'd quit over the mildest reproach, thinking he was doing her a favor. He always came back, but she couldn't afford to lose him today. "Get that stuff off the floor first so nobody slips, don't worry about the rest until after lunch. Any grill orders, use the broiler. Or pan sauté—use your imagination."

Luca brightened. Until he heard Carmen's sarcastic snort, then his ears turned pink again. "Okay, Chef." Head down, he went back to mopping up dirty foam.

"Shirl called in sick," Carmen informed her next.

Shirl was the pasta chef. "Can you cover?"

"Me or Luca, yeah. Slow day today."

"Anything else?"

"You're a waiter short. Only Vonnie and Kris, and Tony's busing."

"We should be okay as long as it stays light. Everything else on track? No problems?"

"Nothing to speak of." Heavy, sweating, red-faced Carmen smacked a chicken strip with brute violence, as if it personally offended her. She was the assistant chef, the sous, Rose's right hand in the kitchen. She was also her cousin, and an old maid like her, so they still shared the name Fiore. Luckily for Carmen, her mother hadn't been as enchanted with naming her children after flowers as Rose's had. Luckily—because it was hard to think of a flower that would've suited Carmen and not sounded like an unkind joke. She weighed two hundred pounds. But she carried it well, and she was strong as a man. The cooks were terrified of her, called her "Sarge" behind her back for obvious, unimaginative reasons—and probably much worse things Rose wasn't privy to. She had a short fuse and a surly disposition, and the lowest tolerance for incompetence of anybody Rose had ever known. But no one was more loyal than Carmen, to the restaurant, of course, but especially to Rose. She couldn't imagine the kitchen without her.

"Did Sloan's guy have some nice crabs?" Rose asked her, backing up toward the refrigerator. "I was thinking of having the salad on that sourdough bruschetta if it's—"

"No crabs. I got sole. It'll be fine, I'll roast it with some lemon and bay."

"What? Oh no. Sole? No, I wanted something lighter and, I don't know, local. Sole?" She wrinkled her face, wanting Carmen to talk her into it.

"I can't do the onion tart, either, there aren't any leeks. I can do a zucchini-parmigiana salad, but it'll have to be with pine nuts because nobody ordered walnuts." The grim pursing of Carmen's lips was more satisfied than sorry, which only confirmed what Rose already knew—she was even less thrilled at the prospect of Anna's visit than Theo was. It bothered Rose, but how could she take offense? In their minds, Carmen and Theo were protecting her. They thought Anna was going to break her heart.

"Is the table set, at least?" she asked, resigned.

"I don't know. Ask Vonnie."

"All right—anything you need me for in here?" She wanted to put on fresh lipstick, comb her hair, gather herself for a few minutes in the bathroom. "You're nervous as a girl," Theo had chided her this morning. It was true.

Carmen smirked. "Well, Flaco's behind, you could help him wash greens. Have to cover up your finery with an apron, of course." Her pale, red-lashed eyes flickered over Rose's black suit with amusement, maybe contempt.

"It's just a skirt!" She threw up her hands and stalked out of the kitchen.

Vonnie had set the corner table with the cobalt glasses and the handpainted plates, and pretty saffron-colored napkins folded under the good flatware. They had enough of this service for small parties, not enough for the whole dining room, which seated ninety-seven. There were freesias in the bud vase, not the usual carnation, and the noonday sun cutting across the crisp white tablecloth made a soft, somehow sophisticated diagonal, Rose thought. She caught Vonnie's eye across the room and gave her a smile and a nod—*good job*. Vonnie, her best server, put up her thumb and grinned in agreement.

Not many lunch customers; the restaurant was only about a third full. That was fortunate under the circumstances, and not unusual for midweek, especially before May when the boaters started coming in earnest, but—what would Anna think? She'd think business was slow, and she'd be right. Would it be *too* slow for her? She'd been working in a very modish-sounding bistro sort of place, the Industrial Strength Coffee Shop or some such; she'd be used to trendy people and high prices, European dance music. The Bella Sorella was going to look hopelessly out of date to her. And dowdy. Boring. If she took the job of running it, she'd do it out of pity.

Through the window, Rose saw about half a dozen elderly women, one with a walker, pass slowly in front of the building and stop under the awning. They had a little confab, scanning the menu, checking the name on the door. They decided to come in, and she thought, *Good, Anna will think we do* some *business.* She crossed the room to greet them, and almost immediately another small group of women, much like the first, came in behind them. "Hello, how are you," she said to the first bunch, white-haired and respectable in low-heeled shoes, carrying guidebooks and maps. A tour group.

"Hi," said their leader, the spry one at sixty-ish—Rose's age. "Do we need a reservation?"

"Oh, I don't think so, not today. How many are you?"

"Twenty-six, or we will be when the others get finished at the Nautical Museum."

"Not a problem," Rose said, smiling warmly, confidently, while her mind raced. Vince was coming in early, he could take over from Eddie and Eddie could help wait tables. That would be three servers plus Tony, and Flaco could help bus—

"We were going to call first, but my sister lives here and she said it's usually not crowded."

"Isn't that nice." They were pushing inside, bunches of women, several with canes and one in a wheelchair, and now a couple of old men, backing Rose up against the host's podium. "Have a seat—welcome, hi—sit anywhere, won't you? Your server will be right with you."

"Yo, Chef, I'm taking off now!"

Rose spared half a second to grin at Eddie, bartender and part-time waiter, while she wiped vinaigrette from the side of a plate of mesclun and goat cheese and slid it down the pickup. "Another one, Jasper, and three plain house with Italian. Eddie, when your drink orders slow down, help Vonnie and Kris—we're short and they're swamped. Where's Vince? I thought he'd be here by now."

"Hey, sorry, Chef, I gotta take off."

She looked up. "Take off? What, now? Are you crazy?"

"Hey, sorry, but I got a doctor's appointment and it's really important. I fixed it up with Vince, he'll be here any sec."

Dupes were coming in as fast as Vonnie and Kris could stick them on the board. "Then don't leave until he gets here."

"But if I don't go now I'll be late."

"You can't leave now, don't even think about it."

"C'mon, these old ladies aren't exactly throwing the booze back, you know?"

"Make drinks till Vince comes. I mean it. Here!" she called before he could get out the door. "Take these on your way—table six."

"Who gets what?"

"Read the dupe." She turned away to help Luca, who was already behind and the big hits hadn't even started. Vonnie came in with more orders. "We're out of ravioli," Rose called to her. "Only three more chicken Carmens, and I'm not sure the fettuccini's—" She stopped. Vonnie's sweet, placid face was chalk-white. "What happened? What's wrong?"

"Guy at a four-top with two women and another man."

"Yes?"

"Kris thinks he's the food critic for *City Week*."

"No. No, no, please no. Oh, my God. Carmen?"

"I heard." Pure terror had drained her face, too. The three women looked at each other with wild eyes for a few still, motionless seconds.

"Okay, then," Rose rallied. "Everybody! Listen up—"

Eddie stiff-armed the door open and yelled from the threshold, "Okay, Vince is here, I'm gone. Lady just came in, she's at the bar. Hey, she looks just like you, Chef, it's amazing. Vince says she's his cousin. What's that make her, your niece?"

3

Anna went dead calm the minute she saw Rose. After all the worry and nerves and second thoughts, watching her sweep across the dining room with her long, still-lithe stride, waving, beaming, vivid as a black-and-white photograph except for a flirty streak of red across her mouth—Anna felt the relief of a soldier who finally hears the first mortar shell blow after an all-night wait in a muddy trench. *It's only Rose*, she thought. Rose, not formidable at all with her glad face and her worried eyes. *She's scareder than I am.*

"Anna!" she cried from a distance, arms open wide. "Oh, Anna, finally!"

Maybe her posture was stiff, maybe she had a look in her eye—they ended up shaking hands instead of embracing, and at the moment when Rose would've kissed her, Anna let go and stepped back. Then they both smiled too hard, embarrassed.

"Really good to see you," Anna said, folding her arms, leaning back against the bar. "You haven't changed." Not true; Rose's big dark eyes and her beaky, theatrical nose were the same, and her smile, so sweet and melancholy, hadn't lost the power to cripple and disarm, if you were stupid enough to let down your guard. But she looked tired. The mystery of her, the dark-saint quality that used to fascinate and beguile, had begun to fade, and the smooth beauty of her face couldn't hide it or stop it. She'd grown older, and finally it showed.

"Oh, you're here, I'm so *glad*, and how beautiful you look." Her voice was the same, still rich and earthy, intimate as a touch on the cheek; Anna had forgotten how easily it could charm her. "I just cut my hair, now I wish I hadn't. How *chic* you are, Anna, that suit is fabulous."

"Thanks." They'd dressed alike, she registered dully, although Anna wore her black jacket and cream-colored shirt with pants instead of a skirt. Another thing she'd forgotten was that they had the same taste in clothes. The same weakness for them, too; unless Rose had changed, they were still her biggest vice.

"Has Vince been taking care of you? I'm sorry I wasn't here when you came—but it's a little hectic in the kitchen right now, nothing terrible, just—oh, you know, the usual."

"Don't worry about it. Anything I can do to help?"

"No, oh no, sit here and relax, please. Do you want something to tide you over till lunch, a salad or something—"

"No, I'm fine."

"—because we might be a little bit late with our meal, is that all right? You don't have an appointment, do you, nothing you've got to rush for?"

"No, nothing. Do what you have to do, I'm happy right here."

"You are so nice. I'll be as quick as I can." Her hands fluttered, giving her nerves away. She looked reluctant to leave, as if this first meeting hadn't gone as she'd wanted and if she stayed longer she could fix it. Anna felt the same awkward dissatisfaction, but she didn't want to fix it. She'd come for a job, not to fix things.

Vince returned from delivering drinks to a table. "Hey, Aunt Rose." He leaned across the bar to finish in a lower tone. "Vonnie told Carmen he ordered mussels, and his date wants the veal chop."

Rose's smile froze.

"Who?" said Anna.

"No one, just a customer." She waved for Anna to sit, sit, be comfortable. "I'll be with you shortly. That's our table over there, so stay here or go and sit down, whatever you like. Do you still like a Strega sour? Just tell Vincent what you want—"

"Go," Anna insisted.

Rose sent her a grateful smile and hurried away.

Vince was Anna's favorite cousin. The youngest of Aunt Iris's five children, the thirty-year-old "baby," he'd been a gawky, scrawny adolescent boy when she left home, but she'd liked him best because he was so funny. And happy, such a good-natured little nerd. He'd taught her how to play chess when she was fifteen and he was nine, and she'd taught him how to dance. When she was in college, she'd given him advice over the phone about girls, and it must've been good stuff because these days, at least according to Aunt Iris, women swarmed around him like gnats.

"Look at you," he said as he poured gin, Strega, and sour mix into a shaker. "You look great, Anna. Everybody's so glad you're back." He had a soft brown crewcut and huge soft brown eyes, a bony, priest's face, and a very cool beard, just two thin strips of whisker running along the edge of his jaw, connecting his sideburns. He was still skinny, but he had broad, handsome shoulders. And beautiful hands; she could imagine women sitting here, ordering drink after drink just to watch him work.

"It's great to see you, Vince. I don't know if I'm back, though," she clarified scrupulously. "I'm here, that's . . . " She smiled, made a vague gesture with her hand. "All I can say for now."

"Oh, yeah, I know, but I'm hoping. We're all hoping."

"Thanks. We'll see."

"It's crazy today," he said, pulling down soft drinks from the tap.

"I can see. What's up?" The place was crowded, but she could see only two servers working the floor and they were getting slammed. She recognized that controlled panic under their smiles, the fast walk that wanted to break into a run. "Is it always like this at lunchtime? I mean . . . a lot of old ladies?"

"No, it's a tour group, they're from Baltimore, Leisure City or whatever. They just showed up, no notice, no nothing."

"Yikes." She stole a look in the mirror at Rose, zigzagging gracefully among tables, asking people how they were doing, if they needed anything, if they were having a nice time. She had a way of touching, the lightest brush on the shoulder, a soft pat on the hand, that could hypnotize total strangers, tame or calm them down, whatever she thought they needed. The tactile opposite of a cattle prod, but with the same result: people did what Rose wanted them to do.

She'd stopped at a four-top, two couples, and out of a well of complicated emotions Anna had to admire the solicitous tilt of her head, the casual, interested but never servile incline of her body, her hands clasped at the waist, and now splayed playfully on her hips as she leaned back to laugh, with just the right amount of sincere appreciation, at some guy's jest. She looked fifty from here, no older, still tall, straight, boyishly slim. She'd never colored her hair, and the new style, artless black and silver spikes that complemented her strong face, made her look rakish, practically punk. Anna had been hoping for *something*, but now she couldn't remember what it was—that Rose would've grown bent and slow in the two years since she'd seen her? That she wouldn't have changed at all? In any case, neither was true. She looked tired, but figuring out what other ways Rose might've changed, exactly what she might have lost or gained—that would take some observation and interest, some attention.

Resentment was a sour, unrewarding emotion. It filled Anna up when she realized that she didn't know anybody as interesting as Rose. Anyone she'd rather observe. Sullenly.

"Yeah, first we get hit with the tour group," Vince was telling her, "and then somebody spots a reviewer."

"A reviewer? Oh, my Jesus." In instant sympathy, her blood ran cold. "Who? That guy?" The ginger-haired, heavyset fellow Rose was bending over?

"I think so, gotta be him or the other guy. I know his name is Gerber and he writes a column for the weekly. Meanwhile, we're short-staffed on the floor, and the pasta chef calls in sick at twelve, she's got cramps or something. We are screwed so many ways."

"No veal chops," Anna guessed.

"Fire in the big grill this morning. But that's not the worst." He loaded the drinks onto a round brown server's tray, then started a vodka and tonic. Anna couldn't imagine how things could be any worse. "The pasta cook, this incredible flake named Shirl, wait'll you meet her—she's got really good penmanship, she's like a calligrapher, so she's been writing up the specials for us on the blackboard. You passed it coming in."

She nodded. Linguini al pesto, scallops Parmesan, mussels in garlic tomato sauce. Nothing very exciting, she'd thought. "What's the problem? Oh—oh, shit."

"Right. She didn't do it today because she didn't come in, and nobody remembered to change it. The food critic for *City Week* wants to order mussels, and it's *yesterday's* special, it's *gone*."

"Oh, Vince." Nothing was worse, or potentially better, in the restaurant business than a food critic's surprise visit. She remembered a family story from before she was born, when a food writer from the Baltimore paper had shown up at the Flower Café—the first incarnation of the Bella Sorella on Severn Street, back when it was only a pizza and spaghetti joint and didn't even have a bar. When Liliana, Anna's grandmother, a very tough customer, a no-nonsense woman not known for squeamishness—another family legend had it that she used to wring chickens' necks barehanded for her papa's little *ristorante* in Ventimiglia—when Liliana heard from the waiters that a critic was in the house, she went outside and threw up. But then she came back in and got to work.

"I know," Vince said, shaking his head. "To tell you the truth, we could use a good review right about now. If he'd say one nice thing, we could run it with an ad in the daily. It would really help."

One nice thing. Even if Rose could coax Mr. Gerber out of the veal and mussels without him even knowing it, something entirely within her powers, Anna could still imagine phrases like *caters to an older crowd* showing up in his column. *Uncommonly slow service. Overwhelmed floor staff.*

Rose had last words at the critic's table and headed for the kitchen, conspicuously not hurrying.

Anna stood up, took off her jacket, hung it on the back of her chair, and followed.

The kitchen was all heat, noise, and chaos. Every station was getting hit, plates wouldn't even fit on the pass anymore, dupes were hanging off the slide like Chinese lottery tickets. "Fire number eight!" a woman was screaming. "Pickup eight, goddammit!" She had her broad back turned, but Anna recognized Carmen's ferocious bellow easily; she'd withered and flinched under it often enough as a teenager, when she'd helped out in the kitchen or filled in for somebody on the waitstaff. Rose was over by the walk-in, throwing a chef's apron over her head, tying it twice around her waist, fingers flying. When she saw Anna, her game face cracked. She came toward her with a chagrined look in her dark, dramatic eyes. Anna had never been able to resist them.

"Good thing I wore the uniform," she blurted out before Rose could tell her to go, overwhelm her with gracious no-thanks. "Black pants, white shirt. Look, I even wore flats."

"Anna, no."

"You're getting slammed, so let me help out, okay? Are the table numbers the same? Somebody can spot me. I won't do any harm—what's some broken glass, a little soup in a lap."

Rose ran a frenzied, indecisive hand through her spiky hair. Then she laughed. "Take the first four tables along the banquette, one through four, back to front. Seat one is six o'clock, they go clockwise."

"Got it."

"Do soups and salads first, if any are still up there. And help Tony, he's your busboy—I think some people never even got bread."

"Right." She started to back up, but Rose seized her by the shoulders and hugged her, a fast, shy grab, before she could step away. *Gotcha.* Anna grinned in spite of herself.

"Anna, thank you—*I'm so sorry.*"

"Forget it, this'll be fun. I used to be a pretty good waitress, don't you remember?" She turned away quickly, dismayed by Rose's delighted smile. *Shit,* she thought, *I* started it. *Rose* was supposed to be the one who got them going on nostalgic reminiscing. Anna was supposed to quell her with blank, uncomprehending stares. She'd had it all planned.

Rose was right, their first meeting wasn't going at all the way it was supposed to.

4

Stop staring, Rose told herself, but it wasn't easy. The rush was over, and they were finally sitting down, and Anna looked so pretty. Her forehead shone, her cheeks were flushed, her black eyes sparkled. With her heavy hair falling down from two tortoiseshell barrettes, she didn't look sophisticated or remote or cool any longer, she looked like herself. She was even laughing—at Vonnie, who set an Aqua Madonna and lime in front of her and laughed back. In the frantic seventy minutes they'd waited tables together, they'd made friends. Rose listened to their banter with a small smile, keeping her face mild, disguising her giddy gladness. Anna retreated when she detected gladness. And she suffered affection from Rose only on her own terms: stingily.

"Oh, God, it all came back to me, why I could never do what you do," she was saying to Vonnie. "My feet are killing me, and I ran around for what, an hour? How do you stand it?"

"Oh, honey, it was a tough crowd today," Vonnie consoled her, a hand on one full hip, a tray tucked under her arm. "Did you ever hear so many allergy stories? And everybody had to have substitutions. But they were sweet, weren't they? Nice old ladies."

Vonnie was the server Rose always asked to train newcomers—nobody else had the patience for it. Divorced, motherly, endlessly good-natured, Vonnie joked about the Zen of table service, but she definitely did her work in a zone of some kind, a state of natural grace. She was a lifer, not in a holding pattern like the others, waiting for a better job to come along. Vonnie wasn't *waiting* for anything, she was here.

"So, honey, did you make any tips?" she asked Anna.

"Yeah, but only enough to cover what I broke."

They laughed again—music to Rose's ears. Vonnie said, "Bet you two are starving, I'll bring your salads right away," and hurried off.

Rose glanced around the mostly empty dining room, monitoring the cleanup, catching Vince's eye at the bar, but what she really wanted to do was look at Anna for an uninterrupted hour or two. Just feast her eyes on her until the connection between the girl and the woman came back into focus. Until she *recognized* her again.

But that wasn't allowed. The key to success was going to be feigned indifference. *None of this matters much, stay or go, nothing important hinges on what you think of me.* They were like a divorced couple, meeting again long after the bitter breakup, pretending all the messy emotions were in the past. At least Rose was pretending; God only knew what was going on in Anna's head.

Already she'd withdrawn a little, if only by rolling down the sleeves of her blouse and putting back on her handsome suit jacket. Back to business. They looked alike, aunt and niece—everybody said that. Rose could see a superficial something of herself around Anna's eyes, dark and heavy-lidded, and most especially in the deep brackets at the corners of her mouth. From smiling, presumably, although she hadn't done a great deal of that so far in Rose's presence. She searched for a glimpse of Paul somewhere, a hint of his humor and warmth—they were there, she knew it. But they were hiding.

What she could never see, now or twenty years ago, or thirty—was Lily. The fair-haired, angel-faced middle child. Lily was the feminine one, they used to say, with her pale skin and high, round bosom, her restless eyes full of mystery and impatience. A different species from the rest of the Fiore women, who were dark and long-boned and languid, practically masculine in comparison. How that must gall Anna. How she must hate looking more like her faithless aunt than her sainted mother.

"Your aunt tells me the last tenants left your house in terrible shape," Rose opened harmlessly—but what a relief to be speaking *to* Anna, not *through* Iris.

"Yeah, that's an understatement," Anna said, scowling. "Who were those people, gypsies? It's a wreck, I'd sue the rental agent if I could afford it."

"Uh-oh. Any major damage?" Lily and Paul's narrow clapboard colonial on Day Street skirted the historic district, but it wasn't a landmark home, it was just old.

"*Everything*, you name it. Number one, the roof leaks. The furnace makes funny noises, I need a new hot water heater, probably new pipes. Wiring. The appliances are conking out one by one."

Rose shook her head in sympathy. Vonnie brought their salads then, and they ate for a while in silence. "Is it . . . " Rose took a sip of water and cleared her throat. "Are you finding it hard to be back? Being in the old house again? I can imagine it might be sad. A little."

"No, it's not sad, why would it be? It's a stranger's house, everything's been painted or paneled over by now, Rose. The Catalanos got erased a long time ago."

Rose, she called her. Not Aunt Rose, not for a long time. "I should've gone over and checked on it for you. I never even thought. Rental agents, I guess all they care about—"

"Why should you have gone over and checked on my house?" Anna pretended that was a straight question, didn't emphasize *you* or *my*. She didn't have to.

"Oh, I don't know," Rose said lightly. "I guess I could've called someone if I'd seen, you know, bomb-making materials in the front yard."

She finally had to smile. "The carpet in my old bedroom is full of BB's. Every time I vacuum, I get up about a hundred more."

"BB's?"

"It must've been a teenager's room. I'm thinking he spilled a big box of BB's on the shag rug and never told his mom."

"Remember—" Rose coughed, covering up the word. No memories allowed today. But she smiled to herself, remembering the day Anna, six or seven years old, had dumped an entire bottle of olive oil on the floor in the restaurant office. Rose had walked in and found her trying to move the heavy desk to cover it, hide the spreading stain. "I was changing things around," she'd invented, then burst into tears. Rose took her in her arms and uncovered the truth—that she'd been making "a fusion" for her mother, a surprise present, olive oil and basil in a pretty jar she'd already decorated with a ribbon. "Don't tell Mommy I spilled, okay, Aunt Rose?" and Rose promised she wouldn't. They'd cleaned the mess up together, and then Rose had taken Anna in the kitchen and showed her how to make a real oil infusion, pureeing fresh rosemary and marjoram in the big food processor. She couldn't remember if Lily, who was managing the out-front side of the business in those days, had ever found out about the accident. She must have—the office had smelled like basil for days, and the rug was never the same. But if she had, Rose wasn't the one who'd told her.

"So," Anna said, "the roof is the first thing, but it's just number one on a very long list."

Rose had an idea. "I know someone who might be able to help you with that. Maybe other things, too."

"A roofer?"

"No, a friend. Of a friend. I have a friend whose stepson built his own house, so he's handy."

"Well, if he can fix an old slate roof, he's hired. Let me have his number."

"No, you should go see him. It's not far. He's always home, but he doesn't answer his phone. Much."

Anna frowned.

"Because he's in his studio so much. He's a photographer."

"But he fixes roofs?"

"Maybe." Rose smiled, shrugged. "Worth a try. Mason Winograd is his name—I'll give you the address."

"Okay," Anna said doubtfully. "But I'd rather just call him."

"You'd have better luck stopping by."

Carmen had roasted the Dover sole simply, just lemon, oregano, and bay. "Mm," Anna said, "delicious," and seemed to mean it. They talked about neutral subjects in low-key, offhand voices, very polite, very aware. Eventually Rose relaxed enough to take a chance and say, "I was sorry to hear about your friend, Jay. That you'd broken up. The circumstances."

Anna nodded. "I don't miss him."

"You'd been together quite a while."

She reached for her glass, sipped. "Two years. I miss his grandfather more than I miss him."

"His grandfather?"

"Nice old guy. We were friends."

"Two years is a long time, though." Her longest ever with one man, as far as Rose knew; and since leaving home, her longest stay in one city. As she got older, the duration of her romantic relationships had gradually been lengthening, and thank goodness for that. There had been a time in her twenties when she'd been with a different man every—*week*, it seemed. Not that she'd ever shared that information with Rose; they hadn't even been speaking back then. Iris was their interpreter, and she'd had hellish tales to tell. An indirect form of punishment, Rose had always suspected, and very effective, too. But mercifully obsolete these days.

"It must've been hard for you," she ventured, "moving out, leaving Buffalo. Your friends, your job."

"No, not really." Anna looked at her with narrowed eyes, and Rose realized too late the trap she'd walked into. "Leaving's not hard at all when two people you trust stick a knife in your back."

She felt her face grow warm. "Oh, Anna." How stupid to think she might have let some of the bitterness go. "We have to talk, I know—I just didn't think we'd—"

"No, Rose, we don't have to talk. We absolutely don't have to talk. We said it all, don't you remember?"

As if she could forget. After Paul died, in fact on the night of his funeral, they'd said all sorts of hurtful, revelatory things to each other. After that, years had to pass before they'd even gotten back to the stage of politeness.

Now it only took minutes—that was progress, wasn't it? After a short silence, during which the food Rose put in her mouth tasted like chalk, Anna's shoulders lost their combative set. The wine was very good, she mentioned; was it a Sancerre? She still had so much unpacking to do, how did one person acquire so many *things*? What a pretty spring they were having—she didn't miss Buffalo at all—was May still the month when tourist season really started?

Pathetically grateful for these overtures, Rose met her halfway with small talk of her own, and the bad moment passed. *So*, she thought. Was this how they were going to deal with each other? Treat their mutual bad behavior—in her old age, she'd learned to spread the blame around a little, not keep it all to herself—as something in the remote past, something they'd already handled so there was no need to mention it again? That would certainly be easier. Another thing about old age: it heightened one's aversion to risk. But would it be possible? It went against Rose's nature to ignore the obvious and bite her tongue indefinitely. Even with everything at stake. And Anna might hate to hear it, but it was true—in that way she was just like her.

. . .

"You know I've never run a restaurant on my own, right?"

"You've run a café."

"Industrial Coffee was tiny, it served silly sandwiches, wood-roasted artichoke and celery root on poppyseed baguettes—it was more of an art gallery than a restaurant. I mean literally—it had an art gallery in back."

"But you ran it."

"I did." Anna shrugged, giving up that point. They were having coffee in Rose's office, which doubled as a storeroom for anything that didn't fit in the laundry closet, the pantry, or the cellar. Anna sat on the section of sofa that wasn't covered with files, papers, and cardboard boxes, and Rose perched on a cleared edge of her desk to be closer to her. "But why can't you manage this place yourself?" Anna asked her. "I don't understand what you need a manager for anyway. You say Carmen's doing most of the cooking now—why can't you work front *and* back? God knows you've always been good with customers."

"Thanks," Rose said, although Anna hadn't made that sound like much of a compliment. In her mind, Rose *manipulated* people—she'd heard that from Iris years ago, when Anna's sense of injustice had been at its high and mightiest. "But the thing is, I don't have time for both anymore. I'd like to keep doing some cooking, I don't want to give that up completely, ever—if I have to stop doing one, I'd rather it was the business. So I need someone I can trust to take over that side. The last manager I had was a disaster."

"Why do you have to stop doing one or the other?"

Anna looked genuinely puzzled, and Rose decided to be complimented by *that*. "My dear," she said, "I'm sixty years old."

"So?"

She laughed. "Thanks again."

"No, but—are you sick?"

"I'm not. But I have a friend who's ill. I'm spending more time away from the restaurant to be with him. I can't do what I used to do by myself anymore, and it's a situation that's—not going to get any better."

"Oh. This is—I forget the name, Aunt Iris mentioned a guy, somebody you..."

"Theo." Rose doubted very much that Anna had forgotten his name.

"Theo, right. I didn't know it was that serious. I'm sorry."

"It's something we're learning to live with."

Small silence. Anna said, "So. Okay, tell me. How's business? How many covers do you do a day? Roughly. What's your food cost? How many people do you employ, total, full time and part time?"

"About thirty-five—yes, I want you to see everything, I want you to look at the books, understand the complete situation." Rose stood up. "I can show you—"

"I don't want to look at books, not now. You just tell me."

She took a breath. "Well. Things are slow. They started slowing down a year or two ago. No, longer than that, three years. We're still in a good location, in fact it's better than ever, and the city's doing nothing but grow—as you see. A new restaurant opened on the water last fall, Brother's, very big and flashy. Doing great business."

"Taking away yours?"

"No, it's not that—but yes, sure, taking some of ours. The owner has a strip mall in the west end, he has movie theaters, some office buildings downtown. He's telling me he wants to buy this place and call it Brother's Two."

"Oh, great."

"I won't sell—I'm not even considering it. But it feels like the sharks are circling. Every year the lease goes up. If we make any major improvements, the assessed value of the building goes up, which makes the rent go up *more*. I'd need a loan to renovate, and the banks don't want to give money to little independents like us anymore, they only like the big chains."

"You're operating at a loss?"

Rose nodded.

"Why? What do you think went wrong?"

"I don't know, I can't put my finger on it exactly. Except for Waterman's Pub, we're the oldest restaurant downtown. Owned continuously by the same family, I mean." There were older buildings that housed restaurants, but they hadn't been in uninterrupted business for over forty years like the Bella Sorella. "Old age—I think that's what it comes down to. We need new blood. On the management side, because I can't afford a sexy, famous chef."

"And you think *I'd* be new blood?" Anna smiled out of one side of her mouth. "You need a twenty-five-year-old hotshot, Rose, trust me."

"Maybe. But there aren't any of those left in the family." She could see Anna mulling what to say to that. Being called "family" rankled—Rose had used the word deliberately. "The staff wants to change the name," she told her. "They think that'll solve everything."

"Change the name? From Bella Sorella?"

"In fact they've got a contest going. Whoever comes up with a name I like—I'm the judge—gets free drinks from the bar for life."

Anna laughed. "I don't know that changing the name is such a hot idea. But I don't know, I'd have to think about it." She looked at Rose boldly. "Maybe it's time to close up shop. You've had a good run. Why not sell out and move to Florida? Take your friend Theo with you. Lie in the sun and read novels."

Rose laughed.

A second passed. Then Anna laughed with her. At the absurdity.

Rose felt slightly dizzy. It wasn't much, but it was the closest they'd been in sixteen years.

Anna stood. She couldn't pace, not enough room, but she could pivot and scowl and gesture. "Okay. Let's see. You don't have a youth crowd. Not to mention a money crowd. You don't have an identity. Are you couples, family, Italian, seafood, eclectic? Your menu doesn't say anything one way or the other. About anything, frankly. When did you last change it?" Rose opened her mouth, but Anna kept talking. Rose swung her legs to the side of the desk to give her more room. "It was like déjà vu walking in this afternoon, I couldn't believe how many things were the same. I mean *exactly* the same. Even the music—wasn't that the 'O terra, addio' you were playing?"

Rose blushed. "I like *Aida*."

"You've got too many employees, you don't need thirty-five. I know what you're saying about bank money, but you could get *some*, and I think you could do a lot on the cheap. Paint the brick walls white, for a start, because it's too dark, Rose, and not in a good way. Keep the pottery and the paintings if you want to, but lose the maps of Italy's provinces, Jesus, they're cheesy. Get rid of the carpet, and I mean *immediately*, leave the floor bare if you don't want to refinish it. Are those the same yellow signs to the rest rooms, the Signore and Signori? *God*, Rose, I mean—And it's too quiet, the hot restaurants these days are incredibly noisy. Or make it even quieter if you want—but first you have to *decide* what you want to be, then go for it."

They could attract a much more up-market diner in this neighborhood, late-twenties to mid-forties, moneyed Gen X overachievers who were into travel, fashion, the theater. Worry about Gen Y in about five years, Anna advised, but in the meantime don't forget the Boomers. Or the dot-com crowd—they weren't local yet, but they were the ones who moored their brand-new cabin cruisers in the harbor, and they wanted a smart place to eat.

"Consider the possibility that your prices are too low. Most people with money really like paying too much, it makes them feel like they're getting what they deserve."

"But if we raise prices, we'll lose our regulars."

"Sure, some. If you want to keep them you could do bar specials, but then you'd probably be spreading yourself too thin. Bottom line, you can't be all things to all people. You have to decide."

She kept coming back to that, the need to *decide* what the Bella Sorella was and then push it hard, *become* it. "I used to know," Rose said wistfully. "We were a friendly family Italian restaurant. That's what we were."

"I know. That's what we were."

"It started with your grandfather's little crab house on East Island—you never saw that place. He called it Fiore's. He had two other restaurants, each one a little bit more successful, before he bought this place and named it The Flower. Oh, but that wasn't Italian enough, so then it was I Fiori, and then it was Tre Fiori. Finally he settled on Bella Sorella, and of course we little girls used to argue over which *beautiful sister* he'd named it after, Lily or Iris or me. He said it was after all of us, that we were all beautiful." She laughed. "You don't remember him, do you? You were so little when he died."

"No, I don't remember him at all."

Enough of that. Rose couldn't tell what Anna was thinking; she was staring at the floor with her hands stuck in the waistband at the back of her slacks, a drift of hair obscuring her face.

"Maybe I should've left it that way," Rose said ruefully. "A friendly family Italian restaurant. But I guess I muddied up the image, trying to keep up with the times. Adding things like mesclun and arugula"—Anna laughed—"and microbrews, and a wood-burning oven I don't have room for and nobody ever orders anything from anyway."

"Nothing wrong with any of that, Rose. Not if you're consistent."

"And you're right—we've got pasta al pomodoro and a grilled Reuben on the very same lunch menu. It doesn't *say* anything. Except that we can't make up our minds."

Anna tilted her head and looked at her. "You know, it might not work no matter what you do. Restaurants go in cycles—it's possible the Bella Sorella's cycle is over."

"No."

"Or maybe this *version* of it is finished. Maybe you rename it, now it's the—the Piccolo, it specializes in steak and pommes frites."

"No."

"Are you sure?"

"I am very sure."

"Good. Because you're lost if you go that way. It never works, it just drags out the end longer."

"Then why—"

"Because it would be a *faster* end, a mercy killing, and if you decide to do it the hard way you might wish you'd gone that route when things get bad. And you know things are going to get bad."

"But then they'll get better."

"No guarantees."

"I don't expect any. Will you manage it?"

It was what they'd been leading up to, and yet Anna looked surprised and defenseless for a second, as if Rose had caught her off guard. Anna was anything but frail but, standing there in her mannish suit with her sharp elbows out, tall and slight, thick-haired and thin-necked, she looked so much like the coltish girl she used to be, Rose's throat hurt. *What if it beats her?* She didn't care so much for herself, she was old and used to disappointment; a long time ago she'd practically made friends with it. But this had to work. They needed something good to happen to them *together*, it was the only chance they had. She wanted it for the others, too, Carmen and Vonnie, Vince, crazy Dwayne, all the ones who depended on her—but Anna looked so vulnerable to her just then. What if the job Rose was begging her to take defeated her?

"Yes," Anna said.

"Yes? You'll do it?" Rose jumped up. All her second thoughts vanished, all she felt was triumph. "Wonderful, oh, Anna, I'm so glad. I've got something—" She went around and jerked open the bottom drawer of her desk. "Here, and glasses, too. We have to drink a toast."

"Oh no. Whoa! You're not going to make me drink grappa."

"Oh yes, you must, it's a celebration."

"Why don't we just siphon some gas out of my car?"

"Call yourself an Italian. Look at this beautiful bottle, it's exquisite, the hand-blown glass."

"Good idea, let's just look at the bottle."

"Here." She pushed a glass into Anna's hand. "To the Bella Sorella. To success." Oh, she should've left it at that! "To your return. Anna, I'm go glad you've come home."

"Wait, hold it."

Rose paused, even though she wanted more than anything to drink, as if by swallowing the bitter brandy fast she could seal the deal. Her own fault—she'd gone too far.

"Let's be clear about what we're doing here. This is a temporary arrangement, Rose. No matter what happens, I'm not going to be here for the long haul. I'm glad to help you out if I can, but I've got other options. I just want to be clear—if you were thinking this would be a permanent setup, then we're not understanding each other."

"Well." Rose laughed lightly. "I don't suppose anything is permanent." She lifted her glass again.

"No, but I want to make sure we're together. I have a friend, we used to work together at the coffeehouse—she's a chef and she's moved back home, San Diego, her name's Shelly. She's working right now on raising capital to start a restaurant of her own, and as soon as she gets things lined up she wants me to come out and run it for her."

"San Diego."

"But you know how it is, it might not work out, in fact it probably won't. But if it doesn't, I've also got other possibilities, and I'll be sending out some résumés as soon as I get settled."

"I see. What about your house?"

"After it's fixed up, I'll put it on the market. But that could be months."

"Months."

"I'll commit to months—that I can do. This is April. Two months to June, that's still when your high season kicks in, isn't it? June, July, August. One way or the other, we'll know by Labor Day if you can turn this place around. Not if you did, if you *can*. After that, we'll leave it open-ended." Finally she lifted her glass. "To the summer." When Rose didn't move, she reached out and clinked glasses. Drank. "Ack. Oh, my Jesus," she rasped, teary-eyed. "Diesel fuel."

"To the summer," Rose said weakly, and took a sip of the colorless liquor. She felt cheated.

"When do you want me to start? And how much are you going to pay me? I need a living wage, Rose, no gouging because it's family. I could start any time, but it might be better to wait till Monday, I'd like to square things away with my house, line up a couple of repairs. Plus I'm really not unpacked yet. But I could come in on Sunday when it's quiet, check things out. Do you still close on Mondays? You might have to rethink that, you know. When does your dinner crew come in? What is it," she glanced at her watch, "three o'clock now, I could stick around till four or so and meet those guys. Want to introduce me to the lunch shift while I'm waiting?" She was moving toward the door. "I didn't get a chance to say much to Carmen, before. God, it's amazing, she looks exactly the same."

Now she only felt half-cheated. "It's family," Anna had said, probably not even hearing herself. That was a start.

"You're better than a priest," Rose had told Theo in the morning. That night, because neither of them could sleep, she lay in bed with the phone to her ear and whispered a few more of her sins to him in the dark. And thought about how odd it was that the only person she could confide in about the first great love of her life was the last.

"Paul's death was so sudden, out on the road like that. Anna and I weren't prepared, no chance to say good-bye to him. We were sick with grief, but we couldn't comfort each other. Couldn't touch, just hurt. We had an awful fight on the night of his funeral—she reminded me of it today. She thinks we said everything then, we don't need to dig it all up again."

"Finally," Theo said, his voice breathy. "Something I agree with her about."

"But we didn't even speak after that. Years. I'd give anything to erase it, because I said ugly things. I said she had a hard heart. A small heart." *I'm so disappointed in you*, she'd said. *To let your father die without forgiving him. Selfish girl, to punish him with your judgment.*

"I made her so angry, Theo, she finally let go of a secret. She'd been hoarding it, and that night it came bursting out of her."

"What secret?"

"That she knew about Paul and me. She'd known it for years, I mean, long before that day she found me in his bedroom. She knew when she was thirteen years old, before Lily died. Before."

Theo was quiet for a time. She listened to the silence carefully, alert for blame. "How come she never said it before? She kept it to herself for seven years?"

"No, only two—Paul only lived two more years after she found out about us. She didn't *know* what she'd seen when she was a girl, it didn't make sense to her until later. When we hit her in the face with it."

"I don't get it. What happened when she was thirteen?"

"I didn't even know at first, I couldn't remember anything she might've seen. She called me a liar, a cheat." *My mother was upstairs dying, and you were already with him! I saw you—I thought you were comforting him!* "But then I remembered. I'd gone to the house one night late, after the restaurant closed, to bring Paul some dinner. He'd just gotten back from one of his sales trips."

"Like you bring dinner to me. You're the lady who brings food."

"To hungry men I'm in love with." She smiled wanly.

"So what did Anna see?" Theo whispered.

"Nothing, really. Nothing to see. Just a feeling, an atmosphere. Paul and I weren't lovers yet—it was just beginning. But she must've *felt* something, and either she was too young to recognize it or she shut her mind and ignored it for the next seven years. I think probably that was it—the latter."

She'd thought about that night so many times. It had changed the direction of her life, and Paul's, and that seemed fair and natural, orderly. Deserved. Not fair that it had changed Anna's, though. No wonder she hadn't found a man to love for longer than a few years at a time, or a place to live. Did she even have a close woman friend? She'd been made to rearrange what she thought she knew about her parents, her well-loved aunt, half her childhood. Because of Rose and Paul, she'd had to learn a very bad lesson—that what you think is real may not be. And the people you love are probably not what they seem.

That night, late, Rose gave Paul his dinner, then left him in the kitchen while she went up to check on Lily. She was dying of cancer, and everyone but Anna had given up hoping for a miracle. Paul's job took him on the road for days at a time, so the bulk of caring for her had fallen to the women, Mama during the day, Anna after school, Rose at night after work. Paul whenever he could. Lily was in the quiet final days, the stage between the last of the chemo and the start of the heavy narcotics. Most of the time, she slept. At the end she needed the bedside lamp on all the time, she couldn't bear the dark. In the low, gold light that night she'd looked younger than her age—only thirty-six. Wobbly and weak, hairless from the drugs, she looked like a baby bird, all bones and blue-white skin. *This is my sister*, Rose had thought, but it wasn't real. *How can I lose her, how can this be happening?* She'd kissed her on the forehead, and Lily had opened her eyes.

"Hi," they said together, and Lily whispered, "I was just talking about you."

"You mean dreaming? You were dreaming about me?"

"Mmm." She shut her eyes and let Rose stroke her face, smooth away the pain lines between her eyebrows. "We were playing poker. The old house. Remember that white kitchen table? Pauley was your partner. You put your cards down and said, 'I win.' "

Rose ran her hand softly along the soft frizz on Lily's head. "You don't have partners in poker."

Lily opened her eyes. She smiled. "You won," she said distinctly. She turned her face away and drifted back to sleep.

The light had been on in Anna's room, too. She'd been studying and fallen asleep in her white blouse and navy pleated jumper, the uniform at her parochial school. Books and ballpoint pens lay scattered across the bedspread, and her head rested on an open notebook. Everything else in the room was sadly, unnaturally tidy. Anna kept the whole house fanatically neat, much neater than Lily ever had—one way to bring order to the chaos her life had turned into. Her grades were slipping, but no one had intervened, not even Rose. No one had time for anything but Lily. How can I help her? Rose had asked herself all the time. How can I be wise and calm when I feel like a child myself? Her own mother was lost in grief, no help to Rose or Anna or anyone else. Sometimes Rose thought Anna was stronger than all of them. At least she still had faith; she said rosaries for Lily, went to mass every morning, fasted, did secret penances. Mama, Rose, Paul, Iris—they'd all given up on saving her, but not Anna. She still clung to the hope that she could pray her mother back to life.

Rose almost woke her, to tell her to get undressed and under the covers. Instead she found a blanket and floated it over Anna's slack, long-legged body, shoes and all. "Love you," she'd whispered, stroking the hair back from her cheek. Dark, coarse, rippled hair, exactly like hers—their mutual curse. "Love you, baby." Anna had smiled in her sleep.

Downstairs, Paul was in the dark living room, looking out the window. It was raining. The streetlight turned the fine strings of water on the glass blue, and Paul's face ghostly. The house felt leaden, as if the heaviness of Lily's dying were forcing everything down, crushing the air out. Rose crossed the room to turn on a light, but Paul said, "Don't," without looking at her. She didn't have to see his face to know he was crying. In all the time she'd known him, she had never seen him weep.

She'd gone to him hesitantly, touched his sleeve. "They're both asleep. They're fine." Meaningless comfort, all she could give him. He nodded. Because he was exhausted, she could see what his long, mobile face would look like in ten years, twenty.

He rested his temple against the glass and tried to smile. "I wish Lily could've been happy," he said. "I was never able to . . ."

"You made her happy."

"I was never able to make her believe I loved her."

"You did love her. Do love her. She knows that." Nothing had been in her head except the need to comfort him, but words stacked up in her throat like cards, she'd had to press her fingers to her lips to keep her mouth closed.

He took the hand she was resting on the windowsill and examined it in the watery light, holding it with both of his, his eyes downcast. A most intimate gesture; only the naturalness of it had calmed her. "Rose, I never did anything to let her know. She just knows."

"What, Paul?" she'd asked fearfully.

"I never told her or showed her, I never did anything to make her think it. I don't think I did. I tried not to."

Were they going to say these things to each other *now*? At first she was shocked. After all the years of keeping the secret—not from each other, they couldn't, but from Lily—*this* was when they would tell each other the truth, in words? He was right, though—Lily knew. *You won*. She'd dreamed it.

"I've always been faithful to her."

She nodded. "Yes," she said, "of course."

"But, Rose. It was you. You I was being faithful to."

Her eyes swam. She'd been true to him, too, even though there had been men. They laced their fingers together, and she thought of all the years she'd forbidden herself to wish for this. At first it was easy, because she was so angry with him—he'd married the wrong sister—but time had passed and they'd become friends again, and nothing she had ever done was harder than pretending she didn't love Paul. Except knowing he was doing the same thing.

They didn't kiss, although she'd wanted to. She'd wanted to know if it would be the same between them or if everything would be different. They were in a spell, they'd spun a truth-telling web around themselves, a cocoon of feeling, not even words anymore. That's what Anna would interrupt and, seven years later, interpret correctly for exactly what it was. But at the time it was enough to hold hands, the deepest intimacy, she could hardly believe her good fortune. Lily's dark shadow had lifted just for that moment, and they were sad and desperate enough to take advantage. If that was a sin, Rose was too far gone then and too old now to regret it.

"Daddy? Mom's calling you. She wants you to read to her." Anna at the bottom of the stairs.

They sprang apart. So—guilty even then, and they knew it, though they'd done nothing yet except long and yearn. Rose's hand had flown to her heart. Anna saw that. "Oh, you startled me!" she said, and laughed—a good, believable laugh, because even though she was worried about Anna, she was glad, practically euphoric, because the pretense between her and Paul was finally over. She left him in the shadows and walked toward Anna, blocking him from her view. "Hot milk," she said, putting both hands on Anna's shoulders, filling her vision. *Look at my bright eyes. Believe it's because I've been crying for your mother.* "Let's make some hot milk, that'll be good. Then you go straight back to bed."

"I've asked myself," she said to Theo, "if I'd do it again. Be Paul's lover while Lily was still alive, not wait the *decent interval.*"

"What's the answer?"

"I don't know. I think I wouldn't, but that's easy to say now. Everything went to hell when Anna found us together. It was her last year at college—that summer she was going to Europe with a girlfriend, and in August I was supposed to meet them in Italy. Anna and I were going to go to wonderful restaurants and get ideas and recipes for the new, improved Bella Sorella. I'd cook and she'd manage." She closed her eyes. "Oh, Theo. Wasn't that a lovely plan?"

"You can't blame yourself because it didn't work."

"Of course I can."

"She's the one who ran away. Why didn't she say right out as soon as it hit her if she knew about you and Paul? Why wait till he died, why hold it in like that? Like a miser. I don't like her."

She waited till he caught his breath, then said, "I think she kept it inside because it was all she had. Being so angry—it gave her some kind of strength against us. And I think she knew if she told us the truth, she'd have to forgive us. We'd make her. She's soft in the heart, Theo. She is. She felt betrayed. She *was* betrayed."

"Crap. She was a grown woman. She wasn't your mother, she wasn't you. What did she know? You were watching your sister die. People do what they do. Lily never knew, and that's what counts."

"No. Oh, I don't know." She stretched her arms and legs in her empty bed. "Are you sleepy?"

"Yeah."

"Good. We'll hang up, and you go to sleep. Sleep all night, don't get up to pee."

"So she's taking the job and you're all happy."

"She's taking the job, yes. I'm happy."

"I guess you got all kinds of plans in your head, how you're going to make it up, be friends again."

"No plans."

"Just be careful."

"Why? What will happen?"

"You just be careful. No parts of you are as young as they used to be."

"You say the nicest things."

"You know what I mean. Your insides."

Theo had a hard time saying certain things. "My liver?" she guessed. "Pancreas?"

She could almost hear him grinding his teeth. "Heart," he said under his breath.

"Pardon? Did you say *heart*?"

"You just watch your step."

She sighed, flooded with feeling. "I wish you were here. What I wouldn't give. I would love to kiss you right now."

He grunted. "Heart" had taken so much out of him, he couldn't reciprocate in words.

"Do you love me, Theo?"

"You know it."

"I'm so lucky," she said.

5

Jay had told Anna he would call. They couldn't leave it like this, he'd said; they would talk when a little time had passed and she'd had a chance to cool down. She hadn't believed him, she'd thought he just didn't have the guts to say good-bye clean. But when the phone rang and she heard that flat, refined, New England drone he couldn't shake, although he'd tried—once he'd affected a tough New York or New Jersey accent, hoping people would think his sculptures were working class or proletariat or something—when she heard his voice, she thought, *I knew it*, and immediately began to rearrange her mind for all the new possibilities. He wanted her to come back—he wanted to marry her—he was calling from down the street. When none of those proved to be true, she felt silly but not really disappointed.

He asked how she was. Fine. He said he missed her. Really. He said he'd sold *Colossus III* to a bank in Boise. Congratulations. He said, "Mac's had a heart attack."

"What? Oh, Jay! How is he, is he okay?" Mac—Jay's eighty-one-year-old grandfather—Anna adored him.

"Yes, he's stable, they say. Evidently it was minor."

"Thank God! When did it happen?"

"The day before yesterday. They're releasing him tomorrow, although he can't go back to the assisted-living place right away. He'll need nursing care for a short time first." Then she thought he was calling to ask if she'd come back and take care of Mac for him. She'd been as close as a daughter-in-law to the old man—she'd hated leaving him much more than she'd hated leaving Jay. Jay loved him too, of course, but Anna was the one who'd called him every week and gone to see him and invited him to dinner at the loft. The one who'd done things for him.

"Jay, I don't know, I don't think I can—"

"There's a rehab facility quite close to the hospital, so they'll just take him there in an ambulance tomorrow afternoon. Would you like the telephone number of the rehab?"

"Oh. Yes, please. And the address." She wrote them down. "So have you been to see him?"

"Of course I've been to see him."

"How is he? How are his spirits?"

"Fair, I would say. He's still a son of a bitch."

She smiled, knowing he meant that affectionately.

"He still enjoys telling me what an asshole I was."

She wound the curls in the phone line around one finger. "In what particular regard?"

"Spoiling things. Between us."

"He knows?" She couldn't believe it. "You told Mac about Nicole?"

"Not—no, I didn't think that would serve any useful purpose. I simply told him—well, what you told him."

"How do you know what I told him?"

"Because he told me."

"What did he say?"

"He said I was an asshole."

"No, Jay, I never, that's not what—"

"I know, Anna. You said things weren't working out and you needed to get away for a while to think. It's safe to say my grandfather drew his own conclusions."

"Oh. Well, I'm sorry." For what, though? For Mac, she supposed.

There was a long, uncomfortable pause, during which she had the distinct impression that she was expected to say she forgave him.

"Nicole has moved in."

She absorbed that, then came up with, "Oh, has she?"

"It seemed the best thing, under the circumstances."

"More convenient."

He breathed the way he did when she was being difficult. "It was what she wanted. Evidently it enhances her illusion that what you walked in on wasn't a meaningless affair in progress."

Breathtaking. "So you did it for her. *Evidently*."

More put-upon sighing.

"You're really something, aren't you?"

"Anna, I'm trying to tell you that I regret what happened."

"I know. That's what's so amazing." She remembered a story he used to like to tell, because he was proud of it. When he was in college at Columbia, for some kind of performance art project he went around interviewing people on the street in a tough section of the city, a tense, mixed neighborhood, and he took photographs of everyone he interviewed. Later he blew up the photos and posted them around the neighborhood, with the verbatim comments of the people in the pictures printed over them. Some of the comments were racist, all of them were in some way foolish or humiliating. What was the point of it? she'd asked, appalled. To make people hear what they really sound like, he'd said. To make them confront the truth about themselves. Mean, she'd thought. A dirty trick.

"Anna," Jay said, "let's talk later."

"Let's not," she said, and hung up.

How could she ever have loved him? What kind of woman couldn't recognize what a selfish, insensitive, uncaring lout he was? And if she saw it now, why did his betrayal still sting like acid? In self-defense, before the self-loathing could start again, she tried to remember his good points. They all came from the early days—they'd met in Philadelphia—the courtship phase when Jay was all charm and heat and dark, exciting passion. She'd been delighted to move to Buffalo with him when he'd asked; she'd left behind friends, a dull job, and any number of failed relationships without a backward glance. Nicole and Industrial Coffee had seemed like serendipity, good luck on top of good luck, a thrilling new man *and* work that might be fun, might actually mean something to her. Jay's good points: he was smart. He was talented. He was good-looking. Too bad all the good points had corresponding bad points—he was proud and condescending because he was smart, he was insecure about his talent, he was vain about his good looks.

He loved his cat. There—a pure, untainted good quality. And completely unselfish, because the cat never repaid his affection except when it suited him. No wonder they got along so well.

Bitter. Yes, she was bitter. She would never get over him, that's what was so infuriating. He wasn't worth it, he wasn't worth it, but *Jay McGuare* was a name she'd remember on her deathbed if she lived to be a hundred. She resented that more than anything. Last night she dreamed he was making a sculpture out of her hair. Strand by strand, she let him pull it out of her scalp and pretended it didn't hurt, that this was fine with her. She woke up before he could start peeling her skin off.

She wasn't ready to think about how much of what must've been wrong between them for a long time was her fault. Intimations crept in anyway, shades of culpability, complicity. Like most women, she always claimed she wanted intimacy, but she'd kept Jay at arm's length while they went through the motions of domestic togetherness, sex, planning for the future. They'd never combined finances, never had a joint checking account, always split everything down the middle, although he made much more money than she did. Even during their most hopeful and idyllic period, when they were *both* talking about marriage, she'd never stopped using birth control.

The deeper, more interesting question was *why*, yet she was even less inclined to explore that right now. But sometimes she couldn't shut out a truly alarming possibility—that Rose and her father had set her up years ago to prepare for the worst. Forewarned is forearmed. Naturally that attitude would seep into your loved one's consciousness by and by, no matter how self-involved he might be. And how far was it from there to pushing him into someone else's softer, warmer, more trusting arms? From guaranteeing that your dread of betrayal and faithlessness became a self-fulfilling prophesy?

She'd lied to Rose about the house. Nothing looked the same, that was true, but she had X-ray eyes, she could see beneath the paint and the god-awful paneling and the dingy wall-to-wall carpets, the quick disguises thrown up to hide its heart. Its Catalano heart. But she'd been straight when she'd told Rose coming home wasn't sad. Even distorted and denatured, her house was a reminder of something she had the interesting habit of forgetting: she'd had an almost ridiculously happy childhood.

The fireplace didn't work anymore, something about an inadequate chimney liner, but she could sit on the furnished tweed sofa and see her mother shaking an old popcorn popper over the flames while her father smacked the logs with the poker and told her to hold the thing a little higher. "Nuh uh, we like 'em burned," her mother would say, winking at Anna, and her father would groan, pretending he was outnumbered and henpecked. That was one of his favorite games, and so of course it was one of Anna's. She played at bossing him around like a haughty queen from the age of about three. "You have to," she'd say, "you're just the man," mimicking him. "You're just the one who brings home the bacon."

She'd sold the piano a long time ago, but it used to sit in the corner between the bay window and the china cabinet, an old black baby grand her father's parents had given him and Lily for a wedding present. He could play ragtime and boogie-woogie, to Anna's delight, but what she liked even better was when he played "soft songs," late at night after she'd been put to bed. They were for Mommy, the soft songs, and that was fine, but she would fall asleep making believe they were for her.

What was now the den used to be a screened-in back porch. She remembered following her mother out onto the porch one bright, snowy morning, and realizing for the first time in her life what *cold* was. "Brr, it's cold!" her mother had cried, racing back in from whatever chore she'd gone out there for, rubbing her arms, and Anna had copied her and echoed, "Brr, it's cold," and understood. The only interesting thing about that memory was that she *knew* she understood, and now, thirty-some years later, she could still remember knowing it. A consciousness milestone.

The kitchen, still tiny and yellow, was the room that years and tenants had changed the least. Anna had no memories of Mom at the stove, bending into the refrigerator, Mom cutting things up at the counter. Her mother hated to cook; she brought home restaurant food and reheated it in the oven. Daddy used to grumble that he was on the road four or five days a week, and when he got home he couldn't even get a home-cooked meal. But Anna had loved it. They got to eat what Nonna and Aunt Rose fixed the customers at the Bella Sorella, and it was heaven. All her friends thought she was the luckiest kid in the world. She did, too.

Why couldn't she trust that happiness again? Why did what happened later taint it so thoroughly, like a dirty watercolor brush in clear water? Why, in the year and a half she'd wasted in therapy, had she focused on nothing but trivial frustrations and childish disappointments, never the good times—why couldn't she even admit there *were* good times?

Revisionist history. At twenty, she'd rewritten her past to accommodate one enormous act of treachery that happened when she was thirteen. But maybe sooner than thirteen—that was the sticky part. The joker in the deck. Maybe much sooner, maybe it existed from the very beginning, how could she know? Things didn't necessarily start when you first noticed them. And no one could tell her the truth now. Her father was dead, and Rose—well. Her testimony was suspect.

Memories of her father were everywhere in this house, even if she had to look for them under layers of time and cheap rehabs. The window over the kitchen sink still stuck—she vividly recalled both times he'd thrown his back out trying to open it. The dark, earthy, oily smell of the basement brought back every repair or home improvement project he'd ever embarked on and usually never finished. At the bottom of the kitchen door, under who knew how many coats of paint, deep, gouged-out scratch marks were still visible from the time he'd brought home a stray dog. Stinky, they'd named her, and she'd lasted about two days before Anna's mother had taken her to the humane society. Anna remembered sitting on her father's lap in his big chair in the living room, heartbroken, snuffling against his shirt, while he spun a long, detailed story about Stinky's new home and how happy she was there, how kind and loving her new owners were. For his sake, she'd pretended to buy it all and be comforted, but she wasn't. Even at six, she wasn't too young to see that his heart was broken, too.

It wasn't fair, but from the beginning she'd felt more betrayed by Rose than by him. Always felt, as her mother's surrogate, more cheated on by Rose than by him. The thought of her father carrying on behind her mother's innocent, unsuspecting back was too fundamental a violation, too painful. She simply couldn't bear it, and so, a long time ago, she'd laid the lion's share of the blame at Rose's feet. It was Rose's fault. Much worse to betray a sister than a wife. The blood tie—meaner, more basic treachery. Men will be men. Yes, it was sexist, but it was also, in Anna's own unhappy, real-life experience, God's own truth. And so she remembered her father with love and sadness and hardly any anger, and she held Rose accountable for every millimeter she'd strayed from the righteous path of virtue and blamelessness.

It rained that night, not hard but enough to motivate her. The next morning, against Rose's advice, she found Mason Winograd's name in the phone book and called him. Surprise—no answer. She looked at a map and found his street, a cul-de-sac in one of the jagged little river inlets north of town. Must be a new development since her day; she remembered that area across the bridge as woods and wetlands, no houses to speak of.

Mason Winograd's house was something to speak of. He had no close neighbors, no neighbors at all that she could see. A downed chain stretched between two posts at the driveway entrance. She drove over it cautiously, into a dense thicket of budding maples and low-growing mountain laurel on either side of a bumpy lane, morning sunshine dappling the windshield, occasionally blinding her. It was only eleven o'clock, but already warm. Through the open car window the racket of birdsong was even louder than the crunch of tires, and she wondered if that was normal for this time of year, bird-wise, or if Mr. Winograd had more than the usual number on his property. Maybe he lured them there with food and other enticements so he could take their pictures. She didn't know a thing about birds. Imagine choosing birds, nothing else, for your sole artistic subject. Maybe he was eccentric.

No, he was definitely eccentric. She had to laugh when she saw his house, although more from shock than amusement. The long, winding drive had prepared her for something interesting, maybe semi-grand, but never this narrow, blind fortress, three flat stories of weathered shingles, windowless, nothing but a big door in the center to break up the sheer gray blankness. *No windows*? Was that even legal? Maybe Rose was playing a joke on her. A friend of a friend, she'd said, somebody's stepson; he'd built this house, so he was "handy." Well, up to a point. But not if you counted windows.

There was no place for her car unless she blocked a late-model yellow Jeep parked in a gravel clearing by the side of the house. She blocked it, and as she pulled the key from the ignition of her car, a movement behind the house caught her eye. Beyond the grassy backyard, a wooden pier jutted into the pretty river tributary. Water, sparkling like a ribbon of broken mirrors, flowed away from the bay; in front of the pier, its bowsprit poking out from the front of a shed or garage, an unfinished sailboat rested on jack stands. Saws and tools lay scattered on the ground next to a couple of sawhorses covered by a length of raw wood. Sawdust everywhere. The movement she'd seen was a man sprinting away from the shed toward the house. She registered fast legs, shirtless torso, long hair blowing back in an urgent wake, before the figure disappeared around the corner and out of view.

Mr. Winograd, she presumed. She'd have said the phone had rung and he was rushing to answer it, except he didn't answer his phone. It was more as if he'd seen something frightening or alarming—her—and he was running away, trying to escape. She got out of her car with misgivings.

Maybe the windowless exterior was a new style of modern architecture; minimalism gone berserk. She'd have to ask Jay. She followed a flagstone path across the front lawn to a one-step concrete stoop. The wide front door was, what else, windowless. She gave it a few raps with her knuckles, and wasn't surprised when half a minute passed and no one opened it.

She could leave. She was feeling vaguely insulted; definitely shunned. She picked her way back along the path to the driveway and kept going, around the sloping side lawn. Beautiful here with the glinting river for a backdrop, cleared around the dock but overhung elsewhere with budding willow and sycamore trees. A lot of birdhouses and bird feeders on tall poles were clustered around the boat shed. Eureka, a window! Airy and wide open on the first floor of the house, perfectly normal, homey even, maybe a kitchen window, and beyond it, cantilevered out from the back, a long, screened-in porch. Flowering vines climbed up the weathered wood sides, and bees buzzed in the sweet-smelling, trumpet-shaped blooms. Pretty.

The man had left the screen door to the porch half open. "Hello?" she called through it. No answer, so she stepped inside. After the blinding sun, it took a few seconds to make out a glider, flaking white with plaid cushions, against the back wall. She saw a small table with an empty plastic glass on it, a wicker footstool. No other furniture, but a large cardboard box took up space in the shadowy far corner, with a scattering of towels and rags on the floor near it.

Through the door opposite, she could see the kitchen. She crossed the porch and stopped in the threshold, called out again. "Mr. Winograd? It's Anna Catalano—my aunt sent me—Rose Fiore. Hello? Anybody home?"

A soft sound made her glance to the right. Nothing there but the kitchen sink, under the window she'd just walked past. No—there was a stick, a limb, a tree limb, resting at an angle on the windowsill. And now she could see two little somethings on it. Birds. Baby birds sitting side by side, staring back at her very quietly. Not moving. They couldn't possibly be real.

"Something I can do for you?"

She jolted up on her toes, barely suppressing a scream. A man had materialized in the doorway to the next room, living room or whatever. *The* man, she could tell by the bare feet and the jeans, but he'd put on a shirt, and he looked perfectly cool and collected, not like a flying fugitive in the least. He leaned against the door frame with his arms crossed, head at a questioning angle. Insolent angle, actually. A serious-looking camera hung on a strap from his shoulder. Maybe he'd just seen an interesting bird and he'd been rushing inside to get his camera. If she'd spoiled some brilliant, once-in-a-lifetime photo, she could understand why he didn't look very glad to see her.

Her heart slowed, and she said, "Hi," smiling at him, trying to look harmless. "I thought I saw somebody, so I, well, just knocked and came in. I'm Anna."

"Anna." He had to clear the gruffness out of his throat. "Rose's niece."

"Yes."

"You look like her."

"Yeah, that's what they say." She was tired of hearing them say it. "And you're—"

"Mason."

"Nice to meet you."

He didn't echo the sentiment. Or offer to shake hands. She couldn't figure out if he was hostile or shy, dangerous, nuts, or just deeply uninterested. He had beautiful salt-and-pepper hair, but he wore it too long, it fell straight down from a high part and hid half of one side of his face. Even without smiling, he had crow's feet at the corners of light, secretive eyes. A deep cleft cut between his straight black eyebrows, the perfect grim complement to his pained mouth, the lips pressed together, pronouncing the letter M.

"Listen, I'm sorry if I disturbed you, but my aunt said you fix roofs. Rooves," she tried when he looked completely blank. "Mine's leaking around the chimney."

"She said what?"

"Oh." So it was a joke. "Sorry," she repeated, laughing, pretending she was amused, "I think I've made a mistake." Maybe she had the wrong house? "Or I misunderstood, I could've sworn—"

"I fixed Rose's window once. At the restaurant."

"You did?"

"Kids broke it. I put in a new pane of glass."

"Oh." *Because you're so good with windows,* she thought.

He kept one hand on the camera at his hip, smoothing the silver metal with long, nervous fingers either lovingly or compulsively. Except for the sawdust in his hair, he looked like a gunfighter. The gaunt, tortured, over-the-hill kind. Something arrogant about him, the way he looked at her, sort of James Deanish recklessness she found equally attractive and irritating. Then he straightened up from his tough-guy slouch, but, oddly, his shoulders stayed uneven, the left one lower than the right by an inch or so.

The phone rang.

He jumped—it was on the wall about two feet from his ear. They stared at each other during the hour-long interval between the first ring and the second. She folded her arms. He rubbed his chest, the place over his heart, with the flat of his palm. She began to feel torn, part of her daring him not to answer—go ahead, *be* as weird as you possibly can be—but the other part drawn to him for some reason, wanting to throw in her lot with his side in the us-versus-them conspiracy—or whatever was going on around here.

He answered the phone.

"Theo." He breathed it in a low, heartfelt, thankful voice, the very sound of relief. "How are you? No, I'm here—I left it out in the—No, I came in without it, this is fine. How're you doing?"

His phone, he'd come in without his phone, she figured out. Theo had called him on the cell phone he must've left in the sailboat shed, and now he was calling him on the house phone. The one he never answered.

"Well, that's good. That's what I'm doing. Right now, it's no . . . I know, but it's what I'd be doing anyway. I'll pick you up, you can have lunch with me. No, it's not a problem. Not at all. Good, yeah. See you."

He replaced the receiver carefully. "That was Theo," he said, more pleasantly than he'd said anything so far.

She nodded, glad for him. "Who's Theo?" Rose's boyfriend, she knew that. So this guy was Rose's boyfriend's stepson.

"He's my stepfather. I thought Rose might've mentioned him."

"Wait, maybe she did. He lives on a boat, is that right? And he's not well, I think she said, he's sick, or he—"

"He has a condition."

"Yes. I'm sorry, I hope he's better. Well," she said, trying to stay on track, "I don't know why Rose told me you could fix my roof, but honest to God, that's what she said."

"I can fix your roof."

"You can?" She hated to bring it up, but—"She said you built this house."

He nodded.

"It, um, has an interesting facade."

He stroked his upper lip with his fingers, as if he had an invisible mustache. Between his hair and his shielding hand, she could hardly see his face at all. "I'm putting in windows," she thought he said; he mumbled it. "Next project."

"Oh. Because the first time you . . . what." She smiled. "Forgot?"

He blinked rapidly. "Long story."

"Hmm," she said interestedly. But he rubbed his chest with his hand again, and didn't tell it to her.

She glanced around at his kitchen, which was sleek and high-tech, no frills but lots of manly stainless steel and industrial-strength appliances. No dirty dishes, no clutter, and all the surfaces shone. Only one thing looked out of place.

"You have two baby birds on a tree limb over your sink."

"Barn swallows."

"Oh. What happened to the mother?"

"I don't know. Someone found them and gave them to me."

"Won't they fly away? Or fall on the floor, not in a cage or anything?"

"No."

One of the gray-blue babies had come down the limb to take a drink out of a pie tin full of water on the slate counter. Bullet-shaped, it wobbled on its way back up, bow-legged, swinging from side to side. Anna laughed. "He walks like Charlie Chaplin."

Mason smiled, too. The temperature in the room went up about ten degrees.

"I've just moved back to town," she offered in the new warmth. "I grew up on Day Street."

"I know."

He must know lots of things about her, she realized, courtesy of Rose, via *Theo*. All the gory details about Jay, no doubt, all about her being the prodigal daughter come home. "What about you?" she said, jutting her chin at him, aggressive. "Have you lived here all your life?"

"No, I left. Like you."

"But now you're back. From..."

"New York."

"Why did you come home? Better birds down here?"

On cue, something squawked. Not the barn swallows, who still sat docilely on their limb, bobbing their chestnut heads. Mason Winograd moved around her, keeping his distance. She followed him when he went out on the back porch. "I wasn't a photographer in New York," he said in a deliberately calm, quiet voice, crouching beside the cardboard box she'd seen before.

She went closer, trying to see inside. "What were you? If not a photographer." He shifted, making room for her, and she knelt beside him, peering gingerly over his shoulder. "Oh," she breathed. "Oh, the poor thing. What happened to him?" It was a bird, blue-gray, maybe a foot long, but it looked smaller all by itself in the big box. It had a thin strip of white tape around its body, and under and across one of its wings. "Did he break his wing?"

"Lawyer. Yes, a broken wing."

"What kind is he?"

"A kingfisher. I found him on the riverbank, trying to take off."

"And you fixed him?" It was a beautiful bird, all bluish-silver except for a pure white stripe around the neck and a white stomach. It kept opening and closing its long black beak. Mason unscrewed the top of a glass jar and took out a lump of fish, or at least it smelled like fish. He set it on the floor of the cage, but the bird wouldn't move, would only look at it out of its bright black eyes. Short-legged, all head and torso, it had an untidy crest of bluish feathers on the back of its head that gave it a cocky look, like a juvenile delinquent.

"Sometimes..." Mason said, and took up another piece of fish, smaller. Anna jumped, but he didn't move a muscle when all at once the kingfisher stabbed its pointy beak at the fish in his fingers and gobbled it up, throwing its head back to swallow. "Sometimes you have to get him started." After that, the bird hopped down clumsily from its tree-limb perch and devoured the piece of fish on the cage floor. Mason put down more fish, followed by thin strips of something reddish and bloody, probably beef.

"How did you get the tape on him? Didn't he move, didn't he flap around? Or was he unconscious?"

"I put him in the foot of a sock."

"You put him in a sock?"

"I cut the toe out for his head, another hole for the bad wing. It calmed him. I put a Kleenex over his head while I worked so he couldn't see me. Movement is what scares them."

"And then you—taped him up?"

"Under his wing there's a little piece of cardboard—see the edge? That's the splint. He had the simplest kind of break, between the wing tip and the outer joint. No broken skin, no infection. He never went into shock."

"Cardboard for the splint, that's amazing. And he'll be able to fly when he heals?"

"Should be. Know in a week or so."

He was on her right, kneeling. He reached down slowly, smoothly, to retrieve an uneaten piece of food, using his other hand to pull his hair back, out of his eyes. For the space of a second, she saw the left side of his face. Scars. Dear God, scars from his temple to his jaw, burled ridges of crimped, puckered skin, alternating livid and pearl-white, an angry ruching of flesh.

He looked up before she could look away. Whatever was in her face, he saw it. Shock? She hoped not, although she was shocked.

He put a screen on top of the kingfisher's cage and stood up, went back in the kitchen. Was he coming back? She began to think about what she would do if he didn't. Leave, she guessed, what else could—

He came back. With a lighted cigarette in his mouth, and he crossed to the screen door and leaned against the post, dragging on the cigarette and squinting out at the sunshine. She hesitated, then went close to him on purpose. So he wouldn't think she was repelled or afraid or anything stupid like that. She slouched against the other side of the door, leaning back on her crossed hands, mimicking his posture. "So, a lawyer. What kind?"

He glanced at her, glanced away. "Insurance."

"Insurance. That sounds . . . weighty. Did you like it?"

He didn't answer.

She went on as if she hadn't asked. "This job Rose wants me to take, it's not like anything I've done before, so frankly, I don't know where all her confidence is coming from. But I guess I've been circling around the business one way or the other since I got out of school. Once I worked as an assistant to the president of a restaurant supply company, so, you know . . . My last job, I was managing a coffeehouse, but that's the closest I've come to running a real restaurant. Anyway, I guess I've been coming around to it all along. Without knowing it."

At least he was looking at her now, not pretending she wasn't there.

"The earliest memory I have is sitting in the kitchen at the Bella Sorella and playing with paper dolls while women all around me were cooking, my grandmother, Rose, Carmen, even my mother if there was a crunch. So I guess I . . . " She wasn't even sure she believed all this, but it seemed important to keep talking. "I guess you could say I come by the profession naturally. Or you can't escape your destiny. Something like that."

He cleared his throat again. He must not talk much. "So you're going to take the job?"

"Yeah. For a while."

"Then leave." His crooked smile didn't look friendly.

"Yes, then leave. What's wrong with that?"

"Nothing. I'm sure you're good at it."

She straightened. "Wow. Who could you have been talking to?"

He held up his hands.

"Hey, you must think you know a lot about me."

"No."

"Well, you don't. Rose doesn't either, she just thinks she does."

"I'm sorry if I . . . " He paused, frowning, and she waited to hear how he would phrase it. She wasn't clear herself on what he had to apologize for, or why it had made her so angry. "Took something for granted," he said finally.

"That's okay. Forget it."

They stared at each other's feet for a while.

"Do you want to know what I've heard about you?"

She lied and said, "No."

"From Rose, that you haven't found where you want to be yet. That you're not satisfied."

She sniffed. You didn't need a crystal ball to figure that out.

"And from Theo—well, you probably don't want to hear."

"Actually, now I do."

"That you're going to be a troublemaker."

"A 'troublemaker'?" She saw that he was trying not to smile, which made her smile. "I can't wait to meet this guy."

"He thinks he won't like you, but he will. When he sees you." Immediately his face shut down, got grim around the mouth. He was embarrassed. Because what he'd said came close to a compliment? He kept his head turned slightly to the left, she assumed deliberately. But now that she knew they were there, she could see the scars easily, even through the protective curtain of his hair. What had happened to him? Rose would know, but Anna didn't want to give her the satisfaction of asking. Why had she sent her here in the first place, what was the point of disturbing this strange man's solitude? To fix her *roof*? Rose must think it would be therapeutic for him, get him out of the house or something, but to Anna it was just insulting.

"You know, I think Rose was just trying to help me out, just gave me your name because she thought you'd work cheap," she said with a laugh. "Obviously you've got better things to do." She gestured around vaguely; he had a sailboat to build, injured birds to feed. Anything else? "So what I'm going to do is get out of your way—"

"What kind of roof is it?"

"Slate. I'm going to—"

"How many stories?"

"Two and a half, but I don't want you to fix it—but thank you, you're very nice. I'll call a contractor."

He said nothing. He'd gone back to his tough-guy pose, arms folded, dusty feet crossed at the ankles. By now she was fairly sure it was a pose, but what he was trying to camouflage with it was harder to guess.

"Well, so. Nice meeting you. Mason." Some perversity made her stick her hand out. He had to take it, he had no choice, but first he started slightly—she'd surprised him out of his Marlboro Man imitation. "Nice meeting you," he muttered.

She went down the two wooden steps to the yard and started away. She hadn't gone far when she heard a light, metallic *snap*. She spun around. He was lowering his camera—which he'd never taken off his shoulder.

"Did you just take my picture?"

He put his hands on his hips, looked thoughtfully down at the ground, then back up at her. "No." Crooked shoulder, crooked smile.

She laughed, it was such an obvious lie.

"There was an egret over there, up in the tree." He pointed over her shoulder. "I took its picture."

She didn't bother to look around.

"Snowy egret, I think. But maybe a cattle egret, hard to tell from here. Gone now."

"When you get the film developed, you'll have to let me know. Which one it was."

"Well, if you're really interested."

"Vitally." She looked hard into his eyes, trying to make him smile again. No luck. Walking away, she listened carefully, but he didn't take her picture again.

6

"What's this, Rose? A suggestion box? I didn't know we had one."

Rose glanced up from the inventory list she was checking. "There's never much in it. Look inside."

Anna hesitated. "Should I? It's not private?"

"Yes, sometimes, but you're the manager, you get all the complaints now." She stretched her arms over her head with exaggerated contentment. "Not me."

"Where's the key?"

She found it in the desk drawer, and Anna opened the small metal box Rose kept on a shelf in the employees' closet. She took out a crinkled Post-it note and read, " 'Venezia. Vesuvio. Sorrento. Adriatico. Alpi. Padua. Genova. Napoli. Toscana. Billy.' " She looked at Rose blankly. " 'Billy'?"

"Billy Sanchez, the sauté cook. He was only in once this week, he's been sick, you probably—"

"The little guy with the toupee?"

"Oh, he'd hate to hear that. He thinks nobody can tell."

"Okay, but what's Venezia, Vesuvio—"

"Suggestions. I told you, there's a contest going on—name that restaurant."

"Oh, yeah. Do you like any of those?"

"No."

"Good." She picked out another note. " 'Dear Rose. What do you think of The Halfway Café? There must be something the Bella Sorella is halfway between. Love, Vonnie.' " Anna laughed. "Well, that's not too bad. Don't you love Vonnie?"

"I'd be lost without her. Is that it?"

"No, one more." She squinted. " 'I don't think it's fair we have to give Tony 15 percent when he's never around and when you do find him he's hooked up with Suzanne in the linen closet. This I have seen with my own eyes. Also last week Fontaine was late and I saw Luca punch her time card.' "

"Anonymous," Rose guessed. "Let me see." She glanced briefly at the cramped, ungenerous script. "Elise—Tony's her busboy. I keep her on lunches because of her attitude."

"That pale girl, practically white-haired? Goes on about how her true calling is fashion design?"

"That's Elise."

"Okay, she's a malcontent because she's not getting the money shifts—but Rose, what's going on with your pastry cook? Fontaine—is that her name? Really sweet, looks like she's about sixteen?"

"Oh, Fontaine. She has lots of problems." All having to do with men.

"Well, yesterday Vonnie told her some guy said the biscotti were soggy, and she burst into tears. She ran outside and wouldn't come back. She was heartbroken, sobbing, absolutely inconsolable. Finally Luca got her to come back in."

"Poor Fontaine."

"Is she okay? I mean, stable and everything?"

"She's pregnant."

"Oh." Anna sat down on the arm of the sofa in the tiny, cluttered office. "That would explain it. How long?"

"About four months."

"My God, she's a *baby*."

"She's not even twenty."

"Who's the father?"

"She won't say. As far as I know, she hasn't told anyone but me she's pregnant, so . . ."

"So I'll be discreet." Anna folded her arms. "You're sort of the mother confessor around here, aren't you?"

Her expression was amused, not censuring, so Rose smiled back comfortably. "I used to be, but I'm delighted to turn the confessional over to you. My worthy successor."

"Oh, no way, I'm just a novitiate. Nobody trusts me—why should they? I'm an outsider. A foreign devil."

She was kidding, but Rose took the opportunity to say something serious. "Strangely enough, that's not true. I thought it would take longer, but this has been, you must admit, an amazingly smooth transition. Vonnie said to me yesterday, 'It's like she's been here for *months*, instead of a week.' " Anna leaned over to wipe a smudge off the top of her shoe, so Rose couldn't see her face. "Don't you think it's going well? Seriously. Don't you?"

"Some things, yeah," she finally begrudged. "I can't say I'm getting a lot of cooperation out of Carmen."

"I know, but be patient. Sometimes she resists change."

"Ha! Let me jot that down."

Rose had to laugh, too; that was a bit of an understatement. "And what have you done to Dwayne? He's turned into a pussycat."

"Dwayne! My God, he scares me to death. I think he could bench press the walk-in." Anna put her hands on her knees, elbows out, and said in Dwayne's guttural grunt, "Not too fuhckin' *hungry*, were they?" and Rose cracked up. Dwayne had been with her for a year and a half—a record for a dishwasher—but he was temperamental. If a plate came back half full of food he'd had no part in preparing, he took offense. "Not too fuhckin' *hungry*," he'd snarl with real anger, genuine resentment. It was a staff joke; now everyone said it, apropos of anything. Except for Dwayne, nobody had gotten tired of it.

"But he hasn't even threatened to kill anybody since you got here," Rose marveled. "What did you do to him?"

"Me? I did nothing. He hypnotizes me. I just stand there waiting for him to put his hands around my neck and squeeze."

They were only half kidding.

"Sometime we need to get serious about cutting back on staff, Rose. You've got too many people working for you. I keep telling you."

Rose kept sidestepping the issue. If she stayed in the business till she was a hundred, she would never get used to or be any good at firing staff. "But you're going to turn things around any day now," she said, smiling cheerfully. "Then we'll need all our people and *more*." That was the tack she'd been taking with Anna, to jolly her out of the mood and off the subject of firing people.

"Shirl, for example. Right now you don't need a dedicated pasta chef, she's redundant. Luca and Carmen can do what she's doing—"

"*Right now*, maybe, yes, but as soon as things start to pick up—"

"Then you hire her back."

"Oh, I couldn't do without Shirl, she's too entertaining."

"Rose."

"Did you know her son is suing her?"

"Rose, you can't—Her son is suing her?"

"Her and Earl, Shirl's husband. Earl Junior, he's eleven years old—"

"Wait. Earl Junior is suing Shirl and her stalker ex-husband?"

"You didn't know this?"

"I—" Anna shook her head helplessly. "I confess, I did not."

Not surprising. Shirl, Rose's longtime pasta cook, a ditzy, round-bodied woman who dyed her hair a different shade of red every week, talked nonstop about anything and everything, but especially her unbelievably dysfunctional immediate family; it was easy to get lost in the stream of consciousness tidal wave and tune out. "Earl Junior's got a lawyer and he's suing Shirl and Earl for... I forget the legal term—"

"Insanity?"

"Being incompetent parents, in other words."

"I'm on Earl Junior's side," Anna said. "Let me know if he needs a character witness. Okay, if you can't part with Shirl, who's next most expendable? I'm telling you, you're fat and inflated, Rose, you need to get lean and mean."

"How about Eddie?" Speaking of lean and mean.

"No, no, he's too good-looking. He brings in the younger women at lunchtime, you can't get rid of Eddie."

"He brings them in when he's *here*, which is about half as often as I need him. Vince covers for him constantly."

"Yeah, but a really handsome bartender is worth almost anything you have to put up with to keep him. Who else?"

"Nobody." Rose folded her arms.

"Nobody? Come on."

"I need everybody else."

"No, you don't."

"I really think I do."

Their first fight. They watched each other with level, speculative gazes, keeping their polite faces mild. "Okay, well, we'll see," Anna said, and Rose tipped her hat to the vagueness of that. Not a threat, but not a retreat. A postponement.

"Okay, smoking on duty. Servers are leaving lit cigarettes in the ladies' room and coming back every few minutes for a drag. It smells like a wet fireplace in there, Rose, I've got customers complaining. Are we together on this? Are you with me that we're opposed to on-duty waiters stinking up the rest room during dinner shift?"

"I'm with you."

"Excellent!" Anna exaggerated her surprise—a little dig. Rose didn't mind. As battle lines went, the one they'd just drawn seemed pretty spongy.

. . .

Sunday night was staff meal night, "family meal," when the kitchen and floor crews took off their aprons or their chef's tunics and sat down for a late supper in the dining room. Often it turned into a party, especially if the last customer had left and there was no reason to keep the noise down. Barring drugs or obvious drunkenness, Rose tolerated all but the roughest carrying-on, because for her that was the point of family meal—to let hardworking employees act for a few hours as well or as badly as real relations. It boosted morale.

For all her good intentions, though, the long table usually ended up divided in half, kitchen staff at one end, waitstaff at the other. Another function of family meal was to try to blur that line, soften the traditional antagonism between the two sides. But unless there was a hot love affair going on between a cook and a server, and usually there was, the invisible border stayed roughly intact. Business as usual.

Tonight the friction was mostly silent, which made it more dangerous. At both ends, stunned or sullen faces stared down at food no one could do more than pick at. Even Dwayne, whose supply of filthy jokes was normally infinite and unstoppable, wasn't talking. He sat with his massive shoulders slumped and his bulbous shaved head down, cleaning his nails with a chef's knife.

"If you were going to be raped, would you rather be clean and neat, like you just took a shower and washed your hair and everything? Or would you rather be dirty? Which would you rather, or would you care?"

Ah, Shirl. What would Rose do without her? She wished Anna were here so she could tell her, "I rest my case."

"Because last night I heard this noise outside the window of my building? And I'm like, oh shit, it's a rapist, and then I start going, oh no, my hair's dirty, and I'm worrying about how I smell and like that. Is that nuts? But I mean, even if it's rape, you've still got your pride."

Rose said in a bright voice, "I haven't heard any restaurant name suggestions in a while. Anybody have any new ones?"

Silence.

"I think of one," Luca said shyly, from the cooks' half of the table.

"No way," Dwayne protested, "he don't even drink. Sardine can't play."

Luca looked confused. "I can't suggest?"

"If you win you wouldn't get nothing, so what's the point?"

"What's your suggestion, Luca?" Rose asked.

He turned his dark, soulful eyes on her. "Is Italian restaurant, *sì*?"

That wasn't as silly as it sounded. Rose had been advised to turn the Bella Sorella into an Indian restaurant so she could name it Curry Favor, and a steak house so she could call it Bone to Pick. "*Sì,*" she told Luca.

"And soon it will be better, yes, because of many improvements?"

"That's the idea. That's what we're hoping."

"So—you name it *Adesso Viene il Bello*. Is good, eh?"

Luca had a flatteringly inflated idea of her fluency in Italian. "*Adesso*," she said slowly, "I know that means 'now.' Now comes the . . ."

"Is a saying. Now is coming the fine thing, the most, the mostest . . ."

"Now comes the best part," Carmen said out of the side of her mouth.

"*Sì, sì*. Is good, yes?"

"It's nice," Vonnie said, and Shirl said, "Yeah, that's not too bad."

Luca beamed.

"It's too long and it's in Italian," said Eddie, the bartender Rose wouldn't mind dismissing; "Ever Eddie," the female bar customers called him. "Nobody could pronounce it."

"Yeah," said Dwayne, "why don't you just call it When the Moon Hits Your Eye Like a Big Pizza Pie?"

Poor Luca. He had the saddest face, droopy eyebrows shadowing tragic, deep-set dark eyes, long-lidded and romantic. Two years ago, just before coming to America, he'd lost his wife and three-year-old son in a car accident. He broke Rose's heart. He smiled at her hopefully, waiting for her verdict.

"It is a little long," she said gently.

"Hah," Dwayne gloated. "I knew she'd hate it. She hates everything." Luca wasn't the only sensitive one—Dwayne was still smarting because Rose hadn't loved his suggestion, Below the Belt.

The table lapsed back into gloomy silence.

Shirl rallied. "Do you think about, like, how you'd clean your teeth if there was a nuclear war? Say everything's gone, all the drugstores and grocery stores and you can't get a toothbrush or toothpaste or anything, forget about dental floss. I think about it when I floss, if this could be, like, the last time. You'd have to find something to get that white stuff off the back of your bottom teeth in front. I have a little pick I got at the drugstore, but if there was a nuclear war, what would you use? And hair, how long would it take before your hair got used to not being washed every day? Nobody would have on makeup, so that would be... except if you were holding your cosmetics case when the bomb went off, then you'd have it. But people would try to steal it off you, so it might turn out to be more trouble than it was worth. Plus it wouldn't last forever. So you'd, like, ration your mascara..."

"Hey, where is everybody?" Anna's voice, in the kitchen. She came around the corner, shedding her wet raincoat. "Hi, guys, looking good. What's for dinner, Dwayne's jockstrap?" Last week, Dwayne had breaded and deep-fried Luca's sneaker and served it to him—Anna's introduction to family meal. "Hey, Rose, hi, Carmen. Vince, my man. Elise, honey, no apron at dinner, it annoys the patrons. They're like, No wonder I can't get a cup of coffee, they're all over there *eating*."

Elise, who might give you the finger if you told her she had lipstick on her teeth, giggled and blushed and took off her waitress's apron.

Rose smiled to herself. Anna thought *she* manipulated people.

"Sit," she said, making room for her between herself and Carmen. "How'd it go? Find anything interesting?" Anna had taken the afternoon off to go to some flea markets and a restaurant supply auction.

"Yes, but I didn't buy anything. Yet." To the table she said, "Hey, I just ate dinner at Brother's, and I'm delighted to report the food was terrible." She frowned when all that got was a few thin smiles. "What's up? Why's everybody so grim?"

"A little bit of a setback," Rose said lightly. "Not the end of the world."

"But close to it," Eddie said from across the table, and reached into his pocket. "We are so screwed. Reviewed and screwed."

Anna looked at Rose sharply. "That thing in *City Week*? It came out?"

She nodded. "I'm afraid it isn't very good."

"It's beyond bad." Eddie unfolded the torn-out newsprint article. "Here's the headline: ALL GOOD THINGS MUST COME TO AN END."

"Here," Anna said, holding out her hand. She looked sick.

Eddie had long, silky black hair he wore in a ponytail, numerous piercings, a diamond-shaped dot on his chin for a beard. Handsome? Rose supposed he was, but he knew it—that spoiled his appeal as far as she was concerned. "No," he said, "I'll read it to you." He cleared his throat theatrically. "It starts out, 'Remember the old Gaiety Theater in the north end? Years ago it was an art movie house, with foreign flicks and independent films you couldn't catch anywhere else between D.C. and New York. Today, alas, the Gaiety is a strip club; naked ladies perform a different kind of act with fire poles, and the closest you can get to *La Dolce Vita* is a lap dance.' "

"Don't read anymore," Vince growled, "just give it to her."

" 'But at least the Gaiety still has some life in it, even if it's the sleazy, pornographic kind. Too bad the same cannot be said for the Bella Sorella, a downtown institution almost as old as I am, and that's saying something. But that's the trouble with institutions: they get older, but they don't always get better.'

"Wow," said Eddie, fanning his face with the article. "And that's just the first paragraph. He goes on. 'Let's start with the service, which veered widely, or rather wildly, on the three occasions I dined at this venerable establishment, between bored and foaming-at-the-mouth frantic.' "

"Three?" Anna said, stiff-lipped. "He came three times?"

"Don't read any more—" Rose said, at the same time Vince leaned over and flicked the paper out of Eddie's hand.

"Hey," he pouted, "just when I was getting to the good part."

Rose already knew the worst by heart, but she leaned against Anna's arm and read it again with her. The menu was "staid and uninteresting, and reads like Basic Italian Cooking 101." The salads were "afterthoughts," the tortellini with sun-dried tomato pesto was "bitter, and if you can get to the bottom of your plate you're rewarded with a pool of oil." The reviewer hated the service, too: "Rarely have I heard so many apologies from the waitstaff," he wrote, "but then, this one had a lot to be sorry for."

Anna moaned and reached out to touch Carmen's arm. She'd gotten to the worst part, Rose saw: "Chicken Carmen comes in a stolid, viscous white sauce, flecked with either red bell peppers or pimientos, it's hard to tell. And what Italian chef ruins lasagne? There's more meat and certainly more flavor in a package of Lean Cuisine than in this runny, pallid, over-noodled excuse for a spinach lasagne."

Carmen hissed, jerking her shoulder to shrug Anna's hand off. It had been a gesture of sympathy, Rose knew, a reflex; but Carmen's pride was scalded, and sympathy would feel like rubbing salt on the burn.

No, the worst part was the end, the last paragraph. "This is a restaurant that's taking up space. With all the talk of preserving our historic downtown from the predations of national chains and franchises, a visit to the Bella Sorella makes one long for nothing so much as a nice plate of rigatoni from the Olive Garden. Or—since the cappuccino machine seems to be permanently on the fritz—a double skim milk latte at Starbucks."

Anna lowered the review to her lap. She kept her eyes on it, even though Rose knew she'd finished reading. She took a soft, shuddery breath and looked up. Into the awkward quiet, she said in a clear, confident voice, "This is bullshit."

The table came back to life.

"Yeah," Vonnie said first, and then others chimed in, "Totally, it's complete bullshit!" and "Who the hell is that guy, anyway?" Anger was better than despair, and Rose was happy to acknowledge a lot of vicious swearing she would ordinarily discourage by pretending not to hear.

"Maybe not *total* bullshit." Anna caught Rose's eye for a second, but the message wasn't clear, Rose didn't know what she was asking for. Permission, she realized, when Anna stood up and said, "You know what this calls for? Champagne. Vince, you and Eddie, would you get us some glasses? And two, no, make that *three* bottles of Schramsburg." She glanced at Rose again, who swallowed and managed to say, "Absolutely," with a carefree smile. What the hell.

Anna stayed on her feet after the glasses were poured. No one drank; they knew she was going to make a toast. "Okay, here's what we're drinking to. Well, wait—first of all, I want to say—this guy is a jerk. There's no question about it," she continued over exclamations of agreement, "we are dealing here with a complete dickhead. The problem is—the problem is, even dickheads get something right once in a while, and this guy Gerber might have ID'd a couple of things we could possibly improve on. Am I right?"

Yeah, maybe, they agreed, yeah, she could be right.

"So now what are we going to do about it? First, let's drink to this moment—because this is the absolute lowest we're going to go. I think that's worth commemorating, don't you? Everybody with me?" She raised her glass. "To the absolute worst it's ever going to get at the Bella Sorella."

Cheers, and everyone drank.

"God, that's good," Anna said in a different voice, an awed aside that got another laugh. "Okay—and now what's the next thing we're going to do?"

Dwayne belched lustily. "Three more bottles."

"Take Tuesday off!"

"No, the next thing, we're going to sit down together, all of us, and figure out how to fix this. I think it's safe to say some changes are going to be made. Not because of this review—this guy can kiss my ass." She touched the newspaper clipping to a lit candle and held on until the flames almost burned her fingers. "Not because of that article," she repeated when the hoots and cheers died down. "It makes a point or two we'll take under advisement—but we want this place to prosper for better reasons than so Mr. Head Up His Ass will like us. For one thing, we want it for Rose."

Heartening applause. Dwayne banged his gigantic fists on the table, upsetting a glass.

"And for Carmen, who doesn't deserve the crap in that pile of ashes. And we want it for *us*, because we have pride in our work and we're good at what we do and we're not taking this lying down. On Tuesday—on Tuesday, we're going to meet, all of us, meet for an hour at four o'clock. Don't worry, you'll get paid. We'll do it in splits, lunch shift can leave at four forty-five, dinner crew comes in half an hour early—that way we overlap and nobody gets screwed. But I want front and back, kitchen and dining room, I want everybody but the part-timers—because this is where we're going to let our hair down, guys, really figure this thing out. I know you've all got good ideas, and Rose and Carmen and I want to hear them."

Rose nodded and said, "Yes, absolutely, yes." At least Carmen didn't snort or roll her eyes.

"This is only a start, and you know I'd be lying if I said it's going to be easy. I see a lot of work ahead. So anybody who's not interested in working hard, now's your chance to go for that job over at the Olive Garden. Last toast." She raised her glass again. "To us. To us, and to the Bella Sorella. And to success."

"That's three," Eddie pointed out.

They drank.

"You can hire all the new line cooks you want, it's not going to make a miracle happen."

"Did I say 'miracle'?" Anna turned her back on Carmen to ask Rose. "Did you ever hear me say 'miracle'?"

"We've got enough cooks," Carmen went on, "too many; if you hire someone new you'll have to fire somebody else to make room. I'm telling you, a new cook is not the answer."

Anna studied her hands.

"No," Rose said calmly, "of course, not the ultimate answer, but maybe it's someplace we could start. I don't like to see you working so hard, and this would help take some of the load off. *If* we found someone you liked and trusted."

Carmen smirked; Rose's try at diplomacy didn't fool or appease her. Anna wanted to hire someone young and fresh in the kitchen, and although she was calling the job "line cook," what she really wanted was an assistant sous-chef. At the least.

"Move on," Carmen grumbled. "You know where I stand, we don't have to keep going over it. I'd like to get to bed sometime tonight."

The staff had gone home; it was just the three of them, still at the big table, sipping coffee instead of champagne. Rose had imagined this scene, Anna, Carmen, and herself at the tired tail end of the day, putting their heads together to think of fun, innovative ways to improve the restaurant. She hadn't thought to include animosity in her daydream.

"All right," Anna said, "we'll move on. I've been looking at some of these online sites that connect restaurants with suppliers. They operate like a co-op, that's how they keep costs down. We could be saving as much as five percent on basic stuff, food as well as equipment, maybe more."

"Rip-off," Carmen said. "Who are they? Strangers. It's taken us years to line up good suppliers we can count on. Local people, so they've got a stake in being fair. And freshness—how're you going to get fresh produce off the Internet?"

"How do you know you're not? How do you know Sloan's Seafood isn't *on* the Internet?"

"Well, that's something to look into," Rose said, "find out more about, because that would be interesting if it worked."

"Speaking of the Internet," Anna resumed after a strained pause. "Our Web site's primitive, it's not linked to much of anything, it's just sitting there. I can fix it, but it would take forever. Don't we employ any computer nerds? And we need to hook up to more sites that make online reservations and also put in a lot of hype for nothing, including your menu."

"Maybe Vonnie's son?" Rose suggested. "He's always playing with one of those game things. How old is he, Carmen, fifteen now?"

Carmen shrugged, not interested. "Food cost, that's all we have to talk about. Ours is too high. End of story."

Anna tapped her fingertips together impatiently. "That's the solution? Lowering costs? Paying less for the food we buy, that's how you see us getting back on our feet?"

"Whose feet? Whose feet is *our* feet?"

"Now," Rose said, "let's—"

Carmen cut her off. "I know a lot of recipes you'd love, honey, they've got all kinds of nifty, trendy ingredients, that asshole in the newspaper would wet his pants telling how great they are. If I made them, we'd go broke in six weeks. The food cost is too high. It's arithmetic, not brain surgery."

Anna made a helpless gesture and slouched back in her chair. "Fine. What's your suggestion?"

"Cut costs."

"And lower prices."

"Not necessarily."

"Oh, I see. So—" Anna closed her mouth, and Rose was glad; she looked ready to boil over. Keeping these two on speaking terms was turning into a full-time job.

"What was that you were saying about dividing up the dining area, Anna?" she tried. "You had a thought—"

"What is the point," Carmen wanted to know, "of cutting the dining room in half? What can you do in one half you can't do in the other?"

"Not in half, I never said divide it down the middle. And the point is *visual interest*," Anna enunciated too clearly. "It *looks* better. The diner thinks he has a choice—I can sit here, or I can sit there. One side's for smoking, too—all you've got separating the sections now is space. Which is wasted."

"What do you want to break it up with," Carmen snarled, "a potted palm?"

"No, something airy, and if possible something *useful*." She turned to Rose again, away from Carmen. "I found a piece of furniture in an antique store today, it's a beautiful old oak and etched glass breakfront or separator or something, it's twelve feet wide, I don't know what it used to be but it would be perfect right—there." She pointed to the area of floor directly behind the U-shaped bar. "You can't see through it, the glass is opaque, but the light coming through is the color of yellow topaz or amethyst. It's really incredible."

"It sounds beautiful."

"How much?" Carmen asked.

Anna drummed her fingers. "We're negotiating."

Carmen shoved up from her chair. "Now I'm really going to bed. I'll sleep like a baby, knowing what good hands all my problems are in."

When she was gone, Anna said a bad word and got up to pour herself a glass of brandy. "Want one?" she asked Rose, who said no thanks. "I don't either. She's driving me to drink."

"Anna, she's hurt. Try to imagine how that review made her feel."

"I know how it made her feel."

"She doesn't show it, but she's embarrassed. It was a blow."

"I know, and I'm sorry, but she's down on *everything*—I could say we ought to change the lightbulbs when they burn out and she'd find a reason why that was stupid."

Rose couldn't deny it.

"She wants to raise the health insurance cutoff from twenty-two to twenty-seven hours a week. *That's* her solution."

"I know."

"You're not doing it, are you? I'm for cutting staff, but I'm not for stabbing in the back the ones you've got. Think what would happen to some of the part-timers, they'd lose—"

"No, I'm not going to do it." Not unless she had to.

"Good. She's just . . ."

"She's just Carmen."

How tempting it would be to go on, sympathize more warmly with Anna's complaints, even add a few of her own. Rose resisted. But it was hard. Nothing brought old antagonists together better than a common enemy, and Carmen was such an easy target. Already Rose felt seduced by the promise of a closeness with Anna she'd tried not even to hope for, not this soon. They'd talked more to each other in the last two weeks than in the last sixteen years. She went around glowing, breathless all the time; Theo wanted to know if she had on "rouge."

"What is her *problem*?" Anna went on. "I mean, has she always been like this? You knew her when she was young—was she an obnoxious little girl, too?"

"No, of course not. Well—no, not obnoxious, but I wouldn't say happy, either. She was always heavy, not what boys considered attractive, so . . ."

"Were you friends?"

"Well, we were cousins, but the age difference was too big. We weren't really close as kids." Would telling Anna a secret about Carmen be disloyal, another way to set up that us-against-her model she'd just rejected? "Something happened when she was young—or not that young, in her thirties—and it soured her on men. Well, life—she was hurt, and it colored everything. She never really got over it."

Anna came closer, wide-eyed. "Carmen had a tragic love affair? Really? Okay, dish."

Rose smiled. "I don't know all the details. Her mother told my mother, who told Iris, who told Lily and me. A lot of it was hushed up because of the circumstances."

"*What* circumstances?"

"She fell in love with a priest."

"Oh my God." Anna pulled her chair out and sat down again.

"His name was Father Benetta—I only remember him because he was young and handsome, not because I went to church that often. But Carmen was devout, went to mass every morning. She was even on the rectory committee, ladies who volunteered to keep the priests' house clean and that sort of thing."

"Ah ha."

"You know, I don't think there was ever anything between them, not a real affair. Although I don't *know* that. I think it was one-sided, but I also think he used her."

"How?"

"By making her believe they were special friends, and that he could confide in her the same way she confided in him. He did tell her personal things, even that he was thinking of giving up the priesthood. Can you imagine the fantasy she must've built out of that?"

"So what happened?"

"Eventually he did leave the priesthood. With the twenty-five-year-old daughter of a parishioner—they were married within a month. He'd been carrying on with this young woman all along—at least that was the gossip—and using Carmen for a shield."

"Oh, Rose."

"It was very sad. She hid it, but she was crushed. If you asked her today, she'd say it never happened. That's how she played it then, too, so you couldn't comfort her. She pretended none of it mattered because she'd never had any feelings for him. She just denied everything."

"And then got sourer and sourer." Anna turned a water glass in circles on the tablecloth. "That's a sad story. Does she still go to church?"

"Oh yes."

"Wow. But still. None of that makes it any easier for the people who have to try to work with her. Right? I mean, it doesn't really excuse a lifetime of bitchiness, do you think?"

"I wasn't trying to say it did."

"No, I know." She got up, began to prowl the darkened dining room, straightening chairs, lining up ashtrays with bud vases and condiments. "What do you think about tables on the sidewalk after the weather warms up? We used to do that. Do you still?"

"No, not for a while. Carmen thought there was too much upkeep." She stood up, too. "Thank you for tonight, Anna, the things you said. It should've been me trying to cheer everybody up, but I couldn't seem to move. Before you came, we were sitting here like mourners at a wake."

"I should've asked you about the booze first. That was an impulse." She wandered closer, running her hands over the backs of chairs, restless. "Was it too much?"

"Not at all. Under the circumstances, I think it was inspired."

"I didn't know what I was going to say till I said it. And now we have to have a *meeting*." She laughed a little wildly. "What will that do? I guess I was thinking action, doing something, even just talking about it out loud, letting people think they had a say—maybe it would help take the sting out. A little. Oh, Rose, that review was devastating."

It made her sick to her stomach. "This is more than you bargained for. I'd understand . . ." Then she couldn't bring herself to finish.

"What?"

"It's more than *I* bargained for, frankly."

"What, you think I'd *leave*?"

"It's just that this must be starting much farther back than you ever imagined. More trouble, everything worse—I'm afraid this can't be what you had in mind."

"Oh. Forget that." Rose's guilt seemed to cheer her up. "Yeah, it's worse, but so what? We made a deal."

"I'd let you out of it."

"Oh, you can't get rid of me that easy."

"As if I'd try."

Their smiles slid away, barely brushing, shy as moths.

"I like family meal on Sundays," Anna said. "It's a nice thing. I tried to get Nicole to do it at the café, but she'd never go for it. So every night the dinner crew just grabbed whatever they could find and ate it as fast as they could, sitting on milk crates in back by the laundry. Not even together. And the food was horrible, always overdone penne bolognese, they said it turned them into vegetarians. Anyway—it's nice. A good tradition. I'm glad you still have it."

A compliment. Rose kept her smile within bounds, but inside she basked.

"It's late." Anna found her raincoat and put it on. "Are you leaving? I'll go out with you, I've got my car in the alley."

"I'm going to run upstairs for a minute. Check, just make sure she's all right." Carmen lived by herself in the small apartment Rose sublet to her over the restaurant.

"Oh. Okay, then. Tell her I said . . . you know, just tell her, not straight out, that nobody thinks Gerber's review is her fault."

Whether it's true or not, Rose could see Anna struggling not to add. "That's nice. I'll be sure to tell her."

"Okay. Night."

"Oh, Anna, I forgot—Iris is coming to town tomorrow."

"Great, I can't wait to see her. I've got those interviews in the afternoon, but we can have lunch."

"No, she can't make it until late, something about the dogs, one isn't weaned or something, and her sitter can't come until the afternoon."

Anna laughed. "Thirty miles away, and I only see my aunt between litters."

"But she's staying the night. At my place," Rose said casually, "so I was thinking you might like to come over for dinner? If you're not busy."

Trapped. She wouldn't want to come to the apartment—too personal, too informal. It would imply all sorts of things that weren't true. "Well, I've got those interviews," she hedged. "They might run late, and I wouldn't want to hold you up."

Flimsy, very flimsy. "Come late, then. If you can't make dinner, come for dessert. Vince will be there."

Anna stared at the floor, hands deep inside the pockets of her oversized raincoat.

"You know Iris will kill you if she comes down and you don't see her."

"Maybe on Tuesday . . ."

"She's leaving early. The dogs."

She gave up gracefully. "Okay, then. Dessert if I can't make dinner. Your place."

Rose would settle for that.

7

Anna's third interview for the line cook's job didn't look any more promising than the first two. At least she wasn't obviously high, unlike the coked-up second guy with the twitchy chin and the googly eyes. This one's name was Mary Frances O'Malley—Frankie—and the logo on her T-shirt said GLUE SNIFFING WHACK JOB. She had dark red buzz-cut hair, a pierced eyebrow, and huge, haunted eyes in a pale, blue-veined, wren-boned face. As soon as she sat down she pulled out a cigarette, then muttered, "Sorry," and started to shove it back inside her beat-up shoulder bag. "Go ahead," Anna said, "everybody else does," and Frankie fired up a Salem Light with hands that trembled slightly, all the fingernails chewed down to the quick.

She was twenty-nine, her application said, born in Chicago. Moved here from D.C. a year ago. Divorced. Suspicious gap since last full-time job. "Why Italian?" Anna decided to ask first. Not all, but the majority of the chef work this woman had done had been in Italian restaurants, some of them high-end. "Why would Mary Frances O'Malley want to cook Italian?"

"It's Tarantino on my mother's side. My grandmother lived with us when I was little—she was from Lucca, which is in Tuscany."

"Yes, I know. My cooking side is Fiore," Anna mentioned, just trying to set her at ease. "They were all from the north, the Ligurian coast, around in there. So your grandmother taught you how to cook?"

"Yeah, she taught me everything. When she died, I took over all the cooking for the family, because my mother was a—an invalid." Rapid eye blinking when she said *invalid*; either it wasn't true or it was so painful she could barely utter it. "But I know other cuisines, I've worked in French and Spanish restaurants, I love Southwestern, I love California. I love food."

She didn't look like she ate much of it. Fast metabolism, maybe; something was always in motion, a foot bobbing up and down, fingers drumming, quick drags on the cigarette.

"What was your first restaurant job? Your very first."

"I used to work summers in high school at a resort outside Chicago, more of a spa, I guess, for rich women. Healthy food, organic, low fat. I bused tables and washed dishes the first couple of years, but by the end I made it to prep cook, and a couple of times I got to fill in on the hot line. I loved it."

"Why?"

"It was exciting. I liked the pressure. Feeling like I was in the calm place in the middle of a tornado. I ditched college after two years and went to the CIA."

The Culinary Institute, arguably the best cooking school in the country. Anna had made check marks at some of the positives on Frankie's résumé, but around the Culinary she'd drawn a big circle and an exclamation point. She'd hired two CIA grads at Nicole's café; one had been good, the other a screwup. The average kitchen worker harbored a lot of contempt for school-trained chefs, but if nothing else, Anna had always thought, a good school grounded you in basic technique and proper work habits. After that you became whatever you were going to be, but at least you'd learned the fundamentals from experts. It only stood to reason that the better the school, the better the training.

Frankie had worked a succession of jobs in better and better restaurants, her application said, first in New York, then Kansas City, L.A., Washington, D.C., and finally here for the last year. The high point was executive chef in an upscale French bistro in Los Angeles for nine months, just before she moved to D.C. Here she'd worked at À la Notte and Jimmy J's, but only for three months each. She hadn't worked anywhere at all since October.

"What kind of hours were you thinking of putting in?" Anna asked.

"It's up to you. I can work noon to ten, ten to ten, I can work six shifts a week, I can work doubles. Whatever you need."

"Uh-huh. You're divorced?"

"Yes."

"Any kids?"

"I have a little girl. Katie. She's three and a half, almost four."

"Do you have somebody to—"

"My ex-husband's got her. I get to visit." She ground her cigarette in the ashtray on her lap.

"That's tough."

"Yeah." She lit up another one. "What else do you want to know?"

"Tell me what you think your strengths and weaknesses are."

"I'm versatile. I can do specials, I can expedite, I've worked every station except pastry. Anything you need, I can do it. I've got moves, I work fast and clean, and I can improvise. I know technique but I'm not hung up on it, I learned it and went on." She stubbed out the just-lit cigarette and rubbed her palms on the knees of her jeans. "The thing about me, what you want to write down in the space for comments—for me it's all about the food. It's all I care about. I'm a cook."

"Okay. You know this is just a line cook's job, though, right? I'm not hiring a chef today."

"I know. Sure." She blushed.

"Right." But she asked anyway, "What's your theory of good food?" She hadn't bothered to ask the cokehead that question, or the guy before him.

"Freshness," Frankie said, no hesitation. "And simplicity. The best, the smartest place I ever worked was Federico's in K.C. That's where I learned everything that matters. They made everything fresh, every sauce, all the stocks, the pasta, the bread, all of it. That was the best food I ever ate. They even grew their own herbs in the courtyard. Nothing fancy, it was basic stuff, peasant food even, but perfect. It was just . . . sublime." She almost smiled.

Anna cleared her throat. Stupidly, she felt apologetic. "I wouldn't call what we do here sublime."

"Maybe it could be." Again the wisp of a smile. Behind the nerves and the bravado, Anna finally saw awareness. Real intelligence.

"Why here?" she asked. "They're hiring up the street at Figaro—why not try there?"

"I did."

She laughed. "Okay."

"But I like this place better."

"Sure you do. How come?"

"Well, for one thing, I heard you hire women. More than most places."

"That's true." Rose used to talk about an all-woman kitchen being the ideal, like an all-girl band, and she'd only been half kidding.

"And also," Frankie said, "it's not pretentious."

"God knows."

"No, it's neighborhood, but it's still a little nervy. You feel comfortable, but like it's still a cool place. Or it could be," she added, seeing Anna's skeptical face. "It's not rigid, so it's got potential.

Really, it could be anything. Sophisticated but not scary—I think that's just right."

Bullshit, maybe, but at least she knew the right buttons to push. Against her will, Anna felt snowed. "That's what I'd like it to be," she admitted. "I'd like them comfortable, but not so they fall asleep. I want a little edge. They come in and they don't know everything about the place, it could surprise them at any moment. But they're pretty sure it'll be a *good* surprise."

"Yeah, that's it. That's exactly it."

They considered each other.

Anna said, "We're about to go through some changes. To tell you the truth, we've got our backs against the wall. It's going to be hard, it's going to be like labor, and in the end this might be the last restaurant in town you want on your work history."

"I'm not afraid to work hard."

"Your career highpoint was the French place in L.A., where you were executive chef. If you came to work here, you'd practically be starting over. I'd like to know what happened."

"Ups and downs, you know how it is, it's like cycles, first you—"

"Screw that."

Frankie stopped massaging her knees and looked at her.

"Be straight with me. You haven't worked in six months. If I take a chance on you, you have to take a chance on me." Trust, she was talking about, and Frankie knew it, she got it.

"Okay." She stood up. *Popped* up, spring-kneed, propelled by nerves. "What happened was, I had some problems. In the past. There was some drinking."

"I see." Shit.

"But I'm straight now, I've been sober since November. I'm in a program, I'm doing the steps, I've got a sponsor." She came close, came right up to the desk but didn't touch it. "I'm turning it around. I have to, because of my kid. I need this job, but mostly I *want* it, and I know I can do it. I can work sick, I never miss, I never come in late—call anybody on that list, they'll tell you. I've never been fired, even at the worst. I quit my last two jobs, yeah, but they didn't want me to go. And I'm healthy now. You won't be advertising again in three weeks—I swear to God I won't let you down."

Jewel-hard determination blazed in the tough little face. Anna stared back, trying to see the truth behind the intensity, thinking Carmen wasn't going to like this. She hated American cooks; they were all lazy punks demanding *respect*—she always sneered when she said that. She was expecting Anna to hire some speechless, hardworking Ecuadorian or Dominican guy she could terrorize, not this white-faced, high-maintenance, overqualified gringa.

"You don't look very strong," Anna noted. "I need someb—"

"I am, though. Give me something to lift. Your chair—get up, I can lift it with one hand."

"That's okay, I believe you."

The T-shirt and holey jeans, the cheap platform boots, the piercings, the tattoo on her biceps—the longer Anna looked at her, the less Frankie O'Malley fit her clothes. They looked dated on her, not hip or retro. She was too old for the look, she didn't have her heart in it anymore. She was like someone who'd just gotten out of prison, wearing the clothes they'd taken from her when she went in.

"What do you do for fun?"

"Fun?" Frankie stepped back from the desk, frowning. The first question to stump her. "I run. You know, jog. Is that what you mean?"

"I don't know. Is it fun?"

She frowned some more. The question just didn't compute. But now Anna could see it—she weighed about one-ten but she probably was strong, nothing but raw muscle and nerve, no fat anywhere.

"Anything else?" she asked.

"Well... I read cookbooks."

"That's good. Anything else?"

"I don't drink." Her smile was a grim tightening of the lips. "That takes up a lot of my time."

Anna tapped her fingertips together, eyeing Frankie O'Malley—and that was another thing Carmen was going to hate. *Irish*, for God's sake. "Do you have a car?"

"Not right now, but the bus is close."

She nodded, thinking she wouldn't care to take the bus home at midnight to the address on Frankie's application.

"You could try me for a week. Trial period. I'll work for nothing for one week."

Anna stood up, embarrassed.

"I can't afford to do it any longer than that."

"Look, it's getting late, my cleaning crew's coming in and I've still got two more guys to interview."

"No problem." Pink-faced, Frankie grabbed her purse from the couch and started to go.

"Hold it, wait—I was going to say—there's no point in me showing you around the kitchen right now, because you haven't even met Carmen yet. You couldn't stick around, could you?"

"Yeah, sure." When her face relaxed, her dark blue eyes got even bigger. With hope. "Carmen's the chef?"

"Pretty much. We call her the sous-chef, though, because technically Rose is the chef. But I can't hire you without Carmen's okay. Naturally."

"No, sure."

"And Rose's," she added, but that wasn't the okay she was worried about. "Hang on a sec, I'll see if Carmen can come down." She picked up the phone, dialed the upstairs number. No answer. "Nope, she's not there." Where could she be? "But listen, now that I think about it, maybe you want to talk to Carmen tomorrow anyway, not today."

"Um, okay. How come?"

It felt like cheating, like giving her the answers to the test, but Anna said, "Because then you can go home and change your shirt. I gotta tell you, Frankie, Carmen's not a big fan of attitude."

She looked down at her chest, looked up. A shy smile spread into a grin. "No problem. I've got another shirt."

"What's it say?"

"Ass-licking boot sucker."

"Oh, much better. Carmen will fall head over heels."

After the last interview, after the cleaning crew left, after finishing her inventory, adding her list to Carmen's and calling in tomorrow's orders for her, Anna pulled her chair closer to Rose's cluttered desk and booted up the computer. "That machine," Carmen called it; Anna should spend more time on the floor and less on that machine if she wanted to improve business, that was Carmen's advice. Anna couldn't wait to tell her about her latest online find—a local computer dating service called "It's Only Lunch." She had some great ideas for attracting couples to the Bella Sorella when they hooked up for that first lunch date. Right now, though, she wasn't cruising the Net for contacts or checking out the competition's Web sites. She was just reading her e-mail.

Aha. A note from Mason. Very short. It made her laugh.

Dear Anna,
Your puny threat doesn't scare me. You are invited to come over and discuss your bill at any time.

M.W.

They'd been writing to each other. Did that amaze him as much as it did her? Polite, businesslike notes at first, but lately, real letters. It was fun. Addictive.

She scrolled down and reread their correspondence in order, bottom to top.

Dear Mason Winograd,
I've tried to call, but I can never seem to catch you in. Rose gave me this e-mail address and said you wouldn't mind if I wrote—to thank you for fixing my roof. You left without a trace, I wouldn't even have known you'd been there, but my neighbor saw you on Saturday with your ladder, etc., and said she spoke to you. I particularly wanted to call you on Monday night, after it rained and not a single drop leaked down the wall in the second-floor bathroom. If you haven't already sent a bill, could you please post back and let me know how much I owe you? Thank you again for your excellent work, and for your trouble. I'm sure it was an imposition, and am sorry if, because of Rose, I somehow put you on the spot. In any case, you were very kind to help out a stranger.

Best regards,
Anna Catalano

P.S. How is the kingfisher?

Dear Anna Catalano,
Was lucky and found box of original shingles in your garage, so didn't need to buy any. Hence, no charge. Glad to hear patch is working.

Kingfisher much cheerier after splint and tapes removed yesterday, although not as ready for flight as he thinks. Another week of captivity, I expect. Then freedom.

M. Winograd

Dear Mason,
Don't be ridiculous. Please tell me how much I owe, and make it a fair price or I'll be angry. I've seen but not yet had the courage to go into my garage, so I think it's highly likely you wasted at least half a day in there hunting for shingles. Now tell me what I owe you.

Anna

Dear Anna,
I forgot to tell you, you have a nest of phoebes in the section of gutter over your back door. I counted four white eggs. Your neighbor spoke to me at considerable length about your renovation plans and mentioned, among many other things, that you intended to replace your gutters. If that's true, you might like to postpone until approx. mid-June. But then you'd want to do it fairly quickly, as phoebes sometimes use the same nest for a second brood not long after they've fledged the first. Just a thought.

M.

Dear Mason,
I'm sorry you got waylaid by my neighbor. Mrs. Burdy is a lovely woman, but I remember my mother hissing at me when she'd see her coming up the walk, "Tell her I'm at the store, tell her anything!" just to avoid an hour-long gossip.

Postponing the gutters won't be any hardship. There's quite a lot of flying in and out of that area right now, so I guess the phoebe eggs must've hatched. I can't say I like their song much, but it is thoughtful of them to say their own name, however shrilly and repetitively; so much easier to identify them that way. More birds should do it, imo.

Anna

Dear Anna,
Mrs. Burdy kept me company while I repaired your roof. Standing at the bottom of the ladder, I should say, not actually beside me on the roof. Consequently, you should know that there's hardly anything about your family, infancy, childhood, and young adulthood to which I have not been made privy. Including the time you, age four, rolled the family car down the driveway and into the garage. (In my shingles search, I had already noticed the damage to the back wall; very impressive.) So please don't apologize to me for Mrs. B., who I found to be a most agreeable and informative companion.

Mason

Dear Mason,
I was six, and it wasn't the family car, it was the car my father's company lent him to drive around four states and the District of Columbia in his job as a book and magazine sales rep. And if you think the garage dent is impressive, you should've seen the car. I, as of course Mrs. Burdy will have told you, was unscathed.

Anyway, that's nothing—I found an archived interview of you online at the newspaper's Web site, and now there's nothing about you I don't know. Including that you're a celebrity. The cover of *Audubon*, no less, not to mention a published book. *That's* impressive. Rose didn't tell me you were famous, I had to find out by accident. Frankly, and I hope you won't take this the wrong way, I thought you were a hermit. Which reminds me. About the bill: don't make me come over there and get it.

There, the ultimate threat. I believe that should do it.

Anna

But no, she was invited to come and discuss the bill at any time. Ha! Well, maybe she would, call his bluff, see how he liked it. At least he hadn't minded the hermit crack. She'd worried about that, hoped it wasn't too personal. She'd meant it, though, hadn't really been joking, and she'd been hoping he would respond to it somehow. Explain himself.

The newspaper article about him was fascinating; she'd printed it out so she could reread it. He'd been the subject of "Sunday's Profile," a weekly feature in the arts and entertainment section, about this time last year. The author, a woman, had gone on at length about his "brooding looks" and "laconic manner." There were two reproduced photographs he'd taken of a clapper rail and a pied-billed grebe, but no picture of him. The thrust of the story was that right here in our little town we had a well-known, highly respected bird photographer and conservation writer, whose latest achievements were a published book and a photo and print essay on the decline of migrating waterfowl on the Chesapeake in *Audubon* magazine. Local boy makes good. Only about five hundred people in the world made their living entirely from nature or wildlife photography, and Mason Winograd was one of them. His father had been a Navy test pilot, killed in a plane crash when Mason was five, his mother an elementary school teacher whose second marriage, when Mason was eight, was to "a waterman." Theo, presumably. His mother must be dead or divorced, then, since Theo and Rose were an item. The article went on about how he'd photographed birds all over the world until four years ago, when he'd begun to concentrate and focus exclusively on the Chesapeake. The writer had missed the real story, to Anna's mind, or else Mason had been so *laconic* she couldn't pull it out of him. In one maddeningly short paragraph she referred to "a serious accident" nine years ago that had "left scars" and cut short his law career, "causing Winograd to reevaluate what he wanted to do with his life." Photograph birds, which he'd been doing as an amateur since childhood, she wrote—but what kind of an accident, and how exactly had it shaped his decision, and why didn't he answer his phone, why didn't his house have any front windows. That's what Anna wanted to know. For starters. She could ask Rose, of course. But she didn't want to.

Dear Mason,
Thank you—maybe I'll take you up on your invitation. I don't think you're ever going to send me a bill, though, so here's a compromise. Come to the Bella Sorella and be my guest for dinner. Any night but Monday, when we're closed. The payment won't be equal, but I think we know whose fault that is.

A.

P.S. If you say no, I'll assume it's because you read yesterday's hatchet job in *City Week*. We're still bleeding.

She hit Send, then automatically checked her incoming mail one last time. Oh—another note from Mason! He'd sent it before he got hers.

"P. S.," he wrote. "That fellow Gerber, did you know he's a well-known pedophile, wife beater, and crack addict? Some say—but this can't be confirmed—also a Republican."

Anna put her hands over her mouth and stared at the screen. She snickered through her fingers, but her eyes stung; she could've cried just as easily. She had pushed the awful review to the back of her mind, because thinking about it made her crazy. Hot anxiety came rushing back now, reminding her of just how much trouble they were in. But Mason's silliness was a comfort. What a nice thing to say.

She wanted to send a note back, something clever and grateful, something to make *him* laugh. He might be online right now—they could have a real-time conversation if she hurried. But she looked at her watch and saw it was after eight—she had to log off, lock up, and go, otherwise she'd be late for dessert at Rose's.

8

"Child," Aunt Iris greeted Anna, "oh, look at you. Oh my, oh my." She gathered her into a rough, crushing, long-armed embrace. "I gave up thinking I'd ever see the day."

"Hi, Aunt I," Anna said, misty-eyed in spite of herself.

"Gave up hope. And here you are. Home at last."

"Home for a while," she corrected out of habit. "How are you? You look just the same." Like a frontierswoman, the tough-skinned, bony-butted kind who sat in front of the wagon and drove across the dusty desert, squinting and not complaining. She even wore her ginger-gray hair in braids on top of her head. She was the oldest and plainest Fiore sister, she'd never had Rose's elegance or Lily's feminine prettiness. In Italy, she'd have been the one who worked in the olive groves with the men, brown as a nut and wiry as a vine.

"Oh," she said, "I miss my puppies, but I'm glad to be here, glad to see Rose. And *you.* Oh, *honey.*" Another squeeze, even harder. "I know, don't tell me, but it's better than cats."

Anna frowned, thinking about Broadway, Broadway and Aunt Iris—

"If I have to get old and ga-ga, it's better that I raise dogs than cats."

Ah.

"You're late," she went on, drawing Anna into Rose's living room, "so you missed Vince, he had to leave right after we ate. He had a date."

"Vince always has a date."

"He's just like his father. I want that boy to settle down so bad, but I don't see it happening in my lifetime."

"Uncle Tony settled down." Anna assumed; she'd never heard otherwise.

"Yes, and that's the only thing that gives me hope for Vincent. Anna, he's so glad you're back."

"Vince is one of the best things about being back." She put an affectionate hand on her aunt's arm, thinking they'd go out on the balcony together—she could see Rose and somebody else out there in the candlelit dusk, a man; she'd thought it was Vince, but obviously not. But Aunt Iris stayed where she was, leaning toward her, lowering her voice.

"We're having an *incident*," she said, cutting her eyes to the side. "Theo fell down just now, lost his balance and went right over backward. He hurt his head and it's bleeding, but he won't let Rose call the doctor. They're fighting."

Anna looked again at the silhouette of a thick-shouldered, shaggy-haired man, sitting bolt upright with his hands on his chair arms. And Rose, bending over him, in his face, talking to him fast and low. He wasn't talking back.

"She wants him to stay here tonight, but he won't, absolutely refuses, says he's going back to his boat. Rose said she's not taking him, so he called his son, stepson, and he's on his way. You know Rose doesn't get mad that often, but she is fit to be tied. I think she'd like to knock him over again."

"Well," said Anna, nonplused.

"It happened so fast—he was coming back from the bathroom and he just sort of stopped in the middle of the living room like he was stuck. Next thing you know, he's flat on his back on the floor. His head missed the rug and hit on the wood, he got a real *crack*."

"Is he okay?"

"Who knows? I think, I *hope*, it's mostly his pride."

Rose came in from the balcony. Her face was pink, eyes wide and glittery. "Anna," she said, unnaturally gay, "you're here! Come and meet Theo."

"Hi, Rose. Are you sure? We can do this another—"

"No, no, he's fine, he's perfectly all right! What's a little blood, what's a lump on the head the size of a kiwi? Nothing at all, not to a real man!"

Anna came closer, staring, fascinated. "You okay?"

Rose growled instead of answering, opening her eyes even wider and drawing her lips back, showing clenched teeth. She was livid. Anna couldn't help but laugh in sympathy, even though she didn't like being drawn over to Rose's side so quickly.

The bay view from the balcony was still intact, she saw with relief; no one had built a high-rise between it and Rose's three-story apartment building yet. A half moon coming up over the water glittered the blue-black surface in silvery ripples. Candles, flowers, dishes from dinner cluttered the glass-topped table, which was set for four. "Oh, sit down," Rose snapped at the man trying to struggle up from behind it, but he batted her hand away, glowering. Then he almost pulled the table over grabbing onto the edge of it while he rocked himself to his feet.

Anna took the dry, scratchy hand he held out to her. Theo squeezed hers painfully hard, even though his was trembling in spasms. He was stocky and thick-chested, shorter than Rose, with grizzled hair and a long, soft-looking gray walrus mustache. His leathery, beat-up face had a mug-shot quality that more than hinted at hard drinking and hard living, and not in the distant past, either. He had a blood-spotted towel slung over his shoulder, a bloody handkerchief in his other hand. He was a little scary. *This* was

Theo? A man less like the kind she'd always thought Rose liked—a man less like her father—she could barely imagine.

"I heard . . . a lot about you," he said haltingly, and he didn't smile when he said it. The words came out light and breathy—something else she wasn't expecting. He looked like a man whose voice would boom out like gunfire. Breathy or not, the message couldn't have been clearer: what he'd heard about her he didn't like.

Were they going to be enemies? She'd been prepared not to like him since Aunt Iris first mentioned his name. But she could see things were going to be a little more complicated. For her, anyway; apparently not for him. He said next, "Nice of you to come—down and put things right for Rose. Very—charitable of you."

"Theo," Rose warned.

"She'd be helpless without you."

"*Theo.*"

He pulled his lips to the side, only slightly chastened. His nose had been broken a time or two; it went off in two different directions, Z-shaped, from a rough bump in the middle. Prizefighter's face.

Anna said, "I've heard a lot about you, too."

"Yeah?"

"I heard when Rose first met you, you reminded her of Hemingway, only without the stupidity and vanity." Aunt Iris had told her that. Anna watched Theo's pale eyes, faded blue in the twilight, blink in surprise and uncertainty. Rose laughed. He didn't have a retort. "I also heard," Anna went on, "that you think I'm a troublemaker."

His lips were still strong and shapely between the two halves of his mustache. Now they almost smiled. "Who've you been talking to? Mason," he answered himself. "I mighta said that. But now that I meet you—" He paused to take a few breaths. "I can see you're sweet as candy. You wouldn't dream of—treating your Aunt Rose any way—any way but fair and decent. Right?"

"Oh, I've always treated Rose just the way she deserves."

A snarly sound came from the back of his throat. Rose started to say something, but he cut her off. "I always felt bad for meeting up with Rose—so late in my life. Least now I can see what she looked like twenty years ago. I guess . . . that's something I have to say thanks for."

Now Anna wasn't sure how to respond. If that was a peace offering, which she doubted, she didn't want to return it with snottiness. "Twenty-four," she corrected lamely. They stared at each other, wary and interested, and hostile, while Rose cleared her throat and rubbed her hands together.

The doorbell rang.

"I'll get it." Aunt Iris sounded relieved.

"It'll be Mason," Theo mumbled. He put his red-knuckled hands on the table edge and gave a graceless yank, clattering the silver and glassware. He was trying to turn around, but his body wasn't cooperating. A moment passed before Anna caught the signal Rose was sending with her eyes—*Go away. He doesn't want you to see.* She excused herself and went inside.

Aunt Iris was running water in the kitchen sink. Anna looked around at the empty apartment. "Wasn't that Mason?"

"He's outside. He said he'd wait."

"He wouldn't come in?"

Iris shrugged. "Strange family."

Outside, Mason had his back to her, arms braced against the balcony railing, staring down at the parking lot in front of Rose's building. He turned around when he heard the door open, and his guarded face opened up when he saw Anna. He looked amazed—as if he couldn't imagine a less likely spot for her to turn up. When he smiled, she had a sensation of familiarity, as if she knew him much better than she really did. The e-mails? "Hi," they said, and she widened the door so he could come in. But he said, "How's Theo?" and stepped sideways, inviting her to join him on the walkway. "Is he all right?"

So she came outside. "Yeah, I think so. He *seems* okay. Rose is furious, though, because he won't go to the hospital, he won't even let her call his doctor."

"But he's all right? He sounded fine on the phone."

"There was some blood, but I think scalp wounds always bleed a lot. But I'm not a doctor."

"This is how he is," Mason said, sounding resigned. "He won't come home with me, either. He refuses to move in with me or Rose."

"He lives on a boat?"

"By himself. It's not a good situation."

"No." If you had balance problems, a boat would not be a good place to live.

They stood with their arms folded across the cool metal rail, watching two women and a man walk across the parking lot and get into a car. Mason always positioned himself on Anna's left, presumably to keep the scarred side of his face out of her view, and she wished she knew him well enough to say something about that. Like, she couldn't care less.

At least he wasn't hiding behind his hair tonight. He fumbled in his pockets for something, probably cigarettes, but came up empty. Nervous habit. *She* made him nervous. She thought of him slouched in his kitchen doorway that first day, affecting carelessness. In fact, he'd been borderline surly. *Something I can do for you?* Tough guy, she'd thought, but not for long; since then, he'd been letting more and more of that cover-up go. She wondered what was underneath, what the last layer might look like. Not that you ever got to anybody's last layer.

"Theo's always moved around a lot," he was telling her, "job to job, place to place. He can't anymore, so for him the next best thing is to live on his sailboat. It's not moving, but everything around it is."

"Did he move around a lot when you were little?"

"Well, he didn't marry my mother till I was eight."

"That's pretty little."

"They split up because he was never around. It only lasted two years. He'd go away on steamer jobs, or barging, or just move down the coast so he could fish in new water. Always had to keep moving."

So by the time he was ten, Mason had lost two fathers. One every five years. "Is your mother still living?" she asked.

"No."

Stars were popping out in the last blue band of color over the treeline in the distance. In the street, a jogger and a guy on a bike passed each other and waved. Bugs milled in the arc of the floodlights beaming weakly in the shrubbery below. It felt like summer. "Is that a bat?" Anna asked, pointing up at a swooping, flickering shape in the almost-dark.

"Yes."

"I hear it's a myth that they fly into your hair."

"Usually."

She glanced over to see if he was kidding. Yes—she thought.

"Or it could've been two bats," he said.

"I just saw one."

"If it was a female, she could've been carrying a baby. They'll do that for a week or so, take the baby on their nightly hunting trips. Till it gets too heavy to carry."

Anna said, "Huh," an ambiguous sound, more acknowledgment than interest. That *was* interesting, but what if birds and bats were Mason's only topic of conversation, his only subject? Then it wouldn't be wise to encourage him. For some reason she thought of Jay's rusty steel sculpture around the bed in the loft, the pretty painted birds with human heads, grinning, deranged. Mason fed wounded birds by hand, put cardboard splints on their broken wings, let babies roost in his kitchen window.

But she didn't want to compare them. That was too easy, and potentially a trap. She wasn't in the right frame of mind to be fair, and anyway, next to Jay any man would look like a prince.

She moved an inch closer to Mason. "Remember when you said Theo would like me once he met me?"

He leaned closer too, expectant, nodding already, ready to be vindicated.

"Boy, were you wrong. He can't stand me."

"No. No." He shook his head positively. "That's not right." If nothing else, his disbelief was flattering.

"Ask him. Not that it matters," she added, lest he think she cared. "I'm just telling you."

They both glanced back through the open door. They could see Theo in the living room with Rose, saying good night to Aunt Iris.

"The thing about my stepfather," Mason said hurriedly, "is that he's very protective of Rose."

"So?"

"So, he . . ."

"Wants to save her from me," she finished when he wouldn't. "Yes, I got that. What I can't figure out is what he thinks I'm going to *do* to her. Steal her money? Run the business into the ground?"

"No, of course not. You really don't know?"

She knew, but she shrugged. "What?"

"Leave."

She laughed, feigning incredulity. "He's afraid I'll *leave*?" But Mason didn't laugh with her, wouldn't even put on a sympathetic facial expression. He was in league with them—she'd forgotten that for a second. She liked him and she thought he liked her, so she'd momentarily lost sight of the fact that they weren't on the same side.

Theo and Rose came outside.

"Ready to go?" Mason put his hands in his pockets and moved closer to his stepfather. "Everything okay?"

"Everything's fine," he said, impatience making his whispery voice crack, "nothing the matter with me. Tripped on the goddamn rug, it's got a—rough place. What I oughta do is sue. Got a bump on the head. Doesn't even hurt."

"Because your head's so hard," Mason said, and Theo almost smiled, liking that. They didn't touch; a pocket of air seemed to separate them, an invisible buffer they had to keep between them. Mason hovered, but didn't touch; Theo accepted, but didn't reach out. A man thing, Anna decided—except Rose was doing it too. Apparently nobody was allowed to touch Theo.

Rose hadn't softened to him yet, though. "I'll go down with you," she said brusquely. "Anna, come with us?"

So they all went down the two half-flights of open concrete stairway, Mason first, then Theo, holding on to the banister and moving slowly, one heavy footstep at a time, Rose beside him but not touching. Anna in the rear.

Mason's yellow Jeep was in the visitors' space by the road. Anna said, "I'm glad we met," to Theo, but didn't offer her hand; she didn't feel like getting it crushed again. "I hope I see you again soon."

He said it back, suspiciously, and after he turned away she couldn't resist raising her eyebrows at Mason. *See?*

"Did you get my last e-mail?" she asked him, while Rose went around to the passenger side with Theo.

"Which one?"

"The one inviting you to dinner."

He stared down grimly at his hand on the door handle, thumbing the lock mechanism, making a *click* sound over and over. "You don't have to do that."

She laughed. "I know I don't have to."

"No charge for the roof. I told you, we're even."

"You don't want to have dinner with me?"

He looked up, alarmed. "Sure. Yes."

"Great, name the night."

"It's difficult—my schedule—I'll be out of town, I'm shooting at Assateague and then Blackwater. There's a program, I have to talk, and then on the Pocomoke. It's a very busy season, spring, hard to say a time—but thank you for the invitation, maybe sometime—"

Rose came to his rescue, by slamming Theo's door and coming around the back of the car to join them. Anna looked on in dull surprise when she hugged Mason in the most natural, warmhearted way, as if they did it often. Old friends. A sour feeling spurted through her. Not jealousy, exactly; more like resentment, its ugly cousin.

"I'll get him in bed and settled down," he told Rose in a soft voice. "I'll stay with him for a while before I go, make sure he's okay. Try not to worry."

"Can *you* not worry?" she snapped back, fierce.

He bent his knees to see into her downturned face. "Do you want me to call you later?"

"No, don't. I'm going to bed."

He glanced at Anna, but she just lifted her shoulders. *Don't look at me, I'm not in this.*

She stayed where she was when Mason started the Jeep and backed out of the parking space, thinking she and Rose would wave and watch them out of sight. But Rose deserted her, strode off with her head down and her arms swinging, ankles flashing beneath the kicked-up hem of her long skirt, and marched upstairs by herself.

"You haven't had any dinner? Go outside and I'll bring you a plate," Aunt Iris told Anna.

"No, I couldn't eat. Let's just have coffee—you come out and sit with me. It's getting late, and we haven't had a chance to talk."

"You'll have some dessert, then."

"No, really, I'm not hungry."

"It's Rose's bitter chocolate truffles."

"Oh, my God." She went out on the balcony to wait.

Rose's apartment was aging gracefully. Fancier, taller, more expensive condos and waterfront villas loomed over it now, crowding it in, but it still had its busy view of the water, and inside it was still airy and uncluttered, practically stark. Anna could remember staying here after her mother died, days at a time while her father traveled on his business trips. She'd sleep on the sofa bed in the living room, terribly conscious of what a *sophisticated* place this was, mysterious, the ultimate to her at fifteen or sixteen in grown-up female freedom. Rose would come home tired but revved up from a crazy night at the restaurant, which was thriving in those days, and Anna could usually coax her into letting her stay up even later while Rose told colorful stories about some amazing or funny or bizarre near-catastrophe in the kitchen or out on the floor. In those days they had the same peculiar perspective: that the Bella Sorella was where life at its most intense and real and interesting went on. Did they still? Anna didn't want to get close enough to her to find out.

But back then they could talk about anything, hour after hour. In warm weather they talked on this balcony, slouched at this table or side by side at the railing with their feet up, watching the lights twinkle on the inky water. Anna would tell Rose about school, boys she liked, teachers she hated, girlfriends who hurt her feelings, books that moved her, clothes she wished she could afford. To this day she associated the taste of Campari soda with a feeling of anything goes. Rose wasn't her mother or her best friend, she was a combination, with the bad parts left out—competition, disapproval, possessiveness—and the good parts left in—sympathy, indulgence, fun. Was it right or wrong to look back on that time from the perspective of history and allow what had happened in between to poison it? And if it was wrong, how did you stop it? What was the antidote? After she found out about the affair between her aunt and her father, she couldn't think of this pretty apartment as anything but a *love nest.* She'd reinterpreted Rose's attention to her as self-interest, her kindness as hypocrisy. She'd divided her life between well adjusted but deluded and cynical but clear-eyed. But what did clear-eyed really do for you? Couldn't it just be an excuse for keeping your heart frozen?

Aunt Iris set a tray of coffee and chocolate on the glass-topped table and took the chair next to Anna's, the one Theo had been sitting in. She wore gray slacks and a black sweater with a white check pattern, always trying to minimize the visibility of dog hair. "You don't want a puppy, do you?" she tried, and Anna said no thanks. "Poor Rose," she said, sifting sugar over her coffee cup. "That man's just breaking her heart."

Anna said, "Hmm," and then for some reason defended Theo. "Although it's not his fault he's sick."

"No, but he could take care of himself. It's a kind of selfishness, if you think about it."

"Is it?"

"Your Uncle Tony wasn't any good when he got sick either, but at least he knew when to slow down. Well, he had to. He sure didn't *fight* it like this." Aunt Iris's husband, a pack-a-day man all his life, had succumbed to lung cancer about six years ago. They'd had a wonderful marriage, but she couldn't speak of him now without a certain sharpness to her voice, a small, unsympathetic pull of the lips. She was still mad at him for dying, pretty much by his own hand from Iris's point of view.

"Tony wasn't so proud of his strength, didn't think of himself as a *physical* man as much as some do. Theo, now, you should've seen him when he and Rose were just starting out. He'd pick her up like she didn't weigh anything, like she was a *paddle* when he'd carry her onto that boat of his."

Anna tried to picture that. Couldn't.

"Strong as a horse, and proud of himself for it. It's who he was. Everything about him was big, even his voice, and this great belly laugh. Bit of a drinker, too, though I never knew of him to get drunk. Now, well, now it's just sad, and all Rose can do is watch."

"It is," Anna had to admit. "It's sad."

"I think she was a little afraid of him in the beginning. Which might've been part of what she liked about him," Iris speculated, squinting her eyes and raising her eyebrows. "He had rough manners and he dressed like what he was, a waterman. He certainly wasn't the kind of man you'd've thought she'd go for, and it worried me at first. She kept telling me he was sweet and gentle, but I never particularly believed it till I saw it."

"What?"

"Well, it was just a little thing. She had a party at the restaurant on Christmas Eve for the staff and her best customers, mostly the bar regulars—of course most of those guys were in love with her, which is why they were regulars. Tony had been gone a year; that's why she invited *me*, so I wouldn't be alone on Christmas Eve. She'd been with Theo for about six months by then, and you couldn't fit a match cover between them, they were at *that* stage. So who shows up in the middle of this party?"

"Theo's ex-wife?"

"No, his ex-girlfriend." Aunt Iris scowled, miffed at her for spoiling the story. "A bottle blonde in a fake fur coat, and she was *loaded.* Her name was Clarice, I remember, very hard-looking woman, and she wasn't a happy-go-lucky drunk, I'll tell you, and she was definitely not in the Christmas spirit. I saw the whole thing. She walked right up to Rose and Theo when they were dancing—oh, you should've seen his face, like Scrooge meeting the ghost of Christmas past, and she proceeds to make a *scene.*"

"How exciting."

"No, it was horrible."

"That's what I mean, how horrible."

"No, Anna, seriously—she started screaming and yelling, curse words I never heard come out of a woman's mouth except in the movies. Rose had a band, and they actually stopped playing."

"Was Rose embarrassed?"

"Yes, of course, and poor Theo, too. The woman threw a drink in his face"—Anna gasped—"something else I've never seen in real life."

"Wow. I have." At Industrial Coffee, although not a drink, a hot hazelnut latte, and in a lap, not a face.

"As soon as she did that, it was over. She burst into tears and collapsed, that was the end of the fight." Aunt Iris bit into a truffle and washed it down with a gulp of coffee. "Oh Lord, that's good. Eat another one, you don't weigh enough."

"Look who's talking."

"The point is, the reason it's stayed in my mind all these years, is what Theo did after that. He could've hustled her out or ignored her or left himself, but he sat this Clarice down in a chair, right in the middle of everything, and knelt on the floor in front of her and took both her hands and started talking to her. I couldn't hear the words, and believe me I tried, but he just kept on and on, talking to her. She'd get all right for a minute, then break down. Once she got to hitting him with her fists, smacking him in the face and on top of his head—and he didn't do a thing about it, just took it till she gave out. He kept kneeling there, and him a big, heavy man, I can still see him switching from one knee to the other when one would get tired. When she finally got quiet enough, he took her home in her own car. He had to catch a cab back. Christmas Eve, this is."

"Was Rose jealous?"

"No, and there was no need, this poor girl didn't mean a thing to him. And of course who knows what all went on between them *before*—Rose might know, but I do not. But I'll never forget how he was with that Clarice, how kind and patient. I thought, if I ever had a man dump me, I'd want him to do it like that. Just a sweetheart.

"Anyway!" She made a shooing motion with her hand. "How are you? I hear about you—Vince says you're settling in like you never went away."

"Oh well. Not quite."

"Are you loving it? I knew you would." She beamed, smug. "I did, I just knew it. Isn't it everything you wanted? Back in a real restaurant, running it yourself, and it's all in the family, that's the best part."

"It's a job, Aunt I. Sometimes it's satisfying, sometimes it isn't."

"Oh, I know, but I'm just so glad you're here for Rose. This is a horrible time for her, and you being here, it's—"

"I'm not here for Rose. She's here, I'm here. We occupy the same space sometimes, but we're not here *for* anyone."

"I know, but—"

"No, don't make so much of it, okay? I'm working at the restaurant, that's all. It's temporary, and Rose knows that. She needed somebody, and I'm glad to help while I can. The timing is right for both of us, but that's as far as it goes, okay?"

"Okay." Aunt Iris held out her crepey arms and bowed from the waist sarcastically.

Anna pretended to think that was amusing. "Tell me about you. And your dogs. This is the best litter yet, you said. How come? How old are these puppies now?" Oh, she ought to let it go, let Aunt Iris spin her homecoming any way she wanted, quit throwing ice water on her hopes. What difference did it make? But she couldn't, and not just because of the likelihood of this conversation being repeated to Rose. She was bent for some reason on scrupulous accuracy, no shading, no rounding up in the interest of harmony and making nice. She'd come to believe it was her only chance of holding her own.

Anyway, the dog diversion worked. She drank sweet coffee with curls of bitter chocolate and listened to Aunt Iris rhapsodize about the most recent batch of genius puppies she'd gotten out of Hillary, the calm, stately Labrador retriever, and Ray, the sharp-as-tacks Border collie. Why did she mix them? Anna had once been silly enough to ask. Wouldn't she make more money by raising pure versions of one breed or the other? No, because people *loved* this cross, once they knew about it. Hillary was a honey of a dog, steadfast, loyal, and true, but not what you'd call *imaginative*—whereas Ray was so smart, he'd hot-wire your car if you weren't looking. Together, perfection. People paid a thousand bucks a pup, then came back for more.

"You sure you don't need a puppy, honey? In that old house all by yourself? Because for you—eight-fifty."

"That's so generous. Why don't you try Carmen?"

"Carmen? And one of my sweet babies? She'd probably fricassee it." They chortled, back on good terms. "Rose asked her to come over tonight, but she was *busy*." They raised their eyebrows knowingly. Sometimes Anna forgot that Carmen was Aunt Iris's cousin, too. "You two getting along okay?"

"She hasn't thrown any knives at me yet."

They kept looking back, through the sliding doors into the living room. Looking for Rose. Her absence weighed them down, kept their conversational subjects short-term and distracted. They talked about Vince and his succession of girlfriends, his indifference to settling down, and whether or not his true calling was tending bar at the Bella Sorella. He had a B.A. in psychology, and Iris lamented that he'd never used it except on his customers. They talked about her other four kids, Anna's cousins; she barely knew them because they were all older than Vince and mostly scattered. When they circled back around to dogs, Anna said, "Oh, gosh, it's getting late, I hate to go but I'd better. I'll just run in and say good night to Rose."

But the bedroom was empty. Sounds of tooth-brushing came from the closed bathroom door. "Rose?" Anna called. "I'm leaving—thanks for dessert! I'll see you—"

"Wait."

Clouds of fragrant steam billowed out when the door opened. Rose materialized in an old black kimono, open over a short pink nightie. Her hair was damp, her face scrubbed, eyes red-rimmed and bloodshot. Anna recoiled from a mental vision of Rose crying in the shower. The smell of toothpaste and soap and Jean Naté sucked her back to her childhood, mixed memories of Rose and her mother, tangled together so tightly she could no longer separate one from the other. She withdrew physically, took a step back from the siren pull of warmth and comfort, soft as a lap, or a woman's bosom.

"I better get going. Those truffles, Rose, my God." She wanted so much to make her smile. "Are you sure they're legal?"

"Take some with you, I won't eat them. Anna, I'm sorry about tonight. Sorry it was so crazy."

"Don't worry about it."

"He's not usually like that."

"Doesn't matter."

"It's hard for him." She sat down on the closed lid of the toilet, out of energy. Anna had no choice but to come closer, halfway inside the hot, steamy room. Rose leaned her back against the commode and stretched her legs out, contemplating her long-toed feet on the bath mat. "And he's getting worse. So fast. I didn't expect that. Nobody was prepared for it to go this fast."

"Maybe this is a phase. It could plateau right here, like a remission. Or even get better. Is that a possibility?" This was as close as she'd come to asking just what it was Theo had.

Rose smiled fleetingly. The fluorescent light over the sink illuminated every line in her naked, aging nun's face. "I hope. They still haven't told us what it is, not for certain. They said Parkinson's at first, then something called PSP. His brain cells are degenerating, that's as much as we know. It started about three years ago."

"How long have you been together?" But she wanted no part of this, this was Rose's melodrama, it had nothing to do with her.

"Five years."

So, since she was fifty-five and he was sixty, give or take. A December-December romance. Were there other sweethearts between Anna's father and Theo? Of course there must've been; that was a nine-year gap, and men had always liked Rose. Anna wanted to know about them, but she'd never ask. Already she could feel herself being pulled too far into Rose's world, and she hated it. Rose was like a spider, extending her web, reinforcing it in silence and secrecy. Before you knew it you were caught inside the silky, invisible strands. They looked delicate, but they were tough as fishing line.

"He used to carve things—he was a woodcarver. Beautiful things, it's how he courted me." She glanced up and smiled. "First with birds and ducks, they were his specialty, but then with busts of people we knew, friends we had in common. Then, figures of me. They weren't true likenesses, not like his other work. More abstract, just shapes, really. He said he worked with his eyes closed. Toward the end, they were just long, curving forms, very strong, very...graceful. Only vaguely human, you know, more like objects. Objectifications of me." She laughed. "Naturally I fell in love with him."

I don't want to know this. But she said, "What do you mean, toward the end?"

"When the tremors got bad. He can't hold a knife anymore. His hands shake too badly."

"Oh."

Mechanically, shoulders slumped, Rose opened a bottle of moisturizer and began to pat drops of it on her face.

"I think I might've found a cook," Anna said brightly.

She nodded, barely listening. Still remembering.

"Carmen's going to hate her, though. Her name's Frankie. You can meet her tomorrow, see what you think."

She nodded again.

"Well, okay, guess I'll go." Rose looked up, resigned. Anna hung in the doorway. "What happened to Mason?" she said instead of leaving. She hadn't been going to ask Rose that, for complicated reasons she used to understand. Now she couldn't even remember what they were.

"Do you mean how did he get hurt?"

Anna nodded.

"A stupid, senseless accident. Nine or ten years ago, when he was living in New York."

"When he was a lawyer."

"General counsel for an insurance firm, yes. Doing well, making lots of money, I guess. Engaged to another attorney. One day he was jogging in the park—on the sidewalk, the path, not on the road or anything—and a car struck him. It came right over the curb, trying to pass another car on the right. He was thrown up in the air—some horrible number of feet, I don't know, Theo tells the story better than I do. The whole left side of his body was just—broken. His arm, leg, shoulder, his face—he came close to dying, several times. He was in a coma for months. When he finally came to, they told him his mother had died."

"Rose, my *God*."

"His hair turned completely white—he's not going gray now, it's the dark coming back in. It was a year before he could walk, then months and months of rehab. Reconstructive surgery. He moved down here to recover, and afterward, he didn't want to be a lawyer anymore."

"The fiancée?"

"Long gone."

What an awful story. Anna had more questions, but a keen look in Rose's face kept her silent. For some reason, Rose wanted her to know Mason. Well, then. Reason enough to thwart her.

So she should've dropped the subject, but instead she said sharply, "You're not thinking about me and Mason, are you, Rose? Any kind of romantic thing, right? Because that would not work out."

"I wasn't thinking much of anything," she replied softly. Thoughtfully.

"Good, because neither one of us is interested. Oh, and I'm on sabbatical."

"You're still getting over Jay."

"In a way." Funny, though, how infrequently she thought of Jay. In fact, it was slightly alarming. "But mostly, I just don't want the trouble anymore, I'm too old for it."

Rose looked amused. "You're through with men?"

"I'd like to be."

"Because you're so old."

"Don't fix me up, Rose. In any way, I mean it."

"All right. Although I don't think that's what I was doing."

"Just so we're clear."

"You're very big on being *clear*."

"Yes, I am."

"I wish . . ." She sighed. "I wish there were ever some *good* news you wanted to be clear on."

Anna backed away when Rose stood up, afraid she might get hugged or something. "Okay, well," she said again. "See you tomorrow."

"I'm glad you came by. Glad you could meet Theo."

"Yeah. Thanks for dessert—wow, that stuff is incredible. How come it's not on the menu?"

"Too expensive. Carmen says."

Anna made a face, but Rose's answering smile was meager, just a reflex. All her troubles had come back to her now that Anna was leaving. She looked so slight and weary in her worn kimono. She looked like a woman anticipating a long night.

Anna, anxious to get away from her, said, "'Bye," abruptly. But then she reached out and touched her on the arm, the elbow, a swift little pat, embarrassingly stiff.

It startled Rose so much, her mouth dropped open.

Anna's, too. They must be mirrors of each other. For the first time in years, she didn't mind the resemblance.

9

Dear Anna,

I don't think I explained myself very well the other night. Spring is the second busiest time of the year, or else it's tied for first with fall, depending on your point of view, for anybody who photographs birds for a living. Right now any number of activities are going on around the Chesapeake because of IMBD (International Migratory Bird Day, second Sunday in May), and I'm set either to photograph migratory species or give talks and seminars on wildlife photography, conservation, ecological diversity, etc., etc., at Prime Hook, Patuxent Research Refuge, Assateague, and Deal Island. In fact, I'm writing to you on my laptop from the Starlite Motel in Smyrna, Delaware, where I'm staying while I shoot hordes of red knots during their annual horseshoe crab egg feast on Delaware Bay. I'm a busy man. Not a hermit at all. On the contrary, I'm a rolling stone. I could tell you many fascinating things about the red knot, but will refrain because of a certain glazed look I noticed the last time we spoke of birds. I'm sensitive to these things.

Mason

P.S. I apologize for my stepfather if he was rude that night. He repented slightly the following day, allowing that you weren't quite as bad as he'd expected. A handsome admission.

Dear Mason,
Handsome indeed! Tell Theo I thought he'd be much uglier. And that I look forward to a long, cordial friendship between us.

I used to go out with a boy from Smyrna. We dated for a whole semester when I was a junior in college. He was going to be either a microbiologist or a bluegrass fiddler, he couldn't decide. I used to be in a band myself. I played the hip, we used to say, meaning I banged a tambourine against my hipbone in time to the rock and roll classics we did our best to imitate. Our most successful cover was "Satisfaction." We felt the lyrics deeply.

What do you do, then, walk around on the beach all day with a camera? That doesn't sound like a serious occupation. They pay you for this? Seriously, it's good that it consumes you—I'm assuming it does. Most people aren't lucky enough to find their life's work, a job that's so satisfying they'd do it for nothing. How did you get started with birds and cameras? If I may ask. What is the most important quality a good bird photographer should have? And I deny looking glazed. That was my *rapt* look—I wanted you to go on and on about bats. What I'm learning in my new job, which I currently do fourteen hours a day, seven days a week, is that the point isn't to become so successful that I get rich—although that would certainly be a nice side benefit. The point is to find a balance. Someday. I think I'm good at what I do, but I could still fail. I'd like to succeed, but not if success means I can never get out, that the restaurant, this one or the next one, becomes my whole life. In fact, I think finding the balance *is* success. Not the money.

But on a good day I purely love what I do. In fact, it's hard to go home. I'll be bone tired, limp as day-old pasta, but still on some kind of endorphin high after all the close calls and near calamities, not to mention the real ones, the floor and kitchen catastrophes that take years off your life. To survive, to get through another night with no fatal wounds—I get this sort of war rush it can take hours to come down from. I always turn music on as soon as I get home. It's not that I want more stimulation, I just need to crash gradually. No wonder half the people in the restaurant biz are drunks or dopers. The insanity gets to you one way or the other, nobody's immune.

Oh, but I love it. Don't tell Rose. Do you love what you do? She told me what happened to you—I hope you don't mind if I bring it up. If you love what you do now, that's wonderful, but I still think you paid a high price for clarity. Was it worth it? None of my business—don't answer if you don't want to.

Anna

"What *is* that?"

Frankie looked up from adding hot stock to rice in a large sauté pan on the eight-burner. "What?" Her serious face flinched; she looked guilty but baffled, as if she couldn't figure out what crime she'd committed this time. Understandable: Carmen treated her like an ex-con. She was in early this morning, as she was almost every day, trying out recipes for the menu Anna was working on with Rose. And with Carmen, when she could be bothered.

"That smell, that fabulous smell," Anna cried, and Frankie's narrow shoulders relaxed. "It's not the risotto, although that looks great."

"No, it's probably the red peppers and eggplant I've got going in the wood oven. Taste this, though. It's not finished, but what do you think of the broth?"

Anna blew on the liquid in the wooden spoon Frankie held to her lips and took a sip. "Mm, chickeny. Yeah, it's really rich. How'd you get it so strong without being salty?"

"Bones. It's pretty good, isn't it? I'm making a wild mushroom risotto, although we've only got porcini and girolles. If I had chanterelles gris, say, and some trompettes de la mort, this would work better."

But Carmen wouldn't order them, Frankie didn't have to add. She'd consider that extravagant, frou frou, not worth the expense. Frankie was Anna's new ally in the war with Carmen, but her strengthened position had escalated the hostilities on both sides. Rose should've stepped in and made peace, but she was acting like Switzerland, clinging to neutrality at all costs.

Frankie glanced at the big kitchen clock. "Okay, you want to try some wood-roasted vegetables?"

"You bet."

Carmen complained the wood-burning brick oven Rose had installed a couple of years ago was more trouble than it was worth, that everything they made in it was either overdone or underdone, oak and mesquite cost too much, the cooks were always forgetting to add it or else putting in too much, the heat from the oven was too intense, the fire danger raised their insurance premium, and nobody ever ordered anything they made in it except pizza anyway.

Frankie said any restaurant that called itself Italian and aspired to anything more sophisticated than spaghetti and meatballs needed a wood-burning oven. It wasn't to be trendy, it was a matter of being serious about food. Wood-roasted vegetable side dishes were a *necessity*, she said, not a luxury, and in fact what they really needed was *two* brick ovens, one for bread and pizza, one for vegetables, fish, chicken, and meat. She was bristling with new ideas for their underutilized oven, but Carmen was still an obstacle. Anna thought of her as a monster eighteen-wheeler overturned on the highway, lying sideways across all the lanes, backing up traffic for miles in both directions.

"Oh, mama," she said around a steaming bite of stuffed red pepper. "Oh, wow. Okay, olives and anchovies," she guessed; "what else?"

"Capers. Garlic, parsley, lemon juice. I used red wine, but you can use balsamic vinegar if you want. What do you think?"

"I love it."

"You can make it cheaper with California black olives, or you can buy commercial olive paste, some of 'em are pretty good. I used Niçoise olives, but you wouldn't have to."

"Where'd you get Niçoise olives?" Anna couldn't remember seeing them in the pantry.

"I bought them."

"You bought them?"

Frankie turned red. She was skim-milk pale, white as a baby vampire, so when she blushed it was a high-profile event. Even her ears turned pink, as well as the scalp under her bristly red hair. The bones in her face and skull were so delicate, she looked like a hungry baby bird. But Anna had seen her lift a forty-pound stockpot full of water and bones with her skinny, ropy arms, and move a cast iron skillet around a flaming stove burner barehanded. There wasn't anything delicate about Frankie except her feelings.

"Yeah, I bought 'em. It's no big deal, I just wanted you to try this right. You know, the first time."

"Okay," Anna said easily, "fine, but I'll have to cost it out."

"Sure."

"It might be too much."

"I know. Here, try this."

"No, thanks, I hate eggplant."

"Try this. Come on, I guarantee—"

"No, I really hate it. Try it on Carmen."

Frankie laughed—a rare sound; Anna didn't hear it much in the kitchen, not from Frankie. She watched her inhale the steam still rising from a pan of eggplant rounds. She cut off a piece and put it in her mouth. She held it there for a second before she started to chew. It was fun to watch Frankie taste the foods she made; her face got comically concentrated as every other sense went out of focus, including her eyes. "Too much oil," she pronounced after swallowing. "Although it wouldn't be, or it might not be, if only we had—"

"I know, I know. I'm working on it." Frankie thought the olive oil Carmen bought for cooking wasn't good enough. It was extra virgin, but Frankie wanted Lucca oil, the most expensive in the world, and the best. Carmen said no, absolutely not, was she crazy? The usual.

Frankie's ex-husband's name was Mike, Anna knew from asking nosy questions; he was a history professor at the local junior college. They'd lived in D.C. until the split, after which Mike had moved here with two-year-old Katie. Frankie hadn't followed until six months later, and Anna theorized, on no evidence at all, that that's when the drinking must've been at its worst.

Frankie went back to the stove and resumed ladling chicken broth into her sauté pan of rice and stirring, stirring. Anna leaned against the counter and watched her deglaze the pan with stock. The smells were getting more and more irresistible. She stirred porcini into the rice next, then the soaking liquid, careful to keep the sand and sediment out. She worked fast, but she never seemed to hurry. Carmen made fun of her for always wearing a formal white chef's tunic buttoned to the throat, checked pants, clogs, and a cook's toque, no matter how hot it got in the kitchen. For these morning experiments, though, she relaxed her own standards and dispensed with the tunic and the toque. She looked like a kid, one with a lot of tattoos, in jeans and a tank top and a backward-facing baseball cap. She was tireless, a machine; Anna had never known anybody who could work so long without complaints or breaks or encouragement. She was starting to worry about her.

"How's Katie?" she asked her—a sure-fire way to get her to lighten up.

"She's great. She's terrific. Wanna see a picture?"

"Absolutely."

She kept her wallet in her back pocket, like a man. She slipped a couple of photos out of a plastic sleeve and handed them over. "These are from Easter. I took 'em."

"Oh my God." Katie, about three and a half, stood at the bottom of a flight of stairs in a seriously adorable Easter getup, a high-waisted pink dress with puffy sleeves and smocking on the chest, pink Mary Janes and pink socks, a patent leather pink pocketbook clutched in both chubby hands. Pink flowers in her hair, which was an amazing shade of pumpkin orange. "Oh, Frankie," Anna said reverently, "she's beautiful." She was, but her saving grace was that she didn't look as if she knew it. It might've been the freckles, which were everywhere, not just a dainty spray across her nose. Or it might've been the excitement in her eyes, a funny, knowing look, as if she was thinking, "How about this outfit! Am I cute or what?"

"I know." Frankie's tender half-smile was sweet, but also painful to look at. "Hard to believe she's mine, huh?"

"Not at all. I think she looks like you."

Frankie huffed. "No, she's got Mike's eyes and everything. All she got from me is that carrot top—I had the exact same color when I was little. Check out Mike, you'll see."

Mike was in the second picture, sitting beside his daughter on the next-to-last stair step, almost as dressed up as she was in a navy blue suit with a vest, a checked tie. Frankie was right, Katie had Dad's eyes, or at least the good-natured joke in them. He looked much older than the man Anna had been expecting; there was gray in his shaggy professor's hair and deep smile lines around his mouth. She wasn't sure what to say about Mike. "He looks nice," she hazarded, relying on the clue that Frankie had never said anything bad about him.

"He is." She stuck the photos back in the wallet, the wallet back in her pocket. She started beating shredded Parmigiano-Reggiano into the rice, stringy arm muscles bulging. "He put up with a lot of shit. From me. For a long time." She glanced at Anna, gauging her interest. Probably her trustworthiness, too. "I'm the one who screwed it all up," she said with her face turned away, beating, beating, adding more butter, now more cheese, putting her back and shoulders into it. "It was all me."

"I hate when that happens. I hate it when there's nobody to blame but me."

Frankie smiled.

"Maybe, you know, someday..."

"Yeah. That's what I'm working on, getting it back. That's what it's all about." Her pale monkey face looked sharp, almost ruthless with determination. "Okay, this risotto's done."

"Let's try it."

But Frankie wanted more ceremony than standing over the stove and taking turns from the same spoon. She got down two plates and spooned a serving of rice on each, adding a pinch more of the grated cheese on top. They sat on stools by the pantry, plates on their knees, and tasted.

"It's great," Anna said instantly, no hesitation. She hardly had to chew to know she liked it. "God, the mushrooms just explode."

"It's good," Frankie allowed, nodding slowly, more judicious. She took tiny bites and drew in air as she chewed, like a wine taster. "It's not really *doing* anything, but I guess it doesn't have to. It's more the texture I was worried about." She often spoke of flavors *doing* things. Sometimes she talked about food as if it were music: flavors had rhythms, ingredients had tones, high, low, medium, and when you arranged them together just the right way, they made chords.

"No, the texture's great. Really creamy, but the rice grains are still chewy." Anna's was all gone. She considered a second helping.

"It'll be a little different each time, but I guess that's okay."

"Depending on who makes it, you mean?"

"No, even if I make it every time. It's just never exactly the same twice."

"I wish Rose could taste this while it's fresh. Write down everything you used and exactly how much. We call it Wild Mushroom Risotto—right?"

"Well, that's what it is."

"How could Carmen hate this?" Anna wondered out loud. "It's real, it's basic. It's practically comfort food."

"You could call it Tame Mushroom Risotto." Frankie ducked her head, blushing again. It was the first time she'd ever said anything about Carmen that wasn't perfectly respectful. When Anna only laughed, she got bolder. "I know how to get her to go for it." She had a crooked eyetooth that showed only when she grinned, which wasn't often. "Tell her it's gotta be either this or my other risotto specialty. Fennel and vodka."

"Gag. That'll do it," Anna agreed, making a face that made Frankie laugh out loud.

Dear Anna,

I'm in Chincoteague. I just had an incredible morning. I'll tell you about it, and you can glaze over or skim through or ignore it altogether, and I'll never be the wiser. It's all about birds.

It's not crowded here yet, too early in the season, so at five this morning I was the only human at the best spot for shorebirds in this refuge, a spit of sand protruding from the salt marsh into one of the channels of Chincoteague Bay. But the birds were there already. I could just make out their silhouettes in the mist. Most were still asleep, heads tucked into their back feathers, sanderlings, dunlins, sandpipers. A couple of dowitchers already awake, foraging along the edge of the water. The only way you can get close enough is to lie down on your stomach, camera and telephoto in front of your face, and squirm forward about six inches at a time. You can also kneel and creep forward slowly, but I can't last at that for long—bad knee. Or you can sit and shuffle closer on your butt, but then you're not low enough, they can see you. No, lying in the cold wet sand on your stomach, that's the ticket. Eventually, you always get to a place where they notice you, even the calmest birds, and that's the critical time. If one spooks they'll all take off, and nothing's more disheartening than to stalk a flock of birds for an hour or two, only to watch them lift up en masse in a panic, leaving you high and dry. Or in this case, low and wet. I was about thirty feet from my mixed flock when I could tell I was starting to make them nervous. Nothing to do but wait. Not enough light for pictures yet anyway, so I framed the closest birds, playing with compositions and angles. You asked what quality is most important for a bird photographer. Patience. And next, some kind of frame or aura or vibe around yourself that keeps birds from being afraid. Some birders say you have to develop this trait, it takes years of experience, but I think I was born with it. I don't even know what it is. Slow movements, yes, and not staring directly into their eyes—that can terrify some birds, especially hawks. But it's something else, too. Can't describe it. A way to breathe. Be. You erase yourself. You become a piece of the landscape.

Nope, can't describe it.

After 15 or 20 minutes, my flock forgot about me and I started to creep up again. At 15 feet, I stopped. The perfect range with the telephoto I was using, and now all I had to do was wait. This is the best part, and also impossible to describe. All there is is bird, lens, color, light, me. Except I almost disappear, and then it's the pure process.

The sun began to burn off the mist, and I began to shoot. The light was perfect, bright enough for subtle saturation, diffuse enough for magic, one of those golden mornings you dream about. Sometimes you know when it's working, you can already see the photos you're taking, and they're great. Two dunlins shouldering each other out of the way, a laughing gull giving itself a shower, one lone willet, huge among the little spotties. I shot a short-billed dowitcher on one leg in still water, his reflection underneath him. I think it's going to be good, as if he's standing on a mirror, nothing but sky-colored water above and below. For fun, not for sale, just for myself, I take pictures of yawning birds. I've got more than 30 different species, a collection, just birds yawning. (Wake up! No glazing!) Today, on this little sand spit, a double-crested cormorant practically yawned in my face. It was completely unexpected; a bird just waking up will often yawn, but this guy had already fed and was perched on a piece of driftwood with his wings spread out to dry. I can't believe I got him, but I did. I even had to focus by hand, auto would've picked up the tip of his bill and I wanted the back of his red throat, the bright blue roof of his mouth. I think I got it, I'm almost sure, and his green eye and the orange around his mouth. What a picture! I think. Hope. I'll know when I get home.

But that wasn't the end. This amazing day, the kind you only get a couple of times a year if you're lucky, wasn't over. In a few minutes the light was going to get too white, and worse, I could hear a car door slam across the marsh. People coming. A great blue heron skidded into the shallow water from—I don't know where, I wasn't looking, I was shooting a black-bellied plover having a tug of war with a marine worm in the sand. (It's good, too, I think. He looks very serious and determined, and the worm is winning.) Great blues are common here, of course, in all seasons, I have hundreds of pix of blues, and they're terrific birds, big and dramatic, always up to something interesting. You can hardly take a bad picture of a great blue heron, and photo editors love them because they look prehistoric. But me, I've never gotten a really excellent shot, something's always not quite right, I fill the frame too full so there's no room for words—eds. need space in the background of a potential cover shot for text—or else my specimen isn't perfect or the light isn't right or the pose is too static or—whatever it might be. I've got adequate stuff, but nothing classic. Nothing I'm proud of.

Today I got something. Because no sooner did this bird land than his buddy landed next to him. Mate? Brother-in-law? You can't tell a male great blue from a female, so who knows. The point is, now there were two of them, and if you can get two birds together, same species or not, you've automatically got twice as good a picture. Potentially. But especially two great blues, who are usually solitary. Except when they're mating, and it's too early, these two weren't mating. I don't think. Anyway—I know, you're not even reading anymore, and I'm just getting to the good part. I back off with my lens, I've learned my lesson, I don't fill the frame with these birds even though they're standing in three inches of water not six feet from each other. No, I back off and shoot, shoot, going on auto, but not shy about shooting, not waiting for something theatrical to happen and not worrying about conserving film, rookie mistake in a situation like this, and all I'm thinking is this is interesting, two blues hunting together—when all of a sudden, blue on the right spears a frog. I thought it was a fish at first but it's a frog, peeper, little guy, and I snap off half a dozen shots of the heron with the frog in its mouth, waiting for the classic moment when it tosses its S-shaped neck back and goes GULP. It doesn't happen. Here's what happens. Blue on the right extends its neck, black plume on top sticking straight up—these are gorgeous, adult, fully developed great blue herons, flawless, a couple of God's best ideas—blue on right extends frog gift to blue on left, between his two yellow bills. Left-hand blue sidles over and opens her (I know it's a female; by some fluke, these two have jumped mating season) mouth, and right-hand blue deposits delicious mating bribe—and I have this moment on film. I have it, I'll know when it comes back from my slide processor, but I trust my instincts. This is good. They both have their feathers furled, and the light's right, they're as glad as I am, this is an ecstatic moment. It's not just that it's unusual for this time of year, and unusual sells. I don't give a damn about selling, but this will sell. (If I got it. I'm scaring myself by how confident I feel.) If it's as good as I think it is I've got something special. Something you don't see. I don't know what to compare it to—you selling out the restaurant on a Saturday night, every seat taken, 6 p.m. to 10, and every customer had a meal they'll never forget. A home run.

So I got my shot. Somewhere in there is an image you don't see very often, and I took it just right. Everything worked out at the same time. Hello? Still awake? I feel good. I can't stop typing.

Mason

Eddie was supposed to come in early and help, but he never showed up. Anna spent the morning standing on chairs, putting holes in the newly painted walls with a portable drill, hanging gigantic, but luckily lightweight, oil paintings by a local, therefore cheap, artist of fruits and flowers. Not generic, not motel room fruits and flowers, more like—well, not primitive, either, and not really surrealist. Hyper-realist? Expressionist? Jay would know, but then he'd have to deliver a lecture along with the answer. Whatever, the paintings were huge and happy, full of color, and best of all, Vonnie said they made her hungry.

Anna loved the shade of peachy yellow they'd chosen over white for the old brick walls. How much brighter and warmer the dining room looked—but not too feminine, Shirl was quick to agree with her. Shirl, pasta chef and nonstop talker, was her chief decorating consultant, and nobody was more surprised by that than Anna. They agreed on everything, so of course each thought the other had exquisite taste, wonderful judgment. Shirl even hated the faded, path-worn carpet as much as Anna did. "Skanky," she called it, and enjoyed dreaming up ways they could expedite its demise, like "accidentally" setting fire to it. And to think Anna had once thought of letting Shirl go.

Carmen rolled in at about eleven, backing her old white Econoline up to the back door. It was her day to browse the Italian market for produce she could get cheaper than from their everyday suppliers. She stumped up to her apartment and came back down with her apron on, ready to supervise lunch. While Lewis unloaded the van, Anna logged in Carmen's purchases on the master inventory.

Before she was half finished, she was fuming.

She waited until Carmen was alone, busy with opening a carton of canned tomato paste in the pantry. Working on keeping her voice curious and wondering, not irate, Anna asked, "Did you get anything on my list?"

"*Your* list?" She was breathing too hard from the small amount of exertion slitting open a cardboard box required. She straddled the carton to open it, broad-backed, biceps as big as ham shanks, blowing her faded hair out of her face.

"The list I gave you last night. To add to your list. I don't see anything I wanted except the Auricchio cheese."

"Yeah, they had that on sale. We could afford it." She straightened up, sweaty and grinning—not in a nice way. She looked older than her fifty years. She looked cooked. The skin on her arms and neck, even her solid legs, especially her round face, was a bricky, rusty red, like roasted pepper. Well, it made sense—she spent every day in 120-degree heat over fires, grills, stoves, boiling water, steam, frying pans. After thirty years of it, more or less, she'd stewed herself.

Sometimes Anna tried to imagine her as a young woman pining for a priest she knew she shouldn't think about and couldn't have, or reeling from hurt when he callously broke her heart. It was almost impossible to picture, but when she did it softened her antagonism to Carmen a little. And she knew one nice thing about her—every night, late, she sneaked food to a homeless guy in the alley, a stumbly, bad-tempered, usually drunken old bum named Benchester. Everybody knew about it, but nobody was allowed to mention it; if they did, Carmen blew up, went on the attack, and denied it. Nothing made her madder than being confused with a kind person.

"They didn't have fresh sardines or your *particular* brand of passata, sorry to say. And you can forget about San Daniele ham. You know how much they want for that per pound?"

"Okay, I was afraid of that, but how come you didn't get the beef? I know they've got it, and it's *cheaper*. But you got T-bone."

"People like T-bone. They don't want that thin, tough *bistecca* you've got a hard-on for."

"Carmen, we wanted to make it with the new fig-basil sauce. I *told* you." One of Frankie's triumphs, it was a fantastic sauce, ambrosia, one of the best meat accompaniments Anna had ever tasted. Too rich for fish, but it was perfect with chewy, flavorful Italian steak.

"Nobody will order it," Carmen pronounced.

"How do you know? It's leaner, sure, but lots of people *like* leaner cuts of meat."

"Wrong. When they order steak they want a steak, not a piece of shoe leather."

Anna slapped her thighs with her hands. "I wanted fresh peas. Were they out of them, too?"

"You wanted fresh peas for a puree on polenta. Believe me, honey, I just saved you from a *world* of embarrassment." Carmen pushed past her and went back out in the kitchen.

Anna followed. "Linguinette! How come you didn't get that?"

Carmen stopped beside Jasper's station, pretending to take an interest in the baby zucchinis he was prepping for a salad special. Jasper was Carmen's pet, her henchman. "*Linguinette.*" She curled her lips, as only Carmen could, in an expression of amazed contempt. "And this designer pasta would be different from linguine exactly...how?"

"It's smaller!" Anna exploded. "That's why they call it linguinette! It's smaller!"

Carmen burst out laughing. Jasper copied her.

Anna lost all caution. "Have you ever even eaten linguinette? Have you? Do you like capellini, or do you think that's funny, too?"

No—she made herself shut up. Carmen would *not* provoke her into a shouting match. Anyway, she'd lose, because Carmen was a master of scorn. Back when she'd had Frankie doing prep work—before Anna found out and rescued her, moved her back to the line—Frankie had made the mistake of uttering the names of a few simple cooking school terms, mise en place, mirepoix, commonplace phrases to her, but which struck Carmen and her gang, Jasper and a few of the others, as unbearably pretentious. Nothing got punished faster in Carmen's kitchen than hotdogging, or at least her perception of it, and the favored form of punishment was merciless teasing. So now Frankie's nickname was "Concassé," after the tomato dice prep she must regret ever mentioning. Jasper never missed an opportunity to call himself the "garde-manger"—and so on and so on. Routine kitchen hazing, but when Carmen joined in it took on an aspect of harassment, if only because she was so good at it.

Big mistake to have it out with her here, now, with half the staff pretending they weren't straining to hear every word. Anna grabbed her temper back, managed to smile, said, "Actually, capellini is pretty funny," and went outside.

Louis was hosing off the front sidewalk. Anna waved back at Roxanne, who owned the jewelry shop across the street. She waved to the UPS man. She petted Fatso, the alley cat all the storekeepers on the block fed. She and Louis talked about how Rose's flower boxes were doing, and whether she'd been right to plant miniature coxcombs this year instead of old reliable geraniums.

Louis had been Rose's odd-job man for as long as Anna could remember. He never changed. When she was a teenager, he'd looked the same to her as he did now, like an old man, gangly and stoop-shouldered, with freckled, ashy-brown skin and close white hair as matted and compact as cotton balls. "What do you think about putting some tables out here?" she asked him. "Not many, six, say. Think we'd need umbrellas? Or a bigger awning, maybe. Where's the sun around cocktail time in the worst part of the summer, Louis? I can't remember."

He scratched the back of his neck, squinting, pondering. "About there," he decided, pointing west, up the crescent. "Slides behind the Ritz Camera around eight. Hot night, it's a sonofabitch."

"Umbrellas, then. I guess. Lot of upkeep," she said doubtfully. "Carmen's against it." Laminated wood furniture would warp, she warned, and plastic would crack, cloud, peel, or disintegrate. All colors would turn gray. They'd be scraping, painting, and replacing for the rest of their lives.

"Well, then," Louis said decisively. Anna wasn't surprised he was against it; after all, he was the one who'd be stuck with most of the maintenance. But then he winked at her. "Ain't that a good reason to do it?"

Dear Anna,
Forgot to say, in heat of heron moment, I'm glad you love what you do. "Don't tell Rose"? You think she doesn't know? She's my friend, not just Theo's, so I hear things. Sorry that bothers you, the fact that Rose talks about you to her friends. You two had an estrangement, but that's all I know, no details. She protects you.

Theo and I, I'm not sure what we had. He's the one who taught me to love birds. He used to patch up wounded ones, gulls and peeps he'd find when he was out fishing or crabbing. I had him, off and on, for a father, but even before he left for good he wasn't around much. My mother was his second wife; he lost the first one for the same reason—not around. He's only here now because he can't leave. And Rose; he stays for her. Am I supposed to be angry with him because he was a bad father? We're friends now, and we've never talked about the past. Manly men.

Dear Mason,
Things are so crazy here—sorry I didn't have time to write back and say congrats on fabulous heron photos. It sounds like meditation when you write

about waiting for the birds to settle and the light to be perfect. The Zen of bird photography. I wish I knew the first thing about birds. I used to go out with a guy who had a cockatiel named Marsha. He bought a record that was supposed to teach her how to talk, but it didn't work, she never said a word. If I were to buy a beginner's book on birds, which one would you recommend?

Re. Theo, Rose, childhood, abandonment, etc., etc.—do you ever feel we're too old for this? How old are you? I'm 36, almost 37, technically a grown-up. I feel very stupid and childish for still having ISSUES with a woman who's not even my mother. When do we grow up? When we have our own children? Somehow I doubt it. I think then we just pretend harder, and show off by dealing with problems of childhood and youth that we really have finally mastered, things like, Don't take dope, Don't have sex yet, knee-jerk "adult" proscriptions that completely hide the fact that we are still stuck in troughs of adolescent angst and indecision and over-all cluelessness.

But that's just me.

I love to read novels, or I used to when I had a life, and my favorite writers seem to be struggling with these questions, but really, my sense is, they understand everything. They write the ILLUSION of confusion, these authors, mostly women, but I doubt any of them are as scattered and hopeless as I am when it comes to being a grown-up. What do you read for pleasure? I like books about women stuck in dire emotional circumstances, abusive husbands, lonely spinsterhood, unappreciative children, etc.,

etc., who triumph in the end because somebody (usually a man, but sometimes, imagine it, the women themselves!) recognizes their worth and rewards them for it. I suppose this has been going on since *Jane Eyre*, but I'm still a sucker for it. I love the happy ending. Cinderella, that's what it is. The prince comes in some form or other, and immediately every rotten thing the evil stepmother ever did is wiped out.

I forget where I was going with this. It wasn't to say that Rose is my evil stepmother, though, or that Theo is your evil stepfather. Although if he is, you've done a lot better job of reconciling with him than I have with Rose. Why do you say she "protects" me? Think about the possibility she's protecting herself.

Your post from yesterday just came today, so you're probably up and out already, shooting albatrosses or something. I guess it's too much to hope for another perfect day, but I hope you have one.

Anna

P.S. How interesting that your father—your real father, birth father—flew airplanes. Am twirling my Freudian mustache over that.

Lunch was light, not what Anna had been hoping for, and on top of that she had to listen to Carmen blame it on the specials. "Too weird," she opined, as if Frankie's monkfish with pureed artichoke had personally scared people away. She spent an hour on the telephone with suppliers, another hour interviewing phone applicants to replace Elise, whom she'd had to let go yesterday for calling Kris a station-stealing bitch. Fine, but not in front of a dining room full of customers. Firing people wasn't any fun, Anna hated it as much as Rose did, but she consoled herself that she'd done Elise a favor by just hurrying along the inevitable.

At three, she grabbed a bite of lunch at the bar. Frankie joined her, looking beat, which was understandable: she'd been on her feet for six hours straight, and she had seven more to go. Vince, who'd switched shifts with no-show Eddie, entertained them with made-up drink names. Vodka, orange juice, and milk of magnesia: a Phillips Screwdriver. Cold Duck and Dr Pepper: a Quack Doctor. It was fun to watch Vince at work, because he was fast, smooth, and obsessively tidy. He made a ceremony out of the simplest drink-mixing; watching him build a martini was like celebrating the Transubstantiation at high mass. He had a lot of regulars, people who came in every day just to see him, get their Vince fix. He could talk on any topic, sports, the stock market, the meaning of life, the movie playing up the street. Aunt Iris said he was good at his job because he was a Fiore, which made him a natural host. It just came out in drink instead of food.

He and Frankie were always arguing. About everything—music in general, but especially what kind they should play during happy hour; whether the TV over the bar was indispensable or an abomination; if they should have a popcorn machine; if the world would end if Rose put in a video game (Vince: no; Frankie: yes). He argued by teasing and bantering, but she was so earnest, she didn't know when he was kidding. Same with flirting: Vince tried out his corny but venerable lines on Frankie, which usually involved exaggerated claims of sexual power, and she responded with blank, uncomprehending stares.

She broke off the current argument—whether happy hour freebies brought in more freeloaders than paying customers—to race into the kitchen and snatch a roasting pan of cherry vine tomatoes out of the brick oven. "Try one," she offered, setting the pan on a folded towel on the bar. The only customers at this hour were a few regulars from the dock and a couple of twentysomethings too wrapped up in each other to notice anybody else. "See what you think," Frankie said. "Careful, they're still hot."

Anna snapped a hot tomato off the bunch and gingerly popped it in her mouth. "Mm, I like." Garlic and thyme burst out when she bit down.

"Yeah, it's great," Vince agreed around a mouthful. "Is this more bar food?"

"Yes," said Anna and Frankie in unison. They were working on a tapas menu, and Vince was their guinea pig.

"I keep telling you," he leaned across the bar to say, "after a few drinks, these guys'll eat their wallets if you put enough salt on. This stuff, the focaccia, the empanadas, they're great, but they'll be wasted on about eighty percent of my customers."

"You sound like Carmen. Where is she," Anna said, "I want her to try these."

"She went to the dentist," Vince told her, picking up the pan and offering some of the roasted tomatoes to the guys on the other side of the bar.

"You're wrong about what people want to eat," Frankie said seriously. "If they're hungry and all you've got is salted wallets, sure, that's what they'll eat, but give them something good and watch what happens."

"Yeah. They'll eat that, too."

"No—okay, yes—but they won't just gobble it, they'll *savor* it."

On cue—"Hey, these are good," one of the regulars, a retired oysterman named Conrad, called over.

Frankie glared at Vince in triumph. "Bar food is an art," she instructed him. "It should be simple but strong, a real hit in your mouth, and you should be able to eat it with your hands. Like chilled oysters. Or like anchovy deviled eggs, like fried potatoes with aioli sauce—"

"Now you're talking."

"Like dates—Anna, here's what I was thinking—dates stuffed with toasted almonds and wrapped in prosciutto."

"Fabulous."

"And also—for happy hour, why couldn't you put out a rapini loaf on the bar? Already sliced, so people just take a piece. You bring it out just once, like at six o'clock, you don't reheat it or anything. There it is, take it or leave it."

"What's rapini?" Vince asked.

Frankie stared, honestly astounded. "What's rapini? It's broccoli rabe."

"Oh."

"You can mix it with garlic and onion and Asiago cheese, and you eat it with bread."

"Ah," Vince said, enlightened. "Like a spinach loaf."

Frankie shook her head, hopeless. "Yes, Vince, like a spinach loaf. Except you hold the mayo. And the water chestnuts," she added, like a punch line. "I've got things to do," she said, slid off her stool, and disappeared.

"Weird chick," Vince said, frowning after her. "She never laughs at my jokes."

"That is weird."

"No, you gotta admit, she's a little intense. I tried to give her a kitten," he said, refilling Anna's coffee cup. "This guy in my building's cat had kittens. You know she lives all by herself, right, out by the warehouse district."

"I know she lives alone."

"A terrible apartment, I mean, not like a tenement but almost. It's depressing. I told her she needed a pet, something to break up the misery."

"How'd that go over?"

"Not well." Anna watched his large round eyes turned mournful. Big waves of affection for Vince came over her at odd times. She wanted to lean over the bar and rub his crewcut head, pat his cheeks, shake him by the shoulders until his head wobbled. She just had an urge to give him an affectionate mauling, like a kid brother or a big friendly dog.

"Oh, good," she said, spying Shirl strolling through from the kitchen. "Here comes somebody who laughs at all your jokes."

"Hi, Anna! Wow, the paintings look incredible." Shirl plumped down heavily on the stool next to hers, dragging a manila folder out of her string bag. "Hey, Vince," she flirted, batting her short, stubby eyelashes. "I love that kind of shirt, that, like, no-collar shirt. It looks rilly good on you."

Vince beamed, he sparkled, back in his element. "How about a lime cola for the lady? No—" He pointed at Shirl with both index fingers. "Ginger ale and bitters. You've got that look in your eye."

Whatever that meant. Vince spouted nonsense to women and they didn't care, probably didn't even hear. Anna interrupted a lot of girlish hair-tossing to ask Shirl if that was the new menu mockup in her folder.

"Yeah. See, look, I did two versions. Earl Junior helped me with the formats. What that kid can't do on a computer you don't even wanna do. So which one do you like better?"

Anna scanned them, pleased with both looks. They weren't the real menu yet, just an experiment with placement and layout. Rose was against changing anything but the logo on the front. "But it's our identity, our signature—the menu is the *face* of the Bella Sorella," she argued. "If you go moving things around too much, you'll disorient people. You know, not *all* change is good change." Well, that was so wrong-headed, Anna had simply ignored it and gone ahead with her plans.

"This one's better," she told Shirl. "Your eye naturally goes here first, top right. So that's where we'll put the specials. And the low-ticket items down here in Siberia, lower right." Eight appetizers, eight entrees, that seemed just right. "And I like the wine list on the back, I like that informality. No separate list. You did a great job,

Shirl. Did it take a long time?" She'd volunteered to do it, but Anna wanted to reimburse her anyway, a little something extra in her pay tonight. Help pay off the lawsuit in case Earl Junior won.

"No," she said happily, twirling a coil of her corkscrew hair, magenta this week, "and I like doing it, it's rilly fun. Which color paper do you like best? The burgundy's for, like, power, but red is sexier."

Vince's ears perked up at that. Anna left them hashing out which was sexier, red or burgundy, and went off to see if Rose was back yet.

She showed up in the middle of dinner service. Anna barely saw her, had time for only a few words before they got steered toward urgent duties in opposite directions. She looked tired but not upset—so she must not have heard any bad news today about Theo. She'd spent the day taking him to therapy sessions and doctors' appointments. Mason usually did that, but he was off in Chincoteague, Anna happened to know, photographing herons.

"I think I'll go home early," Rose told her after the first rush ended. Anna was writing checks at the desk, Rose sitting on a corner of it, scratching her fingers through her hair as if trying to wake herself up. "I wouldn't leave if it was heavy tonight, but it's not." She had on a plain long dress with buttons down the front, brown from the bodice down, dark green above. Fabulous colors on her, Anna registered vaguely. She coveted the dress. "To tell you the truth, I'm running on fumes."

"No, sure," Anna said readily, "no problem. But."

"But. Oh, God." Rose covered her face with her hands, pretending to be overcome. "What?"

"Sometime we have to have a talk. About Carmen."

She slumped lower. "What did she do?"

"Nothing. It's her attitude. Rose—she's grouchy, she's bad-tempered, she's critical. Insensitive. She terrorizes the waitstaff. I've never known anybody so rigid. 'This is the way we've always done it,' she says—like that's a reason not to change anything."

"I know she's difficult." She rubbed her eyes, then scowled down at her fingertips, seeing she'd smudged her mascara. She pulled a tissue out of the box on the desk and wiped her face, and Anna wondered what she thought about her looks, now that she was sixty, if she was vain at all, and what it would feel like, from the standpoint of attractiveness and sex appeal and all that, to be as old as Rose.

"*Difficult*," she said, spoiling for an argument. "She's impossible! I'd like Frankie to be much more involved with planning the new menu, Rose. I want her in charge of it, frankly. She's smart and fast, she has great ideas—and Carmen's got her making marinara!"

"Yes, but it's really *good* marinara. All right," Rose said, sobering when Anna only frowned at that. "I'll talk to her. I will, I promise." She looked as if the prospect excited her about as much as handling snakes. "But not tonight. Please, I have to go home before I fall down."

"Go, I told you, I've got it."

"Shirl had to leave early, did anybody tell you?" Rose got her purse from the file cabinet, then went to stand in the doorway, leaning heavily against the post. "So you're a little short-staffed, but no big deal."

"Yeah, I heard. Cramps again. She was fine this afternoon. I'd say she was trying to get out early on a Friday night, except she looked awful."

"She did."

"Been there," Anna said with a mock shudder. "Not that much anymore, but when I was young. Ugh."

"I remember." She leaned her head back, sent Anna a gentle look down the length of her beaky nose. "Do you remember your first period?"

"Not really. Sort of. Mom taught me how to use a Kotex and all, I remember that."

Rose stayed where she was for a long moment, not moving. Her face seemed to sharpen, then relax; her eyes softened with an emotion that might be sadness or regret—Anna couldn't quite read it.

"What?" Anna said at last, disturbed by the silence.

She smiled. "Nothing. Good night." She pushed away from the door and drifted away.

Anna sat still, staring blankly at the opposite wall and listening to the familiar muffled din from the kitchen, unconsciously separating out the sounds of the cappuccino machine, a tray of glasses clattering out of the dishwasher, Carmen's voice, now Dwayne's, the harsh, intermittent rumble of the garbage disposal. Fontaine, who had finally confided to Anna that she was pregnant, stuck her pretty blond head in the door and asked a question, something about peach puree. Anna answered it. But as much as she wanted to keep it here, her mind was elsewhere. It was back in her house on an afternoon in gray December, the day after her mother's funeral. Or—maybe not the day after, maybe it only seemed that way. Soon after, though, because for years she'd associated the two occasions in her mind: burying her mother and getting her period for the first time. She hadn't lied to Rose about not remembering, at least not in that instant of denial, but now what had really happened came back with a strange immediacy, and she wondered—briefly, not very hard—what other memories she'd mangled or bent or abused in the ongoing effort to write Rose out of her life.

All day—the day after the funeral, or two days, a week—she'd felt heavy and achy, listless, her skin chilly and untouchable, but she'd attributed the symptoms to grief and too much crying, her body's natural reaction to emotional pain. Then, late in the afternoon, she'd found the blood on her underpants, and after a minute of panicky bewilderment she'd realized what it was. She remembered staring at her face in the bathroom mirror, searching for a sign, a clue that she'd turned some corner into womanhood, but all she saw was sickly-pale skin and anxious black eyes. She'd sat on the edge of the bathtub, her arms wrapped around her middle, tense and ill from the first of what was going to be about a hundred, give or take, monthly bouts with cramps and nausea. Eventually her father had knocked on the door. "Annie? You sick? Are you sick, baby?" She wouldn't come out, and she wouldn't tell him why. Was Rose already there or had he called her? Anna couldn't recall—she just remembered letting Rose into the bathroom and quickly closing the door behind her. And a feeling of overwhelming relief, an almost religious unburdening of care, *into thy hands*, except the hands were Rose's.

"Aunt Rose, I got my period."

"Oh, baby—"

"I looked in Mom's closet and under the sink and everything, but I couldn't find anything, you know, any sanitary whatchacallit. I don't think there's anything here." No, there wouldn't have been, she realized now—the chemo would've stopped her mother's menstrual periods.

"That's okay, don't worry about that," Rose had said, "we'll send Paul to the drugstore," and Anna had been glad that Rose was going to tell him. She didn't mind her father knowing, she just didn't want to tell him herself. Rose asked her how she felt, and sympathized with her, and told her how lousy her periods were at first, but then they got better and now she sailed through every month with barely a twinge. "Lily was exactly the same way," she claimed, and Anna believed her, and was finally able to ease into an acceptance of what was happening to her. Stop fighting it or viewing it as an unnatural catastrophe. Move in and occupy it.

Later, Rose had put her to bed with a hot water bottle on her stomach. "Mama used to say put it on your feet, let the heat draw the blood down, but I always liked it better right where it hurts, right there," Rose said, nodding approvingly at the bulge under the blanket over Anna's pelvis. So interesting, she'd thought, intrigued by the notion of her Nonna, a wide, humorless, gray-haired, *sexless* old widow woman, having periods and giving advice about them to her young daughters. Lily, Iris, and Rose. She'd felt connected, not bereft. There were still women in her life, her family, that she could turn to, and she didn't feel so alone.

But she remembered saying to Rose, just as she was about to get up and leave Anna by herself—maybe she'd said it to keep her—"This is the first important thing she'll miss." And Rose hadn't dodged it or pretended she didn't understand or it wasn't that bad, no bromides, no fake remedies. "I've been thinking the same thing," she'd said. "First date, first kiss. Graduation from high school. College. When you fall in love and get married, when you have a baby." Then they'd both started to cry. "Womanly milestones," Rose got out, sniffling.

For some reason that made them laugh. It just sounded funny, like a women's magazine article, "Womanly Milestones"—and yet that's what this *was*, if getting your first period wasn't a womanly milestone, Anna gave up—and so even while they were laughing they'd reached for each other. (*How could she have forgotten this?*) She'd scooted up on her pillow and wrapped her arms around her Aunt Rose, and Rose had put her arms around her, and it was the first time since her mother's death that she had truly felt any warmth or consolation from another person's physical comfort. Even her father couldn't make her feel like this: as if her grief were normal. As if her emotions weren't only natural, they were *next* in a long line of women's natural emotions. Like a totem pole, and her version of her feelings was just the next shape on top, an eagle, a mountain lion, a spear—whatever.

That had been the grace of Rose.

And she'd forgotten it.

Well, but. Still. So what? She'd never said Rose was a monster. She still knew what she knew, that was the point. In fact, Rose and her father might've slept with each other two minutes after Rose kissed Anna's forehead, told her she loved her, and left the room.

She tried to work up some fury over that possibility. Failed.

That wasn't it. She didn't care if they screwed each other's brains out *after her mother died.* That wasn't it.

Before. That's what she cared about, and she couldn't let it go. It was like a lump in her throat, something she couldn't swallow past, a growth. Rose and her father *before*, while her mother—and they loved her, they both loved her!—lay dying. She couldn't swallow past that.

"Hey, Anna?" Eddie called from the doorway, startling her. "You busy?"

"Why?" she asked warily. She was always busy.

"Might have a little situation here."

She looked at him more closely. Ever Eddie was cool at all times, he made a point of it, but he was shifting his weight from one foot to the other and fingering the tiny diamond-spot of beard under his bottom lip. He reminded her of an otter, his black hair so sleek and shiny, slicked back in an elegant, vaguely oriental ponytail. She didn't like Eddie much, but she liked to look at him, the tight clothes and tight body, and always the crotch-accentuating pants. He didn't walk, he strutted, pelvis-first. You just couldn't help yourself.

"What's up?" she asked.

"Got a loud and obnoxious out here."

"Drunk?"

"Definitely. I cut him off and told him to go home, but he ain't moving. I can *throw* him out, no problem there whatsoever." He rolled his shoulders and flexed his fingers, ready for action.

She asked him the obvious question. "How'd the guy get that drunk in the first place?" This was why she wanted Vince on nights, especially weekends, why she frowned on shift-changing. New rules were about to be implemented. If Vince were here, this wouldn't be happening.

Eddie shrugged. "I guess he was hammered when he came in, then all of a sudden he goes off. You can't tell, nobody can tell.

People are still eating, so he's disturbing the peace. A couple of couples at the bar already walked out."

She got up, swearing. "Is he a regular?" she asked, following Eddie out of the office.

"Maybe. Yeah. I think so."

"You think so?"

"I don't know. Somebody called him Bob."

Bob looked like a businessman, fiftyish, well dressed, well built. Red-faced. He sat in the center of the horseshoe-shaped bar, holding forth about something, she caught the emphatic phrase "*and that's not even the half of it*," to twelve or fourteen drinkers who wouldn't look directly at him. So far, shunning wasn't working. She sat down on one of the two conspicuously vacant stools on either side of him, sat all the way, didn't just perch. She could feel the interested, expectant gazes on her, like little flashlights, of about half the patrons in the restaurant, but she didn't look at anybody but Bob. To show she was on his side. "Hi, how's it going?" she greeted him, very familiar, as if they knew each other from way back.

He cut his sleepy, bloodshot eyes at her, then away. "Who're you?" He had a glass of melting ice in one loose fist, a cigarette in the other.

"I'm Anna."

"Where's Rose?"

"She's not here." So he was a regular.

"She was here."

"Yeah, but she had to go home."

"What're you, her daughter?"

"I'm the manager."

He snorted. "Good, then you can make me another scotch. This a bar or what?"

"Listen, Bob. The reason you can't have another drink is"—she leaned forward and said it in confidence, pal to pal—"some people think you've already had enough."

"Yeah? Fuck some people." He laughed a phlegmy *hah hah*.

She chuckled with him, raising her eyebrows, shaking her head. He wasn't a sloppy drunk, no slurring his words or accidentally jerking his elbow off the edge of the bar. A mean look behind the bleariness in his eyes worried her, though. "Yeah, but," she said with gentle reproach. "You're a *little* drunk, right? You gotta admit."

"Not half as drunk as I'm gonna be."

She shook her head some more, disappointed. "See, the problem is, you're no fun anymore. You need to go home and come back when you're your old self. We like having you here, but not like this."

He looked half-persuaded for a second. But then he snapped back into Sullen Bob. "Fuck that."

They went around like that for a while. She ordered club sodas, one for her, one for him. Every time Eddie came anywhere near him, Bob's belligerence level shot up, a thermometer near a heat source. After he brought the drinks, Anna had to make faces at Eddie to keep him away.

Turned out, Bob wanted to talk. He started telling her about his ex-wife. Cathy. Last Wednesday was their anniversary, they'd have been married thirteen years. "I didn't have one drink all day," he swore, weighting the words with heavy significance. "*Not—one—drink*. Not one. Know why?"

"Why?"

"I wouldn't give her the satisfaction." When he smoothed back the silver hair at his temple, a gold cuff link glinted on his shirt-sleeve. Everything he had on was expensive, even his cologne, but she didn't hold that against him. She might have with another loud-mouth rich guy, but more misery was coming off Bob than anger. She could feel it, almost see it, like an aura. "You know she's a lesbian," he confided.

"She is? Really?" But she was determined not to get roped into his life story. That wasn't how you handled a drunk, that just wasted time.

"Big time." He nodded slowly and vehemently. He stubbed his cigarette in the ashtray but it didn't go out, just trailed smoke into Anna's left eye. He began to tear his cork coaster into pieces. "Nah," he admitted, sinking his chin down on his chest, hunching his shoulders under his rumpled suitcoat. Getting small. "I'm lying."

"Oh."

"She's a schoolteacher. Eighth-grade social studies. Social studies," he repeated wonderingly. "What the fuck is that?"

"I've never known."

"The kids're crazy about her, she never has any problem with the little motherfuckers." He caught himself again. "They don't know 'er like I do, course."

"Course."

"Bitch on wheels." He sipped his water absentmindedly. "So, Laura. You married?"

...So now not only do I know all about Bob's life, he knows everything about mine. I remember Vince telling me once it's easier for a woman to handle a drunk, providing the drunk is a man, but if it's a woman it's the other way around. I don't think I really "handled" Bob anyway, I just talked to him. After a while, it started to feel like a date. A really bad date. Rose, I'm sure, is better at this than I am; she'd have gotten him out of there a lot faster, but still with no hard feelings. There's an art to it.

He gave me his card at the end. If I ever need legal advice, Bob's my man. (I don't think so.) Tony and I got him in a cab, and I told him good night, come back any time (taking a chance there), have a safe trip home, etc. The last thing he said, talking to me through the half-open back window, was that it was hard to go home. "There's nobody there," he said. He teared up, but he didn't cry. Thank God, because then I would've.

The thing is, I liked him. The even bigger thing is, I like everybody. Almost everybody. Do I sound like an ass? I didn't have this so much when I worked in the coffeehouse, very serious place, the clientele was all artists and wannabes. Homogeneous crowd, no variety, everybody young and cool and not very interesting (to me). Here—I want everybody to have a good time. I'm so *fond* of them, the regulars, the one-timers who might turn out to be regulars. Lonely guys like Bob, and couples on stiff first dates, married couples who never open their mouths, never say one word the whole meal. Girlfriends who get drunk at lunch and talk and laugh until it's time for dinner. I'm starting to think of these people as *property* of the Bella Sorella, people who must be fed and watered and *satisfied*. Stomachs filled, cockles warmed. It's my pleasure. And I think the secret is so easy—just show that you care. Because all anybody wants is to feel important. Oh, they know me here—they want me! That's it, that's all there is to it.

Oh, and really good food.

Exhausted. Don't know why I'm writing this, except I'm keyed up. That weird high I was telling you about. There's a lot of drug and alcohol abuse in the restaurant business—I told you that, right? Makes sense. Luckily I have other ways to cope when the tension gets tight. I talk a lot, and write e-mails if nobody's around to talk to. Play music so loud the neighbors complain. Or my car vibrates, just the thumping bass audible to passersby—yes, I'm one of those.

Okay, I'll stop. Hope you had a successful day in the marshes. Rose took your stepfather to his dr. appts. today, and apparently everything's status quo. So that's good news.

Night,
Anna

10

Theo's hair on top was hot from the sun, cool underneath when Rose slipped her fingers in to pull it, lock by grizzled lock, away from his scalp and snip it with Mason's kitchen scissors. "Don't cut my ear off," he'd growled at the beginning, and so far she'd managed not to, but she had to be careful around his face and the tender back of his neck because of the sudden, unpredictable head jerks he couldn't control—a fairly new symptom in the progression of his ailment. A minor one, comparatively, and it was a glorious June afternoon, it was Monday so the restaurant was closed, and Theo was having a good day. If she could put a glass box around them, here in the bend of Mason's L-shaped dock, sun-warmed, bird-serenaded, with the blinding-bright river chopping along behind for a background, Rose would have to count herself a happy woman. Right here, right now, what more could she want? Two or three things occurred to her in the next thought, but she pushed them away, like distractions during a meditation. Living in the moment wasn't only good advice anymore, it was a way to keep going.

Theo sat in a folding chair on the dock for his haircut. She put her arms around his towel-draped shoulders from behind and pressed her cheek against his cheek. Their heads moved together in a quick twitch, and he croaked, "Watch it, I'll knock you out." She held tighter, the whole warm armful of him, until he patted her wrist with his shaky hand.

"What would you do, Theo, if you could do anything at all today? This beautiful day. Anything in the world."

"This."

She squeezed tight and then straightened up, so he couldn't see her face. "Me, too."

"And then. I'd go to—the Keys on the *Wind Rose*. With you." The rhythm of his speech emphasized the wrong words sometimes; she wasn't always sure of his meaning until she'd processed the whole sentence. "Take as long as we like, all . . . summer if we want."

"You're assuming that boat's ever going to be finished." The blue-tarp-covered bowsprit poked out of the boat shed behind them; occasionally the whine of a power saw broke the sleepy stillness. Mason was doing outside work today, customizing V bunks to fit inside the narrow cabin.

"Cruise 'er down the coast," Theo said dreamily. "Spend a couple months in the Keys. Maybe—coast over to Nassau."

"In that little boat? Just us?"

"We could sail 'er around the world. She's that tough."

"If we sail her around the world, I definitely want an engine."

"Damn right."

Theo and Mason argued endlessly over whether the all-wood sailing cutter they'd been rebuilding for two years needed a motor. Theo said yes, of course, but Mason, the purist, claimed an inboard engine would desecrate it, all they needed was a stout ash sweep for sculling in tight places. For now they were compromising by putting an outboard bracket on the transom. That way they could postpone the decision indefinitely.

When she'd cut as much of his hair as she wanted, she gave Theo a soft head scratch that made him moan. He'd have fallen asleep right there in the chair, but she knelt beside him and began to massage the muscle in his left forearm—he'd had spasms there last night, one in a cluster of unpleasant symptoms called dystonia—and that woke him up.

"C'mere," he said, and pulled her up, onto his lap. She wound her arms around him. She was afraid she was too heavy on his thighs, she kept the toes of one foot on the ground, supporting some of her weight on them. It made for an uncomfortable perch, but she stayed as long as she could. All this touching, massaging, stroking, holding was essential, they couldn't do without it. It calmed them down. Lovemaking had become almost impossible, but touching was still a compulsion.

"Like to take a sail on 'er with Mason, too. One day."

"That would be nice," Rose agreed.

"Father, son. Better late . . . "

He didn't have to finish that. One of his hardest regrets, she knew, was that his second marriage, the one to Mason's mother, hadn't worked out. He'd wanted to walk into that sweet, ready-made family, a beautiful wife, a little boy who loved him, and be "normal," the kind of husband and father he thought they deserved. But he couldn't stay, and now it was hard for him to forgive himself. Mason had, long ago, but Theo was slow to follow.

"Hot," they decided, and got up. Theo folded the chair, and they ambled down the dock to the boat shed, to get out of the sun and see what Mason was up to. Sharp, sour-sweet smells of varnish and paint hovered in the sawdusty air, dim after the glare outside. Mason wasn't there. No—thumping sounds from the hull said he was belowdecks, doing something in the cabin. Theo kicked the keel, and a minute later Mason came up. He clambered over the side and dropped to the paint-spattered concrete, dragging the long cord of a drill after him. No nails or glue on the *Wind Rose*; the mahogany wood was so hard, all the fittings had to be screwed.

It was a beautiful boat, not that Rose knew much about boats, and not that she was prejudiced by this one being named after her. She loved its classic, old-fashioned shape, and the fact that it was all wood, no fiberglass—but that was another bone of contention between the restorers. Theo wanted to fiberglass the hull, Mason wanted to leave it alone. Mason didn't even want electricity! Oil lamps would do for navigating a day sailer, and the radio receiver could run on flashlight batteries. Simplify, he said. Theo said he was out of his mind.

"Got the chocks on the cabin roof," Theo noted approvingly. Mason said yep, he did that yesterday.

"What are they for?" Rose wondered.

"To stow the dinghy," Mason said, "bottom-up, when you're cruising."

"Nice new fiberglass dinghy," Theo said smugly. He'd won that one. Mason had wanted to build the dinghy from scratch, out of mahogany to match the sailboat.

"Haircut?" Rose offered, snapping the scissors in the air invitingly. Mason grinned, shook his head. He wore his hair long because of the scars on his face, but it wasn't down to his shoulders, didn't hang down his back, so somebody must cut it for him sometime. Did he go to a barbershop? A stylist? She couldn't quite picture that. She could picture him cutting it himself, sawing away in the bathroom mirror, guessing at the length in back. "Sure?" she wheedled. "I've even got the barber chair. We can do it out in the wide open-spaces."

"She's not bad," Theo said, showing off his profile. "She works cheap."

"Tempting." Mason poured paint thinner on a rag and rubbed it over his hands and wrists. "Maybe later. Look at this, Theo."

They examined the rudder, newly painted and varnished, clamped between a pair of sawhorses. Should they wrap the handle in tape or doeskin? Or leave it alone? Naturally they couldn't agree. Rose smiled at the picture they made, short and blocky next to tall and rangy, and thought of how different they were. Because of an accident of marriage thirty years ago, they were rebuilding this boat together, and in some ways the *Wind Rose* was all they had in common. But in others, it was only an excuse, the physical bridge they were using to connect, because their attachment went much deeper than similarities or shared experiences. It must, or Mason wouldn't have let Theo back into his life so generously. Theo had a lot to live down, but Mason had never reproached him for any of it. They'd reversed the Bible story: Theo was the prodigal father, Mason the son who welcomed him home with open arms.

"Mason?" Frankie called from the back porch steps. "Hey, Mason! Phone call!"

"Phone call," Rose relayed faintly when he didn't move, kept polishing a rudder hinge with his shirt cuff. He hated the telephone. He gave out his cell phone number to a careful few, and usually let the house phone ring. Now he was trapped.

She watched his shoulders rise and fall in resignation. "Excuse me," he said, and sprinted for the house.

She and Theo followed him much more slowly. "Should I feel guilty?" Rose said. "I never asked him if I could bring Frankie over with me. I wanted to give her a day off, and if I'd left her at the restaurant she'd still be pounding out pork chops." Instead she was pounding out pork chops in Mason's kitchen, but at least she was getting a change of scene on her one day off. Rose had invited Anna, too, but she'd been vague, "Maybe, I don't know, I'll see," and so far she hadn't shown up. "And then Vince heard Frankie and Anna were coming and asked if *he* could come, and now—all of a sudden—"

"Party," Theo finished.

"Party."

"Don't worry about Mason. Do him good. People in the house. High time."

By the time they got to the kitchen, he was hanging up the phone and disappearing around the corner. Escaping? His house wasn't exactly *teeming*; just two people were in the kitchen, Frankie at the sink washing dishes and Vince opening wine bottles, eight different Merlots, for a tasting.

"Who called?" Theo asked nosily.

Frankie and Vince looked at each other and shrugged. "Don't know," Frankie said, "I didn't ask. A man's voice."

On her own time, Frankie always wore black, and today it was cutoffs and a sleeveless T-shirt with a faded Hell's Angels logo. The contrast with her sugar-white skin was stark, like a shrill abstract painting. From the back she looked like a young boy, lithe and quick, small but long-limbed. When she lifted an iron skillet from the sink to the counter, the muscle in her arm bulged like a knot. "Isn't this a great kitchen?" she said to Rose. "Wouldn't it be cool to have this in your own house?"

"I know, it's marvelous. Do you need any help? How's the pork?"

"No, it's done, it's marinating. Takes about an hour."

An experiment. They'd agreed, Frankie, Rose, Carmen, and Anna, that the new, streamlined, eight-entree menu should have only one pork dish, but they kept vacillating over which one. Tonight's chops were in competition with the all-night wood-roasted, fennel-stuffed pork shoulder they'd done last week.

"Good," Rose said, "then you can relax for a while. Go for a walk, why don't you, go look at the river. Have some fun."

"Get some sun," Theo advised from the table.

Frankie flashed a smile and stayed where she was. "I love looking out at these birds," she said, pointing through the window over the sink at the various feeders and birdbaths and watering holes Mason had in his side yard. "I don't know what they are, though. Well, hummingbirds, I know. And that's a catbird, that gray one, but I only know because he told me. But, like, what's that purply one?"

"A finch, I think. House finch." Rose shrugged when Frankie looked impressed. "I only know what he tells me, too. Where's your little girl today?"

"At the beach with Mike. Three-day weekend. I said it'd be okay." She scrubbed harder at the corners of the sink and pressed her lips together. She was allowed to see Katie twice a week, and Monday afternoons had become one of the regular times.

"You miss her," Rose said in sympathy.

She twitched her shoulders, an annoyed, impatient gesture. Rose wanted to put her arm around her, but she'd have squirmed away in embarrassment. Frankie and Theo got along surprisingly well. One reason must be that they'd both rather be disliked than pitied.

Vince came over with a handful of wineglasses. "These are dusty," he said in a low voice, "can you wash 'em?" Frankie said yes. "I think he uses, like, one glass all the time." He'd lined up his wine bottles along the counter, even set out a basket of baguettes for palate-cleansing between tastes. "We're all set except for Anna. How come she's not here? This won't be much of a tasting if only five of us are drinking."

"She was arguing with Carmen about something with inventory when I left," Frankie said.

"Did she say she was coming?"

"No, but she didn't say she wasn't."

Rose had gotten the same reaction when she'd invited her.

"Where'd Mason go?" Theo wanted to know.

"Outside to smoke?" Vince guessed.

Outside to be alone, more likely. "I'll see," Rose said, and went to find him.

He was on the top step of his front stoop. Brooding, not smoking. She felt a pang of remorse to see him staring off at the woods beyond his yard, hands dangling between his knees, his scarred profile bleak. So her homemade therapy hadn't worked on him. She batted open the screen door and came out, and she had to put her hand on top of his shoulder to keep him from getting up. She sat beside him on the step, remembering to sit on his right side—that meant something to him. "Mason," she said before he could speak, "I am so sorry."

He looked at her in alarm. "Why?"

"I thought you wouldn't mind, but I wasn't thinking. All these people—we've just taken over your house. It's my fault."

"No, I don't mind. I like it."

"You do? No, you don't. You're very nice—"

"Rose—"

"But this is a terrible imposition, and I didn't even ask." On purpose; if she'd asked him, he'd probably have said no. She'd done it *for his own good*—how arrogant, really. Presumptuous. "I apologize. I was—"

"Rose, let me tell you something. That was Dr. Eastman on the phone."

"Dr. Eastman?" She repeated the name stupidly. Mason's doctor; he'd seen him through the aftermath of his accident, all the various surgeries and therapies. She put her hand on his knee in concern. Then she gripped it in sudden fright—Eastman was one of Theo's doctors, too. He consulted with the neurological specialists, he translated their opinions into words Theo could understand. Theo indiscriminately hated all doctors, so Eastman had taken to channeling information about him through Rose or Mason.

"Last week's tests came back."

She girded herself. "What is it?"

"It still isn't definite."

"It never is," she said bitterly.

"But that's the good news. Because they're pretty sure, it's looking pretty much now like it's CBD."

She closed her eyes tight. "Oh no. Oh my God." And yet she wasn't surprised. She realized she'd been expecting it. Was Theo, too?

"I wrote it down, I knew I wouldn't remember." Mason took a scrap of paper out of his shirt pocket. "The last CT scan showed asymmetric atrophy of the fronto-parietal region of the cortex. He said that's more like CBD than anything else. Any of the others we were hoping for."

Corticobasal degeneration. Sometimes they called it CBGD, corticobasal ganglionic degeneration, but it was the same thing. It meant Theo's nerve cells were shrinking and atrophying, the ones in the cortex of his brain, and deeper down in the basal ganglia. There was no cure, no way to slow it down. It was worse than Parkinson's, because it went faster. It was the very last diagnosis they'd wanted.

He folded the slip of paper over, again, again, until it was a tiny, unfoldable square, and put it back in his pocket. "At least we know. That's something."

She wanted to lean against him. She wanted to walk by herself into the woods and lie down on the ground. She couldn't think. "I'm not going to cry," she vowed.

"I am."

She laughed, at the same time tears stung the backs of her eyes. "Now, I mean." She did lean against him then, soothed by his solid arm and the sadness in his answering laugh. "Mason, oh, Mason, thank God for you."

"For you."

"I couldn't get through this if you weren't here."

He took her hand. "When should we tell him, Rose? He'll know what it means."

"Yes, he'll know. Not today."

"No," he agreed.

"Who should tell him?"

"I will. If you want me to."

"Which one of us would he hate it less from?"

"Probably Eastman."

She laughed again. "Maybe we shouldn't tell him at all."

Mason pressed his eye socket against the heel of his hand. "Don't you think he'd want to know?"

"Probably. Oh, I don't know. I don't know."

"I want to finish the boat, Rose. I've been stalling, dragging it out, I think to keep him. I think that's why I've been so slow."

That shocked her. "But he could still have years, it all depends—"

"I know, but I want him to sail it. Soon, while he's able. It's important."

They never decided who would tell him, or when. Or how. They heard the sound of tires on gravel, and looked up to see a little white car nose out of the bend in the drive where the woods started. "Anna," they said together. Rose found herself watching Mason from the corner of her eye, trying to read the emotion in his intent face. He and Anna were writing notes to each other, e-mails, but what that meant she had no idea. Courtship? Information exchange? He'd come to the restaurant once that she knew of, to bring Anna a bird book. He hadn't come inside, though, just loitered out in the alley. They'd ended up going for a walk. Anna had accused Rose once of matchmaking, but she hadn't been. She didn't think. If pressed, she'd have said friend-making.

Anna looked sleek and self-possessed in a sleeveless sundress and sandals, and Rose knew they were both admiring her, she and Mason, as she climbed out of her car and crunched her way over the stones, head high, arms swinging, tanned legs flashing. Life, health, vigor—she was the antidote they needed, and Rose was glad she'd interrupted them. Theo would've been, too. Plenty of time for all that. She jumped up, blinking away the last pointless tear, and made her face calm and her voice gay. "Hi, you made it! Just in time for Vince's wine tasting. Everything okay at the restaurant?"

Mason was more subdued, not as comfortable as she was with role-playing. But after forty years in the business, she knew how to make the show go on. "Hello," he said gravely, keeping his hands in his pockets, keeping his distance. Rose could see Anna pull back on her own greeting, following his somber lead. Inaccurate signals were being sent. She wanted to step in the middle, get between them and explain them to each other.

"Here, I brought something for dessert." Anna handed Mason a paper bag. "It's just a ricotta cake."

"Did you make it?" She said yes, and he looked amazed. "You cook?"

"Well, sure. How could I avoid it? For friends, though, not the masses."

He smiled, pleased to be called a friend. "Thank you," he said formally. "Come on in." He seemed a little dazzled, holding the screen door open for the ladies. *Come on in,* just like a regular host. And in the kitchen, he stood aside with his arms folded and let the women bustle around, setting the table, rinsing dust out of cups and glasses he hadn't used in... well, probably *never*; he'd probably bought them just to fill up the cabinets. Rose could imagine him washing the same plate and fork meal after meal, since Theo was his only regular visitor. But he looked more interested than dismayed, thank goodness, by this takeover of his house she'd engineered without his permission.

"Okay, people." Vince called them to order, marshaling them around the kitchen table. "This is a formal tasting." He'd poured everybody's first glass of wine. "They're all Merlots, but that's all I'm saying. Okay, four are Italian, two are French, two California, one Chilean, but that's all I'm saying. One's incredibly expensive, so if you like it best, too bad." Why include it, Anna asked, if they couldn't put it on the menu? "Because," Vince said reasonably, "I wanted to try it."

"No, thanks, I'm not in this," Frankie said when he tried to hand her a glass.

"What do you mean? You have to be, I need tasters."

"No, thanks."

"Come on."

"I don't drink."

"You don't drink? You don't drink?" His surprise was comical. But how could he not know that? Rose asked Anna the question with a look, and she signaled back, *I have no idea.*

"Just take a sip," Vince coaxed. "You don't have to swallow if you don't want to. Spit it out in the sink, like a spit bucket. All our taste buds are in the mouth, none in the throat. Did you know that?"

"No." She put her hands behind her back, wouldn't even touch the glass he kept pressing on her. She walked backward until she hit the sink.

"Come on," he said, still disbelieving, "I really need your expertise. Think of it as food. You're a great food taster, so just apply all that sensitivity to wine. Come on, Frankie."

"No."

"Please? It's just wine, everybody drinks wine."

"Vince, leave her be," Anna said, "if she doesn't want any, she doesn't."

He wasn't going to give up. "I know, but just—"

"I'm an alcoholic."

"What?" He laughed.

"I'm a drunk." She said it too loud, and then she blushed, embarrassed by her anger. She looked cornered, holding on to the counter behind her with outspread hands, puffing out her chest to defend herself. "I'm an alcoholic."

No one knew what to say. Rose swirled ruby-colored wine in the bottom of her glass and listened to the silence pile up until the room was full. She should have headed this off somehow, but how?

"Oh," Vince managed eventually. "Okay, no problem. Sorry about that. I didn't know."

"Yeah. Forget it." Frankie pivoted, turned on the faucet, started fiddling with a sponge.

Vince looked at Rose, at Anna. He pretended to tear his hair out by the roots.

Before the lethal silence could start again, Mason said in a wonderfully matter-of-fact voice, "I'd call this one soft. That's a wine term, isn't it? It smells like plums. I'd say it's soft and rounded. It's very good. Are we really grading them?"

Normalcy returned, but what a pointlessly idiotic moment. There were so many better ways that could've been handled, and Rose prided herself on handling awkward moments. She half blamed

Frankie for letting it go so far, but that wasn't fair. How could she know what was impossible for Frankie to say and what wasn't?

They tasted the wines. Vince had devised an overly complicated scoring system based on color, clarity, aroma, body, flavor, etc., and it was impossible not to have fun with it at his expense. "*Be serious*," he kept ordering them, but that got harder to do as the tasting went on, especially for Anna. "This gets an eight and a half for pretension," she declared of a Furlan Venezia Giulia. "But I'm giving it a four over all, because even though its assertive bouquet of ash and tangerine insists its heart is in the right place, there's still that faint aftertaste of, well, hypocrisy. And the finish, I regret, is pure Jimmy Swaggert."

Theo wasn't supposed to drink—another reason he hated doctors. He did anyway, although nothing like in the old days. Rose sat close to him at the table, enjoying his deep rumbling chuckle and the tolerant way he was regarding Anna, who was just getting warmed up. Imagine those two becoming friends. Too much to hope for, and she wasn't pushing it. But wouldn't that be something.

"The ideal restaurant wine list," Vince tried to tell them, "is three things: short, intelligent, and affordable. So if we put only one Merlot on, it has to be the best medium-priced one of these eight. If we put two, then we get more of a range, but we have to make a decision about how long our list is going to be."

"There's more seafood on the menu than there used to be," Frankie pointed out from the counter, where she was slicing pears to go with endive for a salad. "Less meat. If you had, say, eighteen wines, you'd weight it toward the whites, ten and eight, eleven and seven, something like that."

"Eighteen," Vince said worriedly. "That's not very many." He was taking a course in oenology at night, he read wine magazines, he picked the brains of the wine reps and the most knowledgeable customers. Trying to become an expert fast.

"No, but it would fit on the back of the main menu nicely," Anna said, always practical. "Are you including sparkling wines in that? And blush wines? They listed blushes separately at Industrial Coffee, but I don't know why, they were just Zinfandels."

The talk turned technical. Mason and Theo were the only ones taking Vince's scoring system seriously. They liked the Scubla Colli Orientali "Rosso Scuro" best, and were sorry to find out at the end that it retailed for forty-five dollars a bottle. The markup made it much too expensive for the Bella Sorella's cellar. But they were also backslappingly proud of themselves for picking the priciest, so theoretically the best, of the eight wines.

Frankie asked Rose if she'd like to grill the marinated pork chops, or season them, or taste the deglaze. Rose knew a polite offer when she heard one and said no, of course not, this was her day off, Frankie was the chef. All the uncomfortableness from before was gone, smoothed over by wine and Anna's silliness—or so Rose thought. Vince got her alone for two seconds while Frankie was out in the dining room.

"Why didn't you tell me?" he demanded in an angry whisper, pushing his face close to hers.

"What, you mean Frankie's—"

"Sh! Yeah! Did everybody know about that but me?"

"I don't know. Anna told me—I don't know who else knows. What difference does it make?"

"What difference!"

"What do you care?"

"*I'm a bartender*," he said fiercely.

"I remember. I don't see wh—"

"She's an alcoholic and I'm a *bartender*." He glanced over his shoulder, but the coast was still clear. "How is that supposed to work?"

"How is it . . ." The light dawned. "Aha."

"Aha!" he repeated like a curse. "She'll *never* go out with me." He made a bitter smile with his nice lips. "Well, at least now I know why."

"She won't go out with you? You asked her?"

"If I told you how many times, Aunt Rose, you'd laugh."

"Never."

"She thinks I'm just kidding around. I keep it light."

Rose was charmed, unreasonably pleased. Vince and women—it was a joke between Iris and her, how much they loved him. If Frankie wouldn't go out with him, it must be a first. How funny. But she made a sympathetic face for his benefit. "Don't give up," she advised. "Women like persistence."

Vince had given Frankie a turtle, Rose found out at dinner. For a present, because she lived alone in a depressing-sounding apartment building where she wasn't allowed to have pets. "Sebastian," Vince had named this turtle, which he'd found in his yard, because its shell was bashed in. "How's Sebastian?" he asked Frankie, after praising the pork chops to the heavens, not to mention the salad and the herb-buttered tagliatelle. "How does he like his bowl? He might need some toys, like a log or something to sit on."

"What?" Frankie was scowling at a piece of meat on the end of her fork, gauging the pinkness. "Oh, Sebastian. Yeah, thanks. He was delicious."

Vince coughed, sloshing wine on the tablecloth.

Frankie grinned. "Kidding."

It was a very merry dinner, and the unlikeliness of that gave Rose pause more than once. All the wine they'd drunk didn't hurt, but they were simply a congenial group. Theo and Anna were on such good behavior, they forgot they didn't like each other. Frankie told funny stories with a straight face about crazy chefs and homicidal dishwashers she had known; Theo and Mason were sure she was exaggerating, but Rose and Anna knew better. Mason had the least to say, but Rose didn't worry about him. She enjoyed the bemused look on his face, as if he still couldn't believe he was here, in his own dining room, with all these *people.* The only time she wanted to cry was when he came back from fetching something from the kitchen and stood behind her chair for a moment before sitting back down. He put his hands on her shoulders, just held them there while the laughter and conversation flowed around them. She felt comforted and weepy, soft inside. In the midst of this lovely, lighthearted meal there was something sad and frightening—Mason's silent kindness reminded her of that. But also of the reverse: that it was possible to endure sad and frightening things in the company of good friends.

They adjourned after dinner to the windowless living room for coffee and ricotta cake. Anna asked Mason something about heron photos. Heron photos? The words made no sense to Rose until she made Anna repeat them, "*heron* photos, photographs of herons, *great blue* herons," a couple of times. Everyone laughed, even Anna and Mason, when Vince teased them on their way out, "Oh, you're going to show her your *heron* photos. Riiight." Very silly, but by then everything was funny. Frankie and Vince got into their favorite argument, what kind of music people wanted to hear in a good restaurant, what kind made them order another drink, what kind made them get up and leave. "I've never even *heard* of these groups," Rose admitted, and they looked at her with similar expressions of pity and agreement. She was afraid to ask what they thought of the Handel recorder sonata or the Mozart quartet for flute and strings, her two favorite dinner tapes. "Play whatever you like," she told them, giving up. "If you can ever agree on anything." They never could, but she was beginning to hear their arguments as flirtation. Vince was courting Frankie by fighting with her. Did she know? She was all business, rarely smiled, took everything he said seriously. Didn't mind telling him when she thought he was a jerk. "You are such a child," she said, disgusted with his goading insistence on junk food and ESPN in the bar. "Time to grow up, Vincenzo. What do you want on your tombstone?" she asked earnestly, poking her sharp finger into his forearm. " 'He served great nachos during the Super Bowl'?"

"Hey, yeah."

"*No*. 'He knew his people and he gave them what they needed.'

That's what you want. 'He was a brilliant bar man. His Cosmo could make you cry.' "

Vince cracked up.

" 'His wine list consoled you when you felt like dying. Everybody who sat at his bar was satisfied. He was a nice man.' "

That sobered him. "Okay," he said after a thoughtful pause. "But can we have the hockey game on while I make the Cosmos?"

Anna and Mason came back into the room laughing. Now there was a sight. Mason, though, was still a man most at ease with a camera between himself and the world, and Rose wasn't surprised to see him slip the Nikon off his shoulder and begin quietly, unobtrusively to take the pictures of his guests. What did surprise her was Anna's easy compliance with his suggestion that she and Rose sit closer together on the couch for a portrait. They touched shoulders, tilted their heads toward each other, smiling at Mason. "That's good," he said, "that's great," angling the camera sideways for more shots.

"God, you two," said Frankie from across the room. "You look so much like mother and daughter, I can never get over it. You even dress alike."

Rose laughed down at her own sleeveless black dress. She'd dressed it up with a scarf around the neck, red and white; Anna had tied a long yellow scarf around her waist. "Great minds," Rose said, leaning close and giving Anna's shoulder a playful nudge with hers. Anna kept smoothing the hem of her skirt over her bare, crossed knee, pressing and pressing the material with her fingers. She didn't look up or smile back.

"Want to see a picture of Katie?" Frankie rummaged in her beat-up shoulder bag. "She might be starting to look like me a little, I dunno. See what you think."

"Is this the Easter picture?" Rose asked.

"No, it's newer, last week."

"I've seen it," Anna said. She got up abruptly and walked to the other side of the room.

"Oh, what a gorgeous child," Rose said. Mother and daughter were kneeling on the grass in front of a plastic kiddie pool, filling it with a garden hose. Each had a hand on the hose, and they were looking over their shoulders at the camera, grinning, squinting in the sunlight.

"Do you think we look alike?"

"Well..." Not really, but Frankie wanted her to say yes. "Maybe," Rose said, "could be, something... around the eyes?"

"No, she's got Mike's eyes." She took the snapshot back, disappointed.

Rose had always wanted to touch her almost-bald head, see what that quarter-inch of bristly red hair felt like. "Maybe if you let this grow," she said, cupping the back of Frankie's head lightly. A surprise: it was soft, not prickly. She couldn't resist rubbing it lightly with her palm. Such a delicate skull, blue-veined above the ears, and something terribly vulnerable about the slender, soft-skinned neck.

"It's curly." Frankie suffered Rose's touch with downcast eyes and a pleased, self-conscious smile. "If I let it grow, it'd be curly."

"Curly? Really? That would be cute."

"You think? Nah, it's easier this way." She pulled away, recollecting herself. "This is me." She shrugged, pushed out her lips, crossed her ankle over her knee. Feigning masculinity was one of her defenses. Against what, though, Rose wondered. Being nice to herself?

Rose excused herself to go to the bathroom, and when she came back Anna was gone. "She went home," Vince explained. "She said she was tired."

Just like that, without even saying good-bye? "That's funny," Rose said. Mason was taking the spent roll of film out of the back of his camera. He gave a slight shake of his head when she caught his eye. *Beats me.* The others nodded, but nobody had any explanations.

Frankie and Vince did the dishes while she sat on the back steps with Mason and Theo to watch the moon rise and listen to the river. "What a nice day this has been," they took turns saying. Rose couldn't resist pointing out that the bird singing its name over and over in the woods behind them was a whippoorwill. "Right," Mason said, nodding, kindly conveying with his voice that that was quite a spot, not a gimme. "They have whiskers," he told her.

"Whiskers?"

"Not the technical term. Looks like little hairs sprouting out around the beak. Like a seal."

This is my family, Rose thought. If she had married Theo, Mason would be her stepson. Whole stretches of time had gone by tonight when she hadn't thought of Dr. Eastman's news. She'd been distracted by the peacefulness, this seductive illusion of normalcy.

Theo was flagging, though. "Stay here tonight," Mason invited him. "Sleep in the guest room. Go lie down right now. Just go." No, he wouldn't consider it. "Want to wake up in my own place." Rose had given up arguing with him. *Fall, then, break your stubborn neck*, she'd said at the end of their last fight on the subject, and neither of them had the heart to dredge it up again. Just thinking about it made her sigh. She didn't realize she had, though, until Theo, two steps below, wrapped his hand around her bare calf. She leaned over and rubbed his back. "I'll drive you back, then," she said. "Old bear."

"Nope. Mason can take me. Right?"

"Sure," Mason said, surprised.

"Why can't I?"

"I don't like you around . . . the marina at night. Been too many break-ins. Vandalism."

"There have?"

"You knew that—I told you. Guy two slips down, Charles, you know Charles."

"Charles Bell?"

"Had his cabin door kicked in—radio stolen, battery—charts, everything that wasn't screwed down."

She went cold. That hadn't happened. No, it had happened, but three years ago, and in another marina. Theo had moved *Expatriate* to the new dock because of the burglaries and break-ins at the old one. To Rose's knowledge, he hadn't seen Charles Bell in two years.

Mild to moderate cognitive impairment. Memory loss and difficulty planning. Those were the symptoms that frightened him the most, the prospect of them. They'd joked about it: "Well, at least if you lose your memory, you won't remember." Was this how it started?

"No problem," Mason said after a tense pause, during which she alternated between hoping and dreading Theo would realize his mistake. "I'll be glad to drive you." Mason knew, too: she could tell by his voice, too quiet, and his still, stricken face.

After that, the party broke up quickly. She kissed everyone good-bye, including a startled Frankie, and drove home by herself in the warm, buggy summer night, trying to see some cheer or beauty in the stars and the fireflies, the dark, wild smell of the water when she crossed over the bridge. An hour ago, in spite of everything, the tempting thought that she wasn't alone had been a consolation, but it was gone now. She felt lonely and overwhelmed, too frail for the trouble ahead of her. All by herself.

So her tired, beaten-down heart lifted when she pulled into the parking lot of her building and saw the little white car with New York plates in the space next to hers. It wasn't the answer to a prayer, because she hadn't asked for anything, but she felt gratuitously blessed, and she gave herself a little congratulatory smile in the rearview mirror. *Look what I get*, the smile said. *Lucky me, after all.*

Their doors slammed together. "Hi," Rose said over the roof of Anna's car. Anna was faster, met her between their two cars before she could get hers locked. "Hi," she said again, softer, doubtfully. Anna's eyes were huge, Rose could see the whites around them. And something electrified about her, as if her hair should be standing on end. "What?" she said, feeling her heart skip. "What happened?" She saw Iris dead, Carmen hurt, the restaurant in flames—

"I know. I know who you are."

"What?"

"Don't lie, Rose. Tell me the truth."

"What are you talking about?"

Anna kept her hands stiffly at her sides, forcing them down, as if she didn't trust what she might do with them. Her whole body was stiff, elongated, she was almost standing on her toes, neck extended, as if a string were holding her up from above. "Admit it. Admit you're my mother."

Rose was so surprised, she couldn't speak.

"Just *say* it. You are, aren't you?"

A laugh slipped out—she couldn't help it. Mistake: Anna looked as if she'd slapped her. "Oh, darling, no. No. I'm not."

"I don't believe you." But she did, Rose could see it in her eyes for just a second, a lost look.

"It's the truth," she said gently. "Oh, Anna. You're Lily's child."

"No, I think you gave me to her. She took me. You and my father—and then she took me because you weren't married and she was."

Rose kept shaking her head.

"I think so. You were always there," she accused, "even before she died. You went to—school things, you did homework with me, you're the one who told me about sex! You were always—" She drew in her breath. Her face flushed darkly; she turned around and braced her arms on the side of her car, keeping her head down. The ticking of Rose's car cooling down sounded loud in the sudden hush. Honeysuckle and hot metal mixed their smells in the soft air.

"Lily was your mother. I promise."

"All right," Anna said to the ground.

"I'm sorry."

She straightened up but didn't turn. "What are you sorry for?" She wiped her face, threw her head back, sniffed in deeply.

"I don't know," Rose admitted. "I guess I'm sorry I'm not your mother."

Anna recoiled from that. "*I'm* sorry," she said quickly. "It all—Frankie was like the one millionth person to say we look alike and—something just clicked. It made sense for about two seconds." She tried to laugh. "God, I feel like an idiot."

"Why?" Because she'd exposed too much, Rose guessed when she didn't answer. Given away not only a wrong guess but a false hope?

"*God*, that was stupid. Can we just forget this happened? Don't tell Aunt Iris, okay? Don't tell anybody."

Inexplicably, her embarrassment thrilled Rose. "Your terrible secret is safe," she said gravely, and had to smile when Anna flushed again. She could see her sitting here in her hot car in the dark, waiting, suffering with hope and dread. Rose was dying to put her arms around her. Did she dare to say this? "I always wanted a child, children. But I only loved one man, so I could never have any. Which would've been very sad, except there was you."

Anna backed up rapidly, as if a hole had opened up in front of her feet. "Okay. Good night. Erase this, will you? This whole—Seriously, this never happened."

"Anna, wait."

"Night." She walked around to her car quickly and, somehow, sheepishly. Rose wished she would come back and laugh with her—this would be so wonderfully funny if only Anna could see it that way.

She felt as if she had about half of her now. A very unwilling half, but Anna couldn't help herself. Cracks were showing, z-shaped fissures; the razor wire and pointy stones on top of the wall had blown off a long time ago. Rose just needed patience. Bad times were coming, but she felt light and airy, almost young again as she climbed the stairs to her apartment. Warmed to her bones by Anna's disappointment.

11

Dear Mason,

I tried to call, but then I remembered you're out of town till tomorrow. Hope you check your e-mail so you don't think I've stood you up tomorrow. I can't meet you after all, I have to fly to Buffalo in the morning for a funeral. A friend of mine has died. It was sudden but not unexpected. Or that's what I was told. It was certainly unexpected by me. Sorry I'll miss our appt.—shall I call you when I get back? Which will either be late tomorrow or early Friday, depending on flights and misc. stuff. Anyway—sorry this is so last-minute. Hope this letter makes sense. I'm kind of a mess.

A.

"You still here?"

Anna looked up to see Carmen's red face in the doorway, scowling at her. "Hi. Yeah, some last minute catch-up. Everything okay?"

"Marco cut himself. Again. He'll live. Everybody's gone, kitchen's quiet."

"Good." She smiled briefly, waiting for Carmen to leave.

"There's no reason you have to rush back here tomorrow night, you know. Rose would tell you the same thing."

"I know, but it might be heavy, Thursdays have been picking up a little. And it's the first day of the street fair."

"So? Flying up there and back in one day, it's too much. We can get along without you for one night."

Hard to say if Carmen meant that kindly or not. "I'll see how it goes. And I'll call one way or the other in the afternoon. Let you know."

"Fine." Carmen fingered a bloodstain on her apron, frowning hard at it as if she couldn't imagine how it had gotten there.

"Okay, then," Anna said helpfully. "Good night."

She gave a stolid nod and started to leave, actually disappeared for a second. Then she popped back in. "I'm sorry you lost your friend."

"Oh—thank you. Thanks. That's—"

She was gone again.

Stupid, but that made Anna cry. She'd managed not to when Jay called; he'd been upset, so she'd concentrated on sympathy for him instead of what she was feeling. Which wasn't as admirable as it sounded—mostly she just hadn't wanted to cry in front of him. Now it only took one gentle word from Carmen, and she was off. She put her forehead down on the desk and snuffled.

The phone rang before she could pull herself together. Rose, probably; they kept missing each other. "Hello?"

"Anna?"

"Oh, Mason. Hi. Hang on." She put him on hold while she blew her nose. "Sorry. Hi. I guess you got my e-mail."

"Just now."

"Oh, good. So."

"Are you all right?"

She inhaled shakily. "Yes and no. You know. It's hit me kind of hard. I loved him. I really—" She started up again. "Really sorry, I just need a good cry, then I'll be fine."

"Is there anything I can do?"

"No. Thanks."

"This . . . is this the man you were . . . "

"Oh—no, no, this is his grandfather, Jay's grandfather, Mac. Thomas McGuare. He was old and not in very good health, but I never thought he'd die, I mean not this soon. This has really blind-sided me for some reason."

"I'm sorry." It was all there ever was to say. He said it as if he meant it.

She reached for another tissue. "So I'm flying up there for the funeral. He died on Monday, and I'm just finding out. He said—Jay said—he wasn't going to tell me at all, because Nicole doesn't want me to come. His better nature finally won one," she said with weak bitterness. "Nicole—she's the other woman, as I'm sure you already know." She rubbed at the incipient headache behind her left temple. "Oh God, it's going to be awful."

"The funeral?"

"All of it. Going back. Seeing them together—I can hardly wait for that. Wait a second." This time she put the phone down while she wiped her face and got herself together once and for all. "Okay, I'm back."

"Anna."

"Yes?"

"Would you like me to go with you?"

"What?"

"Do you want company? I could go with you."

"No, you can't, you're busy, you're working."

"That doesn't matter. If it would be helpful, I'd go with you. Maybe it would make it worse. Just tell me, would it help?"

"Oh, Mason," she got out before her throat closed. She was about to make a complete fool of herself. "Yes," she said in a pathetic squeak, and muffled grateful sobs into a new Kleenex.

He must've changed his mind.

The announcement came on that Flight 3390 nonstop to Buffalo would be boarding in five minutes, and Mason wasn't here. She wouldn't blame him if he had changed his mind: talk about an impulse offer. What she should've done was thanked him and said no, and she *would* have, under any other circumstances. He'd caught her at a low, pitiful point; she'd been sinking and he'd hauled her out of the deep end. She wasn't responsible.

The phone in her purse rang. Ah, Mason. She forgave him in advance. *Don't give it another thought*, she practiced telling him, *it doesn't matter in the least. I'm so much better this morning.*

"Anna, it's Rose. I just heard the news—Carmen called—I'm still at home. I'm so sorry."

"I tried calling you last night—"

"I was at Theo's. He couldn't sleep, and we went for a drive."

"I figured, and then it got late and I didn't want to wake you up."

"That wouldn't have mattered. Are you all right?"

"Fine. I wasn't so good last night, but now I'm okay. I'm at the airport—we're boarding any second."

"I'm glad I caught you. Everything's fine here, don't worry about anything—Well, Carmen says Fontaine came in this morning with a black eye—"

"Oh, Jeez."

"But other than that we're fine, I just wanted to tell you how sorry I am, and if there's anything I can do, anything at all—"

"Thanks, there's nothing."

"Don't come back tonight, that would be foolish—"

"No, I'm not, I decided. But I'll be in by noon tomorrow."

"Okay, but no rush, we can certainly—"

"Oh, thank God, here comes Mason." She stood up so he could see her. "I thought he wasn't coming." She smiled and waved, watching him lope toward her through the crowded corridor, long-legged, long-haired, unsmiling. He had on khaki slacks and a navy sportcoat, a carry-on backpack over one shoulder and his camera on the other. In the last half hour she'd talked herself out of expecting him. Now that he was here, she felt giddy from relief.

Rose said, "Mason?"

"Yeah, he's coming with me."

"Mason? He's coming with you? On the airplane?"

"Yes. He offered, and I was glad—"

"Wait, Mason doesn't fly."

"What's that?"

"He's terrified of flying. He never flies. He can't fly."

He'd stopped in front of her. He mouthed, "Hi," and she smiled and said, "Hi. You're here. Two secs," and looked down at the floor, cupping her other ear with her hand. "Say that again?"

"Anna, Mason's—he hasn't told you?"

"Told me what?"

"He's—well, he's agoraphobic. Sort of, not exactly, it's more complicated than that, and it's been getting better, but he's not good in places he can't get out of. Especially places with lots of people, like—well, like . . ."

"Airplanes."

Boarding went quickly, no holdups. They had seats together; she'd taken care of that last night, called the airline back and arranged it. "Aisle or window?" he asked her after he'd shoved their carry-ons into the overhead. "Oh," Anna said, "you pick, I don't care, either one, I have no preference, I couldn't care less, whichever one you don't want." He looked at her oddly, then took the window.

She watched him from the corner of her eye while the flight attendant went through the safety drill. What should she do? Say something? Let him know she knew? Or not? What would be best? Only now was it hitting her that what she should've done was send him home. But not tell him why, just say, "I'm fine now, this is silly, thanks for everything, that was so nice of you, I'll call when I get back." Too late. He couldn't escape now because they were moving, they'd joined the queue of planes waiting to take off.

The express to Buffalo was one step up from a puddle jumper as far as she was concerned. Seating capacity about fifty. A prop jet. The pilot came on and said there would be a delay. Not much of one, five minutes, possibly seven. He sounded chipper, too human, like a hardware store clerk or your neighbor on Saturday morning. He didn't speak gravely enough. He made jokes.

Mason had a rubber band around his right wrist, and he was snapping it at intervals. The *ping* sound was almost inaudible over the engine roar; she wouldn't have noticed it if she hadn't had every sense concentrated on him. He took the card out of the seat pocket and studied the diagram of the airplane, a DeHavilland Dash 8. He lifted the shade a couple of inches and glanced out at the runway, but the sight made him pale—she actually saw his scarred cheek drain of color. He snapped the shade down and sat back with his eyes closed.

"Did you . . . what were you doing in, um . . . I forget where you were." His nerves had infected hers; she felt queasy, as if she had stagefright.

"Monie Point."

"Monie Point. Where's that?"

"On the Chesapeake."

"I know, but where?"

He shook his head. She thought he wasn't going to answer. "Somerset County. Near Deal."

"Oh, I know Deal, I used to go out with a guy from Deal."

He turned his head toward her slowly. "You have a lot of boyfriends from the Eastern Shore."

"Do I?" Good, he was talking. "Ex-boyfriends, all I have is exes. Did you get any good shots? In Monie Point? Of birds?"

"No."

"Too bad."

"I wasn't taking pictures."

"What were you doing?"

"Helping to extend the singing grounds of the woodcock."

"Ah. What?"

He started to smile, but his whole body jolted when the pilot's too-loud voice cracked on all at once, telling them they were next in line for takeoff, wouldn't be long now, folks.

"The what, now? The what of the woodcock?"

"Singing grounds. Mating fields. Woodcocks need a very diverse habitat in which to mate and flourish."

"Such as . . . ?"

"Early forest and saplings for the females, tall meadows and grassland for the males."

"So you plant stuff—"

"Plant stuff. Clear stuff. Truck in earthworms. I do it with a group of volunteers. Met on the Internet."

"Is it working? Do we have more woodcocks than we used to?"

"Yes."

"Good." He was getting frozen again. "I don't think I've ever seen a woodcock. What do they do, what do they look like?"

He had his eyes shut, jaws clenched. "They're about the size of a quail. Fat, long-billed, big-eyed. Funny-looking. The male has an interesting mating ritual. I saw it once."

"Tell me about it."

The engines revved higher, deafeningly. They were in that pocket of time just before takeoff, standing still while the raw, screaming gathering of power went on underneath them.

"Tell me how they do it, how the males get the females." Mason looked at her. She nodded. She let him see in her eyes that she knew.

He lifted his arm from the seat divider, she took hers out of her lap, and they gripped hands.

"They roost in the long grass, making a buzzy nasal call, to get themselves ready. They take off, explode in the air, flying up and up in widening spirals, so high you lose them in the dark."

"In the dark? It's nighttime?" Smoothly, the plane began to run forward, roll fast like a car, then faster.

"Dusk. You can see them in moonlight. They disappear in the dark, and then they drop. They fall like paper airplanes, twisting, swooping, gymnastics, all the while singing to the females on the ground. When they land—"

Liftoff forced them back, heads flat to their seats. The weightless interval she usually enjoyed made her sick now, in sympathy. His palm in hers was soaked with sweat. She squeezed it tighter. "When they land?"

"When they land—they take off again. Over and over. You can hear the wind in their feathers, a whistling sound when they fly up. They look like leaves when they fall. It's beautiful. A show."

She swallowed to make her ears pop. "Singing grounds. I like that. I guess—we all do better when people help us with our singing grounds." Babble babble. "You could say running a restaurant is a way to make a nice, comfortable singing ground for people. Some people." Luckily, he wasn't really listening.

They kept climbing, but the pressure slacked off and the engine noise moderated. "Well, that's over," she said with exaggerated finality. "Takeoff's always the worst."

"Sixty percent of crashes occur during takeoff."

"There you go."

"Thirty percent on landing."

"Ten percent . . . ?"

"Cruising."

"Well, ten, that's nothing." He must not agree; his death grip on her hand hadn't loosened. "That's like driving your car to the mall.

Jaywalking. Ten is nothing. And that's what we're doing now," she pointed out. "Cruising."

"I'm sorry about this."

"No. Sorry about what?"

"Rose told you."

Denying it would insult him, she felt obscurely. "Yeah. Oh, Mason. Why in the world did you say you'd come with me?"

"I'm much better than I used to be." Which didn't answer the question, she noticed. He opened one eye, bared his teeth in a sick grin. "I'm in a group, therapy group, people who can't fly. We've gone to the airport, sat around. But never flown. That was coming up."

"You're doing great." He had on a loosely knotted tie; she could see it skitter over his chest with every heartbeat. She let go of his slippery hand—he looked helpless for a second, as if she'd stepped away from him in the middle of a tightrope. She pushed the seat divider up, squeezed over, and put her arm through his arm. They rested their newly clasped hands on top of his thigh. "There," she said. "That's better."

"Thank you."

"Don't mention it." She'd probably embarrassed him, but too bad, this *was* better.

He was tense and hard, the muscle in his arm flexed and slightly trembling. His body felt hot through his clothes. "This isn't how I saw myself impressing you."

She smiled without looking at him. "I didn't know you were trying to impress me."

"Shows what a lousy job I've been doing."

"Doesn't show any such thing." Nothing like flirting to take your mind off crashing. He'd invited her to go to the street fair this afternoon. It would've been their first date, not just meeting by accident or going for a walk. But she hadn't called it a date in the e-mail she'd sent, canceling it; she'd called it "our appt." How could she not have realized by now that he was agoraphobic? Or "sort of" agoraphobic, Rose said, whatever that meant. She'd never seen him inside anywhere except his own house, he was always outside, on the street, in the doorway. As far as she knew, he'd never set foot in the restaurant. And now he was sitting beside her on an airplane.

"Does it help to talk," she asked, "or just make it worse?"

"It helps. You talk."

"What does the rubber band do?"

"Distracts me." He demonstrated. "Throws me out of my thoughts."

"Which are dark and scary."

He shook his head, but he meant yes. As in, *You can't imagine.*

"You could do breathing exercises," she suggested.

"I am."

"Oh. Right now?"

He nodded. "It'll be all right, Anna. I won't do anything crazy—don't worry that I'll embarrass you."

"I'm not worried about that." She imagined *he* was, though. Wasn't that one of the big anxieties with people who got panic attacks, that they were going crazy? And that other people would see?

"Talk to me," he said.

"Do you want some water or anything?"

"No."

"They don't give you any food on this flight. But it's only an hour and a half." Thank God.

"Tell me about your friend who died."

"Mac. Oh, Mac was great. His wife died a long time ago, and he lived on his own until this year, when he had to go into an assisted-living place because of his heart. It made him weak, he couldn't go up and down stairs anymore, couldn't take care of himself." Like Theo, she realized. His days of living by himself on his sailboat were almost over, Rose said.

"Mac is tiny, very dark and spidery, a little monkey of a man. Hardly any hair, and bright blue eyes. False teeth and this crafty grin—you just knew he was a terror when he was young. He used to be a railroad man, and he liked to tell ghoulish stories about people or cars or animals that got hit by locomotives, or stories about bums locked in train cars and discovered frozen solid or starved to death weeks later. He liked to shock you, especially if you were a woman. He thought all women were delicate—I loved that about him. He made fun of Jay's sculptures—but lovingly, he was never mean. He'd say, 'Hey, boy, I got an old tuna fish can you can have,' or, 'The lawnmower broke, you want it?' But he was so proud of him. He kept a scrapbook with all Jay's mentions from the newspapers and magazines.

"He used to come to the café to see me. He made fun of it, too, especially the paintings for sale. 'Look at this, a red circle with a white line under it! And only twelve hundred dollars. Can I get two?' He'd say that as loud as he could while he drank his three-dollar cup of latte. Nicole would cringe when she saw him coming. He wore that kind of running suit that makes a lot of noise when you move, and always in some awful, garish color, purple or chartreuse, and *huge* running shoes, as big as his head. Not that he ever did any actual running. He was such a scamp. But very courtly, too, a ladies' man. He had a lot of buddies from the old days, but they were dying off, dying out. So he was lonely. He loved it when I'd come to see him. He really... he loved me."

And she loved him. Love had to go somewhere. She'd closed off most of the conduits to her own family, so Mac had gotten a big, immoderate share. She had no regrets about that.

"You'll miss him," Mason said.

"I didn't call him enough after I came home—came back. I knew he was sick, and I should've gone up there. I wish I could've seen him one more time. I'd like to have told him good-bye." She indulged in a very short cry. They disengaged arms long enough for her to get a handkerchief out of her purse. The flight attendant rolled the drinks cart past them, and they asked for orange juice.

"Now you talk," Anna said, sipping hers, "I'm dried up. Tell me about your childhood." Safe topic. He looked almost relaxed, wasn't even snapping his rubber band. "You grew up on the Eastern Shore, like me. You're an only child, like me."

"No, I'm not. I've got a sister who's twelve years older. Liz. She lives in San Antonio."

"Wow, the things you learn about people. Were you a happy little kid?"

"Yes. Until my father died."

Shit. Not a safe topic—she was just remembering. His father had died in a plane crash. "I'm sorry," she said miserably. "Is that—did you—no wonder you're—"

"I was fine with planes until about four years ago."

"What happened?" When he hesitated, she realized what a stupid question that was, perhaps the stupidest ever in the history of stupid questions. "Don't answer—we don't have to talk about that *now*. I'm sorry. God, what a great therapist I'd make."

"It's all right." At least she'd made him smile. "But I'll tell you later."

"Right, don't tell me now. Whatever you do." She reached over and snapped his rubber band, and he *laughed*. She felt redeemed, maybe not the worst therapist in the world after all. "Childhood," she reminded him. "But only the good parts. What is your happiest memory?"

His happiest memory—he couldn't remember, but his happiest *feelings*, he said, the times as a child he associated with the strongest sense of well-being, were when his father came back from a trip and, later, when Theo came back from a trip. His fathers coming home.

She said it was the same for her, that her father had traveled constantly and she clearly, vividly remembered throwing her arms around his legs in an absolute ecstasy when he returned—and not coming up much over his knees, so she had to have been tiny, three years old, maybe even two.

Mason said he could remember Theo better than his father, who had died when he was only five. He'd loved Theo immediately, no breaking-in period, no resentment. His best memory...okay, he knew what it was—did she want to hear it, his very best memory from childhood? Yes. "We went out crabbing on his old deadrise, the *Sweet Jean*. That was my mother's name, he rechristened it when they got married. We went down to Crisfield, just Theo and me, and we caught crabs all day on the Annemessex River. That's the way I remember it anyway, me working right alongside him, doing everything he did. We went to a bar for dinner that night, one of his old hangouts, this smoky old joint. We sat at a round wooden table in the back room, and he introduced me to his waterman buddies. 'This is my kid, Mason.' I remember that, and watching him, being proud that I belonged to him. I wanted to be Greek, I wanted to take his last name. He was the best of those men, the biggest and strongest, and he told the best stories. That was a perfect night. I was eight, and it was the first time I ever felt like a man. Just a hint of what it would be like. That brotherhood."

She was about to ask what Theo's last name was when the plane suddenly dropped, lost altitude, not much, and then floated back up to where it had been. Minor turbulence. Mason made a sound, maybe his teeth grinding. She said very quickly, "I had something like that, I know what you mean, not exactly like that but the first time I felt like, you know, one of the women. I think I was eight, same as you. It was my grandmother's birthday and we were having a party for her at our house, outside in the backyard because it was summer. Rose and Aunt Iris did most of the cooking, but my mother helped, too, which was rare—my mother hated to cook—and *I* was given the important job of mashing garlic and salt with a mortar and pestle to make aioli. I took it very seriously, mashing and mashing until my arm was burning, but I wasn't going to stop till it was a perfect, smooth paste. What a smell—mm, God, it made me swoon, I never knew what a powerful food garlic is until that day. *Then*—I'd done such a good job, Rose let me mix the two kinds of olive oil and dribble it in, very slowly at first, a few drops at a time, then a thin stream, while she whisked the egg yolks. 'Is it too thick,' she'd say, 'should we add a little water?' and I got to say yes or no. It was the first time I ever really cooked. Rose and Aunt Iris made poached mussels and squid and tiny clams, I remember, and steamed fennel bulbs with new potatoes and green beans, and Chioggia beets, everything on a big platter in the center of our picnic table. And little bowls of aioli all around to dip the fish and vegetables in. 'Anna made the aioli,' Rose announced at some point, and everybody oohed and ahed and said how delicious it was. Even my grandmother said I'd done well, and she was a hard woman to get a compliment out of." She laughed. "That's the day I arrived at womanhood."

They took turns. Whenever the plane dipped or the engine hum changed from one note to another for no reason, he stopped talking and she started. When things righted themselves, she stopped and he started. He told her he'd spotted a brown pelican on his dock two days ago, and how rare that was, what a good sign because they were still threatened and he'd never seen one that far north on the bay before. She told him she'd had to fire the bartender for only ringing in half the drinks he sold and pocketing the rest. "Vince?" he said, aghast, and she said, "No, no, Eddie, the day guy, a jerk, you don't know him. Turns out he's been ripping Rose off for months. I knew he was giving free drinks away to his friends, but that was okay because it was during the day and otherwise the bar would be empty, which is bad for business. I knew he was running drinks to the kitchen, too, which is frowned on but nobody really cares, even Vince does that. I *didn't* know he was stealing about half the afternoon bar receipts right out of the drawer. So good riddance."

Mason told her what birds' pictures sold the best to magazines and stock agencies: eagles, hawks, owls, falcons, osprey, and kestrels. Birds of prey, in other words. How macho, they agreed, but the next most popular was probably robins pulling worms out of the ground, so there you were. Sports magazines wanted game birds, of course, ducks and grouse and wild turkeys, and shots of big V-shaped geese formations never failed. Woodpeckers pecking, especially if they had red heads or tufts. Any bird feeding its young. Cardinals in snow. And you could never go wrong with penguins, especially in couples or groups; people liked them because they looked like them—like people.

She told him the restaurant finally got a good review. In *Chesapeake* magazine, and the critic had particularly admired the service. "Vonnie and I have been working with the waitstaff, and it's paying off. We've got a new rule, the thirty-second rule—a server has to come over and greet you before you've been sitting down for more than half a minute. Because that's what people hate the most—can you believe it, even more than bad food, people hate to walk into a restaurant and be ignored. So now, even if they can't take your order, the server has to acknowledge you, that's our rule. And smile a lot, which they weren't doing. Someone did a study, and waiters who smile with just their lips make smaller tips than waiters who open their mouths and show their teeth. It's true, it's scientific, I think I do it myself. Tip better, I mean. Meanwhile, I'm starting to learn people's names, customers' names. Rose is so good at this, but she's never there so I'm the one who greets people, and I'm starting to know them. The repeaters, not the old regulars, them I already know, I mean new people. So this is good, a sign that it's starting to turn around. But we're stretched so thin, all we do is worry. We're beginning to see a little light, a little profit—of course it's not really profit, everything goes to the debt, which is huge, but at least we're starting to almost break even. Which is a miracle. This is July, the big month, turnaround month. The menu's set and it's good, it's great, except for the soups. Wouldn't you think we could do a decent minestrone? It's a joke now, except Frankie and Carmen don't think it's funny. They still hate each other, I'm still the referee.

I say quit *trying* to make minestrone, I mean, how retro can you get, but for once they agree with each other, they still want to make the perfect minestrone."

She got gum out of her purse for her raw throat, and handed a piece to Mason. She thought they looked reckless and happy-go-lucky, chewing away together. He said they should try bird's nest soup. There was a bird called the edible nest swiftlet; in breeding season it flew against the four-hundred-foot walls of its cave in Malaysia, clung for a second, and deposited a dab of saliva with its tongue. It did this over and over until it made a little cup. "Out of spit?" Yes, dried spit, that was its nest, and people risked their lives climbing the cave walls to get it because it was a great delicacy in gourmet oriental restaurants. Put it in a bowl with some broth, some vegetables—delicious. "How does it taste?" Anna asked.

"Like chicken."

Things got tense again during the landing. Mason shut up and she wondered if he might actually break her hand, or at least a few fingers, while she kept talking, talking, going on for some reason about Aunt Iris's dogs and did he want a puppy, they were great but they weren't cheap, fabulous dogs, she wished she could have one but she was never home, he could train his not to chase birds—

They landed.

She wanted to cheer. Inside the airport, she almost had to run to keep up with him, but she didn't think he was hurrying to escape. He was striding along out of high spirits, and the silence was his way of keeping a lid on his euphoria. He'd done it! He must be singing that inside. After not flying for four years, what a triumph this must be, a real victory, something to crow about. But he didn't say anything, so she didn't either. At baggage claim, they picked up his suitcase, which was enormous, the kind you took on a two-week vacation. She didn't ask what in the world was in it, though; she was following his lead by keeping quiet. But out on the breezy sidewalk, while they waited in the line for a taxi, she couldn't hold back.

"Well—congratulations! Mason, you were great! Don't you think?"

He did; it was obvious. He shook his hair back and took a deep breath of the exhaust-scented air, as if it were the ocean or a flowery meadow. He smiled with his whole face, and it was the freest she'd ever seen him, the most unguarded. "You don't know," he said. "You can't imagine."

"No, I can't, I know. But I still think you were splendid."

"Thanks to you. If it weren't for you, I'd be dead."

"No, you wouldn't."

"They'd be carrying me off on a stretcher right now. A corpse."

"No, they wouldn't!" She wanted to hug him. She almost did—but then he stopped smiling, and the moment was gone.

"Thanks, Anna," he said seriously.

She sobered, too. "No—thank you. For coming with me."

She shied away from asking him why he'd done it, or even from thinking about it. She hoped it was for selfish reasons, to test himself, to achieve this wonderful personal goal, to put a lot of emotional junk behind him. She hoped it had nothing to do with her. She liked him so much. If it had anything to do with her, she was sure to disappoint him.

Mac hadn't had any religious faith to speak of, so the memorial service was in the funeral home, not a church, where more people than Jay must've been expecting showed up. Anna, who had wanted to arrive at the last possible minute, got there just as the service was beginning. There were no more chairs in the airy, parlor-like room, so she and Mason stood in back against the wall. There was no minister; the only people who spoke were friends. Jay spoke, but too briefly, she thought, and nothing he said got to the heart of it, didn't come close to describing the man his grandfather had been. He called him "hardworking" and "a family man." Maybe he was afraid he'd cry if he went too close to the truth. Jay wasn't afraid of passionate extremes, but they had to make him look good. Weeping over his grandfather in front of his friends—maybe that crossed some uncool line.

Or maybe she was simply incapable of giving him a break. It wasn't hard to see him again, not the shock to her system she'd feared it would be. He looked smaller. Not as if he'd lost weight; as if he'd shrunk. She wanted to correct his version of what Mac was like, but she hadn't prepared anything, and the thought of standing up in front of these people made her heart pound. Some of them would think she'd lost the right—Jay had thrown her away, after all. She was about to do it anyway when an old man she'd never seen before stood up and said, "For a pain in the ass, Mac McGuare was the nicest fella I ever knew." That was about right. *Thank you*, she thought, watching him honk into a big red kerchief before he sat down.

At the end, Jay got up and made another little speech. Thanks for coming, Mac would've been so pleased, etc., etc.—in the middle of it he saw her, and broke off long enough to smile slightly and send her a sort of knowing half-wave. Several people, Nicole among them, turned around to see who he was acknowledging. Anna stared back into her old friend's kittenish face, glad she'd had some warning, glad *she* didn't look as shocked as Nicole did. *Didn't think I was coming, did you?* She hadn't wanted Anna here, had even asked Jay not to tell her Mac was dead until after the funeral. If he'd done that—

But he hadn't, so no point in devising atrocious punishments in her mind for him. He'd done the right thing, leave it at that, and don't speculate on his motives. Such as trying to make Nicole jealous. Trying to get two women to fight over him. No, surely that was unworthy of Jay. If it wasn't, she'd thrown away two years of her life on a man who was even scurvier than she thought.

She left Mason and went to pay her respects to the deceased. Mac lay in a closed metal coffin in an alcove of the parlor, surrounded by enormous floral wreaths and arrangements. She'd sent peonies, which he'd loved—she spotted her little bowl among the giant constructions of gladiolus and carnations, and decided it looked small but powerful. Like him. She put her hand on the cool blue metal of his casket, over the place where his heart would be. *Hey, pal.* Then her mind went blank. He was dead, and she couldn't go any further yet; everything past that was just a dark sadness, too new to penetrate. She said a prayer for him, an old one from her childhood. She didn't have much faith either, but nobody had even mentioned God at his service, and that seemed stupid. She got out her handkerchief and wiped her eyes.

"Anna. I'm very glad you came." Jay held out his arms.

They embraced, and she thought, what a complicated minute this is. She truly wanted to give him her sympathy, only a little more than she wanted to sock him in the eye. "It was a nice service," she said, pulling back. He kept his hands on her shoulders, so she pulled back farther. "He'd have liked it."

"Yes, I believe he would have."

"Will he be buried now?"

"No, cremated."

"Oh. Is that what he wanted?"

"He never said."

Jay wanted to be cremated; he'd told her that a couple of times. So he was cremating his grandfather. Well, what difference did it make? Except now she'd never have a place to visit Mac.

"I've invited some people to come up to the loft this afternoon—I hope you'll come. It's a little reception. Drink a toast to the old man."

This was so uncharacteristic, she could hardly process it. Jay *hated* parties; she'd had to fight for or trick him into every dinner party they'd ever given, and cocktail parties—forget it. She looked around at the quiet crowd, still twenty or thirty people milling, trying not to greet each other too boisterously. Funerals were so weird.

She spotted the man who ran the Monkfish Gallery, and there was Monica Loren, Jay had been courting her for years, trying to get her husband, who was on the city council, to put his sculptures in pocket parks downtown. Ah, it all became clear. A professional opportunity.

"Thanks, Jay, I don't think so."

"Please do come. For Mac."

Right, for Mac. "No, I really—"

"Hello, Anna," Nicole purred, gliding up silently on cork-soled espadrilles, black and beige, Anna had helped her pick them out on a shopping trip, girls' day out, lunch and gossip. Had she already been sleeping with Jay?

"Nicole." She took a step back when it looked like her old friend meant to hug her. Was everybody insane?

"I've asked Anna to join us, after," Jay announced. "At the loft."

"Oh, great." Nicole visibly paled. "Do come."

Oh, yeah. She'd like that. As much as she'd like to chew glass. It made the decision so much easier.

"I'm with a friend." She gestured toward Mason. Jay and Nicole turned to look at him, and she saw for the first time, at least consciously, that he was exactly the sort of man Jay hated. He was tall, for one thing, and uncategorizable, so not easily ridiculed. And mysterious. Oh, and the scar, Jay would loathe the scar. How wonderful. She regretted in passing that her motives for accepting were no better, possibly even worse, than Jay's for inviting her. "Thanks, we'd love to come."

12

"I've always had a strong connection to the crumbling, rusting remnants of the city, call it the wasteland of our industrial past. In my art I reassemble, I reconfigure these found artifacts in new ways, in order to give a voice to what's been left behind, to make you see it again, the economic and social past of the urban landscape."

Anna took Mason's arm and led him away, out of earshot. Listening to Jay explain his *oeuvre* to Monica Loren had the dual effect of embarrassing her and making her feel sick. "Let's go in the kitchen," she muttered. "I happen to know he keeps the good booze in there."

Mason went willingly.

Sure enough, she found Chivas in the cabinet over the refrigerator. "You're drinking, right?" she asked, pouring out a couple of shots.

"Definitely."

They looked each other over. "How are—" they said at the same time. They laughed. "I'm okay," Anna said. "You know, considering."

"Considering this used to be your house."

"Yes, and now I'm the unwanted guest. What about you? Is this excruciating?" She'd interrogated him all the way over in the taxi, trying to make sure she wasn't torturing him, that he was coming of his own free will, and that he wouldn't hyperventilate in the elevator or black out in the loft. He'd said, "I just spent two hours on an airplane. You think your boyfriend's apartment can scare me?" A major piece in the puzzle of Mason Winograd had dropped into her lap this morning, but now it was almost as if she'd known about it from the beginning. It was so obvious in retrospect; she must've been blind not to see it.

"This is excruciating," he said, adding an ice cube to his drink. "But I wouldn't have missed it."

"That's how I feel." They smiled grimly, comrades in arms. "What do you think of Jay?" she asked, casual.

"Don't ask me that."

"Sorry."

"What would be a good answer?"

"You're right. Nothing."

They sipped their drinks, backs to the sink, and watched him talk and gesticulate in front of a ten-foot-high rebar and scrap steel construction called *Convergent Sprocket 3*. So he was working on his sculptures in the loft again. Or—could he have moved this piece into the yawning cavern that used to be their living room just so he could tell Monica, whom he'd lured here under the guise of eulogizing his grandfather, how important it was? Yes, Anna realized on a wave of dismay. It was more than possible.

"He *looks* like an artist," Mason observed.

"I know." It was part of Jay's success, she'd always thought, the fact that he looked so fierce and reckless with his crazy hair and archless eyebrows and his gloomy, petulant mouth. "He looks brooding and intimidating, I know. He actually scares people. But believe me, he's just thinking about what's for dinner."

And she'd gotten some pleasure, especially in the beginning, out of being Jay McGuare's chosen mistress. Living in his showy, gratifying, reflected glory, such as it was. She couldn't deny that. She'd put up with an amazing amount of crap, too, for the privilege. How much, she was only starting to realize. His self-obsession. His unholy ambition. The way he lived in this loft or in his studio as if he were alone, occasionally noticing someone else—she—was with him, mostly when he wanted sex or a meal. He was like a not-very-well-trained animal. And women were mad for him—that had always struck her as funny. It didn't anymore, of course; it had only been funny when she'd thought he was hers.

"You're probably wondering what I saw in him." Leading and disingenuous, but she was feeling the need to explain herself. Apologize for herself.

Mason passed a hand over his face. "Yes and no."

"Oh, well. Never mind, then. No, you're right, anything I could say would just be self-serving. But I'll tell you this: he was better than a lot of men I've hooked up with. In my checkered past." True, but she'd probably exaggerated Jay's good points to herself—he did have some—to encourage the delusion that she was making progress with men.

"Don't expect me to drink to that," Mason said.

"Do you think we get who we deserve? Most of us?"

"Probably."

"I think so, too. Except—there's this girl at the restaurant, a sweetheart, and she falls in love with the worst guys in the world. It's pathological, it never fails. Since I've known her she's had three different boyfriends, and every one of them treated her like crap." And now one was actually *hitting* Fontaine, according to Rose. "No way she deserves *that*."

"No," Mason agreed.

She eyed him curiously. "What about you?"

"What about me?"

"You were engaged once. Rose said. Was she nice?"

He bowed his head and stared down at the floor, arms stretched out behind him along the counter. She wanted to see his face. She slipped a lock of hair behind his ear with her finger, and he turned his crooked smile on her. "I thought she was nice. I could say self-serving things, too, but to tell you the truth I can hardly remember her. Her name was Claire. When I think about her now, mostly I remember her arms."

"Her arms?"

"She did ballet for exercise, and I remember how her arms looked in the air when she danced, jointless, like long white scarves. But that's it. I thought I was in love with her, and she's a blur. Except for her arms."

He didn't speak of Claire with bitterness, but Anna disliked her on principle. She'd abandoned him, hadn't she? She wanted to tie Claire's long white arms around her neck. Maybe it was the drink, but somewhere along the way she'd started to enjoy herself.

"You know what Jay said to me once? Love is like a cup of coffee. It starts out hot, it'll burn you if you're not careful. Then comes the long spell in the middle when it's just right, every sip is warm and stimulating—actually he didn't say it this eloquently, I'm paraphrasing. And then the last stage, when what's left starts to get cold. And the final stage is so bitter, you can't swallow it."

"Profound."

"I know, but what's amazing is that I never saw *us* in that analogy. That's what love is for *everybody else*, I thought, but he wasn't speaking metaphorically at all—he really meant it. Don't you think that's amazing?"

"That he meant it, yes. Not that you believed it wasn't for you."

People interrupted them, separated them; guests she knew well enough to have to speak to, talk about Mac to for a little while, then about herself. They wanted to know how she was doing, naturally, what she was up to, if she was coming back. Mostly they were avid for some revelation, intended or not, even a visual, about her and Jay, her and Nicole, some juicy tidbit to chew over later with their mutual friends. She couldn't blame them. It was fairly delicious, drinking scotch in what used to be her kitchen, watching Nicole pretend she was too sophisticated even to notice that something was wrong with this picture as she passed Industrial Coffee hors d'oeuvres to Jay's friends. He wouldn't help her, either—best she figured that out early. She'd probably like to stay tethered to his arm, hoping for safety in numbers, but counting on support from Jay was always a risky proposition.

"I want to talk to you."

Speak of the devil. He grabbed Anna's hand and led her over to the brick wall he still had nude drawings of her tacked to. Now *that* was nerve. "How are you, Anna?"

"I'm great." She looked around for Mason, saw him by himself, examining the lewd painted figures on the screen around the bed.

"No, how are you *really*."

"How am I really." So many things she could say. "I'm looking forward to the moment when I can get out of here. When are we drinking that toast to Mac, Jay?"

He waved that away, but at least he had the grace to blush. "I'm cut up. That's how *I* am. I didn't expect it to be like this. Stupid, but I didn't think I'd feel this way. Work is all I've got now."

"So, nothing's changed?"

"Everything's changed. It has to be the same for you, too."

"I'm sorry, are we talking about Mac dying or me leaving?"

He cursed. But she'd given him the idea. "That's hit me almost as hard," he said earnestly. "I've just got nothing inside anymore, I can't work."

"I thought—"

"Anna, I think you should come back. We're both in trouble. We could help each other."

Across the room, Nicole sidled around the man she was talking to so she could look over his shoulder at Anna and Jay. Anna could almost feel sorry for her.

"You know, Jay, I just don't see that happening."

"It's not working out with Nicole. If that's the problem."

"If that's the—" Stunning. He'd reduced her to staring.

He had a way of shifting his weight quickly from one foot to the other, as if he were planting himself in the dirt before some physical contest. It meant he knew he was right but he wasn't getting anywhere. "Who's the guy? How long have you known him?"

"Who? Oh, Mason, I told you, I introduced you. Mason Winograd—maybe you've heard of him? He's famous. In a way, you know," she qualified modestly, "in his field." Well, she couldn't resist, and besides, it was true. But mostly it was the surest way to prick Jay, who wanted fame more than anything, certainly more than excellence.

His dark, Celtic face turned blacker. This unlikely jealousy couldn't go on much longer, his ego wouldn't let it, but she could enjoy it while it lasted. "Are you together?" he demanded, jerking his head backward. "You're with him?"

"Well." She smiled. "Obviously." That was true, too, as far as it went.

"Fast work," he sneered. "For you."

"But not for you. You hold the record." When he laughed, she knew he'd given up. "I'm sorry about Mac, Jay. I know you loved him. I came up here for him, and to say that to you. That's all."

"Right." He backed away. He was finished. From now on, he could say he'd tried to make things right but she wouldn't cooperate, she was too bourgeois or conventional or too puritanical or too narrow and hidebound or too anything he liked. From here on in, it wasn't his fault.

"Hi—what's funny?"

Nicole could make her catlike face into a shy, beaming picture of sweetness and caring, really an artwork of kindheartedness, and it wasn't always a disguise. But usually it was. Anna used to admire her for it, wish *she* had such an ingratiating skill, so handy in the restaurant business. But how silly, how pitiful that Nicole thought the sweet face could work here, now, on *her* of all people.

Jay looked ever so slightly disconcerted, not much, to find himself standing between his old lover and his new one, as if he'd caught himself wearing a tie that didn't quite go with his shirt. "Nothing's funny" was his exit line, and he turned his back on both of them and escaped.

"Well, that's for sure," Anna said cheerfully.

Chewing the inside of her lip, Nicole watched him walk away, her eyes narrowed with suspicion. *Here's the payback*, Anna thought. *You'll never trust him.* If she'd tried, she couldn't have devised a fairer comeuppance. "Anna," she said, "I was hoping you and I would get a chance to talk."

"Were you?" She arranged her face into receptive, nonthreatening lines. She was beginning to feel depressed, though, over how little any of this mattered. She disapproved of how easily she'd gotten over Jay, and it appalled her to think that her best woman friend in Buffalo had been this shallow, feckless cheat. She knew everything about Nicole, her social worker ex-husband, her twelve-year-old son with ADD, her icy, inattentive mother, her flirtation with Buddhism, her Pilates phase, how she fudged her corporate income taxes, her fear of cats. They'd belonged to the same book club, gone to the same hairdresser, liked the same movies. And yet, Jay's betrayal had hurt her much worse than Nicole's. In some strange way, she might even have said Nicole's was no shocking surprise. Not that she was expecting it, not that she could have predicted it—just that, unlike Jay's faithlessness, it wasn't a complete bolt from the blue. So what did that mean? Anna was even stupider about women than men?

"I never got a chance to tell you I was sorry about what happened," Nicole said. "The *way* it happened. I mean, what a terrible way for you to find out, and I just feel bad about it."

"Do you?"

"Yes, I really do, because we were friends, and I hate to see a friendship break up."

Anna laughed.

Nicole stiffened and stopped apologizing. "Well, anyway. I just wanted to say that to you." Like Jay, she was now off the hook.

"Jay's vague on how long it was going on," Anna said agreeably. "Can't really get a straight answer out of him. I'm curious—was it weeks? Or months?"

Nicole had thick, tawny hair she wore down her back in a braid. When she was nervous, she stroked it over and over on her shoulder or her breast, like a small animal that needed soothing.

"Days? Years?"

"*No.*"

"Not years. Well, that's something. Oh, forget it, I don't care anyway."

"Anna, I'm so sorry."

"Yeah, we did that. So. How's the café doing?" She was more curious about that than the length of Jay's affair.

"It's doing great! Really great. Marsha and I are both managing now, splitting the job, and that's working out well. We're having a very good summer. *Very* good."

"Marsha's managing?"

"With me, as I said. It's working out fine, better than I hoped." Marsha was the part-time pastry chef; until last year she'd worked out of her own house. She was nice, smart, reliable, but what Marsha knew about restaurant management wouldn't fit inside a profiterole.

"Good," Anna said. "Glad to hear it."

"And how are *you* doing? How's it working out at your aunt's restaurant? Jay said you were having some problems."

"Not anymore. No, we're having the best season ever. It's fantastic. I'm having the time of my life."

"That's wonderful."

Just in that moment, they didn't despise each other. Understanding bloomed in the tacit knowledge that they were both lying about how splendidly things were going, both for the same good reason. When it came to the business, they were in rare agreement: the show must go on.

Like most city residents, or in her case former resident, Anna had no idea where to stay overnight in her own town, what hotels had more than pretty lobbies, which ones were worth the cost. Rather than give it any thought, she'd booked a room, and then another when she'd found out Mason was coming with her, at a chain motel on the outskirts, halfway between the city and the airport, in the middle of a high-tech office park. She regretted it as soon as the taxi pulled into the heavily mulched, Bradford pear tree–lined crescent flanking the sterile brick and black glass exterior. They should've stayed downtown. At least some of the architecture was interesting, and they could've gone for a walk, she could've shown him her former favorite places—the bookstore she liked, the Stetson hat store, the park where old *women* played chess.

"Sorry about this," she said to Mason at the front desk, out of the hearing of the check-in guy. "Pretty boring."

"No, it's fine," he said, but what else could he say.

"What's *in* there?" She pointed to his enormous suitcase on wheels, thinking that was a question, not to mention a tone of voice, she wouldn't have dared to use on him as early as this morning.

"Things." He made a grin or a grimace, hard to tell which, and nervously stroked the long carrying arm of the case with the side of his hand.

"Oh, *things*. Wish I'd thought to bring some of those."

Definitely a grin this time. "Tell you later," he said.

They had second-floor rooms across the hall from each other; her view was of a parking lot and the highway, his was a parking lot and two identical blue glass office buildings. Except for a cracker at Jay's, she hadn't eaten all day. She was starving. She unpacked, which involved putting her toiletries bag in the bathroom and throwing tomorrow's slacks over the back of a chair, and called Mason's room. "Shall we eat here or go out?"

Whichever she liked, he didn't care, he had no preference.

"I just want food," she said. "Okay if we stay here? Try the dining room?"

Fine with him. He'd knock on her door in fifteen minutes.

Fifteen minutes? What was he doing in there? Sometimes she thought she knew all about him and other times, like now, it hit her that she didn't know much of anything. She turned on the all-news channel, and thirteen minutes later he knocked on her door.

The dining room wasn't open—too early. They ended up in the coffee shop, eating grilled cheese sandwiches and french fries. She apologized until he convinced her, through repetition, that he really didn't give a damn where they ate. Or, within reason, what they ate. She clucked over that, told him it was no way to live, food was a gift meant to be enjoyed. How could he not care about food with that gorgeous kitchen of his? Frankie lusted after it, she revealed; she was pretty fond of it herself, and she wasn't even a cook.

He didn't argue or defend himself. He seemed content to agree and let her keep talking. She took to teasing him a little. It made him laugh. She wasn't surprised that he liked it; he struck her as a man who didn't get teased nearly enough.

Over coffee, she talked some more about Mac. It seemed only right, since he'd been cheated out of his tribute at Jay's. It felt good to tell Mason why she'd loved him and what he'd meant to her, how much she was going to miss him. By the time they were ready to get up because they were tired of sitting, she felt as if she'd done Mac justice, as well as she could for today. She was even glad now that she'd gone to the loft and seen Jay and Nicole, put them together there in her mind as a couple. The end. Another phase of her life, call it the Industrial Coffee phase, was over.

They went for a walk. An aimless one since there were no sidewalks, just parking lots and asphalt accesses to office buildings full of companies with the word "Systems" in their names. It was late afternoon; the sun that had baked the acres of parking lot all day was gliding down behind the steel and concrete complexes and the neat plantings of cherry and holly and Japanese maple trees. Men and women in business clothes began to stream out of the buildings, clogging the walkways on the way to the parking lots. The sound of cars starting up became a symphony. To get out of the way of the cars and the pedestrians, they sat on a bench under a flagpole in front of the QualSystems Building. "What are those called?" Anna asked, pointing at low-growing rows of purple and green plants that looked like cabbages. Mason didn't know. She said, "I always wonder if you can eat them. Frankie might know. She's fighting with Carmen over whether we can afford to serve a green called mâche, which grows like a weed but for some reason is ridiculously expens—"

Mason kissed her. Shut her right up by putting his hands on her waist and his mouth on her mouth—for a second she felt like the girl at the piano, that picture of the girl taken unawares by the piano teacher, getting kissed while her startled hands were still on the keys. And then, just as quickly, she stopped being astonished. It was like hearing the first two or three notes of a song and being mystified, then hearing two or three more and recognizing it. Oh, *that* song. I *love* that song.

They got up and started walking again. The parking lots had grown treacherous. A minivan almost backed over them; they had to walk single file on an uneven hillock between rows of cars to escape. Under the concrete pillars holding up the portico of the Systex Building, they stopped to kiss again. "I've forgotten where we live," Anna said, squeezing her fingers around Mason's hard shoulders, the left one a little lower than the right. He'd changed his shirt during the thirteen-minute wait. This one was denim and smelled like clean laundry. "I'm turned around."

He remembered. He led them up and down curbs through the maze of lots and driveways, past bleached mulch slopes of begonia and petunia plantings and waving tufts of ornamental grasses. The lobby of their building was cold and quiet, a relative haven. One of the women behind the registration counter nodded at them in a knowing way as they crossed to the elevator, or at least Anna interpreted the nod as knowing. But she was reinterpreting everything, she was like a computer tax program that comes up with a set of numbers, but then somebody sticks in a new one on line C and *bam*, everything changes. All new total.

"Your place or mine?" You said corny things like that when your mind was jumping ahead, wasn't altogether engaged to begin with.

"Mine." Mason whipped his key card out like a six-gun, and that reminded her of the way he'd slouched in the doorway when they first met, his hand on the camera at his hip, gunfighter style. She'd changed her mind about him a dozen times since then. She'd half concluded he was, among many other things, a tentative man, but there was nothing tentative about him now.

His dim room was a replica of hers. They sat at the foot of the king-size bed that wasn't covered with stuff, mostly clothes, the contents of his gigantic suitcase. He'd left his TV on; they unbuttoned each other's clothes while on the screen an attractive Asian woman in a red suit told about a warm front coming up from the south. "For some reason," Anna said, "I wasn't aware . . . I didn't know we wanted to do this," stroking his hair back, kissing his face. "Now it's just . . . I mean, it seems so obvious."

"I was always aware." He got her undressed and then went in the bathroom and came back nude, with condoms. "Better hope these work," he said, opening one with his teeth. "They're antiques." He smiled to show her he was joking, or maybe that he wasn't but it was still funny—but his smile faded when he saw how she was looking at him. She couldn't help it. "Pretty bad," he said in a terrible voice, such a failed try at carelessness. She grabbed his hand and pulled him down beside her before she ruined everything.

"Look what happened to you." She touched a corner of the garish faultline of raised skin roping his left arm, shoulder to elbow, like twisting strings under the flesh. The left side of his chest was all scar tissue, but the worst wounds were lower, under his ribs and on the side of his belly, and especially devastating over the bone in his hip. She reached across his lap to put her hand there, held it still, didn't caress the maimed flesh—he might not like that. And she didn't embrace him, but that's what she wanted to do most, press her healthy body to his wrecked one, as if that could neutralize the trauma. "Did you break *everything*?" she asked, resting her cheek on his collarbone, rubbing his back.

"Not everything."

"What broke?"

He held himself stiffly, wouldn't touch her with his hands. He began to name bones and body parts. Spleen. Lung. Ilium. Femur, clavicle, sternum. Kidney—

She put her hand over his mouth. "Did anything not break?" Relief flooded through her when he began to smile. Oh, thank God, she hadn't ruined it. "You have the most beautiful mouth," she told him, tracing the shape of it with her fingers. "I'm so glad it didn't get hurt." She could make a sex joke now, she could touch his penis and make a crack about how glad she was that it hadn't been hurt, either. And then they could make love. With Jay, if the circumstances had been the same, she would have. But she wanted this to be real, not easy.

She still wanted to touch him, though. So she did, but without the sex joke. And after that, everything worked out all right.

"It's about this suitcase."

Mason opened his eyes, scrubbed them with the heels of his hands. Stretched. "Whatever could you be talking about?"

"You're not going on another trip right after this one, are you?"

"No."

"Like, around the world?"

"No."

She held up a pair of jeans and a pair of dress slacks. He shrugged. She held up a pair of sneakers and a pair of hiking boots. A raincoat and a collapsible umbrella. A bathrobe. A hat—no, two hats.

"You just never know."

"What's this?" Two boxes of dried soup mix, a package of trail mix, a water-heating coil, a plastic bag full of teabags. A coffee cup. She held it up.

"My lucky mug."

That figured; it had the Nature Conservancy bird on it. "Is this your lucky pillow?" And books, magazines, a lot of camera stuff, films and filters and batteries and such. That made sense, but the rest—"Why do you need all this stuff?"

"Just in case."

"In case what?"

He sat up. He looked like a tall drink of water—that was the phrase that leaped to mind—long and rangy, his scarred skin dark against the white sheet between his legs. Scarred or not, he was all man, as the saying went. "Do you know anything about panic disorder?" he asked.

"You mean like panic attacks?"

"Panic attacks can be part of general anxiety disorder. GAD—isn't that a good acronym? There's something called PDA, panic disorder with agoraphobia. That's mine. For the last five years."

"Five *years*." She put her hands inside his size-twelve loafers and tapped the soles together. "What's it like?"

"It's like normal anxiety times a thousand. You worry about everything, obsess about every possible thing that might go wrong. To keep the panic manageable, you try to control everything around you. Because losing control—that's the ultimate terror, see. That you'll be so scared you do something crazy and people will see. And you'll be humiliated. So you shrink your world down. Farther and farther, until the only place you feel at home is—home."

She walked his shoes along her thighs, up and back. "And so all the things you pack for a trip..."

"I might get hot, I might get cold. I might get hungry." He smiled lopsidedly. "Have to be prepared."

"How did it start? Was it just a gradual thing—"

"No. It happened in the hospital. I'd had some surgery, I was ready to come home." He touched his left cheek. "The last reconstructive surgery I had. I was getting dressed, that's all. Nobody was around. Nothing provoked it, but all of a sudden I couldn't breathe. I thought I was dying, I thought it was a heart attack. I was terrified, sweating, shaking, the walls were closing in, the light blinded me—these are the classic signs of panic attack, but I didn't know it, I just knew I was afraid and there was nothing to be afraid of. You think you're insane, or you will be if you let go, if you let anyone see what's happening to you."

"God. It sounds horrible."

"After the first attack, what you're afraid of most is the next one. That's how you become agoraphobic—you keep narrowing down the places where you feel safe."

"And then you..." She put his shoes aside and looked at him. "You build a house with no windows."

"Just in front." He lay back on the mound of pillows. He crossed his arms over his forehead. "I haven't gotten around to fixing that yet. That was stupid. That's hard to explain."

"You don't have to explain it."

"The funny thing was the timing. The accident was behind me and I was feeling good again, like my old self. Even professionally, I was having good luck, some photo sales that took off, moved me up to the next level. I bought the property on the river and started to build a house. Then I had my last surgery and my first attack. After that... If you think I'm bad now..."

"I don't."

"I'm a standup comedian compared to what I was like then. I could hardly go out at all. I was stuck. I could work on my house if nobody but Theo helped me. He should've stopped me, but he let me do it—I installed the wood siding right over the framed-out windows."

"Because it was safer?"

"I guess."

"Like a fort."

"Yes. Like a fort." He said it to the ceiling, wouldn't look at her.

"I have to say, Mason, that seems a little extreme. I wish I'd known you then. Because I'd've been happy to make you some curtains."

He had his face covered with his folded arms. She started to grin when his stomach bumped up and down. She jumped up and tackled him, and they rolled together.

They went across the hall to her room, mostly for the fun of it but also because she wanted a cold drink and his minibar refrigerator was broken. Somehow they ended up in the shower. Apparently all the talk about his body had given him the idea that it was okay to talk about hers. "Anna, how could your boyfriend keep naked pictures of you on the wall when he's got another girlfriend?"

"Incredible, isn't it?" More incredible was how Mason could tell they were pictures of her. They looked like the sexual fantasies an adolescent boy had created with his Erector Set, nothing but harsh lines and sharp angles and prominent genitalia. But Mason said no, they looked just like her. "Oh, thanks," she said, "thanks so much."

"But they're beautiful. *You're* beautiful."

"Thanks. If you think so. Really."

"You don't think so?"

He was spreading soap over her breasts and her stomach, so it was easy just then to feel beautiful. "I never wanted to look like Rose. Well—later, after I grew up, I mean." As a girl, she'd loved it that she looked like Rose. "I wanted to look like my mother, who was small and curvy, very feminine. She had blue eyes. She was *comparatively* voluptuous. Don't you think that would be better? Tell the truth."

"You can't really feel that way."

"Why not? Jay used to say I had a great shape, but frankly, I don't *want* to look like some elongated Moore sculpture, it's not flattering. I'd rather look like a woman than a modernist mobile."

He shook his head, baffled-looking, and put his arms around her. Obviously he didn't get it. They rubbed their soapy fronts against each other, and the argument began to seem irrelevant. "I love the way Rose looks," he said. "I love the way you look. Modigliani women."

"That's nice." She almost told him about her most embarrassing moment. Right then she could *almost* have admitted to him that she'd thought, for one minute only, that Rose was her mother.

"Don't laugh," he said, "but I envied Theo when he met Rose." He had his hands on her bottom. He dipped his knees a little, abashed. "I almost wished—ha—that I'd met her first."

She pushed him away. "I don't like that." She rinsed off under the warm spray by herself. "I'm sorry, but I don't like that. At all."

"What? What?"

"I'm sorry, but I have trouble with that."

"No—Anna, you don't—"

"No, it's not that, I'm not *jealous*, I don't care if you wanted to *sleep* with Rose. Wanted," she pointed out; "past tense."

"Then—"

"This is my problem, Mason. I understand I'm conflicted. I have lots of, how you say, issues. So let's drop it. I'm getting out, but I'm not mad. Okay?"

She got out. She felt silly, but there was nothing she could do about it. He'd said the exact wrong thing, but she couldn't hold it against him. She didn't understand herself, so she could hardly expect him to.

To make up, she told him he was a better artist than Jay. Lying beside him in her own king-size bed, she said, "You like being successful because it means you're good at what you do—Jay is an artist so he can be successful. It's exactly the opposite. He studies trends and courts people who can help him and gets smothered in the politics. Meanwhile, you take pictures of yawning birds. You should be shooting the eagles, the, what is it, the birds of prey because they sell best, but instead you do studies of herring gulls because you think they're interesting. You have *passion*. Your photos—and I don't even know anything about bird photography, and I know you can't really compare what you do and what Jay does, but your photos are playful, they're not forced, they're honest. Jay's sculptures are all mannered and premeditated and clever and trendy. He's so jealous of you he could spit."

Mason liked that a lot. To repay her, they made love again.

They fell asleep for a while, and when they woke up Anna remembered she'd forgotten to call Rose. "I said I'd call after the funeral. What time is it?" Nine-thirty. They were starving. First she called room service, then she called Rose.

"Hi, it's me. I know, sorry, I meant to—no, everything's fine, I just didn't think about it till—How's it going there? That's great. Terrific. Oh, that's great. Well, you know, it was sad, but... Yeah. Um, he's fine. Yes, no problems. No, it went very well. Is he—no, of course he's not here." She sent Mason an indignant look, to match her tone. "Why would he be here? Well, if so, it's because I'm rushing, I want to get to dinner before the dining room closes. Um, because I fell asleep. I know, now I'll be up half the night. Well, I don't know, Rose, I imagine he found food on his own somehow, he's a grown man. Why don't you call his room and ask?" She pretended to pound her fist on her head wildly—this was getting out of hand. "Yeah, okay. Right, see you tomorrow. No, my flight gets in early, I—yes, I told Carmen, she knows everything. Right. 'Bye. Okay. 'Bye."

She hung up and screamed softly. "She said I sounded funny. Did I? She thought you were *here*."

"You couldn't tell her?"

"Tell her you're here? Oh my God, no, it would give her too much satisfaction. Absolutely not." She laughed, keyed up for some reason. This was so high school. She felt as if she were sixteen and Rose was her mother. Mason didn't laugh with her. "You don't understand, Rose has been wanting this for months. She denies it, but it's true. No, I could never tell her, I'd cut my tongue out first."

The food came. They'd ordered like children, shrimp cocktails, mashed potatoes and gravy, hot fudge sundaes. They ate the sundaes first, in bed, watching a hospital drama. Mason could hardly believe it when she told him she'd never seen it before. When did she have time to watch TV at night? He explained what doctors were in love with each other, which ones had drug problems or trouble with their mothers. They turned it off when she remarked, after the second or third emergency operation, that maybe it wasn't the best show to watch while you ate your dinner.

Later, they argued about Rose again. Mason started it. She said something true but semi-snide about Rose's ingratiating manner, what a born schmoozer she was, how perfect for her profession, how she could hypnotize you if you weren't careful—she sort of got on a roll and couldn't stop. Mason watched her in silence for a while, then said, "You know what feels really good?"

She grinned at him and stood up from the table, where she'd gone to scavenge the last piece of shrimp. He was stretched out on the bed in his khaki slacks, nothing else, and she was drawn by the sight of his long, bony feet—maybe she had a foot fetish; first his shoes, now his feet. Sleeping with him wasn't what she'd expected. Not that she'd been expecting anything. But if she'd been expecting something, it wouldn't have been what Mason was like. Very passionate. Appreciative. He had a way of moving, smooth and quiet, unobtrusive, feline. It mesmerized her, especially after she put it together that he'd probably *learned* to move that way after years of bird stalking. She liked to watch him, say, reach for something. He put his arm out just a little more slowly than other people, a subtle, fluid gesture. Effortless but aware. He made love that way, too.

"What feels really good?" she asked, strolling over.

"Letting people off the hook. Forgiveness."

She halted. "What's that supposed to mean?"

"I want to ask you something. It's personal."

She wasn't going to like it, she could tell. "So ask."

He patted his fingertips together over his chest and looked up at her through his lashes, trying to disarm her. "Did you ever make it up with your father? Before he died, I mean."

"Look, Mason."

He held up his hand.

"Maybe you don't know everything. You know? Maybe you don't know everything you think you know. About me *or* Rose."

"Come over here."

She thought about it, then shrugged and sat down on the edge of the bed. She folded her hands in her lap when he'd have reached for one. "My father. Yes, since you ask, we were okay when he died."

"Good." He curled his wrist around her knees.

"We were speaking and everything. If that's what you mean."

She resented him for making her think of the last time she'd seen her father. He'd come to see her in Baltimore, where she'd moved to get away from him and Rose. She wasn't proud of herself for that now, but at the time she'd been glad to hurt them that way, the only way she could think of—that and withholding what she *really* knew about them: that they'd been lovers forever. She'd hoarded that bit of information for a long time, a way to torture them, she'd thought. Her anger had kept them baffled and worried, but they couldn't call her on it because they *were* guilty. It was the opposite of a healthy situation, but she'd seen it as a way to get back a little bit of the power. Mean-spirited, yes, but it had felt good.

One night her father came to take her out to dinner. He wanted to really put things right, he said, once and for all, get back to the way things used to be. They went to a Spanish restaurant downtown. She remembered his long, craggy face in candlelight, creased with earnestness, full of worry and affection. She'd loved him so much. She'd been easier on him than Rose—she still wasn't even speaking to Rose. Rose must've seduced him, she'd decided, hypnotized him and then sunk her claws into him. But it was time to forgive her father completely, and that night she was ready to do it. Until he lied to her. He'd looked her right in the eye and told her that day she'd caught Rose in his bed was their first time together. "Isn't that something? Talk about irony." He shook his head at the wonder of it. "It was as big a surprise to me as it was to you, honey, to find out Rose and I had feelings like that for each other."

For a salesman, he was a lousy liar. She'd felt embarrassed for him, and contemptuous, and brokenhearted all over again. She pretended to forgive him—"Ancient history, Pop, forget it"—but she was brittle and cool, and they both knew that nothing had changed.

A few weeks later, he was dead.

Afterward, when she tried to comfort herself, she'd focused on his sunny nature. Unlike her, her father was altogether an optimist. She had to believe he'd known she would come around eventually.

To Mason she said, "Listen. I know what you're saying, and forgiveness is fine, but there's not just one way to—I mean, you and Theo, I'm very glad for you. I think he treated you like shit when you were little, and it's great that you've let bygones be bygones, more power to you. But possibly these situations aren't exactly the same, you know?"

"Yes."

"Maybe abandonment is one thing, betrayal is another."

"Maybe they feel the same."

"Okay." She laughed angrily. "I give up, you're a saint, I'm a bitch. I'll stipulate to that if it'll make you happy." She stood up, went to the window, pulled back the curtain, glared out across the parking lot.

Mason came over. This room was too small. Why couldn't they have gone to the movies on their first date? He put his hand on her waist, using the other to draw her hair back so he could put his mouth on the back of her neck. "Are we through arguing?" she said in a querulous voice. He touched her through the thin material of her robe; carefully he undid the sash. Rather than flash the parking lot, she dropped the curtain back into place, then leaned back into the slide of his fingers on her warming skin. She pressed her hands to his over her breasts. "Are you angry with me?" she asked, beginning to lose her breath.

"No."

"Is this just a way to shut me up?"

"Yes."

She turned. His kind, serious, currently preoccupied face was becoming very dear. He kissed her on the throat. He kissed her mouth without using his tongue, but it was a deep, slow, delicious kiss, it broke her down. He had extraordinary hands, they could make her come apart, they and the excruciating slowness of all the things he did. She was always a move or two ahead, at least in the wanting, and it was agonizing to have to be patient. He did it deliberately; he'd found her pace, before, studied her like a boxer, so his countermoves were always good but always late. She knew what she wanted quite a while before he gave it to her.

They moved to the bed. She thought to get a little of her own back by seducing him now, being the aggressor, but he kept confounding her by making it mean something. Or feel like it meant something. Sex wasn't romance unless you pretended; she had a personal history to prove that. Sex was nerve endings and synapses and lucky timing. She didn't even *want* romance, just decent treatment, a little cheerful reciprocity between the sheets. Mason was doing things, in the heat of the moment she couldn't say what, doing things to make it feel... significant. Of a purpose. What was he doing? Saying things in her ear, pretty things, not to turn her on, just to say them to her. She forgot what they were as soon as she heard them; their intimacy unnerved her. And he was touching her, but not in that premeditated, sure-fire, cause-and-effect way she was used to, could predict in advance and found subtly depressing. Nothing he did was *in order*.

He came inside her, finally, and she thought, *Got you now.* My game, my turf. Finesse-wise, men folded after penetration, all but the cold-blooded, and Mason wasn't cold-blooded. No, and he lost control but he didn't stop, he didn't come, he was waiting for her. They kissed sweatily, and Anna said, "Mason—God, this is—God, you know this is only for tonight—"

He paused, and she bucked under him, not interested in another stop-action tease now. She didn't like the quality of the silence all at once. "What," she said when he raised up over her. He bent his head to kiss her, and she didn't like that either, it felt like rue, not passion.

"If you wanted to repay me," he said against her lips, "you could've just said thanks."

"*Hey.*"

He pulled away and began to hunt for his clothes.

"Wait. Mason. I didn't mean 'tonight,' that was—I was speaking figuratively, not *tonight*, literally, I mean—ha—what kind of girl do you think I am?"

He found his pants first and put them on, then he found his shorts. He stuffed them in his pocket.

"Mason, wait. I meant *temporary*, that's all. This is temporary. But *everything's* temporary, right?"

"Right."

She got up, scrambled her arms into her robe. "Look, I'm sorry, but what do you want? Really, what do you want from me?" She laughed again. "You don't want to *marry* me, do you?"

He had everything now, shirt, shoes, pocket contents. He headed for the door.

"Well, this is rude," she hurled after him, disbelieving. "You're crazy. You won't even talk to me!"

He turned around. "Sorry. I'd stay and fight it out, but I'm not in shape right now. You'd wipe the floor with me."

"I don't want to fight. I want to have an affair! Can't we have an affair?"

He went out. She stood in the middle of the room and listened to the door open across the hall, then close with a definite-sounding *click.*

Ha! She walked around in a circle. She wanted to be furious, aggrieved, the injured party. "Prick," she said out loud a couple of times. "Insane bastard." What was his *problem*? How—how *womanish* of him. Wasn't that what *she* was supposed to do, leave in a huff when the guy accidentally revealed his one-night-stand intentions?

"Just for tonight"—she had no idea why she'd said that anyway. A figure of speech. She'd just meant it wasn't *permanent*, but why say anything at all, especially at that moment? So that was stupid, but he was even stupider. "You could've just said thank you," something like that—how insulting, as if she'd sleep with him to pay him back for being nice to her. He couldn't possibly really think that. What a jerk.

She studied herself in the bathroom mirror while she brushed her teeth. She'd done the same thing about an hour ago, when she'd come in to pee. She'd made funny faces at herself then, amused because she'd looked so—goofy, like she'd just won a car in a raffle. She didn't look so damn chipper now. She looked like she'd been sucker-punched.

She threw the rumpled spread over the old bed and got in the new one, the untouched bed. She could still smell sex, though, all over herself. She debated taking another shower. She hated the feel of her anger draining away, like a reverse blood transfusion. She wanted it back, but a low, sorry voice was starting to say something in the shadowy back of her mind. She closed her mental ears, but presently she heard it anyway. *I fucked up.*

She called Mason's room.

"What did I do?" she asked him. "Whatever it is, I'm sorry. Write me an e-mail. Tell me in a letter what I did wrong."

"It's all right. You didn't do anything." He sounded exhausted.

"Obviously that's not true."

"It is true. Try to understand, Anna. It's not your fault that you're my worst nightmare." He hung up the receiver very gently.

13

"I thought that was your car."

Anna jumped up and whirled around in one fast move. "Rose." She'd left her thirty minutes ago at the Bella Sorella. "I've got some errands to run," Anna had called across the kitchen, and Rose had waved and called back, "Fine, me too—see you later." And now here they both were.

"I didn't follow you," Rose said with an anxious laugh, watching her feet as she came across the lumpy, just-mown grass in her flat-heeled shoes.

"I know." Although, for a second, the thought had crossed her mind. But it really wasn't much of a coincidence that they would both show up today at her mother's grave. It was Lily's birthday.

"Oh, those are pretty." Rose gestured toward Anna's salmon-colored roses. "She loved roses. I brought these," she said deprecatingly. "Lilies. Not very imaginative, but it's what I always bring." She knelt down in the grass and placed her orange and yellow bouquet by the greening bronze marker, near Anna's roses but not touching them; a respectful distance away.

"Rose, put them in the vase. They'll die there."

"No, I don't want to crowd your roses, they're so pretty."

"No, put them together—"

"This is fine. This is fine. I should've brought a vase, but I always use the one in the marker, and I just wasn't expecting—anyway, this is fine." She stood up, slapping wet grass blades from her hands. "Looks pretty this way. More of a show."

They stood beside each other, looking down at the flowers on Lily Fiore Catalano's grave, admiring the bright pastels against the dark green lawn. "One thing I've always wished she'd lived long enough for me to thank her for," Anna said.

"What, honey?" Rose turned to her consolingly.

"Not naming me Daisy."

Rose let out a bark of laughter that sounded loud, almost raucous in the quiet cemetery, no other sound but birdsong and the faint whiz of cars on the highway beyond the hill. It had rained this morning, but the clouds were sliding away on a fresh-smelling breeze, throwing speeding shadows on the ground between blasts of blinding sunshine. One of those days when you had to keep taking your sunglasses off and putting them back on.

"Iris called this morning. She can't make it down—sometimes she does, and we come here together on Lily's birthday. Either way, we always call each other."

Anna tried to imagine those phone calls. It was odd to think of Rose and Iris mourning her mother together, this long after she'd been gone. Twenty-three years. "Another thing I've always wished," she said, "is that I had a sister."

Rose nodded. "Sisters are a blessing." Anna glanced at her, looking for irony or awareness. "They keep us from feeling like we're alone. More than men do."

Anna pondered that. "Are those for him?" she said too curtly. Speaking of men. She pointed at a clutch of red and white petunias, the stems wrapped in a wet paper towel, that Rose had left on the ground after putting her lilies on her sister's grave. Hoping Anna wouldn't see them?

Rose bent to pick them up. "I stole them out of Louis's planter in the front window." She eyed them critically, plucking away the tan, tissue-thin dead petals and blowing them off her fingers. She went across to the other grave, the one on the far side of Lily's. BELOVED HUSBAND, the marker read; Lily's said BELOVED WIFE. Squatting, she placed her damp, straggly bouquet beside the bronze plaque. She paused, resting her palms on the grass; the side of her face Anna could see looked serene and fond, peaceful. She'd done this often enough to be soothed by the sameness. A ritual. Then she straightened, pushing up with her hands on her knees with a little sigh of breath. Getting old, Anna thought with an unfamiliar pang. Rose said, "Shall we go sit by the water for a minute? Do you have time?"

Anna shrugged. "Sure."

They went down the path to a small, man-made pond that lay between two tiers of graves on the long, sloping lawn. Concrete benches at discreet distances surrounded the pond, but they were all empty today, probably because of the rain. Anna spread her raincoat out on one and sat down. "What a dreary place. Why would they plant weeping willows here?"

"It does seem a little obvious." Rose sat down on the piece of raincoat beside her.

Lily pads floated on the black water in the shady end, but Anna had never seen them bloom. Two little ducks, speckle-breasted, gray-headed, were all that kept the place from being unbearably melancholy, and they weren't doing that good a job. What kind were they? One of the most monogamous birds in the whole bird kingdom was the American black duck, she happened to know, courtesy of Mason. It had come out in some context or other that night. Their one and only night. Oh, she remembered the context—she'd asked him how birds had sex. They did it the same way people did, pretty much, except their equipment was more rudimentary.

"Your mother would've been sixty-three today," Rose said.

"Yes."

"I wonder what she'd look like. If she'd still be beautiful."

"Was she beautiful?"

"Oh, she was. You've seen pictures. You remember."

Anna nodded. She'd just wanted Rose to say it. "What was she like? As a person, not a mother. What sort of a grown-up woman was she?" And why were these questions possible now when they never had been before? Something about the coincidence, or the flowers, the sad black water.

Rose didn't look at her, but there was care and thoughtfulness in the quality of the pause before she answered. "Lily. Oh, Lily was like air and light. Always changing and moving, you couldn't catch her."

Yes, Anna thought; *Look at me, Mommy*—the refrain of her childhood.

"Your grandmother used to say she had a short attention span, but that wasn't it. She was moody and quick, flighty, hard to pin down. Elusive, I guess is the word."

"Was she happy?"

"Sometimes. She had such highs and lows."

And as soon as she got sick, that was the end of the highs. What Anna remembered most about the eighteen months between her mother's diagnosis and death was her closed door and her darkened room, and the necessity to be quiet. She had longed to be with her, make tea, rub her feet, read to her, but her mother had hardly ever felt well enough to let her come close. So Anna had cleaned the house.

"But everyone loved her. In her good moods, Lily was wonderful fun, everybody loved to be around her."

Light and air, present and absent. Interested, indifferent.

"How did she meet my father?" And how strange, that no one had ever told her the story.

"How did Lily meet Paul?" Rose crossed her legs and clasped her hands around her knee. She wore slim black pants and black ballet slippers; the white stretch of ankle between them was bare and trim, blue-veined. "Oh, they met at the restaurant."

"Really? He was a customer?"

"He was living in Baltimore, just starting out selling books and magazines. He had several accounts in town, and one day he came in for lunch."

"And they talked?"

"Yes," she said after a slight pause. "Lily was hostessing that day, so, yes, they talked." Her face softened; she smiled. "Your father had on a plaid shirt and a corduroy sport coat. And he had that New Jersey accent, but it was even worse then. He looked like Tony Perkins—Lily thought. We both thought that."

"You saw him, too?" Rose should've been in the kitchen; that's where Anna had put her in her mind for this story.

"I saw him. It was so funny—he got up to pay and he couldn't find his wallet. You should've seen him blush and stammer—before that he'd been flirting. We ended up lending him five dollars for gas to get home."

"That's funny."

"He left, but then five minutes later he came back, triumphant and vindicated—he'd found his wallet on the floor of his car."

"And so then . . . what? He called her and they just started dating?"

Rose turned to look at her. She smiled, but her eyes had a shuttered look. "Yes, that's right. To make a long story short."

If that was painful, Anna was sorry for her. If she'd fallen in love with Paul that day but he'd fallen in love with Lily, Anna was sad. But in light of the way things had turned out, her sympathy had boundaries.

She changed the subject, began to talk about the restaurant. They'd had another good week last week, and the best weekend yet. "It's fantastic," Rose said, her face lighting up, "I can't believe we're doing so well in such a short time."

"Yeah, it's pretty good. But it's the busiest time of the year anyway, you have to keep that in perspective."

"But everything's working, everything all at once. I haven't had that feeling in so long."

"But don't forget, we've had perfect weather and the economy's good—that means *everybody's* business is up."

"You're right," Rose said. "It's important to guard against too much optimism."

Anna started to agree, then realized she was teasing her. "What did you decide about the floor? Have you thought about it? You can't keep putting it off, we have to *do* something."

"Do we? I'm just not sure what. I'm not convinced a bare floor is that much better."

Bare floor; she always made it sound like a prison cell, like solitary confinement. "We'd refinish. You've got pretty pine boards under that carpet, Rose, it could be beautiful."

"But that would cost so much. And we'd have to close for days, and we can't afford to right now. The timing's not good."

"It'll never be good. You could do it in mid-week, Monday, Tuesday, probably be open for business Wednesday night."

Rose sighed. "But then think how noisy it would be. My old customers, the ones who've been coming for ten or fifteen years, my *friends*, Anna—they'd hate it."

"It's a tradeoff. Yes, you lose a few of the old-timers, but you get more families and young people. *Young* people, Rose, the ones with the cash."

She sighed some more. "Oh, I don't know, I just don't know."

"Well, think of it this way—those old folks are going to have to leave anyway if you keep things exactly the same and then fold."

"I'd hardly say we're keeping things exactly the same."

"Not everything. I exaggerated." They weren't moving nearly fast enough for her, though. Rose wasn't like Carmen, thank God, backward and reactionary for the hell of it. Still, when you cleared away the camouflage and looked past the personal styles, you saw that, deep down, they were pretty much on the same team.

"Yes," Rose said, "you exaggerated. Those paintings!" She laughed too cheerfully, like a mother pretending her teenager's new tattoo was charming. "They've changed the whole look of the dining room."

"Well, wasn't that the idea? I thought you liked them."

"I do. I do. I never *hated* the maps, though. I know you did—"

"The maps? You're kidding."

"—but I thought they were kind of homey."

"They were *yellow*. Look, it all goes back to what you want, what style of restaurant, and I thought we'd agreed on that a long time ago."

"We did agree."

"We must not have, because I want clean, warm, and upscale—you want dingy, friendly, and family."

"I do *not*."

"You do, Rose. If not, why is it like pulling teeth to get you to change anything?"

"Now that is *really* an exaggeration."

Was it? Maybe arguing with Rose about the restaurant was a safe way to fight about something else. Maybe the restaurant was a scapegoat. That wasn't an altogether brand-new thought. This one was new: maybe Anna wanted to change everything about the Bella Sorella, make it *her* restaurant, not Rose's, to pay her back. Steal it from her, the way she'd stolen Paul from Lily.

No, that couldn't be. She wouldn't be staying around long enough, even assuming such a devious plot had seeped into her subconscious. That reminded her.

"Listen, Rose, you know my friend Shelly?"

"Who?"

"The woman I told you about, we used to work together at the café, she moved to San Diego. The one who's starting a restaurant? She wants me to come and manage it?"

"Yes, I remember."

"Well, that's not looking very hopeful all of a sudden. It looks like the people she was counting on for backing aren't coming through after all."

"Oh, dear." Rose's try at a commiserating look was a failure.

"So that option may not be viable anymore, but there's this guy. His name is Joel and he's an old friend, I've known him since I lived in Hudson." Where she had moved for a few years, back in her late twenties, with a man named Tyler. Tyler had wanted to go back to the land, but his main crop on their rented farm in upstate New York had turned out to be marijuana. "Anyway, he's still there, and he's got a vegetarian restaurant he wants to redo, bring it upscale, try to turn it into gourmet vegetarian."

Rose gaped at her. "Is this that—dope grower, that man you—"

"No, no, that was Tyler, this is Joel. Completely different guy. Anyway, he wants me to come up there and help him make the change. I haven't said I'll do it, but it's a fallback if Shelly's thing definitely fizzles. It's a contingency, that's all, and I wanted you to know about it." What could be fairer?

"Thanks," Rose said faintly. "Contingencies, options, and fall-backs. I do appreciate your keeping me up to date on all of them."

Anna tried to read her stiff, half-smiling profile as she looked out over the black pond and the grave-dotted hill behind it. The two little ducks were dabbling at the very edge of the water, so close she could see the yellowish-orange of their feet under them, steadily paddling as they poked their black bills among the weeds.

"I'm just telling you," she said reasonably. "We had an arrange-ment, and it seems to be working out for both of us. That's great—right? But it was never supposed to be any kind of a lifetime commitment, Rose, it was always open-ended."

Rose kept her eyes on the distance. She let her knee go and uncrossed her legs, rubbing the tops of her thighs as if the circulation had gone out of them. She clasped the gritty sides of the concrete bench and rocked back, looking up at the high coasting clouds. "Theo's worse. Mason's staying with him on the boat now, or I am, since he refuses to move in with either of us. It can't go on this way. We haven't told him. He has a disease called corticobasal degeneration."

"Oh, Rose."

"It means he only has another year or so before he's completely immobile. Then maybe two more years after that. That's all."

"I'm so sorry."

Rose looked at her. "*I'm* sorry," she said, blinking fast. "I should not have told you that. I did it for the wrong reason." She gave Anna's forearm a quick, hard squeeze and stood up.

Anna stayed where she was, watching her move across the lawn toward the pond bank. The ducks paddled backward, then turned in unpanicked half-circles and glided away with soft, irritable quacks. From ten feet, they turned again to look at Rose, who was bent toward them in a graceful L, rubbing her fingers together as if she had food in her hand. They wouldn't come any closer, though. They didn't trust her.

Confession wasn't the same as exoneration. And manipulation, even if you went all guileless and owned up to it, was still manipulation. Admitting you'd done something for the "wrong reason"—was that supposed to cure it? Anna hugged her arms, avoiding the sight of Rose by getting up and walking back to her parents' graves. She began to tear the crabgrass away from the plaques, making neat earthen borders around them.

Mason had never written that letter telling her what she'd done wrong. The morning after their one-night stand in Buffalo she'd called his room, but he'd already checked out. She still didn't know how he'd gotten home, if he'd taken another flight, the train, a rented car. In a few days her anger, which was complicated anyway, mixed up with too many other emotions to give her any satisfaction, died away altogether, and then all she felt was sheepish. The rest of July had been the month of sheepishness.

But it flared up again, her anger, when he hadn't invited her to the launch of the *Wind Rose.* They'd had a little party outside on his dock to celebrate, Rose and Theo and a few of their friends, even Frankie and Vince. But not Anna. And then, insult to injury, he hadn't responded to her casual e-mail, which had simply said, "M: Want to go to the movies or something? A." No answer at all, not even "No," just silence. When Rose mentioned he'd gone to some island in Maine to photograph puffins, Anna had thought, *Aha, no wonder!* and waited for him to come home. But then, again, nothing. After that she didn't feel anger, just disappointment. A hole.

She'd done a stupid thing in Buffalo, and in the aftermath she'd decided it was Jay's fault. Seeing him again had stirred up the poison in her, which had been lying harmless at the bottom, covered up with normal, wholesome emotions. Proximity to Jay soured everything in the glass, and she'd reacted by pulling away from Mason. Who hadn't done anything wrong, hadn't slept with anyone she loved behind her back, didn't deserve to be lumped in with all the ones who had. But that was like reaching a "breakthrough" in therapy—Aha, my little brother hit me when we were on top of the Empire State Building, that's why I'm afraid of heights! Just *knowing* why you did stupid things didn't cure you of stupidity.

At least Mason had never tried to manipulate her. She almost wished he had. And he'd certainly known when to quit—Rose kept trying. She was standing with one hand on her hip, shading her eyes with the other; the sun had broken through again, dazzling on the water. While Anna watched, she turned and came striding toward her, long-legged, arms swinging. Her face was clear again, determinedly cheerful. "It's clearing up. Good, we can eat outside."

"Eat outside?"

"Did you forget? It's somebody else's birthday, too."

"Oh, that's right." She stood up, slapping the dirt from her hands on the seat of her jeans. "Katie. I almost did forget." Frankie's little girl was coming to the restaurant for a little party this afternoon—Rose's idea.

"Well, I'll get going. You stay if you like, there's still plenty of time. I interrupted you."

Anna looked at the pretty roses and lilies on her mother's grave, the wilting hank of petunias on her father's. "That's okay." She'd paid her respects, finished her business. "I'll go back with you."

They walked up the winding asphalt path together, toward the parking lot. Halfway, they had to move aside so an elderly gentleman coming down could pass. Rose put her hand on Anna's back, guiding her, and the old man moved past. They resumed their way, but Rose didn't take her hand away. Anna didn't move over or shrug it off. It felt nice, that light pressure on the back of her waist. Companionable. Warm. *Fine*, she thought, *but I'm still leaving.*

She'd seen pictures of Kate, but for some reason she was expecting the reality to be a sort of miniature Frankie. But no. Frankie's almost bald head and flat chest, and especially the long, baggy shorts and sleeveless jersey she had on today made her look like the world's smallest professional basketball player. Freckle-faced Katie hardly even looked related to her in a yellow pinafore and a starched white blouse, yellow patent leather shoes and matching yellow pocketbook on a shoulder strap. Inside the pocketbook, she was proud to show you, were all the things a young lady might need, comb, mirror, pretend lipstick, a tiny bottle of cologne, a tissue-thin hankie. Marbles. And she had ringlets today, beautiful long, curling trails of carrot-colored hair down to her collarbones. Side by side, Katie and her mother looked a lot like Shirley Temple and Eminem.

They had the party at three o'clock, the slowest time of the day, around one of the new umbrella tables on the sidewalk. It was one of those clear, perfect afternoons, rare in early August; it wasn't hot and the air smelled clean and the sky looked just washed. Rose had bought party favors and hats, in spite of Carmen's prediction that passersby would mistake the Bella Sorella for Chuck E. Cheese, and Frankie had made Katie's three favorite foods, hot dogs, spaghetti with meatballs, and corn on the cob. The guests at the table kept changing as cooks and servers came and went, popping up to do something in the kitchen or on the floor and then coming back, but Katie was too excited to notice. She was at Mommy's restaurant.

"My mommy's a cook," she told everybody she met. "I *know*," they'd exclaim, captivated. She delighted them all, even Carmen, who just this morning had tried to sabotage Frankie's dinner special by "borrowing" the key ingredient—even scary Dwayne, who carved Katie a dolly out of a bar of soap with a boning knife at the table. Dwayne had a lot of extremely vulgar tattoos on his thick, wrestler's arms, but luckily all the bristly black hair growing on them obscured the details. Luckily, too, Katie couldn't read. She got many hastily purchased dime-store gifts and she loved them all, puzzles and games and stuffed animals, a harmonica, a deck of cards. Rose accidentally hit a home run, though, with the best present of all: Ballet Star Barbie.

Frankie sat beside Katie and didn't say much, helping her open packages and exclaiming over them, occasionally coaxing softly, "What do you say?" She was quietly radiant, her small, foxy face lit up with pride and love, madonna with a nose ring. She and Fontaine had collaborated on a three-layer chocolate cake for dessert. They lit Katie's four candles and everybody sang and ate cake and vanilla gelato.

Luca fell in love with Katie. He'd lost his own family, Rose had told Anna, in an accident a few years ago in his native Sardinia. Whenever a child had a birthday at the restaurant, he'd always come out of the kitchen and sing "Happy Birthday" in Italian. "*Tanti auguri a te,*" he sang to a giggling Kate, "*tanti auguri a te. Tanti auguri, carissima* Katie, *tanti auguri a te.*"

"Rose, what do you think of this?" Fontaine said when the singing was over. "Cake and Eat It."

The staff couldn't sit down to a meal anymore without bombarding Rose with new restaurant name suggestions. It was getting a little silly, since she never liked any of them. "Cake and Eat It," she said slowly. "Hmm." If nothing else, she was always polite. "Well, if all we did was desserts..."

"Oh, yeah, I guess." Fontaine gave a good-natured shrug. She was about seven months gone, Anna gauged. She had corn-silk blond hair and a sweet, blue-eyed, baby face that suited less and less her expanding waistline. Rose didn't need a full-time pastry chef, but she was letting Fontaine work eight-hour shifts anyway so she could make some money before she had to quit and raise a baby. She wasn't coming to work with any more bruises these days, but that was the only good thing going on in her life. She'd finally confided in Rose who the baby's father was. "Guess," Rose said to Anna. "Think of the worst possible person." "Someone we know?" "Someone we used to know." Then it was easy. "Eddie!" Yes, Ever Eddie, the crooked schmuck of a bartender Anna had fired last month. He couldn't be the black eye–giver, though, because he was long gone by then—to California, somebody said, and somebody else said Las Vegas. Either way, he was out of the picture. Why would a girl as sweet and harmless as Fontaine consistently let one rotten boyfriend after another abuse her? What sort of satisfaction did it give her? "Happens all the time," Carmen had pronounced—like she would know.

Rose listened patiently to more restaurant name suggestions. Vonnie said, "How about the Open Arms? Doesn't that sound warm and welcoming? Or Heart's Content. I thought of Creature Comforts, too."

Rose pursed her lips and looked thoughtful.

"Sweet Home," Vince piped up. "Like that? 'Let's have dinner at the Sweet Home.' "

"Sounds like soul food," Frankie objected.

Luca said he thought Fontaine's suggestion was very good, then bashfully offered one of his own. "*Il Caffe delle Tre Forti Donne.* Eh? Is too long?"

"The Three Strong Women Café," Anna translated over the laughter. "Who would these three strong women be, Luca?" As if she didn't know.

"You, of course," he answered gallantly, "and Carmen, and Chef Rose."

Rose sent Anna an arch look, veiled and playful. "Why, that's not bad," she said in encouraging tones, "not bad at all." But then, when Luca looked stunned by his good fortune, she had to tell him, "It is a little long, though."

"She hates everything," Dwayne muttered, a litany with him now.

"It's true, Rose," Anna said, to pay her back for teasing. "Nobody's come up with anything you'll even consider. Is this a real contest or not?"

"No, no, these are all wonderful suggestions," she denied, laughing, "it's just that—if we really changed the name, the new one would have to be *perfect*, and I know it can't be. Whatever we choose, it'll leave something out, something important. Essential."

"But that's true for anything."

"I know, but—if we call it Open Arms or Heart's Content, it says we're a warm, cozy place, but nothing about the *food.* And if we call it Pasta Pasta"—Shirl's suggestion—"it's the same thing but the other way around. If we call it Con Brio, which is a lovely name, it says we're gay and lively, but also that it's *noisy* here, maybe it's not dark and romantic enough. You see? The Chesapeake Room—I love that, but doesn't it sound like a men's club? I see fishing prints on the walls, and no women eating. Same with Capriccio and

A Capella and Raincheck, Chin-Chin, New Leaf—these are all nice, but they all leave something *out.*" She held her palms up in a helpless gesture. "Sorry. Keep trying. Really, I love them all!"

Anna said, "Okay, how about the Love and Happiness Restaurant. Or the Love and Happiness Café. Come on, what does that leave out? Let's call it Love and Happiness."

Rose just laughed.

"You don't like that, either? Not inclusive enough?"

"Not inclusive enough."

"Also," Frankie said, "it sounds Chinese."

"Okay, the Love, Despair, Happiness, and Death Restaurant. How's that?" Anna loved making Rose laugh. "Too long? Luca says it's too long. Then just pick the best two. Come on, Rose, you're the boss, you can pick the two you like best."

But Rose flapped her hand and rolled her eyes, and that was the end of that.

Katie's party ended at four, time for everyone to go off shift or back to work. Mike, Frankie's ex, was due to pick Katie up at four-fifteen, and some of the staff who usually went home at four hung around to get a look at him. Frankie had some prep work in the kitchen that couldn't wait, so Vince put Katie on top of two phone books on a bar stool and did magic tricks while she waited for Dad. He was wonderful with her, and that was a bit of a revelation to Anna—Vince the ladies' man was absolutely charming with children, or at least this child. He had big, round, beautiful eyes, a mobile, expressive face. A clown face, it turned out, and it could send Katie into gales of giddy, skittering laughter.

"Daddy!" Katie cried when she saw Mike. Vince came around and helped her off the stool. There was a funny moment when he could have handed her directly to her father, who was smiling, arms out, ready for her, or set her on the floor. He set her on the floor.

"Hi, I'm Anna. Obviously you're Mike."

"It's good to meet you."

"Sorry you've just missed Rose, she had to leave early."

Mike said he was sorry, too, he'd heard a lot about Rose. He had a nice smile. He looked like an assistant professor, which was what he was, in wrinkled khakis and a blue work shirt, a tweed jacket over his shoulder.

Vince introduced himself, and the two men shook hands. Anna said she'd go get Frankie.

"Mike's here."

"Oh, okay." Frankie was making ribollita, a sort of pureed Tuscan stew. She called it an acquired taste; Carmen called it mush. "Listen, this is finished, all except for the spices that go in last. Luca knows, I told him the whole deal."

"Okay, no problem. Go have fun." Frankie was taking a rare night off. She, Katie, and Mike were going back-to-school shopping, then out to dinner for one last little birthday fling. She'd been talking about it all morning, as thrilled as if they were taking the Concorde to Paris.

She took off her dirty tunic and threw it across the room in the laundry pile. She got a gauzy red shirt out of the employees' closet and put it on over her tank top and baggy shorts. "What do you think?" She stopped at the mirror by the door, the one the waitstaff used to check their lipstick or their hair just before going out on the floor. What was Frankie checking?

"Looks great," Anna said after a startled moment.

"Yeah? I don't know if he's taking us someplace nice or not, after. Could just be Mickey D's. So I look okay?"

"You look fine."

In the mirror, she lifted her chin and opened her eyes wider. Then she scowled. "Oh, fuck it," she said with a nervous shrug, and went out.

Vonnie and Kris had come over, ostensibly to say good-bye to Kate but really to get a gander at Mike. Dwayne, Jasper, and Shirl wandered out of the kitchen for the same reason.

"Hi," Frankie said.

"Hi," Mike said. "How'd it go?"

"Terrific." She was *shy*, Anna saw; she looked at Mike when she thought he wasn't looking at her. "A great time was had by all."

Mike put his hand on top of Katie's head. "Hope she didn't eat too much."

"Forget that, she ate everything in the kitchen. I don't know what Carmen's gonna serve for dinner tonight. Didn't you?"

"I ate everything," Katie confirmed. "It's okay," she told Vince, "I got Mommy's meta-blisa."

"Mommy's metabolism," Mike said. Everybody laughed.

"Okay, we ready to go? Daddy'll have to carry that bag of loot, kiddo, it's too big for me."

Mike put his hand on Frankie's arm. "Uh, slight change of plans. I wanted to call and tell you, but I didn't find out till late."

"You have to work? No problem, we—"

"No, um . . ." He gave a weak, embarrassed grin at the audience, and everyone started backing up. "Talk to you a sec," he muttered to Frankie, pulling her the other way. Katie followed him. "Hold it," he said when he saw her. He leaned down. "This is a birthday secret, okay? I need two seconds—"

"Birthday secret!"

"Two seconds to talk to Mommy. You go over there for two seconds." He pointed to the bar.

"Secret!"

"Go, go." He turned her around and gave her a little push, and Katie ran straight for Vince.

Anna didn't have to hear what Mike told Frankie to know it was bad. Frankie's stiff posture said it all. The conversation lasted about two minutes, not two seconds, and it probably would've gone on longer if Katie hadn't run out of patience and crashed it. She ran to her dad and wrapped her arms around his legs, demanding to know the birthday secret *now*.

Anna tried not to listen, not because she wasn't curious but because Frankie's flushed, unconvincingly gay face broke her heart. "The surprise is at Colleen's," she told Katie, "so you and I are going shopping *next* week. Next Monday, just the two of us, and we'll have a great time. I promise."

"It's at Colleen's?"

"Yep, the surprise is at Colleen's."

"Are you coming, too?"

Frankie went down on one knee to straighten the crooked collar of Katie's blouse and fluff her hair. They talked in soft voices, low and calm, high and childish, while Mike shifted from foot to foot and jiggled the change in his pants pocket. Anna couldn't help liking him, before. Now she couldn't stand him. Colleen was the woman he'd been seeing off and on—she'd heard all about her from Frankie. She taught art at Mike's college; she lived on a small farm; she had a pony; Katie liked her a lot.

Frankie hugged Katie for the last time, waved to her and Mike at the door, and rushed back into the kitchen without looking at anybody.

"Great," Vince said, "this is just great."

"Sucks," Anna agreed.

"Do something."

"Like what?"

"I don't know, talk to her."

"Oh, she'd love that. Nothing Frankie likes better than a girl-to-girl chat about her love life."

Vince blushed. Anna rubbed the back of his neck for comfort. "I gotta go work," he told her. They didn't talk again until after dinner.

Dinner service was busy but not crazy, no emergencies, no heart stoppers like running out of all the specials by seven-thirty. It was the kind of night when restaurant management didn't seem like an insane career choice. All the elements in the big machine were humming along in harmony, food preparers, food servers, food consumers, and food, and all a conscientious overseer had to do was oversee. That left plenty of time for the fun part, and for Anna that meant schmoozing with the bar regulars and making nice with the customers. She was a host. That was her job and she was good at it, and it had only taken about twenty years to figure that out. Slow learner.

Rose had left her to-do list on the desk. It never seemed to get any shorter. Glancing at it, Anna couldn't help noticing that she was the one doing most of the crossing off. "Order straws, sip-sticks, p. towels for bathrooms, aspirin, masking tape"—she'd done that. "Louis: Sharpen knives, clean capp. machine, wash front window"—Anna had passed that message on. "Run off new schedule & time sheets, call dishwasher man, tell Dwayne—vacuum dust in refrig. compressor units, clean grease trap"—Anna had taken care of those. That left "Reschedule grill fire inspection guy, call workman's comp rep, rewrite phone book ad, trash pickup Tues.?" Not to mention paying a stack of aging bills from the phone company, the laundry service, the water softener service, the building landlord, and eight or nine separate food and beverage suppliers.

Anna didn't begrudge the time Rose was spending away from the restaurant to be with Theo. Not at all—how could she? He was sick and Rose loved him. By the same token, though, didn't it make sense, wasn't it only fair that the one doing most of the work got to make most of the decisions?

She was totaling up receipts when Vince slumped into the office and flopped down on the couch, arms and legs sprawled as if he'd dropped from a height. "I thought you left," Anna said. "I thought you had a date."

"Called it off." He watched her punch numbers on the adding machine for a while. "I asked Frankie if she wanted to go to a movie."

"Yeah?"

"She said no. So then I asked her if she wanted to go for a walk. It's hard to come up with things that don't involve booze."

"I guess."

"She said no. I asked her if she wanted to come over to my place and watch TV, get a video or something. No. I asked her if I could go over to her place and watch TV. No."

"By now you're probably starting to get the idea..."

"She hates me."

"No, she wants to be by herself."

"I don't want her to be, not tonight. You know what I'm scared of, Anna, don't pretend you don't."

"Okay, I won't, but Rose says there's nothing we can do. If she's going to fall off, she'll fall off. We can't stop her."

"Half of all recovering alcoholics relapse in the first six months. Ninety percent do at least once in the first four years."

Anna had nothing to say to that. Frankie got a DUI last year; it's what had finally made her stop drinking, the shock of it. "That was low as I could go," she'd told Anna in a rare confidence. "The bottom. I couldn't get any worse than that." Did Vince know? Frankie was stingy with personal information.

"She ever tell you about her family?" he asked.

"A little. Not much."

"Her father took off when she was seven because her mother was a drunk. Frankie took care of her till she died. That guy Mike." He jabbed his thumb into a hole in the sofa arm, enlarging it with unconscious violence. "How could he toss her out like that?"

"Oh, Vince. You of all people..." But now didn't seem like a charitable time to remind him of what drunks were like.

"I know, but she's *okay* now, she's sober. But he's got *Colleen*." His lips twisted with distaste. "Guess what I did. I bought her a case of nonalcoholic beer. You know, for a present."

"That didn't go over?"

"It's got alcohol in it. Just a fraction. I didn't know, plus she says the smell of it triggers cravings." He hammered the top of his head with his fists. "Smart present, huh?"

"Oh, Vince."

"I just wanted to hang with her tonight, that's all. No moves, just company."

"She'll be all right. She's tough."

"Wrong. She's not tough at all."

After he left, Anna thought about calling Frankie. But what good would it do? None, probably, and it would definitely annoy her.

She picked up the phone.

The low, toneless "Hello?" sounded terrible, but it sounded sober.

"Uh-oh. Sorry—it's me—were you asleep?"

"No. What's wrong?"

"Nothing, I was just calling to say hi." She laughed nervously. "Kate's incredible."

"Yeah, thanks again, you and Rose," Frankie rallied to say, "you made it really nice today."

"Our pleasure. So. How are you?"

"I'm fine. I just can't talk right now, I gotta go."

"Wait. Could I come over?"

"What?" Incredulous. "No."

"Okay, but—do you want to talk or anything?"

"No, I don't. I just said that. Look, I'll see you tomorrow."

"Okay, for sure. See you tomorrow. I might come in a little early myself, get a head start on the inventory. Maybe—maybe you could help me?" Silence. "Or not, I was just—"

"You want me to come in early and help you with *inventory*?"

It even sounded ridiculous. She couldn't tell if Frankie was amused or insulted. "Yeah."

"And that would be why, so I'll lay off the sauce now, get a good night's sleep, and have a real clear head tomorrow for inventory?"

Okay, insulted. "Sorry," she said, miserable. She deserved that. The problem was, she didn't know what she was allowed to say and what was off limits. They were friends, but Frankie's drinking had never been open for discussion. "I'm sorry. I just—"

"I'll see you tomorrow, Anna," she said shortly. "At the usual time, if that's okay with you."

"That's okay with me."

They hung up.

Anna listened to the stillness, nothing but the low hum of machines that heated or cooled food or washed dishes. Rose always said she liked this time of the day best, when the restaurant was empty and quiet. "Like a problem child who's finally gone to sleep. And I'm like the mama who hangs over his crib and thinks, 'Oh, what an *angel*, I forgot how much I love you.' " For Anna, it was the opposite. She preferred the craziness of a full house, when the joint was jumping and chaos ruled. It felt like a family when everybody was here, the whole staff on a good night, a big, noisy, unruly, semi-functional family. Sometimes everybody hated everybody and homicide seemed like the next logical step, but most of the time they got along, and once in a while there was so much love—no other word for it—it was as if they were all drunk on it.

This was new. She could just barely remember it being that way in the old days, after her grandmother died and Rose took over the Bella Sorella. Certainly it had never been like that at Nicole's, where kitchen help lasted about three months and floor help about five. Employee loyalty? No such thing. Nobody's identity was tied up in Industrial Coffee except Nicole's, no sharing, no community, no *us*. At Rose's, the lowest-paid prep cook actually gave a damn. Billy and Shirl and Vonnie kept stuffing the suggestion box with new restaurant names, and not only because they wanted free drinks for life. They wanted to see the Bella Sorella flourish. They really did.

So they were a motley, crossbred kind of a family, scrambling along more or less together to get through the frantic day. But then the last customer paid up, the waiters settled with Vince, the cleaners finished in the kitchen, Anna totaled up receipts, Rose locked the safe—and everybody went home. They scattered, they split off like spokes from the hub of a wheel. Vince lived alone, Frankie lived alone. Carmen, alone upstairs. Vonnie was divorced, her last kid almost gone. Louis, Luca, Fontaine, they all lived alone. The women Dwayne and Jasper and Flaco slept with were mostly in their heads; after work they went drinking, together sometimes, then they went home by themselves.

Before she started feeling sorry for herself, Anna shut off the computer and gathered up her stuff. She was turning off the desk lamp when the phone rang.

"Anna?"

Mason's voice. She left the light out so she could listen to it in the dark. "Hi," she said.

"I called your house. I thought you'd be home by now. Late night for you."

"Yes, I'm the last one here."

"How are you?"

"I'm great, I'm good. You?"

"I'm . . ." A pause, as if he was checking his pulse or taking his temperature. "Fair," he decided. "I'd say I'm fair."

She had so many conflicting feelings, it made it hard to take an approach. How was she supposed to be with him? She'd done one dumb thing, but he'd overreacted—that was still her version. And then he'd ignored her, which made it two to one, her side. Not that she was keeping score. And over all that was this asinine tingling in her chest because of his voice in her ear. She hadn't felt it since she used to get his e-mails. His screen name was SnapShot; she'd see it in her In Box and get that fleshy thrill, miss a heartbeat or two.

"I hear you went to Maine," she said. "Rose mentioned it."

"Macias Island. Somebody canceled at the last minute and I took his spot."

"There's a waiting list?"

"Yes. To photograph puffins."

"Puffins. Puffins. Aren't they sort of like parrots?"

He laughed, an infectious huff of his breath. "Sort of. Maybe if you crossed a parrot with a penguin."

"Did you get any good shots?" Funny how giant emotional upheavals could just drift away, seem like trivia after a few minutes of chitchat. If you were inclined that way to begin with.

"I got a few. Anna. Listen." Silence.

"I'm here," she reminded him.

"I'm sorry I've been . . . invisible."

"Yes, well." She had a sense of giving in too easily, but why? The him-me lines were blurring so quickly; the longer Mason talked, the harder it was to remember, really keep in mind what the problem was.

"You even asked me to the movies."

"Yeah, and you didn't even write back. How rude." She was smiling when she wasn't talking, trying to keep her voice straight so he wouldn't know. She wasn't a connoisseur of making up; she could foresee regretting the speed with which they seemed to be reconciling. She should drag it out for fun, but it wasn't in her. "Luckily," she said, "I'm willing to overlook that."

"Good, because I'm calling to ask if you'd like to go to the movies."

"It doesn't have to be the drive-in, does it?" How reckless: she'd jumped several steps ahead by teasing. She waited for his reaction on a nervous edge.

He laughed.

It came rushing back, why they were good together, everything she liked about him, why keeping away from each other hadn't made any sense. A little taste of anger came back, too, though, like indigestion; she remembered exactly how *cheated* she'd felt when he'd walked out on her. Look at what he'd deprived them of. Who knew how soon she'd be gone, but soon, and look at the time he'd wasted. But she set that aside—bygones—in the interest of expediting a truce. How magnanimous. She felt expansive.

"What are you doing right now?" she asked.

"Um..." He was startled into confusion. "Sitting on the dock, looking at the boat, Theo's boat—"

"Which I've never even been on board," she pointed out.

"What are you doing?" he countered.

"Nothing. Thinking about going home." To an empty house that was too big for her. Her aging clapboard reminder that she was literally back where she'd started.

"Come over here," Mason said.

"Give me twenty minutes."

14

Too many people. Too many helpers. Rose had almost finished packing everything Theo would take to Bayside Gardens before Anna and Mason even got there, so there wasn't much for them to do. It all fit in a couple of moldy duffels, meager-looking on the *Expatriate*'s cockpit deck. "It's temporary," Theo insisted. "I'll be back as soon as this heals"—his wrist.

He'd broken it exactly the way Rose had dreaded and feared that he would, by falling down the companionway steps. He'd frozen on the second-to-last one and lost his balance, and when he'd tried to break his fall, he'd snapped his wrist. He kept saying, "Coulda been my neck," as if that was supposed to comfort her. After the shock and fear wore off, she was *glad* he'd fallen, glad the cumbersome cast was on his right hand because it crippled him so effectively. Nothing else could have gotten him off this damn boat and into a place where at least he'd be safe. Miserable, but safe.

And *still* he wouldn't move in with her, or with Mason. As much as he hated the idea of a nursing home, he'd rather be taken care of by strangers than by people who loved him—"people who aren't getting paid to wipe my butt," was how he put it. It was probably too late now anyway; his disease had progressed to the point where he needed the kind of skilled care she or Mason couldn't give. And he was never going to get any better.

"Theo, what about these?" Mason called up the steps, unrolling the soft cloth containing Theo's carving tools, each one in its neat felt pocket.

"What is it? I can't see, what you got there—"

"Chisels, files, awls—"

"That's my woodworking tools. Leave 'em be."

"Okay."

"Take them with you if you like," Rose said quietly, so Theo wouldn't hear. Mason was helping her down in the cabin while Anna tried to keep Theo occupied above. What those two were talking about Rose couldn't imagine, and she was dying to know. Their voices were too faint to hear.

"Take them?" Mason said.

"If you think you could use them. His fishing gear, too."

Mason didn't pretend to misunderstand. He ran his fingertips over the exposed handles of the tools, worn smooth from all the years of use. "I remember when he'd carve things for me. Airplanes, horses, things like that. I wish I'd saved them, but they're gone now, lost or thrown out." He looked up. "I'll leave his tools here, I think."

"All right."

"Anyway, he's already given me the dog to look after. That's enough for the time being."

"And then some," she said, smiling back. "But Cork is so sedentary, I'd be surprised if he gave you any trouble." She could see the old mutt from here, sprawled on the seat next to Anna on deck, his chin on Theo's thigh. "It's nice of you to take him."

"I hate this," Mason said with sudden heat. "All of it. What it comes down to. His whole life in two bags."

She put her hand on his wrist, afraid Theo would hear.

"Rose, is this the right thing? I hate it that he thinks he's coming back."

"But why, if it makes him happy?"

"We're tricking him. What if we're wrong, what if he'd want to know?"

She moved her knees so he could sit beside her on the narrow bunk. If he stood for long in the cramped cabin, he got a stiff neck from keeping his head bent so it wouldn't hit the ceiling. Theo, six inches shorter, had never had that problem. "You're the kind of man who would want to know the truth. You'd *have* to know it, and no one would think of keeping it from you. But Theo's different. It won't always be this way, but right now, Mason, I don't believe he could stand knowing what's going to happen."

"Okay."

"It's too soon."

"All right."

"But we have to be together on this." They'd talked about it for hours. "If you still have doubts—"

"No, I don't, I'm with you. I just don't like it."

"I don't, either. Thank God for you." She told him that all the time.

"For you," he always said back.

She ran her hand along Theo's pillow, the scratchy wool of his blanket. Her mind shied away from the thought that neither of them would sleep on this hard, narrow bunk again, together or apart. "Look at those two," she said, nodding up at Theo and Anna. "I never thought I'd see the day, did you? What do you suppose they're talking about?"

She watched Mason's face as he followed her gaze, and she knew it wasn't the sight of his stepfather making him look intent and fascinated. "Dogs, probably."

"Theo's halfway decided Anna's all right," she said. Because she made Mason happy. Rose didn't say that, though; she left the implication blank, so Mason could fill it in himself. Maybe even elaborate.

He said nothing.

She sighed. Which one was more annoyingly discreet, him or Anna? "Because you seem to like having her around," she tried, conscious of the lameness of that, not to mention the obviousness. But if she was going to get information out of either of them, her chances were better with Mason; nothing sent Anna into clamlike uncommunicativeness faster than a reference to her and him as any sort of item whatsoever. The maddening part was that there was no *reason* for her reticence except spite—she just didn't want to give Rose the satisfaction.

Well, too bad, she was satisfied anyway. Two people she loved dearly, one more than anyone else, two people she had *put together,* don't forget, wittingly or not, were finding each other. They talked on the phone, e-mailed, went on dates, actual dates, walks, picnics, late suppers at Mason's house. That by itself was something of a miracle, Mason walking around in the world, out and about, big as life—"Like he owns the place," Theo said. He was flying again, going on trips up north and out west to photograph birds he never had before, the marbled godwit, the prairie falcon. What a change! Flying with Anna to Buffalo had started it, but Rose wasn't allowed to ask about that. They'd come back changed, both of them, and she'd have said not in a good way, but now everything was fine, so what did she know?

Nothing. That's what was so irritating.

Mason smiled, and roused himself to say, "Yes, I like having her around."

"Good, good," she said encouragingly. "Good."

Nothing.

She gave up. No, one last try. "I take credit for that, you know. I'm the one who told Anna you could fix her roof."

His eyes twinkled. He knew what she was up to. She wasn't going to get any juicy information out of him, that was clear. Anna's doing; he was keeping her secrets, not his own. Did he know what he was getting into? Too late now, but the old *Be careful what you wish for* adage flashed across Rose's mind. Matchmaker, beware.

They went up on deck.

Anna was telling Theo a story about the old man who had died, Mac, her old boyfriend's grandfather. Theo's facial paralysis hid his laughter these days; you had to look for it in his eyes. Anna's story made them light up and the breath wheeze softly through his parted lips. Rose hadn't thought anything could make Theo laugh today. "I'd'a liked that fella," he sighed to Anna, and she smiled at him and said, "He'd've liked you, too."

"All set, I guess." Rose straightened from setting down a cardboard box full of Theo's chess set, some of his books, his favorite coffee mug, next to the duffel bags on deck. "Can you think of anything we've forgotten?"

"A file."

She bent toward him, not sure she'd heard. "A what?"

"So I can saw my way out."

"Oh." She ruffled his hair and helped him to stand up. The cast on his wrist had a side benefit: it was on his shakier arm, and the added weight helped keep it steady. "Are we ready to go?" Mason came around on his other side. Supporting him, they got him safely over the gunwale and onto the dock. Mason went back for the duffels, Anna took the box, Rose took Theo. Slowly, carefully, Cork leading, they made their way down the marina pier, passing the sail and working boats and cruisers of Theo's neighbors. The farther they got from the water, the closer to land, the better Rose liked it, even knowing it was the opposite for him. For almost a year she'd lived with the nightmare fear that he would fall off his boat and drown. Now at least he was safe from that.

At the chain-link gate, he stopped short. Taking shuffling steps, he turned himself around. It was a heavy, cloudy late afternoon, with a wind coming up from the water to cool down the mugginess. The bay, inky black glass an hour ago, rippled like corduroy with a shallow, monotonous chop. Theo lifted his left arm and slowly pointed.

"The clouds?" Rose guessed. He shook his head.

"Osprey nest," Mason said, and Theo nodded. Rose saw it, a messy construction of sticks and moss on top of a buoy about sixty feet out in the water. She thought she could see a head poking out, but it could've been a stick.

"Wanted to be here. Chicks about to fly. There's two. Any day now."

Mason squinted across the sparkle of the water. "I could photograph them for you." Theo snorted a laugh. "I could. You're right, it's any day now. The parents will keep bringing them food while the fledglings learn to fish. That's a sight. Want me to?"

But Theo flapped his good hand and turned himself back around. Didn't answer.

When they got to their cars, Rose's and Mason's parked side by side, Theo said he wanted to go with Rose and he didn't want Mason and Anna to follow. Rose could get him settled at Bayside Jail—he never missed a chance to call it that—and Mason and anybody else who cared to—she guessed that meant Anna—could come and visit if and when it suited them.

Mason looked surprised. "You sure? I thought I'd come with you—all of us. Show of force, let 'em know who they're dealing with."

Theo gave his wheezing laugh again, but shook his head. He looked so weary. Rose tried to guess what was in his mind now. Did he think the nursing home was a humiliation? An end for him that he wanted as few witnesses to as possible? Mason helped him into the front seat of her car and got him buckled in. As soon as he stepped back, Cork jumped up on Theo's lap. They all laughed, and exclaimed over his spryness, and how they hadn't thought the old boy had it in him. Theo laughed, too, but he bent his head and pressed his face against the wiry fur on Cork's neck. When he didn't move, Anna took a few steps back and turned away. Mason hung on the door, staring at the ground. Rose rubbed Theo's shoulder. "He can visit," she said thickly. "I'll bring him, Mason will bring him. We'll both—"

Theo lifted his head. "I don't want to go," he whispered. His pale eyes swam. Rose nodded, unable to talk. "I don't want to go, Rose."

"I know."

"I know I gotta." He lifted Cork's grizzled head. "You miss me?" He kissed his dog between the eyes. "Here, take 'im." Mason reached in and lifted the dog gently from his lap. And held him while Rose closed the door, went around to her side, and started the car.

"I'll call you tonight," Mason leaned in the window to say. "See how you settled in. And I'll come out tomorrow. First thing in the morning." Theo nodded, looking straight ahead. "Next weekend maybe we'll take the sailboat out, cruise down to Deal or Crisfield for the day. Sound good?" He nodded again. "Take it easy," Mason said softly. "Okay?"

"Yeah."

"Give 'em hell."

He grimaced for a smile.

Bayside Gardens wasn't beside the bay, but it did have a garden and Theo's second-floor room looked out on it, neat beds of white daisies, black-eyed Susans, and heat-weary coneflowers. He hated it.

"But why? It's pretty. It's south-facing, you'll have the sun all day. You can look out at the people taking walks on the path."

He said a bad word.

Rose sat down on the edge of his bed. "Now, look."

"Don't," he whispered. "Lecture me. I know."

"You know, but I'm lecturing you anyway. You're off to a bad start, mister. You can't hate everything. Not after..." She looked at her watch. "Four and a half hours." He hated dinner in the perfectly nice dining room downstairs. Hated the announcements for meals and activities that came over the intercom in his room. Hated his neighbors, hated his nurses, hated his bed, his room, the air conditioner, the wheelchair he was supposed to use when he wasn't using the walker.

"Can," he said. "Do."

"Theo." She picked up his twitchy old hand and held it to her cheek. "I've asked you to come and live with me—how many times? A hundred? Mason, too. But you won't."

"Nope."

"This place is no good, I know, because there's no water under it. But what can we do?" She scuffed her cheek with his knuckles. "Try to make the best of it, I guess. I don't know what else to do. If I could think of anything—"

"I know. It's okay."

She nodded against his hand. "It will be. It'll be okay. Tough at first, but then better. You'll get used to things."

"Yeah."

"If not, we'll move. This isn't the only place in town." It was supposed to be one of the best, though. "At least you don't have a roommate," she pointed out.

"That'd be hell," he agreed.

"And hard on you, too."

He shoved at her shoulder, telling her he got that joke.

She bent over and laid her head on his chest. The slow, steady thump of his heart was as precious to her as her own heartbeat. It was getting late. Outside, voices echoed faintly; occasional footsteps passed by the closed door. "Don't want you to go," Theo said. "Wish you could stay."

"Love me, Theo?" she murmured.

"You know it."

She kissed him on the mouth. He wasn't much of a kisser anymore, and she missed it. Nowadays she had to do all the work. She sat up and went to the little desk under the window. She got the matching chair, carried it over to the door, and set it at an angle under the doorknob. Just like in the movies.

Theo blinked at her.

"They really ought to have a lock. Guess they're afraid you'll lock them out." In the middle of the room, she smiled at him and began to unbutton her shirt.

"Hey, now," Theo said, sitting up higher. "What're you doing, Rosie? Aw, now."

She stripped for him slowly, letting the shirt fall to the floor, coming closer to take off her bra. Black bra today, how fortuitous. She dangled it toward him, then flipped it over her shoulder, thinking, if your body was sixty years old, you'd better have an appreciative man to show it off to. Luckily for her, Theo had always been that man. She swayed a little, as if there was music, unzipping her slacks. Theo shook his head, amazed, almost smiling, his eyes full of love and fun. Like old times.

She kicked off her shoes and shimmied out of her slacks. Nothing left now but panties and knee-high stockings. She laughed as she got rid of them.

She ran her hands through her hair, as if it was long and black again, as if she were young again. "See anything you like, sailor?"

"I like it all. Always liked it all," he said, wiping his cheek. He was weeping.

She had to help him with his pants. His erection was a precarious thing, flushed with hope. She stoked it tenderly, the small spark, trying for a flame. "This ain't going to work," he warned her.

"Yes, it is." She kissed him again and again and moved over him, onto him, cradling his face with her arms. "If anybody comes," she whispered, "this is a therapeutic massage."

"I can't do it, Rosie."

"You don't have to do anything. You get to just lie there."

And for a little while it did work, she had him like her old Theo, lusty and sure, everything she needed. She pressed his rigid hand to her breast, calling him by the old names, telling him how much she liked it, loved him, how good he was. Then he groaned and she felt him slip, diminish inside her. They moaned together, and she wanted him to laugh but he couldn't. He turned his face away, wouldn't let her kiss him.

"Christ, Rosie. I told you. Oh, Jesus Christ." He started to curse. He was ashamed of his tears, so she pretended she didn't see them. She slid down beside him, fumbling for the rumpled sheet.

"It doesn't matter." And she wasn't sorry she'd tried. She hugged their hips together with her outflung arm, pulling him hard against her.

He swore some more. "I hate when a woman says that."

She raised up over him. "You mean this has happened *before*?" But he wouldn't smile. "Oh, Theo, I know, but it really doesn't, it just doesn't matter."

"Matters the hell to me."

She stroked his stomach under his T-shirt, fluffing the soft hair under his navel. "Are you sorry? I'm not. Anyway, I don't have to make love with you to love you."

"Wouldn't hurt, though."

She wanted to cry, too, but she never did in front of him. She could cry for months. She went around like a woman at the end of a pregnancy, full, tight, but with sadness inside instead of a new life.

"When I get outta here." Theo tapped the fingers poking out of his cast against her arm. "It'll be better. We'll take that trip."

"On the *Wind Rose*."

"I need to get outta here. This is no place. For me. We'll take that trip."

"We will."

"Not ready. Not done yet."

"Absolutely not. We are not done yet."

She held him until he drifted off to sleep—a blessing; insomnia was one of his plagues. Then she slipped away like a ghost.

15

Hot. Anna's and Mason's sweaty hands stuck together, so they strolled back to the restaurant from the town dock without touching. Not much would have gotten Anna out in the broiling August sun at the hottest time of day on the hottest day of the year. Sex might have, but they hadn't so much as kissed. Too hot.

With her own two hands she'd made crostini with red peppers and goat cheese for a picnic, and they'd taken it out to a sweltering bench by the blinding water in the middle of a swarm of sweating tourists ogling the sailboats in the harbor. They'd stopped in the bookstore afterward, just for some shade and air conditioning, but she didn't have time to dawdle, too much work to do this afternoon.

Just the same, in front of the Bella Sorella, where a few wilted diners were still picking at lunch under the umbrellas, and it was time to say good-bye and part ways, Mason said, "Let's go around to the alley," and she said, "Okay."

If anything it was hotter here, and God knew it smelled worse, especially in the little nook behind the Dumpster. Their special place. It wasn't even private; kitchen staff came out in the alley to cool off, and Frankie came out to smoke. Everyone else smoked in the kitchen, which was expressly forbidden but ignored, but

Frankie wouldn't dream of it. It went against her code of conduct for the serious cook.

Leaning against the gritty brick wall in the aromatic shade of the garbage stockade, they started out with kissing, mouths touching and nothing else because it was so hot, but that didn't last. "Yuck," Anna mumbled, encircling her damp arms around Mason's damp neck and pressing against him.

"Yuck?"

"It's an endearment."

She thought about how close she'd come to missing out on this. "You are," she said between kisses, "the nicest man I know. I like everything about you. I like your nose. I like the way your fingers smell like photographic fixer." The scars on his face barely registered anymore; they were like someone else's mole or port-wine birthmark, there but irrelevant.

Sometimes this public petting they did in the alley got out of hand. They took it too far, and then they either had to cool off or do something about it. Once they did something about it in the office with the door locked, but too many people wanted in, and once in Mason's car, which was a Jeep with no backseat. That was an experience she wasn't anxious to repeat.

He smiled, but he didn't reply to her compliment, didn't say, "I like everything about you, too." She was used to that and didn't mind. She was the one who put things in words in this relationship. Their unspoken deal.

"I have to go away," he said. "On Monday, for four days."

"Where to?"

"Montana."

"*Montana.* What for?"

"Spruce grouse, blue grouse, wild turkey. It's for a magazine story about the Bitterroot Mountains."

"Wow, aren't you the gadabout these days. Will you fly?"

"Yes."

"Who'll hold your hand?"

"Whoever's in 12D."

"Will you take your gigantic suitcase?"

He had a way of dipping his knees and ducking his head when she teased him, like a boy, abashed and delighted. Consequently, she loved teasing him. "I've already got it packed."

"You're not even kidding. Did you pack your lucky bird?" She'd given him a stuffed toy vulture for a present, three feet high, hunched and menacing, cartoonishly fierce.

"I bought it a seat."

"Twelve F. You'll be surrounded." He could fly now, although it was still an ordeal, but he wasn't over being afraid of having another panic attack. Fear of fear, he called it, the core symptom of his disorder. And he still preferred to be either outside or in his own house, but he made himself go places, especially her house or the Bella Sorella. So far, so good.

"I'd better go in," she said. "Stuff to do."

"Me, too."

"We've got a full house tonight. First time this summer."

Their good-bye kiss turned into a prolonged grope. She was addicted to the way the shapes of their bodies fit together, just the right meeting of curves and flats. She loved it that he kissed with his mouth closed until *she* was ready for tongues. She hummed in his ear, not wanting to let go. "Dee-lish," she said in a sibilant whisper, making him shiver.

Another thing they never talked about was how they'd gotten back together. She didn't know why he wouldn't, but the reason she never did was because it seemed unkind and in poor taste to point out that she'd won. For the first time ever, she was carrying on a relationship completely on her terms. Fun, physical, and fleeting, she called it to herself. It was more than that, of course, but she liked the careless sound of the alliteration. Even though it was deceptive. They were living in the moment, and it was just what she wanted. Even Mason had to be feeling grateful to her by now for holding out for this. She was most men's dream lover. Clues that he wasn't as committed to the idyllic temporariness of things turned up from time to time, not in words but intangibles, looks, touching, that sort of thing, but she wisely ignored them. Not to acknowledge the thin line between dream lover and worst nightmare was one way to maintain the satisfying status quo.

" 'Bye," she said definitely, stepping back.

" 'Bye."

"See you tonight? I'll come over. It'll be late, though."

"I'll be home."

She blew him a kiss. Walking away, she heard a click, and knew it was his camera. A little habit of his she'd almost gotten used to. Strange, strange man. She couldn't wait for tonight.

"Where's Frankie?"

Carmen looked up from the red wine fish broth she was deglazing at the stove. "Outside. In front, talking to her ex."

"Really? Talking to Mike?"

"She left those duck breasts half done. Look at that. They're drying out," she complained, pointing her big spoon at the finely scored yellow breasts on the counter. "While she takes care of her personal business."

Anna walked out without answering.

She found Vince by the front window, peering out from the side in the shadow. "We're spying," she mentioned at his elbow.

"Something's wrong. Look at her."

"I can't see her face."

"You don't have to."

Mike was doing the talking. No jacket today; he had his sleeves rolled up, tie at half mast. Sweat made dark arcs under his arms and stuck his shirt to his back. He rubbed his neck, combed his beard, gestured. Talked and talked. Frankie kept her hands in the pockets of her enormous carpenter pants and her eyes on the sidewalk. The bill of her ball cap shaded her profile, but Vince was right. Something bad was happening.

She straightened up suddenly. She either cursed or said a very short word, and when she pushed past Mike her shoulder struck his, tilting him sideways. She came into the restaurant so fast, Anna and Vince didn't have time to pretend they were doing something else. It didn't matter: she marched back to the kitchen without looking in their direction. Mike stared at the front door for a while longer, a pained look around his mouth, eyes crinkled in distress behind his glasses. Then he clasped his hands behind his neck and walked away.

After a quick, hot debate, Anna convinced Vince their best course was to say and do nothing. None of their business, and if Frankie wanted to talk—not likely—she would. If she didn't, they'd only alienate her by pestering her.

"My prep's done, everything's set," Frankie announced an hour later in the office doorway.

Anna looked up from the computer. "Oh. Great. Well—"

"So I'm going home. I'm sorry, I can't work tonight, I'm sick."

"You are?" She stood up.

Frankie stepped back. She took a cigarette out of her T-shirt pocket and lit it one-handed, with a folded-over match in a matchbook. She waved it out in the air, the whole matchbook, and blew a hard stream of smoke at the ceiling. "Yeah, I've got something, don't come near me. Contagious."

"I heard Mike came by, Carmen mentioned it. I hope you're not upset—"

"Yeah, he came by, we talked. So, nothing. I need to go home. Can I? Carmen says she can live without me."

"Sure, of course, if you're not feeling well." Frankie had never taken a day off before, never so much as come in late.

"Thanks." She pivoted.

"Frankie?"

"Yo."

"Um, are you okay? I mean—"

"No, I'm *sick*. Didn't I just say that?" Her eyes blazed and her pale, tense face flushed. "Jesus Christ!"

"Okay—sorry—"

"Okay!" She disappeared.

She didn't come in the next day, either. Anna got the message from Carmen, who had trouble disguising her satisfaction. "Says she's got a bug, she doesn't want to spread it around." She had her thick arms folded across her middle, her chef's toque jammed low on her forehead. The singed-looking reddish hair sticking out around the sides gave her a sinister-clown look, especially when she scowled and smiled at the same time. "She didn't sound good."

"Well, if she's sick—"

"Sick, yeah, right."

Anna turned her back, unable to stomach the sneer. Carmen infuriated her. "At least she called."

"Before she couldn't dial."

"You'd like that, wouldn't you?" Fighting with Carmen was a no-win, but she felt goaded into it. "You'd love it if she fell off the wagon and ruined her life. *And* her kid's life."

"What?" Carmen looked genuinely shocked. "That's crap."

"Whatever." She left her in the kitchen and went to find Vince.

He was dropping glasses in the bar, he was so distracted. "She's never sick, never. That guy did something to her. I'm calling her up." The chef's knife he was supposed to be slicing lemons with was making a fine dice instead. Soon it would be zest. "Did you talk to her?"

"No, she called Carmen."

"How'd she sound?"

"Carmen says not good, but—"

"I'm calling her." He picked up the bar phone and punched the number. With his back turned, he reminded her of Frankie the last time she'd seen her: same cocked-gun stiffness in the shoulders, same brittle, balls-of-the-feet nervous tension. They both wanted a target, and there was nothing to shoot.

"No answer." He slammed down the phone. "No machine, even—and she's got a machine."

"She could be trying to sleep. If she's really sick, she—"

"She's not sick, you know it. Anyway, if she was sleeping, she wouldn't take the machine off so the phone could ring a hundred times."

"Okay. So—"

"She's in trouble. She's drinking. I'm going over there."

"Vince, I don't think that's a good idea."

"Why?"

"Well—probably she doesn't want to see you."

"You go, then."

"Me?"

"You're her friend. She likes you, she'd talk to you."

"She likes you, too. She's your friend, too."

They went around like that for a while. Then they both went to see Frankie.

They didn't tell anyone, meaning Carmen, where they were going. They said "an errand," and anyone who overheard assumed it was something to do with wine or liquor, Vince's department, an emergency pickup or a meeting with a wholesaler. "Back in an hour," they said.

Vince drove his car as if he knew where he was going. Frankie's neighborhood was south of town, a mean, dreary collection of run-down apartment buildings and beat-up duplexes on a four-lane boulevard famous for late-night drag races and drug busts. She could do better than this. She'd gotten three raises in four months, she could afford something respectable or at least quiet. She talked about moving out as soon as she got joint custody of Katie—as soon as having a nice place mattered. Until then, she was saving every cent. She'd bought a used car, but that was it; everything else went into a savings account for Katie, even though Mike didn't particularly need the money and that wasn't part of the divorce arrangement. She was building up credit for the custody judge, she said, proving she could be a responsible parent.

The parking lot beside her yellow-brick building was crowded with cars for midafternoon on a weekday. All the first-floor windows had bars. The front door was dark green metal, scratched and graffitied, with a deep dent down around car bumper–height. It wasn't locked and there was no buzzer.

The foyer smelled like cooking oil, dog shit, and pot. O'Malley, 3F, one of the tinny mailboxes said. They walked past the out-of-order sign on the elevator and took the stairs. On the first landing, a nursing mother, just a girl herself, sent Vince a sleepy smile. On the second, three boys, all about twelve, casually turned their backs to hide whatever deal they were negotiating, a joint, a gun, a dirty magazine. The third-floor hallway was empty, but behind the thin doors came canned television voices and the high, complaining squeals of children.

Vince knocked at 3F and stood back, flexing his shoulders, smoothing the line of beard on his chin with his knuckle, trying to look casual when he was jumping out of his skin. No answer. He knocked again. They cocked their heads, listening like dogs to the silence behind the door, weighing its sincerity. "She's in there," Vince decided. "Frankie?" He knocked harder, using his fist instead of his knuckles. "Hey, Frankie, it's me and Anna! Open up."

"In the interest of total harrassment," Anna said, rooting her cell phone out of her purse. She dialed Frankie's number. Faint ringing inside the apartment and in her ear: stereo. But no answer. "Hey, hold it," she said, alarmed when Vince started using his foot on the door.

"I don't care, she's in there."

"Okay, but still, we can't break the door down."

"Why not?"

"Vince."

They were staring at each other hopelessly when the clump of fast footsteps on the stairway made them turn. Frankie walked around the corner, hands on her hips, head down, panting; she didn't see them until she was midway down the hall. She stopped. She had on tight black running shorts and a sweat-soaked tank, a terry headband around her egg-white skull. "Hey," she said, more accusation than greeting. She approached looking stoical but disbelieving. "What's up?"

"We... we wanted to see how you were feeling," Anna came up with. "Guess you're better. That's good."

Frankie bent over and scrounged a key out of the side of her sock. Unlocked the door, went in. She didn't invite them in, but she left the door open behind her. They looked at each other. Anna felt sheepish, but Vince looked nothing but glad. They went inside.

The apartment was one room and a kitchen. Frankie slept on a sofa-bed, currently out and unmade. She flipped it closed with one hand, rumpled sheets and all, then tossed cushions on it. Her body language broadcast carelessness and disdain and resentment. She dripped perspiration from every pore, like a prizefighter after a tough ten-rounder, flyweight division.

"Want anything?" She had a waist-high refrigerator in the postage stamp kitchen. "All I got is water."

"Oh no, thanks," they said in unison.

She took out a bottle and drank half of it without stopping. Still not looking at them, she put her hands on the wall and began to do leg stretches, extending her ropy calves behind her, flexing slowly, athletically.

Except for the unmade bed, the place was depressingly tidy. More mess would've disguised the grimness. The smell of stale cigarette smoke hung in the under-air-conditioned air, but even the ashtrays were clean. The decor was Early Katie, with pictures either of or by Katie taped to the walls and various constructions of clay or papier mâché on the horizontal surfaces. No TV, but a cheap boombox on the radiator, surrounded by stacks of CDs by rap and hip-hop singers Anna had never heard of. Cookbooks littered the back of the couch, and one paperback novel with a clinch cover—a romance. Anna turned her eyes away from it quickly. She'd seen something she wasn't supposed to see. It moved her in a funny, painful way.

"Hey, look here, you got him a bigger bowl."

Anna went over to see what Vince was crouched over on the deep windowsill. A turtle, brown with yellow spots on his dented shell. Sebastian, she assumed. Vince picked it up, and it retracted its sleepy head halfway and waved its scaly, sharp-toed feet in the air. "And toys," he said wonderingly. "You got him a water slide."

Frankie snorted. "It's not a water slide. It's just—I found a rock when I was out running. It slants, that's all."

"Does he like it?"

"Jesus, Vince. How the fuck do I know?"

He set the turtle back on its slanted rock carefully and stared out the window.

"Sorry we disturbed you," Anna said stiffly. "Vince and I, we didn't know if you were okay or not and we came over to check. We didn't mean to intrude on your privacy."

Already flushed from her run, Frankie's cheeks bloomed redder. "Yeah, it's fine. It's—nice to see you."

"We were afraid you might be upset."

She looked between them, worry-eyed, clenching her hands indecisively. "Mike's getting married." She let her shoulders sag. Just like that, she gave up being tough.

"Oh, Frankie, no."

Vince didn't say anything.

"Yeah, and it kinda hit me, that's all. I'd been thinking something else might happen, so this one blindsided me, that's all. I didn't drink. If that's what you were worried about." She sneered that, but the defiance died out as fast as it flared. "Not that I didn't want to. Last night... well, anyway. Bad night, but I take 'em one at a time, so. So that's it."

"I'm really sorry. I know you were hoping..." It was hard to sympathize with Vince here. Talking about how cut up Frankie was over Mike couldn't be any fun for him. She wished she'd come alone.

He finally said something. "The guy's an asshole."

Frankie frowned, puzzled and disapproving. Then she gave a crooked grin. "Hey, but here's some good news—Luca wants to marry me." She laughed when all Anna and Vince could do was stare. "Yeah, instant family. Whaddaya think? A girl could do worse."

"Um," Anna said, feeling her way. "Well, um—"

"*Are you out of your mind?*"

"Relax," she told Vince, who was all but standing on his toes, "I said no. Anyway, it's Katie he wants, not me. Luca just wants a kid, and I happen to have one."

Anna didn't think it was quite that simple, but she approved of Frankie's decision. Poor Luca.

"So, okay," Frankie said, "I'll be in to work tomorrow. I'd come in tonight, but I got a meeting. I can't miss it."

"That's okay, forget about tonight. But tomorrow, that would be great."

"Okay."

Nothing to do then but leave. Anna said, "Maybe we could do something after work tomorrow night. You know, if you feel like it." Not since Nicole had she suggested such a thing to another woman, she realized. A girlfriend invitation.

Frankie said, "Yeah, maybe."

At the door, Anna looked questioningly at Vince, who hadn't moved.

"Be down in a sec," he said.

"Oh. Sure. See you," she said to Frankie, and hurried out.

Vince had the key to his locked car. She didn't have to wait long in the hot parking lot, just long enough to consider how easy it would be to fall back on old bad habits if you lived in a place like this. How strong you'd have to be in yourself to stay clean and straight here. It wasn't a real slum, not even a project, but it was depressing as hell. No wonder Frankie didn't mind long hours in the kitchen. There was chaos there, too, but she could control it, master it. The one place her toughness worked.

Vince stalked out. He wore a black scowl and he didn't talk. He ground the gears and left rubber in the parking lot peeling out.

"What happened? Are you all right? Would you mind slowing down?"

They came to a red light, so he had to. "She's driving me crazy."

"What's going on?"

He glanced at Anna, then back at the road. "I hate where she lives, so I asked her if she wanted to move in with me."

"You did?"

"Like a roommate, share expenses, that's all. Pool resources."

"She said no," Anna guessed.

"She said"—he mimicked Frankie's nastiest voice—" 'Hey, yeah, Vince, that's how I'll get my kid back, I'll shack up with a bartender.' "

Anna made a disgusted sound, for sympathy. "She didn't mean that. Frankie says stuff."

"Then it was like she felt sorry for me, or she was just sick of dealing with me. She said, 'Look, you want to hook up? Okay, let's do it, let's just get it over with.' "

"Oh, Vince."

"She says, 'Gimme five minutes, I'll take a shower.' " His voice was raw; he sounded close to tears.

"What did you say?"

"Nothing. I left."

"Good."

"I can't help it, I can't let it go. She's got me. I think I'm in love with her." He tried to laugh. "It's not even physical, you know? If we ever made it, it would be bad, it would be terrible. I mean, it's not like she's even sexy."

"Love stinks," Anna said. "I don't see how anybody makes it last."

He drove in silence for a while, at a reasonable speed. "My folks did. They were nuts for each other till Pop died."

She thought of Aunt Iris and Uncle Tony, how they'd seemed younger to her than her own parents when she was little. They'd had a flirty way of fighting, and nicknames for each other, "Sugar Babe," "Pretty Boy," exaggerated endearments they used for laughs. Seeing them hold hands or put their arms around each other had fascinated her as a child, because that sort of thing rarely happened between her parents. Aunt Iris and Uncle Tony had been a little shocking.

"I'm not giving up," Vince said, rallying, confirming Anna's suspicion that between them, she was more cynical in the love department. "Frankie doesn't know me, that's her problem. She doesn't take me seriously. Now Mike's out of the picture, maybe she'll look around. I've got nothing but time." He sat back, drove the car with his wrist over the wheel.

"That's the spirit. Frankie won't know what hit her."

You wanted what you were used to, she supposed. The play your parents performed for you in your childhood. She thought of Mason, and what she wanted from him. Not much. That seemed about right.

16

"You have got to do something about Carmen. No, Rose, I'm serious, you have to do something."

"What is it this time?" The headache she'd been fighting all morning began to throb again behind her right eyebrow. Migraine? She hadn't had one of those since menopause.

"It's—she's—" Anna came into the office in a burst of jerky negative energy. She probably didn't mean to slam the door, but the sharp bang jolted through Rose's system like jagged electricity. "It's the kitchen. She won't listen."

"Ah. Be more specific."

"Frankie's got great ideas for redoing the layout to make things flow, you know, keep people from banging into each other, cut down on the steps you have to take to get from one—"

"Right, yes." Frankie wanted to do things like move the plate elevator, which was directly behind the big range, closer to the dishwasher so Dwayne or his daytime counterpart didn't body-slam servers on their way to and from the line.

"Carmen won't cooperate! Every suggestion, she shoots it down like it's the stupidest thing she's ever heard. And everything's personal—it's like Frankie wants to rearrange the furniture in Carmen's bedroom. I'm sick of dealing with her. She's stubborn, she's shortsighted, she's impossible."

I'm sick of dealing with both of you, Rose thought but didn't say. Sometimes, when she was feeling especially empty and wrung out, she suspected Anna enjoyed making things up to fight about. Otherwise, they would be getting along too well, and she couldn't have that.

"So will you talk to her?"

"Yes, all right," Rose said, although she had no energy for it. She felt... finite, her brain only able to hold so much, and all the available space was currently taken by Theo. It was hard to care about all this kitchen sniping, hard not to resent strong, healthy Anna striding around, venting her petty frustrations over Carmen, when Theo could barely swallow solid food anymore.

"It's more than that," Anna said. She braced her hands on the desk and leaned in close.

Rose leaned back. Guilt was all that kept her from snapping, "I don't have *time* for this." Anna spent more time in this chair than she did these days; she felt as if she should get up and switch places.

"Rose," Anna said earnestly, "most chefs would rather work alone, that's just how they are, but a good chef has to fight that impulse and work with a *team*. Don't you agree?"

"Yes," she said cautiously.

"It's not even enough to be creative and motivated and imaginative and innovative—none of which Carmen is, if you ask me, all she is is a hard worker. A real chef has to know how to get the best out of people, *inspire* people. Whatever the chef's like, the kitchen's going to be like, because the chef sets the tone."

"All right."

"Fun, grim, nightmare, paradise—the chef is the one who—who—puts on the music everybody else dances to. Am I—"

"Yes, Anna, I—"

"Okay—but not only that, she has to really care about *people*. Right? She has to *like* them. She has to be a generous person inside herself, or else what's the point of making food? Where's the passion going to come from year after year, hardship after hardship, if you don't give a flick about the people you're supposed to be trying to serve?"

"What are you saying, you want Carmen—what? Out?"

"I want her not to be the chef." Anna straightened up, turning stern and righteous. Getting to the point brought out a militaristic streak in her. "Frankie should be the chef. If you can't fire Carmen—"

"Fire Carmen!"

"—then give her a new title, I don't know what. Not executive chef, something meaningless, and tell her you're worried about her health or something, you want her to consult."

"Consult?"

"Kick her upstairs." She jerked her head toward the ceiling—a pun, and another sore point with Anna, the fact that Carmen sublet from Rose the apartment upstairs for almost nothing. A sinecure, she called it, disapproving because Rose hadn't raised Carmen's rent in about fifteen years. With money so tight, Rose should either make her pay what it was worth or lease it to someone who would. That's what Anna thought.

"Slow down," Rose said, "let's take this a piece at a time. First of all, let me talk to her, maybe I can smooth it over, this kitchen design thing."

"You probably can, and then something else will pop up tomorrow."

"Then we'll—"

"Rose, she's not a nice person. She's bitter, she's an old maid, she's not happy."

"She's family."

"The Bella Sorella is family! Billy Sanchez is family, Vonnie's family. The people who love it and want it to work, they're family. Carmen—she knows food and she works hard, okay, and she's not a bad cook, but she stopped learning anything new about twenty years ago!"

"She *can* change. I'll speak to her. Anna—Anna, put yourself in her place. Of course she resents Frankie, she's everything Carmen isn't, young, strong, excited about the business—"

"Exactly! She's excited about the business. That's what you want for your chef!"

Rose shook her head. "I said I'd speak to her, but my dear, Carmen is the chef. We'll have to solve this some other way."

"Right." She marched to the door.

"Wait—don't be angry."

"I'm not." But obviously that wasn't true. This time when she slammed the door, she meant to.

Rose pressed the heel of her hand against her throbbing right temple. That used to work in the old days. For a minute or two. Migraine at her age? Ridiculous; stress, more likely. Her fault. How had she gotten herself into a relationship with Anna where only one of them was allowed to get mad?

Iris called on Rose's cell phone when she was sitting with Theo, reading the newspaper to him while he half listened, half dozed on the bed, propped up on his pillows. They chatted for a few minutes, then Rose carried the phone out into the hall so she wouldn't disturb him. And so she could tell Iris how he really was.

"He's not mad anymore—that's what scares me the most. He just lies there."

"What do you mean, he's not mad anymore?"

"He used to say this was temporary, as soon as his wrist healed he was moving back to his boat. He *hated* this place. He still hates it, but he doesn't care anymore."

There was a pause, and Rose knew Iris was trying to think of a way to turn that into a positive. Iris the realist, the blunt, plainspoken, some would say the tactless sister, had turned into a Pollyana where Theo was concerned. Rose found it an unexpected comfort to be the pessimistic one for a change, the deliverer of unadorned bad news, at least with one other person. With Iris she could sound as hopeless as she felt.

"Well," Iris said staunchly, "acceptance is a good thing, isn't it? And what a relief for you, not to have to keep the secret from him anymore. You hated that, not telling him what was going on."

"But we've never talked about that."

"Oh. You haven't?"

"Mason and I decided to let it go for now, so I don't know what he thinks. About the future. He still talks about us taking a trip someday on the sailboat."

"Well, that's good. I guess, something to look forward to."

"It's a new kind of lethargy. The aides get him up a couple of times a day, and I make him walk with me when I come, just up and down the hall. Mason takes him outside. But if we didn't make him get up, he'd lie in that bed all day, staring out the window."

"Oh, honey."

The night nurse on the wing, a stout, platinum-haired woman named Shirley, walked by. With raised eyebrows and a pleasant smile, she tapped on the face of her watch.

"I've got to go, Iris, they're shooing me out."

"They're not too strict about closing at ten o'clock, are they?"

"No, they're wonderful. I stay till eleven almost every time I come." It was quarter to eleven now.

"Give Theo a hug for me."

"I will."

"Night, Rose. You try not to worry."

Theo had turned off his bedside table lamp. Did he think she'd gone home? The night light he hated—because he couldn't turn it off—glowed palely in the corner, bluing the room and casting faint shadows. She padded to the bed on tiptoes; if he was asleep, she didn't want to wake him just to say good-bye.

No, his eyes were open. He blinked at her, the only way he could smile these days. "Hey, babe," she whispered. "I'm going to go on now. It's pretty late."

He moved his lips, preparing to say something. His speech became more halting as the day wore on; by nighttime, he was often too tired to talk at all. "Jean," he said. His rigid hand fluttered on the sheet over his chest. "Wondered if you'd come."

She kept her face soft. This had happened twice before, so it didn't sting quite so much this time. "It's Rose." She took his hand between both of hers. "It's Rose, Theo."

"Rose." He nodded, agreeing. "Better—get going. Late."

"Yes, I'd better." She kissed him, letting her lips linger on his for a moment, and when she straightened, his eyes were alive with tenderness and appreciation.

"Love you," he got out. Without prompting, for once. "Love you, Rose."

Sometimes he couldn't let go once he'd grasped something; she had to pry his fingers, one at a time, from their stiff grip around her hand. She'd make a joke, "Just can't bear to let me go, eh?" Tonight she didn't have the heart.

Driving home, she let herself cry for a minute, really just a few seconds. She started at a red light, and by the time it turned green she was all right, herself again. Theo calling her by his long-dead ex-wife's name, Jean—Mason's mother—that's what had set her off, but not because of jealousy. She'd never been jealous of Jean, a woman Theo had loved but should never have married. He could have called Rose any name—*that's* what upset her, the fact that, three times now, he hadn't known her. There were other examples, little things, losing his way coming back from dinner, forgetting what she'd just told him, or not understanding it, making her explain the simplest thing over and over. The doctor had said, "Yes, in part," when she'd asked if it was because of the medications he took for his muscle spasms. She didn't like *in part.*

Summer was almost over. This morning she'd seen yellow poplar leaves falling on the dry wind like fireflies. At night the cicadas were deafening, drowning out everything with that raucous, panicked drone they made at the end of their cycle, end of their lives. The days were still hot, but there was a tiredness in the air that said fall was coming, no mistaking it. All the trees looked weary, burdened. Too heavy to last much longer.

The phone in her purse rang. She hated talking on the phone in the car. She almost let it ring, but what if it was Theo, some emergency at the nursing home—

"Hello?"

"Carmen fired Frankie."

"What? Anna?"

"I just heard. I wasn't there, I'm at home."

"What happened?"

"I'll tell you what happened. After dinner service, Carmen told Frankie she had to clean out the grease trap."

"No. No, I'm sure that was a misunderstanding."

"No misunderstanding. She did it on purpose, because she knew Frankie would refuse because it's not her job, it's ten o'clock at night, and it's—it's punitive, an *insult.* She did it so she'd quit." Anna's voice sounded metallic with anger, vibrating with it.

"Well, we'll straighten it out tomorrow," Rose said, taking her hand off the wheel to put on her turn signal. "I'm sure it's—"

"I already hired her back."

"Ah. You—"

"They can't work together, Rose, one of them has to go."

"Well, that may be true. That may be true."

"I want you to fire Carmen."

She turned her face upward, not wanting Anna to hear her tired sigh through the mouthpiece. "We went through this before."

"I want you to make Frankie head chef."

"Yes, I know. But I can't do that."

"Then Frankie's going to quit."

"I hope we can avoid that. I know I haven't given enough attention to this problem, I've been—"

"And if Frankie goes, I go."

Rose braked hard for a light she didn't see until she was almost through it.

"It would just be sooner rather than later. I was going anyway, you knew that. So—it's nothing new. Just sooner instead of later. Rose?"

"This is the excuse—this is what you're going to use? This business with Carmen?"

"It's not an excuse. What do you mean?"

"But why now? That's what I don't understand. Was it getting too good?"

"Pardon me?"

"Did you catch yourself—not even remembering why you were so angry? What it was about me you hated? That must've been scary for you."

"Look. That's—I don't even—Could we stick to the point here? Are you going to fire Carmen or aren't you?"

"No, of course not."

"Fine. Here's my two weeks' notice. I'm not mad, Rose. This is one of those things, an honest difference of opinion. As I said, it's just happening sooner instead of—"

"*I'm* mad," Rose said, and clicked off.

What has my life been? Losing Theo slowly, one day at a time, had a side effect of exposing dusty corners, dark places Rose normally kept covered up; not buried or hidden, just decently out of sight, if only because they weren't useful or profitable. *What has my life been?* She had had two lovers, innumerable friends, the community of her restaurant. She had a sister. But it was Anna she had loved the most, Anna, the one who had given her the most pain. She'd lost her father, her sister, her mother, Paul, now Theo, but

Anna's ill-will and her disappointment were the chronic wound, the one that would not heal. Rose had never been able to revile her for cruelty—her own guilty conscience would've called that hypocrisy. But this was too much. She hadn't done enough to deserve this.

At Harvard Street she turned left instead of right, back toward town. Heat lightning flared in the pink haze of sky over the black treeline. Anna's neighborhood, oak-shaded Cape Cods and modest colonials, hadn't changed much over the years. Rose would drive past the house, Paul's house, once in a blue moon, pulled by nostalgia or homesickness, but she hadn't been inside since his funeral. Not since she and Anna had had their last fight, as it happened. A fitting setting, then.

She parked on the street near the tiny driveway, sending the neighbor's dog into a bored frenzy. Lights were on downstairs, not upstairs. Good, she was still up. Not that Rose cared.

She wouldn't get sidetracked by memories. She knocked smartly on the freshly painted red door, and when Anna opened up she greeted her with, "Don't you know not to open your door at night until you know who it is?"

"Rose. What a . . ."

"Unexpected pleasure." She moved inside when Anna couldn't seem to form the words "Come in." The house had a neglected, unlived-in look. Anna talked about refurbishing it to sell, but then she never did anything. It looked different and the same, the small foyer, the living room on the left, dining room—still with packed cardboard boxes in stacks on the table—on the right. Maybe Anna had never unpacked them; maybe they traveled with her from town to town, year to year, bulky tributes to impermanence.

"I was making some tea," she said, staring hard at Rose, searching for a clue to tell her what was going on. She was barefoot, but still in the same clothes she'd worn all day: wrinkled straight skirt and tight white blouse. Her face was shiny with fatigue and tense with watchfulness. "Have a cup with me?"

"I didn't really come here for tea." But Anna either didn't hear or pretended not to, and Rose shrugged to herself and followed her into the kitchen.

Same and different again. The table was chipped enamel instead of scarred oak, but still in the only place it could be in such a small room, on the back wall by the door that led to the den. She'd helped Anna with her homework at that table. Talked and listened to her, cried with her over Lily. Cried with Paul, too, and served him meals he ate at midnight, tired from his long drives home. Had she stolen Lily's family, then? Was that what Anna thought?

She was fiddling with cups and saucers, teabags and sugar. Pointedly, Rose took the steaming cup she handed her and set it on the sink counter without tasting it. "I think it's time we had a talk."

"What about?"

"Your mother and father."

"Oh, I don't."

"I do. You'll be leaving soon, and I want you to know something before you go."

"You won't change my mind."

"Of course not. That might prove you've grown up."

Hot fury flashed between them. Anna's head snapped up and her nostrils flared. Just as quickly, she caught her temper and beat it back under control. Rose followed her lead; it would feel good, but they'd get nowhere shouting bitter things.

She leaned back on her hands against the counter. "You asked me how Lily and Paul met."

"In the restaurant. That's what you said. Was that a lie?"

Rose stared at her until Anna had to drop her eyes, stirring and stirring her dark red tea.

"He thought I was his waitress," she said slowly. "He asked me for some ketchup. I told him I was a cook, that I was just taking a break. He liked that, that I was a chef. He started talking about Italian food, and what a terrible cook his mother was. He was sitting at a front window table, the one in the corner. He talked a lot, but he was shy. Very handsome. I told him I liked his accent—he said he didn't have an accent. He was so embarrassed when he couldn't find his wallet. I teased him to set him at ease. Comped him his three-dollar lunch and lent him gas money to get home. He promised to come in and pay me back the next time he was in town."

"Where was my—"

"Lily was hostessing. When he came back with his wallet—remember, he found it in his car—I introduced them."

"Yes? And then?"

"He asked me to have dinner with him."

"You?"

"Not Lily."

Anna's eyes were unreadable, her lips a tight, skeptical line.

"Mama let me out of dinner service, and he took me to a band concert on the water. He talked through the whole thing. He was an amateur inventor, he played the trombone and the banjo, he was a reader of great books, a correspondence course taker. He wanted to have his own bookstore, he wanted to sail down the Mississippi on a houseboat, he wanted to live in San Francisco, see Europe, raise collies. When he brought me home, we sat on the front steps and talked for two more hours. Oh, how he could talk. Mama liked him. She said he reminded her of Papa."

"Well. Go on," Anna said when Rose paused. "This is fascinating."

She ignored the implication that it was a story, something she was making up. Let Anna keep her defenses as long as she could if it made her feel better.

"We fell in love," she said bluntly. "First time, for me—I was only twenty-one. Young, I know, but it felt like love. It was love. Lily claimed not even to like him. She made fun of how skinny he was, how he talked too much, how he could never do all the things he said he wanted to do if he lived six lifetimes. I was used to that, though. Lily never liked it when I had something she didn't."

"My mother was jealous of *you*?"

"Hard to believe. She was the pretty, vivacious one, everyone said so. But she could still be jealous. And selfish, and possessive. She was insecure. Do you really not know this? She couldn't be happy for long. I loved her because she was funny and sweet and generous—if it was just us, nothing outside the two of us for her to crave or to covet, she was a wonderful sister. But she couldn't stand it that Paul loved me, and she took him away from me."

"I don't believe you."

"I know. It happened when we went to the beach for a long weekend. Six of us rented a cottage at Bethany—Iris and Tony and little Theresa—she was four, their only child then—and Paul and me. And Lily. Iris and Tony were the chaperones. There were three rooms—"

"I don't want to hear this."

"I don't want to talk about it."

"Bullshit. You're *dying* to tell me."

Was she? She wasn't dying to tell her that Lily had played and flirted with Paul all weekend in a strange, confusing way, touching him as she passed by, a hand trailing across his back or his shoulders, or pinching him teasingly, leaning against him to laugh at something he said. Rose had watched Paul watch Lily—who was so lovely, fair and feminine and shapely, not straight and tall and dark like her. Lily was a natural flirt, sexually powerful, and unlike Rose, not a virgin. But Rose had only been angry, not worried. And only angry at Lily, not Paul.

"She seduced him. On the last night."

"I can ask Aunt Iris if any of this is true, you know."

"Please do."

Anna's eyes burned with a look that could only be called loathing. "Why tell me this now?"

"Because I'm sick of keeping it from you."

"I know why—for the same reason you told me Theo's worse, Theo's dying. So I'll feel sorry for you. So I'll stay." She came closer, enunciated clearly. "Fat chance." She set her teacup down with a clatter and walked out.

Rose followed. "Lily and I had a room together. She waited until I was asleep and then she went to him. He had no excuse, none. He wouldn't vilify her, afterward, but she overpowered him—that's what happened."

Anna laughed. "*Overpowered him*?" She prowled around the dusty living room, unable to sit, picking things up and putting them down.

"The next day, she told me what she'd done. She couldn't wait to tell me. She said they loved each other. She was so sorry they'd hurt me, but it was too strong, they couldn't help themselves. Paul—Paul—"

"Yes? Don't stop now."

"Paul couldn't explain what he didn't understand himself. I broke it off. I wouldn't listen to his apologies, which—" she laughed thinly—"were not very sympathetic. And so Lily got him. Six weeks later, they married." She might've left it at that, but Anna had a sour, triumphant look on her face that was galling, as if Lily's victory were *her* victory. Rose was sick of protecting her. "They married because she was pregnant. With you."

Anna went paper-white. She sat down hard on the arm of the sofa.

"Mama wasn't even angry. That felt like another betrayal to me. But she loved Paul by then. Lily *should* get married before me, she said, because she was older."

"Why don't you just cut to the chase." Anna's wavery voice sounded high and childish. "When did you start cheating on her?"

"You know when."

"No, I don't."

"That night you saw us. Here. Right in this room, right by that window."

"That's what you say."

"Do you think I'm lying?"

"For thirteen years you just—*pined* for each other?"

"Yes."

She snorted. "Why should I believe you? For all I know, you were sneaking around behind her back for years! Maybe from the beginning—your own sister—maybe you made her whole marriage a lie."

"No. You can believe what you like, but we never touched each other until that night. At first, it was easy. I was so *angry*—I didn't *want* him. And we all pretended so well, all three of us, a conspiracy of silence for the sake of peace. Years went by before I knew that nothing had changed between Paul and me—no, that's not true, everything was much worse because we were older. I was a woman, not a girl, and I was afraid he was the only man I could love. Lily had a husband and a child, but she wasn't happy because she couldn't believe she could keep them.

"Once when you were very little, only a baby, she—wouldn't let me hold you. We couldn't talk about it, we *never* talked about it, but that time, just that once, I said, 'Lily, you've got Paul, can't you let me love this little girl?' After that, she let us be whatever we were going to be—you and me. It was the kindest thing she ever did. I always thought of it as—a recompense."

Tears kept welling in Anna's eyes and spilling down her cheeks, uncontrollable. She backhanded them away angrily. "Say anything you like, put any spin on it you can. She was *dying*. The cruelest time, the ugliest time—why couldn't you wait?" She stood up, shaking. "Was my mother taking too long?"

"Did you know—the world doesn't revolve around you? That what happened between your father and me had *nothing to do with you*? Can you *ever* realize that?"

"Why couldn't you wait for her to die?"

"Who are you? You're not me, you're not my mother. You can't know what it was like to be losing a sister, to be grieving—"

"Grieving, ha—"

"To have lost Paul to her and to see him beaten down by the lie his life had turned into—"

"Why couldn't you wait! Why!"

"Because I didn't want to! I wanted him back. *While* she was alive—yes!"

"To even the score."

"Yes! She stole him from me—I stole him back!"

"People don't *steal* people. You betrayed your own sister, that's what you did."

"All right—that's what I did."

"And I'm not getting over it. It hurts." Anna's face collapsed like a child's.

"*Life* hurts. And you're right, people don't steal people. That woman you hate, that Nicole—she didn't steal Jay from you, either."

Anna blanched. *Low blow*, her dark, naked eyes said, but Rose didn't agree. "I don't forgive you. I never will." She spun around. Her purse was on the gateleg table in the hall; she fumbled in it for something. Keys: they fell on the floor with a clatter.

"If I needed anyone's forgiveness, it wouldn't be yours, it would be Lily's."

"That's not true. You need mine, but I don't forgive you."

"Are you *leaving*? How perfect. How perfect."

The straps on Anna's purse were tangled; she kept pulling, tugging, trying to get them to go over her shoulder.

"You could tell *me* to leave. But I guess that wouldn't be as satisfying."

She gave up on the purse and strode to the door.

"To think I actually considered firing Carmen for you."

Anna sent her a bitter look and yanked open the door.

Rose went after and called out into the dark yard. "Talk about 'family'! Carmen knows about loyalty—she'd never leave like this—for nothing, for another job that doesn't even exist yet, for strangers—for nothing!"

She'd set the neighbor's dog off again. Anna had trouble unlocking her car door. When she got in, she slammed it repeatedly before it closed right, the last time with such force, it shut the dog up for a second. She backed up without looking, and screeched off down sleepy Day Street as if monsters were chasing her.

"That went well," Rose said out loud. It didn't work, though, didn't save the day with a little bravehearted levity.

The truth, whatever that was, had never seemed so insignificant to her. It didn't change anything, not if the damage had already been done. She'd thought she had nothing to lose by telling it, everything to gain if the gamble paid off. But she'd bet wrong, and now she had less than before. As soon as this high wore off, this righteous, anger-fueled elation, the poverty of what she had left was going to sink her.

17

She felt set upon, besieged. Victimized, but not like Sylvia Plath. More like St. Stephen, shot through with arrows. Why the shock, though, why be surprised? Rose had always been able to hurt her, this was nothing new. But she felt blindsided, caught off guard. Lulled by Rose into a false sense of security, then *whack*, cut off at the knees. She turned the radio up for a distraction, but the staticky rock station only stretched her nerves tighter. She felt endangered. She needed a safe haven.

In high school she used to go to a cove on the Severn and neck with a boy named Scottie McGrady. Baldwin's Cove, it was called, nothing but a spit of sand between pine wood tracks, a little bit of beach and some boulders. She'd even gone by herself once in a while, to hang out and think, sit on a rock and throw pebbles in the water. Plan her life.

But they'd killed it. Now it was Trelawny Landing, a gated community of million-dollar wooded estates hugging the river. She backed out in the turnaround beside the guard's kiosk and drove north. Another high school habit was circling the Baltimore Beltway, but in those days driving was the end, you went around and around in your parents' car for the pure pleasure of being on the road and on your own. Anna got as far as the Pikesville exit, turned around, and came back.

She couldn't stand it, she hated how she felt, half-born, as if she was in labor but she was the child instead of the mother. She couldn't go home. She didn't know what to do with herself.

She'd go see Mason. That had been her first impulse, but she felt prickly and sharp, cactus woman, no one could fit next to her, not even him. Or was it some intimation that he wouldn't be as sympathetic as she needed him to be? But she loved his generosity, the way he would let her use him if he knew she needed to. She took him for granted already, and that was odd—it wasn't as if she'd known a lot of men like him before. Something in her must think she deserved him.

His house was dark. What time was it? Christ, midnight already. He kept healthy hours, in bed by eleven-thirty, up at seven. When she stayed over, she disrupted his schedule, but he didn't mind. He said she made it worth his while.

Her car tires on the gravel made a loud crunch, and her slamming door exploded in the silence, startling the crickets. From inside the house, Theo's old dog didn't make a sound, though: he was deaf. "Ow, ow, ow," Anna muttered, hopping and limping across the sharp stones. Stupid to leave home with no shoes, but she'd been in a hurry.

She used the knocker on the front door, and presently she heard sounds inside. Mason should get a peephole. The problem with no front windows was that he never knew who was at the door until he opened it.

"Hi."

"Hi." His sleepy grin was the nicest thing she'd seen all day. He had on cutoff sweatpants and nothing else, and that looked pretty nice, too. Cork sidled around his legs, saw who it was, and wagged his tail.

"Sorry it's so late. Guess I woke you up. Can I come in?"

"Sure." He looked at her more closely. "What's wrong?"

"Oh...I just need somebody to tell me I'm not a selfish, heartless bitch." Was she going to cry again?

"I can do that."

"Preferably with their arms around me."

He put his arms around her, and she relaxed into his drowsy warmth, liking his skin and his shaggy hair, the friendly prickle of his whiskers. *Now I'm okay*, she thought, and wondered if she was in love with him. She wanted to go to bed with him, no question about that. She wanted the sweaty ritual of sex, and especially the obliteration at the end. She wanted to use him.

"What's wrong?" he asked again. "What happened?"

"It's Rose."

He pushed her away to see her face. "Is she all right?"

"Yeah." She shrugged his hands off her arms. "She's fine."

She went past him, through the dark living room to the kitchen. She turned on the bright overhead light and got a glass from the cabinet, filled it at the sink. Mason, leaning in the doorway, watched her drink tepid tap water.

"No shoes," he noticed.

"I had to move fast." She prowled around the neat, shiny room. "No wounded birds today." They were doing a replay of the first time they'd met. Except she'd been in a better mood that day. "What's this?" On the kitchen table, wide folds of nylon cloth in camouflage colors, sewed onto big plastic circles—hula hoops, they looked like.

"Something I'm making."

"What is it?"

"A hoop blind."

"What's it do?"

He came over, took the voluminous contraption out of her hands. "Well, you get inside. It covers you up completely. This is for a telephoto lens, this hole. It's for taking pictures from the water—the hoops collapse the farther in you wade. You can go in up to your chin."

"You must look pretty silly."

"Yes, but that's the idea. The birds relax because they're laughing so hard."

"Rose and I had a fight. It's been coming on for a while, I guess. Although *I* didn't know it—I thought we were doing pretty well."

"What did you fight about?"

"My mother. My father."

Mason sat on the edge of the table, crossed his feet, crossed his arms. Waiting for the story. The possibility that he might not automatically take her side occurred to her again. It gave her a queasy feeling.

"I don't want to get into it," she decided, "all the gory details. Too boring for you. Suffice it to say, she tried to rewrite history, but it didn't work on me. I still like my mother."

She had a cache of memories, a collection of the good times, sweet times. Her mother with her hands over her face, shoulders shaking, trying not to laugh in church—her mother letting Anna miss school the next day so they could stay up late and watch the Academy Awards—her mother yelling delicious obscenities at the neighbor woman whose obnoxious son had pulled Anna off a seesaw and bloodied her nose. At the Bella Sorella, she'd worn straight skirts and crisp, tailored blouses, and her high heels had made a smart, decisive clacking sound, so businesslike and irrefutable. She'd had a gay, controlled laugh, slightly theatrical; Anna had delighted in it and tried to provoke it, but it hadn't come often enough.

She had other memories, not such nice ones, and it rankled that Rose's so-called *revelations* had opened the door to them as well. She remembered when her mother had been inaccessible to her, literally not there because she was in her bedroom with the door locked, usually in the wake of a fight with her father. "She's just tired," he would explain to Anna, the two of them at the kitchen table eating his improvised supper of canned chili or scrambled eggs, furtively listening for a sound overhead. They would treat each other with strained care and extra politeness, and her father would minimize the last shouting match by calling her mother "high strung" or "not quite herself." Her mother wasn't so reticent. "Stupid *sciocco*, I can't live like this, I'll go mad!" and then the inevitable slammed door. Anna would skulk around the house as if one false step might blow it up, but she never knew what was best to do, make noise, be quiet, act natural, act like a mourner at a wake. Nothing worked twice anyway; her mother had her own agenda, and her sudden recoveries were as unpredictable as her declines.

Mason made his voice irritatingly reasonable. "Do you really think Rose was trying to discredit your mother? Blacken her memory for you—"

"Yes, Mason. Yes, I do."

"Because it doesn't sound to me like something she'd—"

"I told you, we were fighting. Gloves off. She told me"—this would wipe that *patient* look off his face—"she told me my father fell in love with her first, and my mother took him away from her. *Seduced* him, she claims."

"You don't think it's true?"

"What if it is true? What if it is? What if every fucking thing she said is true, what difference does it make? What does she think I'll do now, Mason, say, 'Oh, *that's* what happened—oh, no wonder, poor Rose, all's forgiven'? Nothing's changed! She still did what she did."

He glanced away from her. To hide his disappointment, she assumed. "Anna." He tugged gently on the cuff of her shirt. "Haven't you ever made a mistake?"

She pulled her arm away. "Yeah. Moving back here."

"You don't mean that."

"I gave Rose two weeks' notice. There's a job in New York I can have any time I want. So I've decided to take it."

He stood up and backed away. His shocked face looked too naked in the stark light, she wanted to glance away from it, out of modesty. "Why?"

"Why? Lots of reasons, not just this business with Rose. Carmen fired Frankie and Rose won't do anything about it, that's the main thing. But mostly, because it's time. I told Rose in the beginning that I'd give her the summer. I've done that. The restaurant's turning a corner, it'll either make it now or it won't, me sticking around won't change that."

Mason didn't speak.

"I'll be sorry to go. I'll miss—you. I don't want to leave you. I don't feel like Rose has left me any choice. But you're the one I'll miss." The way he was looking at her made it impossible to expand on that, not now—but how inadequate it sounded. It didn't represent the whole truth. "And a few other things, but . . . this isn't my home anymore. I've found that out."

The red streak of scar stood out from the pallid flesh of his cheek like a smear of warpaint. "So you're leaving."

"It's just a matter of sooner rather—"

"The geographic solution."

"Oh." She stiffened. "Is that how you see it? I'm sorry."

"What did you come here for?"

"Don't be angry. Oh, Mason—"

He picked up her half-full water glass and hurled it across the room. She shrieked, throwing her arm up to cover her eyes, jolting backward against the kitchen table. Glass shattered in the sink, too far away to do any damage.

"Don't go." He said that in a quiet voice, but he was in a cold fury.

"I have to. I can't stay. Rose has made it impossible."

"I doubt that. Don't go."

"You doubt that? I'm lying?" Her anger wasn't cold at all, it was burning hot. "Rose can do no wrong, I forgot—I always forget whose side you're on."

"You sound like a child."

She wished *she* had something to throw. She swept his stupid hoop blind off the table with one arm and started away, making a berth around the glinting glass shards on the floor in front of the sink. In the living room, she tossed back, "You know what, I'm really tired of people telling me I sound like—"

He snatched her from behind, one hard arm around her waist and the other across her chest. She gasped in shock—he wasn't playing. She strained away, plucking at his fingers to loosen his grip. They pivoted, grappling, fumbling, neither one speaking a word. She used her feet to kick back at him, savage stabs that never landed, and then finally one heel connected with his shin. They went staggering against the coffee table, scattering the chess set. The dog, startled out of a nap, got to his feet arthritically and began to bark, wagging his tail with excitement. Anna's leg tangled with one of Mason's and she went down hard, taking him with her. They hit, half on the floor, half on the carpet. Her elbow struck something sharp and she squeaked in pain.

He let go.

She got one knee underneath her and started to spring up, but Mason yanked her back with his hand around her bare foot. She shouted a curse and kicked at him, kicked away, hopping backward, out of his reach. She made a mad dash for the door, batted the screen open, slammed outside. When she looked back, he was getting slowly to his feet.

They stared at each other through the screen, baleful-eyed, breathing hard. But he stayed where he was, didn't come any closer. It was over.

The ripped shoulder of her blouse hung down around her elbow. She felt battered and bruised and stupidly exhilarated. On the brink of something. She was shivering all over. She took a couple of steps toward him. "Okay. I hurt you and I didn't mean to. I never saw this coming. I hate it. But I can't be Theo's—replacement, for you or for Rose. Look, Mason, people leave, and you can't change it. Do you think you're not worth staying with? Because of all the ones who've left you? You can't believe that." She wanted to touch him, but she was still wary of him. "You're a good man—please, don't let this *mean* anything. Anything more than what it is."

She stopped talking when he came toward her, scared of him again, but he stopped on the other side of the screen. "Don't let this mean anything." He braced his hands on either side of the door. Backlit, he looked like Christ on the cross, his head down, his lean, scarred body tilted. "Okay," he said. "I'll try that." Careful not to slam it, he shut the door in her face.

Mason finally called, but not for a week.

In the meantime, Anna told Joel she would definitely take him up on his job offer. She needed about a month to square things away at home, but she looked forward to being in New York well before the end of September. He seemed glumly pleased. She liked Joel because he was levelheaded and smart, but she'd never met anyone as gloomy. He was on his third wife; the other two had to get away from his dark life philosophy, in which everything that possibly might go wrong was bound to. That had advantages in the restaurant business, but it also made Joel a lot more effective in the kitchen than the dining room. That was where Anna was supposed to come in. Maybe they would be a good match, but not if he was expecting her to be the hopeful one. Between them, they made up about one quarter of an optimist.

"Come with me," she told Frankie. "Joel's no prima donna, he'll make you the sous as soon as he finds out how good you are. I could probably talk him into it right now, in fact. Vegetarian gourmet. Think about it. Come on, it'll be fun."

But Frankie wouldn't leave Katie, and Anna hadn't really expected her to. Rose had hired her back, and the situation was status quo, no better or worse than before with Carmen. Anna warned her to start looking for another place. "As soon as I'm gone, Carmen's going to find a way to get rid of you, you know she is, and this time for good." Frankie agreed; she was keeping her eyes open for something in town.

So everything was winding down. Besides a lot of pain and confusion, Anna felt smothered by anticlimax. She'd never worked so hard as she had in the last four months. It was as if she'd entered a contest, the decathlon, say, and just before the finish line of the final event she'd been yanked out of the race by—something stupid, a broken shoelace, a cramp. She was exhausted, but she had nothing to show for it. She hadn't won or lost, she'd just—stopped.

She dragged in to work every morning, tired before the day started, ready to collapse by dinnertime. She ought to have *more* energy, not less, with the prospect of a brand-new job, new opportunity around the corner. But a blanketing sense of incompleteness smothered any enthusiasm she could work up.

It didn't help that everyone was angry with her. Not openly—well, except for Vince. And "angry," no, that was too strong. Probably paranoid, too. It was just that she wasn't one of them anymore. Dwayne didn't include her in his vulgar practical jokes on Flaco—a silly example, but it meant something to her. Louis's face didn't light up when he saw her, and he didn't saunter over to smoke a cigarette and shoot the breeze in the morning shade under the awning. Shirl consulted Rose instead of Anna about the new logo for the sign out front. When Luca got his feelings hurt, he confided in Fontaine, and lately even Vonnie wanted to go home after her shift instead of hanging out with Anna and a bottle of Peroni and talking about how the night had gone. Family meal wasn't the same. Nobody shunned her, nobody was rude; they just didn't think to include her anymore. She was a lame duck.

Vince simply couldn't believe she was leaving. "What are you trying for, a raise?" When she convinced him she was really going, he was openly hostile. "Upstate New York? Are you out of your mind?"

"It's a nice town. I thought you'd be glad—there's a winery not far away, I thought you'd like to come up—"

"Why don't you just move to Canada? Or Japan? They like tofu there, you'd fit right in. What the hell is the matter with you? So you had a fight with Rose, so what?"

It was no use explaining to him that she'd never been going to stay forever, that the plan all along was to see how things went, with the option to leave if she liked after giving Rose the summer. "You should stay," he declared flatly. "Leaving's a cop-out. It's stupid." And the final dig: "It's not like you're getting any younger."

Just because she was miserable didn't mean she was wrong—she was down to telling herself that by the end of the exhausting days. Nothing worse than being misunderstood by people who used to like you. Oddly, or maybe not, the one who was nicest to her was Rose. Anna didn't trust her gentleness at first—*it's a trick*, she'd think, *she's trying to kill me with kindness*. Neither of them ever referred to the night she'd stormed out of her own house, never revisited any of that evening's painful disclosures. No need; they hadn't forgotten anything, and what was there to add? They got through what was left of Anna's tenure by treating each other with a rueful, impersonal warmth that was more demoralizing than ire or blame or rancor could ever be.

She tried not to think of that night, but it haunted her. She hated the phrase "geographical solution," hated it with a visceral repugnance verging on nausea. When she felt strong, she lumped Rose and Mason together and made them the common enemy, in cahoots with each other to make her feel guilty for being who she was and not who they selfishly wanted her to be. When she felt weak, they just defeated her.

When Mason called, she was on the phone with the fish supplier. She put him on hold and told the fish guy she'd call back.

She sat up straight behind the desk, as if Mason could see her. She lined up the papers and invoices and moved the stapler over so it was centered in front of the lamp. She brushed a smear of flour off the bosom of her shirt. Neat and tidy. In her mind, everything was chaos, like waves in a storm, everything dark blue-black and whirling. But order was coming, it was a button-push away. Whatever Mason would say, it was going to stop all this suffering and second-guessing and confusion. Thank God, because she had really needed rescuing.

"Mason? Sorry, I can talk now. I had to get rid of—"

"Is Rose there?"

"No. I mean yes, she's in the kitchen, so it's okay, we can—"

"Can I speak to her?"

She took the phone away for a second, as if it had burned her ear. "You want to talk to Rose?"

"Yes, fast. It's important."

"All right. Just a minute, please."

She put the receiver on the desk and stared at it. It flashed through her mind, a picture of herself smashing the phone against the edge of the desk, beating it against the edge until the desk was splintered and the receiver was just wires in her hands, everything else shards of mauve plastic scattered on the floor.

Rose was in the pantry, laughing with Carmen. Frankie hadn't come in yet; she worked normal dinner hours now, she didn't bother coming in in the morning to test specials or start an early prep. Lunch service would begin in half an hour, so the kitchen was already hot, loud, and crazy.

Rose saw her and came over.

"Phone call," Anna said. "Mason."

"Thanks." She took it on the wall phone by the ice maker. "Hello?"

Anna, sullen as a jealous child, felt torn between walking out and staying to listen. She compromised by pretending to care about the dough Shirl was pinching into farfalle on the floury counter. Rose said, "Oh, my God," in a low, panicky voice.

"What happened?" Anna said, coming closer.

"I'll meet you. I'm leaving now." She hung up. She swept past Anna and headed for the office.

"Rose, what's wrong?" she said, following.

Rose jerked open the bottom desk drawer and got out her purse. "Theo. He's gone."

"Gone?"

"They were outside—Mason went in to talk to the floor nurse about his meds, and when he came back out he was gone. And Cork—and Mason's car." She was ash-pale, barely moving her lips. When she passed Anna in the doorway, their shoulders bumped awkwardly. "Sorry—"

She left.

Anna stood with her mouth open, staring. When her wits came back, she bolted after her. "I'll go with you!" Rose didn't hear—she had to run to catch up with her.

18

Rose saw Mason leaning against the decorative split-rail fence edging Bayside Gardens' parking lot when she drove in. The sight of him moving toward her with his slouchy, long-legged stride calmed her a little. His expression was concerned but not desperate, not panicked. He slid into the backseat over Anna's protests—"No, sit up here, Mason, I'll get in back"—and reached his hand over the seat to squeeze Rose's shoulder.

He said, "I've called the police, given them the license number and all that. Told them what he looks like."

"What did they say?" She started to drive out of the parking lot, even though she didn't know where she was going. But idling, not moving, not doing anything was intolerable. Mason might be calm, but she wasn't; her foot shook on the accelerator, her hands on the wheel were damp with sweat. She should've let Anna drive. "What did the police say?"

"Not much. They wanted to know if he had a valid driver's license. They kept asking me if he'd stolen my car."

"You should've said yes!"

"I did, finally." He caught her eye in the rearview mirror and they laughed, a little wildly. "I could see it was the only way they were going to do anything. So now they're looking for him. They say."

"Can he even drive your car? It's a standard shift, isn't it?" Nightmare visions of Theo plowing into something or somebody had plagued her all the way over. He could barely walk, barely feed himself—how could he drive a four-wheel-drive Jeep with a stick shift?

Mason shook his head and didn't answer.

"Where am I going?" she asked, stalled at the stop sign in the first intersection. It was starting to rain. She turned on the wipers, smearing the windshield. "I don't know where I'm going."

"Could he have gone to the marina?" Anna offered. "Where he used to live? Maybe he's just gone back—"

"Wait," Mason said, "listen. Theo kept talking about the *Wind Rose* today. More than usual. About taking a day trip, sailing to Tangier Island, going someplace with you, with me, maybe with some of his old buddies."

"Yes—my God, the *Wind Rose*, it's all he talks about. Mason, you don't think he's taken it!"

"I don't see how he could have, but he might've gone there. He might've gone just to look at it."

"Or he could've gone to the restaurant," Anna said. "To see you, Rose."

Rose drummed her fingers on the steering wheel, fluttery inside from indecision.

"I'll call the restaurant," Anna said, fumbling in her purse, "while you drive to Mason's."

Good. People telling her what to do, that's what she needed. She turned left and drove through the increasing rain to Mason's house.

His Jeep sat in the driveway at a skewed angle, twin ruts of gravel gouged out behind the back tires. The driver's door hanging open chilled her; something alarming in the jaunty haphazardness of it. And when she got out of her car and went close, the sound of the warning buzzer—because Theo had left the key in the ignition—sawed through her like a dentist's drill. She started to run.

Her shoes slid on the wet slates in the grass in Mason's sloping side yard. She'd outdistanced him, but he came up from behind and took hold of her arm, steadying her, trotting beside her. "It's gone," she panted, but she kept on running. The sailboat should've been tied at the end of the dock, but it could've drifted in its moorings, it could be behind the boat shed, invisible from here—

"It's gone."

They halted together, halfway down the slippery wooden pier, hovering in the angle of the turn. The rain came faster, thudding on the dock, hissing on the green-gray river. She strained her eyes, trying to conjure the *Wind Rose* out of empty air, but the lines dangling from the wooden cleats at the side of the dock dropped off into nothing. Nothing, no clue left, not a gas can, not a stray work glove, no bait bucket, no weather-beaten cap. None of the benign, commonplace objects that went with the *Wind Rose* in her mind. Nothing, just rain, washing away the evidence, obscuring the view.

"Come inside," Mason said. "I'll call the cops again. And the Coast Guard."

"Yes, go. I'll stay here."

"Come with me. You'll get soaked out here."

"No, I'll stay."

He hesitated, then sprinted for the house.

Anna took his place beside her. As she had in the car earlier, driving to the nursing home, she tried to encourage Rose by thinking up hopeful scenarios. This time it was that Theo was just out joyriding on the river, taking the sailboat out for a spin, using the engine—he couldn't put the sails up, could he?—and cruising around because he knew Rose and Mason and everybody else would never let him go out by himself. "He's escaped, Rose, he's on a lark, he'll be back as soon as he gets tired."

Rose patted her on the hand absently, not listening.

Mason came back. He made Rose put on his heavy gray slicker. He opened a wide black umbrella over her head, but the wind made it hard to hold. She wrapped her hand over his around the handle and pulled him up close beside her.

"Anna," she said, "would you mind—"

"What, Rose? What?"

"Would you go inside and listen for the phone?"

Her face fell. "Yes. Sure."

Wind gusts blew the rain in Rose's face. Mason put her behind him, to shield her from the worst of it. She watched the silver lines blow sideways from behind his left shoulder, holding on to his waist with one hand, the umbrella with the other. Summer was gone; the smell of fall had settled in the brackish tang of the river. What was Theo wearing? Was he cold? No, he was never cold. And he was still strong, but what would this unkind wind do to his little sailboat?

"We should go in," she told Mason, and he nodded, but neither of them could leave the scent, the trail, the last place they knew he'd been. It would seem too much like giving up. Like leaving him out there by himself.

"Mason, why did he do this?"

"I don't know."

"Is it good or bad that he took Cork with him?"

"I don't know."

"You know how he's been. Not always himself—in his mind."

"Yes."

"What was he like today? How was he when you saw him?"

"He was fine, in a good mood. But quiet. Calm. We mostly talked about the boat."

"Did he say anything, anything at all . . ."

"He said you'd come to see him last night. You'd brought him some pudding."

Ricotta pudding. His favorite. But he'd had trouble swallowing it.

"When he talks about you, you know, his face always relaxes. You're like medicine for him, Rose."

She rested her cheek on his shoulder.

The rain dwindled to a misty drizzle; the wind fell. A bird flew up from one of the tiny marsh islands across the way in the river. A coot, Mason said. It flapped an awkward arc against the low gray sky before it dropped down and disappeared from sight.

"It's wrong," Rose murmured, "it's too soon. I'm not ready to lose him. I've been preparing, trying..."

"Yes."

"But this is too soon. I still have things to tell him. I thought there was time."

The rain stopped. Mason closed the umbrella, and immediately she missed its dark, safe cover. They were too open out here, no protection from the dangerous, lightening sky. Something was going to happen and they weren't going to be able to stop it.

Even before she saw Anna's face, she knew. It was in her stiff shoulders and the careful way she walked, her arms out a little from her body, as if she were balancing on an edge. She came up on the dock, her light footsteps shaking the planks, eyes still on the ground. Behind her, Rose felt Mason's chest expand in a deep, defensive breath.

"The police just called." Her voice was clear and steady, but her face had a helpless, pleading look Rose could barely tolerate. "Some boaters, a family, they came on the *Wind Rose* out in the bay. They were heading back in because of the storm warning, a squall—" She waved her hand at the river, the sky. "They thought it looked funny—they came alongside to see why it was still, why there was nobody on deck. Just a dog barking." Her eyes filled.

Mason said, "Is he dead?"

"They found him. He was in the water, next to the boat. His leg, his foot was caught in a line. Yes, he's gone."

"He drowned?"

"Yes."

Rose pushed her face against the front of Mason's shirt, taking handfuls of the damp cloth. She could taste it, cotton and salt, bitter on her lips, indistinguishable from her own tears. Gone. Dead. Drowned. It didn't mean anything. It was sad, but she didn't know why yet, it wasn't real. She wasn't surprised, but she didn't believe it.

"Where is he?" Mason said.

"They brought him on board. They're coming in, towing the sailboat. The police said they were making for someplace called Dutchman Point. They said it's—"

"I know where it is," he said.

"I want to see him."

"Oh, Rose, no." Anna put her hand out.

"I'll take you," Mason said.

They'd thrown a blue tarpaulin over his body. Mason spoke to the two policemen on the deck of the cruiser, and then he came and got Rose and helped her on board. One of the policemen pulled the tarp away. Rose went down on her knees.

Nobody had closed his eyes. She was afraid to touch him at first. And then, as soon as she did, it was all right. It was only Theo. She brushed her fingers over his scruffy mustache, caressing his parted lips. His cheek was icy; she put her cheek next to it to warm him. What made her cry was his green wool sweater, sodden and twisted at his waist; she'd given it to him for Christmas. One of his shoes was gone, the sock half off. He looked disheveled and reckless, his grizzled hair a wet tangle on the deck.

"He looks like himself," she said to Mason. She meant, he looked more like himself than he had in a long time. Dying had loosened the stiffness in his face and let the old familiar lines, the sweetness and heart come back. Now it was real. Theo was gone, this Theo, the one she knew best. She threaded her fingers through his and pressed his big, blocky hand to her heart. *Did you do it on purpose?* She hoped so—she hoped not. Either way, she couldn't bear it. Mason touched her shoulder, and she thought, *Whatever you say, I'll believe. You decide. I can't.*

"Love me, Theo?" she whispered. She put her ear to his lips and listened for his answer.

19

Anna broke down at Theo's funeral. She was mortified, stunned, she couldn't believe it was happening. One minute she was sitting quietly in her pew behind Rose and Mason, half listening to irritating, generic organ music and wondering what Mason would do if she pulled on the little thread sticking out of the back of the collar of his dark blue suitcoat. In the next she was doubled over her knees, desperate to muffle hoarse, croaky sobs, feeling crushed under some kind of racking sorrow. *What was this?* She had no idea, but she couldn't control it. Aunt Iris's patting hand on her spine only made it worse. She hadn't felt like this when *Mac* died. It was as if Theo's funeral was all the funerals of her life, and she was mourning him and every other person she'd ever lost. When the service ended and it was time to go to the gravesite, she asked Rose if she could be excused.

"Do you need me?" she said, eyeing the cars lining up for the procession to the cemetery. "I'll go if it'll help." She was too far gone to phrase that any better. "Really, truly, I'll go if you need me."

Rose put her hand on Anna's hot, swollen, blotchy cheek and said, "No, I don't need you." At least she softened it with a smile.

No, she didn't need her, she had Mason, who'd hardly left her side since Theo died. They had each other.

To Anna's knowledge, Rose had only wept in public once, last night at the funeral home. She'd seen her sway and start to fold in on herself as she stood at the head of Theo's open coffin—Anna had risen from her chair and started to go to her, to catch her if she fell—but Mason got to her first, and supported her in his arms until she recovered. Otherwise, Rose had been calm and steady, practically serene. Or else she was simply shutting Anna out of her grief. That was probably it. Either way, her composure made Anna's highly visible collapse at the funeral feel even more inappropriate and excessive.

Mason stood at Rose's side on the church steps and regarded Anna with a penetrating expression she couldn't decode. *Hysterical female*, he was probably thinking. Maybe he resented her distress—maybe he didn't even believe in it. She wanted to speak to him, but she had nothing to say. She'd already told him how sorry she was, asked if there was anything she could do, said all the things you could say to someone to show you cared and felt sympathy and wished you could console.

But they were reduced to the most excruciating kind of politeness, like strangers but worse, and no matter what she did she couldn't break through. "Thank you," he answered to everything she said. It was almost funny. And he said it *kindly*. Rose was taking the same tone with her, an at-a-distance gentleness that had felt good at first, then frustrating, then intolerable. It was the most infuriating passive-aggressive punishment—although she wasn't so far gone as to think they meant it to be. But she would take a wrestling match with Mason any day over this horrible, aggravating kindness.

Last night, late, determined to have a real, true conversation, she'd waited in the parking lot of the funeral home for Mason to come out. She'd forgotten that he and Rose were joined at the hip; they came out together and saw her at the same time. What did she want? They'd looked at her curiously, possibly with dread, certainly with suspicion, as she crossed the empty lot to where they stood next to their side-by-side cars. She hadn't known what she was going to say to Mason anyway, but she had no idea what to say to *both* of them. Especially since she'd just told them good night.

"I just wanted to say again how sorry I am."

They'd nodded tiredly. They were exhausted, and they'd heard that sentence a hundred times in the last couple of hours.

"And if there's anything I can do . . ."

They murmured, waiting for her to finish and go away.

"I really liked him," came out of her mouth next.

Rose had tipped her head, resting it tiredly on Mason's shoulder.

"He didn't much like me, I know. He was afraid I'd . . ." Had she really blundered into this? At least it was *real.* "Afraid I'd do something to hurt you," she said, looking at Rose. "He was very protective. He loved you so much." Did that sound patronizing? Presumptuous? As if Rose needed Anna to tell her Theo had loved her. She blushed.

"Anyway," she plowed on. "I think he might've started to like me a little, toward the end. That day on the boat, when we moved his stuff to the nursing home—he said to me, he said something like—we were talking about Cork, and he said, 'You seem like a dog person.' I knew he meant it as a compliment. So—that was something. We had a good talk that day." She ran down.

"Anna," Rose said. *Kindly.* "Theo didn't dislike you at all."

She flushed again. Oh, this was dreadful. She'd wanted to make some kind of a connection with Mason, but instead she'd made a little speech that turned Theo's death into a misfortune that was all about *her.* They must think she was such an ass.

"Good night," she'd said, on the brink of tears. "See you tomorrow." She'd worked up the nerve to touch Mason on the sleeve of his jacket.

"Thanks," he'd said. "Good night."

Now she watched them go off, arm in arm, to the town car Rose had hired to follow the hearse to the cemetery. She wanted to run after them and tell them she'd changed her mind, she wanted to go with them after all. She *was* an ass—she couldn't stand herself any more than they could. She liked it better when they were yelling at her. Or tackling her. *Stay, stay*. She'd succeeded so well at self-extrication, nobody gave a damn now whether she stayed or not. She didn't feel free, as a consequence, not like a woman keeping her options open and her horizons refreshingly clear. She felt dismissed.

After the funeral, Rose took some time off from the restaurant. Labor Day was coming up, the end of the season; business would drop off afterward and the summer hires would go back to part-time or back to school, back to something. Anna told Rose she'd be happy to stay on for a while, to help with the transition. "For a while": that's how she'd phrased it. Afterward she'd asked herself why, where time was concerned, she seemed to be congenitally incapable of definiteness. But Rose had said, "That's fine, if you think you can manage it with your friend in New York. Don't jeopardize anything there on our account." She was being earnest, not sarcastic. "We'll get along."

"How is she doing?" Anna called Aunt Iris to ask. "Is she okay? She seems fine, but I don't see that much of her."

"Oh, I expect she'll be all right."

"I know, but does she talk to you? How is she? She *looks* all right. She's only been coming in for a couple of hours a day."

"It's a slow process."

The last thing Anna had expected was her trusty source of intelligence on Rose to dry up. "Yes, but is she depressed? Does she cry? How would you say she *is*, Aunt Iris?"

"I'd say she's doing as well as can be expected under the circumstances. So, dear, have you put your house up for sale yet?"

And that was that. After years of being the go-between, Aunt Iris had chosen sides. It was hard not to feel betrayed, and even harder not to feel sorry for herself. In fact, that was impossible.

Why don't they just book my flight for me, Anna took to wondering, *start packing my bags?*

At the Bella Sorella, she became not so much obsolete as unnecessary. She was used to organizing the family meal, making it a little more special than it had been under Rose's regime by introducing wine and olive oil and ice cream and anchovy tastings for servers and kitchen staff alike, and by letting the cooks take turns preparing the meal, which could be as experimental, as ethnic, as bizarre as they liked; in fact, she'd encouraged weirdness for the fun of it, and some of the dishes they'd eaten together late on Sunday nights had been exceedingly strange, definitely unpredictable. Staff morale had never been higher, Vonnie had told her weeks ago, before Anna gave notice. She'd suspected that was true, but it had meant a lot to hear Vonnie say it—even more so than if Rose had, because of course Rose's motives weren't pure.

But now—now it was *Frankie* who was organizing the last family meal before the Labor Day layoff. *Anna's* job. All the plans were made before she even knew about it. She felt superfluous when she found herself sitting at the big back table between Dwayne and Flaco, sipping an Australian chardonnay with Luca's Sardinian mother's Welsh rarebit with smoked cod in caper sauce and sautéed mustard greens, and toasting the sad, imminent departure of four part-time servers and two cooks.

Shirl announced that she was getting back together with Earl, her stalker ex-husband. He wasn't really her ex, it turned out, because the divorce had never gone through, so instead of remarrying they were just having a simple vows renewal in Atlantic City. Nothing Shirl said shocked anyone anymore, so when she told the table, "Earl Junior's so excited about being ring bearer, he's dropped the lawsuit," people just nodded and hummed and went on eating.

"Luca, this is fantastic," Frankie said, waving her fork over her plate. "How'd you get the cheese sauce so smooth?"

Luca, whose feelings had been hurt when Jasper said he wished there was a dog under the table to feed his mustard greens to, smiled beatifically. "Secret recipe," he answered, and everyone groaned. "You, I tell later," he said in a softer voice to Frankie, who winked at him.

Vince was still in love. Anna watched him watch Frankie, cast sidelong glances down the table whenever she said anything, cock his ears to catch the softest syllable. She wasn't really mean to him, or no meaner than usual; the one time Anna had made a casual reference to his devotion, Frankie had said, "Yeah, well, too bad I'm not interested in being anybody's girlfriend. I'm a mom and a cook, that's all I've got room for."

Rose stood up, interrupting the hilarity of watching Dwayne discover Fontaine had made his piece of tiramisu with spackling compound instead of mascarpone. The table quieted down instantly. Since Theo's death, even the rowdiest of the kitchen crew treated Rose with the most extraordinary gentleness, clumsy and almost embarrassing to watch, but touching, too, because the only explanation for it was that they loved her.

"Let's have a toast. To Kelli and Marco, Popper, Diego, Lorraine, and Bobbie. We're really going to miss you guys. Thank you for all your hard work—and here's to great success wherever the future takes you. And happiness."

They drank, then Jasper brought in a new dessert, Carmen's *torta delizia*—delight cake—because it was a special occasion. More toasts, lots of jokes and jests. In the middle of an unexpectedly tearful farewell speech from one of the departing waitresses, Anna saw Rose get up and slip out. She would go home, not come in again till late on Tuesday. What did she do with herself? In Anna's dark imaginings, she stayed in her small apartment, sitting alone or hanging over the terrace rail at night, staring out at the dark bay. Always by herself, always grieving in solitude. It wasn't right. Iris said it was natural, it would just take time, but to Anna it felt as if they'd abandoned her.

After dinner, Frankie waited till Carmen was out of earshot to corner Anna in the kitchen. "Hey, listen," she said, fingering a buckle on the old army knapsack she used for a purse. "I wanted to tell you first, even before Rose."

Uh-oh, Anna thought, even though she'd been urging Frankie to go for weeks. "You're leaving."

"I got this offer from the Rio Grande, it's kind of an upscale café in the 'burbs—"

"I know it."

"Yeah. And sure, it's basically Tex-Mex, but they want me for chef, so... And the pay's a little better, not much but I have to think about stuff like that."

"Of course."

"I figure it'll help round me out a little, and after a year or so I'll move on to something more interesting. But meanwhile I get a different experience, and it looks eclectic on the old résumé..." She gave *résumé* two syllables, a joke, but she didn't look happy. She had a worried face at the best of times; now it looked dissatisfied, too.

"No, it'll be great." Anna tried to sound cheerful. "It's local, it's something completely different, and you'll be the boss. I'm not seeing a downside."

"Yeah, except I'd stay if I could. If it weren't for Carmen. And you leaving."

Two big obstacles. "How are things otherwise?" Anna asked. "In your actual life."

"In my actual life." Frankie grinned and looked down at her feet. "Not too bad, believe it or not."

"No kidding?"

"Me and Mike, we sorta came to an understanding. We're not getting back together," she said quickly when Anna's face lit up. "This was more like... Hah, more like an intervention, only I was sober."

Anna folded her arms and leaned against the pantry shelf, signaling she had all the time in the world. It was tough to get Frankie to open up; you had to be cool about it, and the last thing you could show was sympathy.

"We had a long talk, that's all. He said he knew how I was, you know, hurting about Colleen and all. He wants me to have partial custody of Kate."

"Oh, Frankie. Oh, that's fantastic, I'm so glad."

"Yeah. It's everything." She lifted her face, and it was glowing. "What happened was, he forgave me. Katie did, too. I didn't know how that would feel until it happened. You're Catholic, right?"

Anna looked at her in alarm. "I used to be."

"Yeah, same here. I always hated confession, that was like the worst, humiliating or something, I never felt better because some guy mumbled a prayer through a screen. But..." She stuck her hands in the back pockets of her camouflage pants and contemplated the floor again. "I pulled so much shit when I was drinking. You don't know. Stuff I thought I'd feel dirty about for the rest of my life. And Mike said it was all okay. And it was like...I don't know." Her ears turned pink. "Extreme unction or something."

Anna wanted to curve her hand around the back of Frankie's skinny white neck and just hold it there. She refrained.

"All along I've been working through the steps, you know, trying to make it up with the people I've let down, and it was like—Mike skipped ahead or traded places or something. He made it right with *me*."

"What a guy," Anna said softly.

"What a guy. I get credit for picking him at least." Her laugh had a hitch in it. "And Katie's so sweet, she doesn't hold anything against me. And she could, too. But she just loves me." She swiped at her eyes. "So anyway, that's the long answer to your question. How I am in my actual life."

"Sounds pretty good."

"Yeah, well. It's a start."

Anna was too familiar with her own tricks and devices for guarding against that dangerous enemy, optimism, to tell Frankie it was a lot more than a start.

The evening wound down. The waitstaff closed out with Vince, the cooks went home, the cleaners finished in the kitchen. Another week over. Anna couldn't decide whether to come in tomorrow or not. They were closed, but she'd hardly missed a Monday yet, there had always been so much work to do. Her own house needed attention—the realtor didn't want to list it until she got new carpeting and painted the outside trim, minimum. But she kept putting it off.

"Rose! My God, you scared me to death, I thought you'd gone home. You *did* go home."

"Then I came back. I'd forgotten these."

Anna moved into the dim office tentatively, careful of Rose's mood. She was sitting behind the desk with the lamp on low, a messy spread of papers fanned out in front of her, a glass of something by her hand. "What's all that?"

"Papers of Theo's, insurance, things like that. I'm the executor of his estate."

"You are? I didn't know that. Is it hard?"

"No. Because *estate* is a bit of an exaggeration." She gave a wan smile. She looked slight and bony, her jaw unnaturally sharp, an aging woman in a black dress in a large black chair. She sat back, folding her hands in her lap. "He had just enough money left in his bank account to pay for his funeral. He'd have liked that. If he knew it. I wonder if he did."

Anna waited in suspense, wondering if she would say something now about the way Theo died. They'd ruled his death an accidental drowning, but Anna had doubts, and she would be amazed if Rose didn't, too.

"Luckily there aren't many other bills. He didn't own a credit card. He never wanted things; if it didn't fit on his little *Expatriate*, he had no use for it."

Anna went closer. She sat on the very edge of the desk, careful not to touch Theo's papers. "How are you doing?" She felt shy asking.

The melancholy smile came and went again. "I'm all right."

"Maybe you should get away for a while. Go someplace exotic, take a vacation." Even while she was saying it, it sounded like a silly idea.

"I'm better off here. With family. The restaurant is family."

"But it must be so sad."

She leaned her head back and let her heavy-lidded eyes close. "I miss him the most at night. If we weren't together, we always talked on the phone. Last thing, both of us in our beds with the lights out. I miss the sound of his voice in my ear. In the dark. That closeness. Sometimes the telephone ringing interrupts a dream, and I'll think it's him." She opened her eyes. "But it's Carmen. Or you, or someone wanting me to change my phone service."

"Oh, Rose."

"It'll be hard getting used to being on my own again. I did it once before, when Paul died, but it seems harder now. I guess because I'm older."

"You're not on your own."

"No."

"You're *not*."

"I know. Just feeling sorry for myself."

That wasn't true, either. Anna was the one in this family who specialized in feeling sorry for herself.

"Well." Rose finished what was left in her glass and stood up, began shoving Theo's papers into a folder. "Do you need to get in here? I'm going, I'll be out of your way. You should go home, too, it's late."

"Rose?"

"Yes?"

"What can I do?" Anna was embarrassed when tears started. "How can I help you?" she said in a thick voice. "I'd do anything."

"Sweet," Rose murmured. "There's nothing."

"I mean it. Just ask me. I'd do anything."

Rose came around from behind the desk. Now her smile looked indulgent. "That's very kind of you—and I mean *that.* Oh, Anna. There's nothing I'd like better than to stop time, but my life is going on. Your life is going on. We came together for a while, and I'll always be thankful for that. But don't be afraid that I'll ask you to stay." She put her hand on Anna's shoulder, leaned over and touched her lips to her cheek. "Go home soon." She whispered, "I love you."

Anna listened to her footsteps fade, then the back door close, a car start in the alley. She listened to the silence flow back for as long as she could stand it, then she got to work, going through the last of the receipts, getting the bank deposit ready for Tuesday morning, stashing everything in the safe.

She finished too soon. *Go home*, Rose said, but she didn't want to. She told herself it was because she'd painted the second-floor bathroom last night, and it would still smell. It would keep her awake, that paint smell. Rose had left the computer on. Despite a dull premonition of defeat, she checked her e-mail. Right the first time—nothing from Mason.

She kept an electronic folder of all his letters. The last ones he'd sent were from Montana, where he'd gone to do a piece on the Bitterroot Mountains. She clicked on the second one, her favorite. He'd written it in a bar on his laptop.

Dear Anna,

Here I am at Bender's Tavern in the town of Stevensville, about 20 miles south of Missoula, waiting for the rain to stop. Can't take pictures in the rain. There's only one thing to do in Stephensville when it's raining—drink beer at Bender's. There aren't so many photographers here that we trip over each other's tripods, not like Macias last month. I got some good pictures, I think, yesterday and this morning, before the sky opened up. As usual I overshot, but if you wait for the perfect photo you end up not shooting a single frame. Shoot fast and shoot often, that's my motto.

Birds I have spotted so far at Lee Metcalf Wildlife Refuge: wild turkey, blue grouse, pileated woodpecker, spruce grouse, red-breasted nuthatch, rufous-crowned sparrow, osprey, long-eared owl, misc. ducks, geese, herons, swans. No surprises here; that's what you expect to see this time of year in the Bitterroots. Most exciting for me—and I know this will delight and amaze you, have you hopping a plane ASAP to see for yourself—a flammulated owl. Yes. My first sighting. You see this tiny, elusive creature, only about 6 inches high, in pictures but rarely in life because he looks exactly like a slab of bark. I shot fast, but if I got anything at all, it's dark and blurry and useless for selling. Too bad, but at least I can add him to my life list. Cause for great joy and excitement.

Speaking of lists, you know we're mental about listmaking, we birders. Some of us—not I—enjoy the lists more than the birds. "Listers," we call these people. It's all in the competition for them, they might as well be counting traffic lights or telephone poles. They have lists for all occasions, birds seen on TV, birds seen from the window of the bus, first bird seen today, dead birds. I know a guy who keeps a list of birds seen from his bathroom window while he sits on the john. Birds spotted while brushing his teeth or showering don't count, he has to be sitting on the actual toilet. He says it's a short list; he keeps sighting the same finches and house sparrows year after year. He's thinking of planting trumpet vine under the window, try to get some hummingbirds.

How are you? I called Theo this morning, didn't talk for long. I miss you. I think about you whenever I'm in a restaurant. Other times too, but definitely in restaurants, where I observe everything much more keenly than I used to. The waiters probably think I'm a food critic. Something I've always wanted to know—how do you keep all the ingredients you'll ever need for every dish on the menu at all times? Especially the ones nobody ever orders. I'm looking at the menu here at Bender's, which is a very good name for a bar, and here's a tongue sandwich. Who would order a tongue sandwich? For all I know it's the most popular sandwich in Stevensville, but for the sake of argument let's say that the vast majority of people here feel about a tongue sandwich as I do, i.e., aghast. But here it is on the menu, so they must have it on hand at all times. Months go by, staff changes, one day somebody orders the tongue sandwich but by now no one currently employed at Bender's remembers how to make one or even where it is. I had no appreciation of the difficulties of restaurant ownership until I met you.

Still raining. Another beer? I'm not much of a drinker. Makes me think I have a lot to say.

I've been watching two men at the bar. Locals, not birders or hunters—you can tell because they don't look out the window every five minutes to see if the rain's stopped. One's fiftyish, going bald, starting to spread, has on a plaid flannel jacket. The other one is late twenties, taller and straighter, has a sandy, receding crewcut. They've got the same nose, almost the same rough-edged profile. They both smoke Camels and drink Pabst. They don't say much to each other, and when they do they keep their eyes on the auto race on TV. The older guy put his hand on the other one's shoulder, and I heard him say to the bartender, "Larry here..." I missed the rest. The old one looked smug and proud, the younger one looked shy and pleased.

I thought about my father, something I don't do often because I don't remember him very well. After he died, I used to dream about him coming back. I fantasized that it was somebody else's charred body, not his, in the wrecked F-14 Tomcat. He was a secret agent—that's why the government had to fake his death. I'd pretend he was watching me in my yard or out on the playground at school, always in disguise, not allowed to approach me. As much as he wanted to. Even after Theo came, I kept him in the back of my mind, the way a devout Catholic kid probably keeps God in the back of his mind. Exactly like that—my dad was everywhere, and he could read my thoughts.

Right now I'm thinking what it would be like to sit in a bar with him, drinking beer and watching the stock car races.

Write back if you have time. I miss you. I think this day is shot. I think I'll have to order the tongue sandwich and sober up. Should I call you tonight? No, I'll be asleep. You call me, doesn't matter how late. Wish you were here. I picture you in camouflage and hip waders, a pair of two-pound binoculars around your neck. Then I picture you without them.

Mason

Oh, Mason. What if she wrote him now? She felt caught up in something she used to have control over, but now it was out of hand. She didn't believe in fate, but lately her life had taken some sort of Calvinist turn. Everything was ordained, as if she was acting out a plan that somebody else had devised a long time ago—except it wasn't somebody else, it was her. And the plan used to seem vital, but now it was just painful.

Dear Mason,
Do you think it would be possible for us to stay together even if I didn't live here? A long-distance relationship? I am trying so hard to think of a way not to lose you.

She hit Delete.

Dear Mason,
You're like collateral damage, you were never the one I wanted to hurt. I did anyway. I did that stupid thing they do in the movies, I lumped you in with all the rotten men because of one rotten man who screwed me. Once I looked at you—we were sitting out on your dock, remember that night we

saw the two shooting stars—and I thought, he could be like Jay. He could do that to me, they all could. I caught myself, but the thought was there, it was like a pebble in my shoe. I'm sorry, I apologize. I was gun-shy, that's all I can say. I was like a war veteran who jumps, years later, when a car backfires. So you were like a car backfiring and I thought you were a bomb. I wish we could—

She deleted that, too.

Dear Mason,
It goes back much farther than Jay—he's not the one who's making me crazy. But it's all tangled up now, Jay and Nicole, Rose and my father, you and me. I think I have to go away, but I don't want to leave you. I'm so sorry I'm your worst nightmare. I'm so sorry your mother died while you were sleeping. I think the way she left you was worse than anything, worse than your father's plane crash or even Theo dying. I wish I could be the one who stays. Oh, Mason—

She turned off the computer.

Selfish. Mason was fine. The poison had finally settled to the bottom, and she had the nerve and the ego to try to stir it up again. How irresponsible and mean. She disliked herself intensely.

She moved a case of tomato paste cans and lay down on the sofa in the dark. Lousy couch for sleeping, lumpy and not long enough. It had the shallow, ghost indentation of Rose's body, though, S-shaped, from a thousand little naps and rests, and Anna's fit the same outline precisely. Her eyes went to the square of grainy light around the curtained window from the streetlight in the alley. A siren wail grew louder, peaked, died away.

She fell asleep and dreamed about a little girl in an open railroad car, flying through the Old West, craggy mountains in the distance, dots of cactus in the desert foreground, prickly balls of sagebrush blowing by. The ground was bright yellow, and the railroad car sent up billowy plumes of choking dust in its wake. "It won't stop," the little girl said. Her hands were stuck to the handles of the push-pull thing—it wasn't a railroad car anymore, it was a handcar, and the little girl's back kept bending, straightening, bending, straightening, as she pumped the car through the Old West. One of the craggy mountains loomed up. The tracks ran into a hole in the side, a black, inverted U, like a cartoon mouse hole. "It won't stop," the little girl, who was Anna, said, and the handcar flew straight into the hole and disappeared.

She woke up with the smell of dust in her nostrils. So real. No, not dust, paint. But—she was *here*, she was in the office, not at home. She sat up, groggy.

Smoke.

She leaped off the couch and lunged for the light switch. Was it smoky in this *room*? Where were her shoes? Under the desk. She kicked into them and ran out in the corridor. Slow-moving smoke from the door to the kitchen coiled thick around the ceiling. She raced inside, saw orange flames licking up the front wall. Under the smoke was an electric smell, like burning wire. The ice maker was invisible behind hissing, spitting flicks of fire.

Her mind went blank; she couldn't remember where the fire extinguisher was. They had two. *Where?* The main light switch was behind the worst of the fire; she could only see by the dim glow from the glass-doored refrigerator. There—the extinguisher, on the wall beside the big range. Of course; where else? She grabbed it, fumbled for a minute with the red pin thing, then aimed it at the highest flames, below and behind the ice maker.

It worked for a few seconds; the foam stifled the fire at the bottom. But as soon as she aimed at the flames crawling up the wall behind the machine, new ones bloomed under it. She continued to spray, but she had to keep stepping back, back, as the heat and the smoke increased.

The smoke detector in the dining room went off, then the sprinklers in the ceiling. She hadn't been scared before. As soon as the smoke detector went off, an ear-piercing shriek that felt like a blade slicing through her brain, she was afraid. Not panicked, just frightened, heart racing, blood pounding. *What'll I do? What'll I do?*

Wake up Carmen.

She ran for the back door, then stopped, skidding, almost falling, as it hit her it would be faster to call. Racing back into the smoky kitchen, she grabbed the phone—it was *hot*—off the wall beside the linen closet. She only had to push one button. Good thing, because she'd never have remembered the number.

"Hello?" Carmen's sleepy, groggy voice still managed to sound irritated.

"Can't you hear the smoke alarm? There's a fire in the kitchen. Get up and get out, because I don't know what it's going to do!"

"Did you call the fire department?"

Ice water replaced the blood in her veins. It thawed and she came back to life when she remembered, "No—it dials automatically. As soon as the sprinklers go off in the dining room, it calls the fire department."

"Okay." Carmen hung up.

Anna turned in a circle in the middle of the kitchen, coughing, watching fire flicker above the door and hesitate, as if it couldn't decide if it wanted to eat the big clock or go around it. It was raining in the dining room, not very hard, though, fifteen or twenty delta-shaped deluges pouring out of the smoke-veiled ceiling, drenching tables, chairs, floor. The wet room looked pretty in the blue glow from the reach-in behind the bar; exotic or something. Tropical. Night in the rainforest.

Shit, shit, shit. The smoke and water were going to do more damage than the fire. But just in case, she dashed back to the office and opened the floor safe, grabbed the canvas bag of cash and receipts she'd put in it an hour ago. She took her purse, too. Papers, documents? No, and this was silly, the fire wasn't even that bad. But on the way out, she plucked a framed photograph off the wall—Rose and Theo, hand-in-hand on the deck of the *Wind Rose*—and stuck it under her arm.

The whole front wall of the kitchen was on fire! She couldn't see the dishwasher or the pantry through the flames, and they were moving toward the linen closet. "Jesus!" she shouted. All the clean and dirty laundry would go up like paper.

Carmen burst in from the back door. "Holy Mother of God." She had on flip-flops and a billowy sleeveless yellow nightgown, knee-length. "What are you standing there for? Get out." She went to the maintenance cabinet over the steam table, jerked it open, rummaged around, and pulled out a power screwdriver.

"What are you doing?"

The brand-new meat grinder, Carmen's favorite piece of equipment, was attached to a stainless steel counter in the prep corner. She went down on her knees, her burnt-orange hair sticking out like a rooster's comb, and started unscrewing screws.

"Carmen, what are you doing?"

"Go out in the alley, wait for the firemen."

Anna stared at her for speechless seconds. Then she looked around. "I'll get the microwave."

"No!"

She unplugged it, then took a closer look. She could barely get her arms around it. A cart—Dwayne had one at his station. She tipped a mountain of clean plates and silverware onto the floor and rolled the cart back over, loaded the microwave on it with a lot of graceless shoving. She only ran into walls six or seven times on her way to the back door.

What else was portable? Pasta maker next. Knives. Knife sharpener? "The cappuccino machine! Carmen, help me."

"No, it's gone, it's too close to the fire." She was still working on the meat grinder. "Anna, get the hell *out*."

The enormous range-grill stood next in the fire's path. Besides lights and fans, its exhaust hood had built-in fire prevention equipment. Heat detectors set it off—all at once wet, slimy foam whooshed from the bottom of the hood, soaking the grilltop and dripping down the sides, puddling on the floor.

Carmen yelled at her over the increasing noise and smoke, "Are you sure the sprinklers called the fire department?"

The fire on the front wall had turned the corner and gone into the dining room. The phone was gone, melted. Anna dashed through what was left of the door and stood under one of the inadequate sprinklers, turning her hot face up. Swallowing water, she gasped a chestful of smoky air and fought a dizzy feeling. What if all of Vince's wines got destroyed? He'd picked each bottle so carefully. They should have a cellar, storing them up here was stupid. She couldn't stop coughing. What if the walk-in caught fire? Somebody should save the expensive meats, at least, and that new shipment of she-crabs—

The breakfront! The firemen would never save it. If Carmen was unscrewing the meat grinder, she was rolling the antique oak and beveled glass breakfront out the front door.

She got one shoulder against the wet, slippery side and shoved. It moved a few feet, then caught on a floorboard. The constant shriek of the smoke detector made her deaf. She pushed again, got a few more feet. The smoke was sinking; it didn't hug the ceiling anymore, it had sunk to head level. Nose level. She bent her knees, but she couldn't get enough leverage, couldn't budge the damn breakfront. Sharp popping behind her—bottles breaking. Her muscles weren't working right. This was stupid. Where was her purse, where was her picture of Rose and Theo? She would just get them and get out.

"Carmen!" she tried to scream through the door. She thought it was the door. It looked like the entrance to hell. The stench of her own nose hairs stung in her nostrils.

"Anna!"

They yelled something to each other at the same time. Anna stopped to listen.

"Get out!"

Good idea. She tried to scream it back, but she couldn't get enough air. Her lungs felt scalded. She was wheezing instead of breathing. As soon as she turned around, something exploded behind her. The concussion hit between her shoulder blades and blew her forward; she plowed chest-first into a table. The last thing she heard was glass breaking. She hoped it was men with axes smashing in the plate-glass window.

20

Doctors were impossible to find. They'd either just left or would be there any second, then never materialized. In the afternoon, Rose finally tracked down a nurse with a minute to speak to her, in the hallway outside Carmen's room.

"It's a pretty straightforward SI case, smoke inhalation. They checked her blood gases and now she's getting Albuterol. That's just a bronchodilator, it relaxes the muscles so she can get more air in her airways. We're giving her humidified oxygen and keeping her quiet. Luckily there weren't any serious burns. We'll keep her overnight, make sure there's no infection or anything, no complications, then she can go home, rest there instead of here. The main thing she's going to be is exhausted."

Carmen opened her eyes when the chair Rose pulled closer to the bed scraped the tile floor. No burns, but her eyebrows and eyelashes had singed brown tips, spiky-looking, more like wires than hairs. She wasn't allowed to talk. A clear plastic mask covered her mouth and nose; through the condensation Rose saw her sardonic, one-sided smile. That was progress. In the ER, she'd only been able to grimace.

She took Carmen's big, fleshy hand, inert on the coverlet, and was rewarded with a strong squeeze. They'd cleaned her up since Rose's last quick visit. She'd been ashy-gray all over from soot and smoke, especially around her mouth and nose. The medicine had stopped the convulsive coughing; she looked relaxed, almost comfortable.

"How are you feeling? You don't look bad. Everything considered, you look pretty damn good."

Carmen rolled her watery eyes.

"They say you can go home tomorrow. There's some smoke damage on the second floor, so you'll come to my house while we clean it up. You're just supposed to stay quiet, and you can do that at my place as easily as yours. The main thing is not to worry. Just get well."

Carmen nodded tiredly. It hurt to see her like this, weak, helpless, taking orders from others. It wasn't natural. Behind the mask, she said something Rose couldn't understand.

"How's the restaurant?" she guessed. "Well, the good news is that the wall that burned wasn't weight-bearing, so there's no real structural damage. Thank God. We had some losses," she said airily, evasively, "equipment and so forth, but almost everything in the dining room can be saved. I just talked to the insurance man, and he's being a little cagey but I guess that's his job. It could've been so much worse," she said, and Carmen nodded her head on the pillow, blinking her eyes in thanks. "And," Rose added, "thank *God* we've got our meat grinder, because without that—" She gave a dramatic shrug and raised her eyes to the ceiling. Carmen, whose cheeks were already flushed, turned a little redder. She stuck her tongue out, and that made Rose laugh. A first in the long, hellish day.

"Iris sends her love. I told her not to call because you can't talk, so she says to tell you she's thinking about you."

Carmen smiled and nodded.

She leaned closer. "Okay, I'm going to go now, leave you to sleep. Remember not to worry, because there's nothing to worry about. Anything I can do before I leave? Anything I can bring you? Okay, then." She kissed her very lightly on the cheek, awkward, careful not to dislodge the oxygen mask. She whispered, "Crazy lady. I don't know what I'd do without you. You know that?"

Carmen whispered.

"What? No, don't talk—"

She whispered it again, and Rose heard it through the plastic mask. "Same here."

Unlike Carmen, Anna was a lousy patient.

"Why can't I go home now?" She wasn't supposed to talk, either. She didn't have a mask, she had a cannula—prongs in the nostrils—so there was nothing to shut her up. "They're not even giving me any medicine, so why can't I leave?" What was left of her voice was just a scratchy croak, like a crow with a sore throat.

"I think they have to monitor your blood to make sure it's got enough oxygen in it."

"They already did that. It hurt like hell. Look at this bruise." She held out her arm. "I want to go home."

"Also, you're supposed to shut up."

She swallowed, making a face when it hurt. "The worst is my chest," she complained.

"Your lungs? I can imag—"

"No, my chest. Look what I did." She pulled her washed-out seersucker hospital gown down in front, showing off a wide, alarming, blue-black bruise across her breastbone.

"Oh, honey, that looks terrible. Does it hurt?"

"Yes, it hurts. A lot." She winced to prove it when she tried to sit up straighter. Rose hurried over to help with her pillows. "I went headfirst into a table right after something blew up in the kitchen."

"The gas line to the range. Thank God Carmen was out by then. *Would you stop talking?*"

"Bluh. I feel like I'm going to throw up."

"That's from swallowing smoke. Carmen's sucking ice chips for the nausea."

"I finished mine. Could you get me some more?"

This was a side of Anna Rose had forgotten about, but it was coming back to her quickly: the whiny, querulous, self-pitying sick person. She sighed. "I'll be right back." She went for more ice chips.

When she returned, Anna was trying to get out of bed. "But I have to pee," she sulked when Rose made her get back in.

"Wait for the nurse, you'll pull out your IV."

"It's just saline anyway. You could help me. The nurse is incompetent. If she sticks me one more time, I won't be responsible."

"I'd forgotten how bad you are at this."

"What?"

"Being sick."

She actually pushed her bottom lip out. They hadn't done as thorough a cleaning job on her as they had on Carmen; she still had smoky black smudges around her eyes. The pouting lip reminded Rose—"Remember when you had measles? We took turns staying with you, Lily, Mama, and me." Anna shook her head. "You don't remember? Oh my God, you were awful. It was like baby-sitting a fox terrier puppy. The only thing that would keep you quiet—"

"*The Hobbit.*"

"Yes, *The Hobbit.* You loved it."

"I still do. I read it about every ten years. You read it to me first—I'd forgotten that."

She'd forgotten a lot of things. Rose was almost used to it, the memories Anna had either lost or mixed up, confusing her with Lily, sometimes the other way around. Rose, after all, often confused Anna with a daughter. A real mother couldn't have gone through more hell than she had last night, beginning with a 2 A.M. phone call from the police. Fire in the restaurant; significant damage; two women ambulanced from the scene, conditions unknown. She hadn't lost her faith—that seemed like a miracle now. Speeding in her car through mercifully empty streets to the hospital, taking corners at desperate, death-defying angles, she'd kept asking God,

What now, what now, what now? Aghast at the possibility of another loss, a worse loss, surely this would kill her—but not *angry*, thank God. Yet. She'd never berated Him. She had an old Catholic God, not like Anna's good-natured relativist God. Hers would not have been amused if she'd berated Him.

"Here's some good news," she remembered to tell Anna. "Fontaine had her baby this morning. It's a little girl, and they're both doing fine."

"That's great. But, Rose, how in the world . . ."

"I have no idea." With no help from her family, how Fontaine was going to make it on her part-time pastry chef's salary with a brand-new baby, Rose couldn't imagine. "By the way," she said, "you and Carmen are heroes at the restaurant. Staff's been coming in all day to look at the damage, Louis and Billy, Dwayne, Shirl. Vince and Frankie."

"We weren't heroes, we were idiots."

"Well, now, there I couldn't agree with you more." She put her hands over her cheeks. "What in the name of God were you thinking? Both of you? No—don't tell me, don't talk."

"Is the breakfront okay?"

Rose took her hands away.

"Well, is it?"

"Yes. It's pristine."

Anna gave a satisfied nod. Around an ice chip, she said in a garbled voice, "So what's the damage?"

"The bar is fine, the sprinklers saved it. Vince is so disappointed—he wanted a new one with a zinc top."

"I heard bottles breaking."

"Just the wines in the display rack. They're gone, but the bar wines and liquors are all right. Filthy, but all right."

"What else?"

"Well, the kitchen is bad. The rubber mat melted and now it's stuck to the floor, so that'll be a fun job. About half the major appliances are gone, either destroyed by the fire or damaged so much by smoke and water that they're useless—the dishwasher, the salamander, the smaller range, the smaller refrigerator, all total losses. But the big range and grill are okay, which is a miracle, and the walk-in freezer will probably be all right after it's cleaned up. So that's two big, expensive items we can save. They're still figuring out what happened with the air ducts to the second floor, and that could be a huge expense if it's bad."

"Carmen's apartment?"

"No fire damage, but it's a mess. There's a sticky film from the smoke over everything. She doesn't know that yet, so don't mention it when you talk to her."

"What about the insurance? Are we covered for everything?"

This was the other thing she hadn't told Carmen. "We may not be. I don't understand it, but the agent wasn't all that reassuring. Everybody thinks the fire started with an electrical short, probably in the ice-making machine."

"Right. It did."

"Well, meanwhile, the fire prevention equipment in the grill exhaust hood has to be serviced every six months, and we missed it in August. Technically, it wasn't in compliance."

"You missed it?" She said that too loud; she winced and put her hand on her throat.

"It's my fault. We skipped the last inspection because I didn't want to pay the fire security company that does the cleaning—simple as that. Cash flow. We weren't having a code inspector visit till the end of this month, so I thought we had plenty of time."

"But if the cause was electrical anyway—"

"Yes, that's the point. It's a technicality, it has nothing to do with anything. It even *worked*—the foam stuff, the flame retardant or whatever you call it *came out*—that's what saved the grill. But Mason says they'll do anything to try to lessen their liability. The other thing the insurance man said is the O rings in the sprinkler heads were corroded, so maybe they're not liable for all the smoke damage in the dining room."

"My God."

"I know."

"What if they won't pay?" Anna's teary, bloodshot eyes went wide. "What will you do?"

Rose shook her head. "I can't even think about it."

Anna's roommate was a frail, elderly woman, in for overnight observation after falling and breaking her arm in the bathtub. They listened to her light snoring through the yellow curtain that separated the two beds.

"I was numb at first," Rose said, speaking softly in the confessional silence. "I couldn't make it sink in, not even when I walked around and made myself look at everything." The grim, boarded-up front, every storeowner's nightmare, the stench inside, the vicious damage, everything charred, blackened, stinking, wet, distorted, the rape of the business she had loved and hated and nursed and cursed for two-thirds of her life. "I couldn't make it real. It was like watching myself in a movie."

"Shock," Anna said.

"Iris said I should retire. That's when I woke up. She said I should cut my losses and get out. Because I'm old and tired—she didn't say that, but that's what she meant. I should sell out and move to Florida. For a little while, I have to say, the idea appealed to me."

"No." Anna's outraged face was gratifying.

"Yes. Like falling asleep when you're freezing to death. Just let go. How much easier it would be. I *am* old and tired."

"Bullsh—" She broke off to cough.

Rose laughed. She got her purse from the floor, her sweater from the back of the chair. "But now, do you know how I feel? I'm not numb anymore, that's for sure. My heart's broken. It's as if I'm grieving for a sick person, some injured loved one—and I can't wait to nurse it back to health. They'll have to drag me out of there now with chains and pulleys. Because here's a tragedy I can finally do something about."

Anna grinned. She looked at Rose expectantly.

She leaned over to brush a dirty lock of hair back from Anna's forehead. "I'm going now. Sorry I stayed so long. Do you need anything?"

"Oh, you don't have to go."

"You're exhausted. I am, too. I'll call in the morning, see when they're springing you and Carmen. Vince will probably pick you up and take you home."

"Rose?" Anna croaked.

She turned back at the door. "Hm?"

But then she didn't say anything, just stared across the room at her with her red-rimmed raccoon eyes.

"What?" Rose said.

"Nothing. Thanks for coming." She sank back down on her pillows with a rattling, dissatisfied sigh.

Much later, close to midnight, Anna called.

Rose wasn't asleep. She'd been sleeping badly for weeks, even before Theo died. Every night she told herself to get up and do something, clean a closet, write a letter, at least make insomnia productive. But she was too tired and spiritless to do anything except lie in the dark and drift from memory to memory, worry to worry. Tonight the worries crowded out the memories, and the phone's ring made her cringe. A call this late—what else could it be but more bad news?

"Hi, it's me," Anna said, as if the raven's croak wasn't a give-away. "Sorry if you were asleep."

"No, I wasn't. Are you all right?"

"Yes, I'm fine. I just, um . . ."

Rose glanced at the clock and sat up, scratching her head to clear it. "Couldn't sleep?"

"Yeah, I mean, it's bright as a bus terminal in here, plus the nurses think nothing of gabbing all night in the hall right outside your door." She went on in that vein for a while, complaining about everything, until Rose remembered—

"Hey, you're not supposed to talk. Why are you calling? You shouldn't even have a phone."

"Oh hell, I can talk, all it does is hurt my throat. Carmen can't talk—she won't even answer the phone in her room. The roommate answers, very unpleasant woman, she sounds very unhappy."

Rose sank back down, burrowing into her pillows. Were they going to have a chat? Fine with her.

"Aunt Iris called after you left. You know, just wanting to know how I'm doing and all."

"She's coming down tomorrow."

"Yeah, she said. She couldn't come today because of some dog's hernia or something. I told her there wasn't anything for her to do anyway."

"She's worried about you. And Carmen."

"I know."

Pause.

"And, um, Mason stopped by," Anna said casually.

"Mason came to the hospital?"

"Mm hm. Just for a minute."

"Really? He hates hospitals. I don't think he's been in one in five years." The doctors wanted to do more surgeries on his face, but he wouldn't cooperate.

"Wow," Anna said. "Well, he was uncomfortable, that's for sure, but I just figured it was because of, you know, the situation and everything. And what he wanted to say to me."

"What did he want to say to you?" She wouldn't have asked, but Anna was in such a forthcoming mood.

"Oh, you know. Not to go, stuff like that."

"I see." She smiled to herself. "He hasn't said that before?"

"He has, but not in a long time. Not lately."

She stifled a yawn. "And what did you say?"

"Nothing," Anna said, sounding dejected. "I told him I couldn't talk. Which was true—my throat really hurt."

"I expect you'll tell him something eventually."

There was another long pause.

"I have to get up early tomorrow," Rose hinted. "I've got another meeting with the insurance agent."

"Oh. Okay, sorry. I'll let you get some sleep."

"You get some sleep, too."

"Rose?"

"Yes?"

"How come . . ."

"How come what?"

She either laughed or coughed. "You know, everybody asks me to stay. Except you. So I was just wondering—maybe you don't even want me to, and that's why you don't ask."

Rose closed her eyes. "You want to know why I haven't asked you to stay?"

"Well . . . yeah."

"Because it wouldn't have done any good. You'd only have gotten angry."

"No, I wouldn't."

"Anna—"

"*Before*, I might've, okay. But why didn't you ask me again? Tonight when you were talking about rebuilding, starting over—you could've asked me then."

"I guess I could have."

"How come you didn't?"

"Because it's a foregone conclusion. Frankly, I'm surprised Mason didn't know that. He's usually good at that sort of thing."

"What do you mean? What's a foregone conclusion?"

"That you're staying."

"How do you know?"

"Oh, Anna, you're not going anywhere. You almost died last night."

"So? Anyway, no, I didn't, it was never—"

"You almost died because of a thousand-dollar piece of furniture."

"It was fourteen hundred, and I never—"

"You risked your life to save as much as you could of the Bella Sorella. So did Carmen. It was an incredibly foolish thing to do, and I know you weren't thinking straight, but that's what you did." Silence. No need, but Rose connected the line between the last two dots. "Does that strike you as normal behavior for a person who's just passing through?" Anna mumbled something. Rose said, "I didn't hear you."

"I don't know." More rusty mumbling.

"What?"

"You still could've asked me."

Rose laughed helplessly. "Would that make you feel better?"

"Yes."

She sighed. "Will you stay and help me put my poor, burned-out, under-insured restaurant back on its feet? Again?"

"Okay."

"Even though it may not work? Even though this time we'll probably fail and go down in the ashes and get—bitter and hopelessly broke and in debt and old before our time?"

"You bet. Can't wait."

They snickered together. "You're just my kind of partner."

"Crazy, you mean. Runs in the family."

Rose smiled in the dark. "Good night, Anna."

"You could've said that sooner, you know."

"Good night?"

"No, the other. I could've been fast asleep by now."

"Me, too," Rose realized.

21

Anna hadn't spent so much uninterrupted time in bed, at least alone, since last winter, when staying under the covers had been the simplest way to keep warm in Jay's loft. She was sick of sleeping, sick of being horizontal. At three in the afternoon, she threw off the covers and padded downstairs. Aunt Iris had left a pot of soup this morning when she'd stopped by to see how she was doing. Chicken soup? Vegetable? Hard to say; cooking wasn't Aunt Iris's strong suit. Anna heated a cup in the microwave and ate it leaning against the counter, staring out the window at the bird feeder. It was supposed to be squirrel-resistant, but there was a big bushy one right now, hanging upside-down from the wire, stuffing its face. She rapped on the glass, but it just looked at her with its liquid eyes and kept on chewing a sunflower seed. She knocked harder and waved her hands. "Beat it!" Finally it did, but first it twitched its tail at her in a rude, suggestive way. "Up yours, too." She used to like squirrels, but now they were pests, scarfing up bird-specific food she'd gone to no small trouble and expense to select, like millet for song sparrows and raisins and peanut butter for mockingbirds. The most interesting bird she'd attracted so far was a scarlet tanager, lured with a banana. She'd seen it during the period she and Mason weren't talking to each other, though, so she couldn't call him up and brag about it.

Tiredness was the only symptom she still had, no more coughing or nausea from breathing smoke. Before she finished her soup, she felt too lethargic to stand up. She got as far as the couch in the living room and collapsed.

Poor Carmen had to stay in the hospital another night—she had bronchitis. Anna was dying to talk to her, but Rose and Iris said not to call, she needed her rest. It was hard. Anna was dying to hear her grouchy voice, ask her if she didn't think it was pretty damn funny that they were still alive. Considering what idiots they had been. That was their new bond, she guessed; they had both behaved like complete lunatics. She could still see Carmen in her blowsy yellow nightgown, a human fire hazard, hunkered down under the metal counter while she tried to unscrew the meat grinder. She had, too—Rose said she'd saved it, not to mention a thousand dollars' worth of chef's knives and specialty pots and pans. Really, on the craziness scale, Carmen ranked much higher than Anna, who'd merely tried to save a room divider. She wanted to call her up and tell her so.

She wondered if Carmen was getting as philosophical as she was. Forty straight hours in bed—you couldn't sleep all of them away, so that left plenty of time for thinking. Time enough to figure out that the thing about righteous indignation was that it didn't go anywhere. It just sat there. It had nothing to feed on but itself, so it got fatter and fatter. Its diet consisted of nothing except outrage, reproach, and helplessness, and she could hardly think of three less appetizing ingredients. But she'd dined on it like the world's most unimaginative gourmet since she was twenty—a long time to spend chewing and swallowing an emotion that was indigestible to begin with.

The hardest thing to admit was that she was responsible, not Rose, for just about everything that had ever gone wrong with her adult life. That included the disconnectedness and isolation, the fact that she'd never sustained a relationship with a man beyond a couple of years, she had no best friend, and no home. Not only had she blamed Rose for all those deficiencies, she'd pretended they weren't failures at all, but choices. She'd held a grudge for almost half a lifetime over a perceived wrong that was never any of her business anyway. Four-year-old Katie forgave her mother for *real* sins, but twenty-year-old Anna had gotten on her very high horse and stayed there for almost twenty more. What a jerk.

She cast around for something to occupy her mind besides her inadequacies. In addition to soup, Aunt Iris had dropped off an armload of amusements, magazines and paperback novels, crossword puzzle books, a box of chocolates, a photograph album. She must expect Anna to be laid up for days. She chose the least mentally challenging, the chocolates and the photo album, and hauled them both onto her stomach, settling on the couch under the knitted throw. It was an old family album with puffy white pasteboard covers, yellowed from age, an embossed "Memories" in gilded script on the front. She turned the rusty pages curiously. Why would Iris leave her this? She'd seen most of these old snapshots before in her own family's photo albums.

She could never get over how skinny, about a hundred years ago, her Grandmother Fiore had been. She remembered Nonna as a wide, florid, unsmiling woman, always cooking, as muscular as Carmen and only a little sweeter-tempered—but here she was in a scoop-necked sundress and wedge-heeled sandals, graceful as a dancer. And Nonno—he looked like a gigolo! On their wedding day they'd posed in front of an old rattletrap car, not quite a Model T but almost, proud and excited in their black and white finery. But mysterious too, like silent film stars. Next came the baby pictures, Iris first, already cuddling the family dog, who was bigger than she was. Here she was at three or four, holding her parents' hands in front of their first restaurant, the tiny crab house on East Island, Fiore's Crabs & Beer, the hand-lettered sign in the window said. Then came Lily, then Rose, and here they were together in a sandbox, two cute little girls in corduroy jumpers and sandals with ankle socks. Time went by in photographs of Fiore birthday parties, First Communions and Confirmations, picnics and family reunions. And two more restaurants, a pizza parlor called Luigi's—named after nobody; Nonno, whose Christian name was David, had just wanted something that sounded Italian—and a spaghetti place called Banchetto that also sold homemade gelati to passersby from a sliding window beside the door.

Now pictures of Aunt Iris's wedding to Uncle Tony, with Lily and Rose as the pretty teenage bridesmaids. They'd had their reception at, where else, the Flower Café, Nonno and Nonna's brand-new restaurant on Severn Street—the first incarnation of the Bella Sorella. Anna kept turning the pages, waiting for the point, the punch line, but the album gave out in the late 'fifties with a color photo of Uncle Tony holding Anna's cousin Theresa in his arms, Aunt Iris's first child, on the steps of St. Luke's Church.

She turned the last page and found a few loose photos between it and the back cover. Color shots, more family pictures. Fiores at the beach. She looked at them more closely.

Theresa was about four now, building a sand castle with a red plastic bucket in the surf while thirtyish Aunt Iris hovered over her, grinning hugely, thin and shapeless in an electric-blue one-piece bathing suit. Next, a picture of Lily, lying on her side on a striped towel, one hand resting on the high curve of her hip, gazing into the camera with a sleepy, enigmatic smile. How sophisticated she looked, and much older than her age—twenty-two, according to the date on the back. Had she bleached her hair, Anna wondered, or was it sun-streaked? She thought of old photos of Julie Christie—her mother had that look, sexy but smart, not just a pinup.

Beefcake: Uncle Tony and her very young father faced the camera with their hands on their hips, legs spread, rather shockingly naked-looking in their skintight nylon suits. He-men. Tony was bigger, hairier, actually quite a hunk if you liked that sort of thing, and obviously Aunt Iris did. But Anna thought her lean, black-haired father was much handsomer. She stared at his tan, grinning face and marveled that he'd ever been so young. Either he hadn't shaved in a few days or he was going for a little hippie beard. He looked beautiful to her with his wire-rimmed glasses and shaggy hair, a careless cigarette clamped in his teeth.

The first of the two remaining pictures confirmed what Anna had already deduced—this was the long weekend in Bethany that had changed three people's lives. Possibly the weekend she'd been conceived. Her father and Rose, unaware of the camera, sat beside each other on a white blanket, Paul cross-legged, Rose with her long brown legs folded modestly to the side. She had on a black tank suit, the kind racers wore, not especially flattering but she'd loved to swim—she still did. Her long hair was streaming wet, and stuck to her forehead in lanky waves, styleless and therefore timeless. Everyone else looked right at home in the mid-sixties, but Rose could've come from any era. She rested her hand on Paul's bare knee, her head turned toward him, listening carefully, paying attention—there was so much tenderness in her faint smile and her downcast eyes. He was telling her something earnest and serious, his eyes full on her face. He could be talking about world peace, he could be talking about what kind of beer they should buy tonight for the clambake—either way, it was impossible to look at this photograph and not know they were in love. Solid, delighted love, no doubts, no games. They trusted each other. They thought this was going to last forever.

In the last photo, Paul posed with Rose and Lily in bright, shadowless sunlight, the blue and white Atlantic swirling around their calves. He stood between the two sisters with his arm around Rose's waist, but Lily had his other arm. She was pressing it to her side, her breast. His grin didn't look hip or cool in this one, it looked sheepish. Punchy.

Anna looked again at the photograph of her mother, alone on the striped towel. She studied it, the way she lay with one hand on her hip, the other pulling a pair of sunglasses down her nose so she could stare, languid-eyed, at the photographer. She had pale golden skin, flawless; the bust of her turquoise two-piece pushed her breasts up and out in a showy, generous display. Anna wasn't sure what her smile meant, whether it was flirtatious or bored, or both. Or was there a good-natured joke behind it? She looked and looked.

She wondered again what Iris's motive could've been for leaving her these pictures. Surely it wasn't to nail down Rose's visible, indisputable first claim on Paul; surely it wasn't to unmask her mother as some jealous, man-stealing femme fatale. Iris could not possibly think that would provoke in Anna any kind of epiphany. Besides, she had to know by now that there was no point: Anna and Rose had reconciled, the fight was over, it was ancient history.

Maybe it was simply to show her a picture of the past. These photos had been withheld from her until now. Maybe Iris only wanted her to *see* Rose and Paul in love, to look into their faces and let the years fall away. To believe in it and be glad for it, give up her last confusion about it. Accept the painful, grown-up truth that the mother she'd loved had not been chosen by the father she'd loved.

Fine, she'd done that. Mission accomplished.

She had a nagging sense, though, that there was more. One last lesson to learn. For a long time she'd been avoiding the tiresome, unappealing possibility that her highest, most enlightened life task was to forgive Rose. Now she had to look into the eye of another unpalatable possibility: that she wouldn't really be free until she forgave her mother.

Late in the afternoon, she went to see Mason.

Technically, she wasn't supposed to get out of bed until tomorrow, but she felt well enough after sleeping most of the day away. The thought of calling him on the telephone or, worse, sending him an e-mail left her cold. Literally; a slight but definite chill was coming from Mason's direction. He might be better at e-mails than talking, but she wasn't. She didn't think her own disembodied words would be the medium to thaw the ice.

She pulled in next to an unfamiliar car in his driveway. Sports car; a hunter green convertible with the top down. Who the hell was here, and how dare they? She felt unreasonably aggrieved. Cork lay fast asleep on the shady side of the porch, ineptly guarding the wide-open front door. He didn't see or hear Anna until she touched him on the head; then he jerked up as if he'd been shot. She jumped too, not in fear, just reaction—Cork didn't have a violent bone in his arthritic body. They soothed each other's nerves, she by petting him, he by wagging his tail, while she listened to the faint rise and fall of voices from the back of the house, Mason's and a woman's. Fatigue washed over her unexpectedly; she had to sit down on the top step. She stroked the dog and listened to the voices come closer.

The screen door opened. She turned around but didn't get up when an attractive blonde, fortyish, expensively dressed, stepped outside, followed by Mason. Neither one looked particularly surprised to see her; in fact, the woman smiled briefly but didn't stop talking. Mason pretended to listen to her, but Anna could tell she didn't have his attention anymore. When she paused—they were talking business, making some kind of a deal—Mason looked at Anna and said hi. "Hi," she said back. He said, "This is Cathy Doran—Anna Catalano," and the women said hi to each other.

"I know it's exactly right, I mean it's just what he wants, I absolutely know it." Cathy sounded excited. She was leaving; she said this as she walked across the flagstone path toward the driveway. Mason followed, but she stopped halfway to finish the conversation. "I honestly don't have any qualms about doing this on my own."

"But just in case—" Mason said.

She interrupted, as if they'd been through this already, "No, I have a guy—I told you, I know someone who'll take it down to St. Michael's on the weekend. All I have to do is arrange it. Oh, this is perfect—Frank's birthday is Sunday, it'll be the most incredible surprise." She laughed gaily. "We have a sort of contest going. He'll *never* top this."

Whatever the deal was, they shook hands on it; Cathy said she'd call Mason in the morning, then walked off to her car. He stayed put while she got in. She pulled on a Ravens ball cap at a jaunty angle, started the burbling, low-throated engine, backed out, and pulled away.

"Who was that?" Nosy and none of Anna's business, which was why she asked. She meant to insinuate herself back into Mason's life, and one way would be to take it for granted that she belonged there.

But what she really wanted to say was, "Boy, you sure are a sight for sore eyes." He sauntered over and put one foot on the step beside her, stuck his hands in his back pockets. Last night in the hospital he'd looked a little green around the gills, but today he looked good. Healthy and ruddy-skinned in the slanting sunset, streaky-haired, as if he'd been working outside. Which she guessed he had; according to Rose he'd just gotten back from a trip to Cape May to photograph birds heading south on the flyway. She had a potent urge to touch him, reach inside the bottom of his pants leg and massage his calf. Press her fingers up and down the hard bone in front.

"She wants to buy the *Wind Rose*," he answered her question. "For her husband."

Anna absorbed that with a shock. "You're selling it? I thought—I didn't even know—" She hadn't even known the sailboat was *his*; for some reason she'd assumed it was Rose's.

"Theo and I owned it together, and he left me his half in his will," he said, reading her mind. "But I doubt if that's what he really wanted. He'd have given it to Rose if he could."

"Why couldn't he?"

"Fairness, his notion of it. He couldn't work on the boat much for the last year or so, less and less the sicker he got. I think he meant to pay me back by leaving it to me."

"But you don't want it anymore?" Considering how Theo had died, she couldn't blame him.

"I've got a better use for the money."

And she knew what it was. It came to her in a flash— "You're going to give it to Rose."

He tried to look simultaneously noncommittal and slightly offended. He took his foot off the step and moved back.

"You are, aren't you? You're giving it to Rose because the fire insurance money might not come through—or it might get delayed while the lawyers fight about it. That's all right," she said hastily, "you don't have to tell me, none of my business. But do you think she'll take it? Maybe if it's a loan. Well, anyway. Wow, that's... Okay, we don't have to talk about it."

He scowled at her, foiled and confounded. "Do you want to come inside?"

Good way to change the subject. She noticed she wasn't tired anymore as she got up and followed him into the house. He hesitated in the living room, as if debating where to put her, then proceeded on to the kitchen. "Do you want a cup of coffee or something? A drink? How are you feeling?"

"Have you got any fruit juice? I'm okay. I can still smell smoke in my nose, but that's about it. Thanks," she said when he handed her a glass of orange juice.

He folded his arms and leaned back against the refrigerator. "Sorry about last night," he said, watching her drink.

"Why? I thought it was very nice of you to come." Especially since he was phobic about hospitals.

"I wasn't very nice when I got there."

"You weren't?" Truthfully, she couldn't remember much about his visit. *Was that really Mason who came to see me?* she'd halfway wondered, especially after the nurse gave her a sleeping pill. The standout moment was after he left, when she'd gone into the bathroom and finally gotten a good look at herself in the mirror. She'd let out a croaky obscenity, startling her roommate. Mason had seen her looking like *this*? Dirty eyes, sooty nose, filthy, ashy hair?

"I shouldn't have said you were stupid."

That's right—he'd called her *stupid*. It was all coming back to her. "No," she agreed, "you sure shouldn't have. Very bad sick person etiquette."

He'd said she was stupid to think she was leaving, was what he'd said. Not angrily or hatefully; quite nicely, in fact, but how gentle could you be when you were calling someone stupid? She'd wanted sweetness and sympathy from him, and he'd never even touched her. Clearly he'd noticed the same incongruity Rose had, that she was sucking oxygen in a hospital bed after risking her life to save a place she kept insisting had no emotional hold on her. He and Rose had certainly twigged to the contradiction there a lot faster than she had.

"Why'd you come to see me if you were just going to yell at me?"

He shook his head at her, as if he considered the question disingenuous but he'd be a good sport and answer it anyway. "To make sure Rose wasn't humoring me. I wanted to see for myself that you were all right."

She melted.

Something squawked, a raspy, wooden-sounding quack from the direction of the back porch. "What's that?" she asked. "A new patient? The bird hospital is open again?"

He smiled. "Come and see."

Out on the porch, a white and black bird, medium-size, sat on the bottom of a big metal cage, a real cage, not a cardboard box this time. She followed Mason's lead as best she could and approached it with slow, nonjerky movements. "What is it?" she whispered, squatting down beside him. "What happened to him? Poor thing. Is it a tern?"

He looked at her with unflattering amazement. "What kind?"

"What kind? I don't get credit for knowing it's a *tern*?" It sat quietly, apparently unafraid, blinking its beady eyes and bobbing its long, forked tail. It had a light gauze bandage on its bright white breast, and a splint, an actual splint, on its foot—a tiny cardboard platform taped between each of its clawed orange toes. "What happened to him?"

"Forster's tern," Mason said. "Wait a sec." He went in the kitchen and came back with a plastic container, the contents of which became obvious as soon as he took the lid off. Stinky fish. "Herring," he explained, transferring pieces from the container to a shallow dish inside the cage. "He likes canned clams, too."

"What got hold of him, a cat?"

"More likely an owl or a raccoon. Cork and I found him on the riverbank. They breed out on that marsh island you can see from the dock. Something nocturnal got him."

"Wow, he looks like you were just in time. Did he break his foot?"

"Just a toe. That's why he can't perch. His beak was cracked, too, but that's already healed. Although he'll always have a slight overbite."

She looked at his straight face and decided that wasn't a joke. "Did you give him stitches?"

"Yes."

She'd been joking. "You did? No, you didn't. Really?"

"I was out of silk thread, so I had to use dental floss. Want to see?"

"That's okay." If he was showing off, it was working. She decided to show off, too. "Terns" she said, "are neotropical migratory birds. Which means they spend the summer here and then fly to South America for the winter. This guy should be leaving in a couple of weeks. Think he'll be up for the trip?"

Mason sent her a sly, appreciative look. She followed him back to the kitchen and watched him wash his hands at the sink.

"The distances some birds migrate are truly incredible," she mentioned. "Take the blackpoll warbler. It can go nonstop from Canada to South America in seventy-two hours. That's about thirteen hundred miles. That's like a human being running four-minute miles for eighty consecutive hours."

"Amazing."

"It's a very hazardous journey. Lots of birds don't make it, they get blown out to sea in storms, or they land and find out the place they've been stopping over to rest and eat in for years has turned into a shopping mall. Or they fly into office buildings at night, thousands and thousands of songbirds especially, they fly into the lights of tall office buildings and die. Cities should pass laws making these buildings turn their lights out at night, it's ridiculous."

Mason dried his hands on a paper towel and threw it in the garbage. He watched her.

"I'm against migration," she said.

"You're against migration?"

"It's too perilous. Much safer to stay where you are. Just stay home once you get there."

He went to the refrigerator and took out a bottle of water, opened it, downed a few swallows. Stared at her some more.

He wasn't getting her migration analogy. She decided to stop beating around the bush.

"I've been behaving badly. In particular, I haven't been fair to you. In fact, I've been a real ass. I didn't come here to ask if we can still be friends. You keep doing things that make me think you must care for me, otherwise I can't figure out why you'd do them. That's what gives me the guts to say this to you now. Because, as you know, I'm not very gutsy. In this area."

He wasn't jumping in to disagree with anything. He had his hands on the counter behind him, elbows jacked out, head down, contemplating his tennis shoes.

"I'm suggesting another try. If it doesn't work out, I won't be leaving, after. And if it does work out, no matter how terrifying that is, I won't be leaving, either. I've landed. I'm like the great blue heron," she said recklessly, "I live here now. All year."

"In fact," he said, "the great blue heron is rare around here in the late summer. In winter, we might get New England's great blues, while South Carolina gets ours. Range overlap, that's called. So it's true we have them year-round, but they're not necessarily the same—"

"Oh, for Pete's sake, I'm trying to make up here." She grabbed hold of him. "I'm sorry I was a lousy girlfriend. I can do a lot better." She stood on her toes and kissed him.

He said, "I don't see how."

This was what she needed. Active forgiveness; somebody's arms around her. Making up with Rose on the phone was satisfying, but not in the same way as making up with Mason in bed. She felt like she'd been without him for years, not weeks. Even when she'd had him, she'd kept him at a distance, thinking she was freer that way. A woman who traveled light.

"I have to ask a stupid question," she said while she rooted around in his closet, hunting for his flannel bathrobe. She found it and tied it around her naked self, burying her nose in the shoulder. She'd missed that smell. "Well, not so much stupid as annoying. For you."

She flopped down on the bed and sat cross-legged, facing him. "Mason, what do you see in me? Why do you want to be with me? But wait—first I'll tell you what I see in you, because I don't want this to be all one-way and self-centered. But then back to me, because I'd really like to know. Why you care about me at all when I've been such a jerk."

"But you haven't been."

"See, that's one of the things I love about you. You're so nice." She traced the long scar that went from his rib cage to his hipbone, stroking it very lightly with her fingertips. "You're just...nice. And for another thing, I've never known anybody like you. You're mysterious—but that's not too important," she backtracked, "that's like being good-looking, it doesn't mean anything, because eventually all the mysteries get solved. That's just infatuation. What else? I like it that you know things I don't know anything about. I find that sexy. And I trust you. Even when you tackled me, I wasn't truly frightened, not deep down."

"That was a little crazy," he conceded.

"Yes, it was. You don't talk much—I don't know if I like that or not. But you're a man of action, and I know I like that. But the thing I admire most is how brave you are." She knew that would embarrass him, and sure enough, he crossed his arms and legs and made a scoffing face. "No, you are, you do things you're scared to death of doing. And sure, they're irrational, I mean, they're intrinsically nonscary things, but they absolutely terrify you and you do them anyway. I love that." All this "liking" and "loving" of "that" or "that in you" was getting a little silly. How hard would it be just to say, "I love you"? Really, how hard?

"Okay, now you tell me what you see in me. Not that that's the end of the list for you—I've got more, I'm just taking a break."

He sighed. Oh, she'd missed seeing him smile. She loved thinking she could make Mason happy, that she could change his moods and be good for him. She'd forgotten to tell him that she loved the shape of his head, and his snobby, aristocratic feet, and his skinny butt. Later.

"You," he said. "What do I see in Anna. I won't say Rose—that never gets me anywhere."

"You can say it if you want. I'm not as weird about that as I used to be." She lay down beside him, sharing the pillow.

"I never meant you *are* alike. Only that you look alike."

"Why do men always put looks at the top of the list?" she butted in. "We never do, but you guys always say, the very first thing, 'she's pretty,' or 'she's attractive,' when you're describing a woman. Always. Why is that?"

"We're shallow."

"Anyway." She snuggled closer, not wanting to be disagreeable just when he was getting to the good part. "Do go on."

He took her hand and frowned, absently moving his thumb between her fingers, web to web, pressing down. He did that with his own hands when he was thinking hard, and now he was doing it with hers.

"Well?" He was either choosing his words carefully or he was having to dig down awfully deep to come up with reasons he liked her. Or loved her. Whatever.

"Before I met you, my favorite way of looking at things was through my camera. Framed." He held his hands in the air, making a box with his fingers, sighting through it. "I could be right there, between the black sides of the lens, inside the dark box with whatever I was photographing. Safe, like being in an empty movie theater. I kept order by framing a thing exactly the way I wanted, and then I reproduced it. Took its picture. Whatever I wanted, whatever I thought was beautiful, it was mine, and it couldn't fly away, I captured it. Not just birds—landscapes stood still for me, too. They were caught. And people."

She thought of the photographs he used to take of her, Anna leaving, Anna walking away. From the first, he'd been trying to make her stay.

"But people can't be caught," she told him urgently. "They leave. I was trying to say that to you when we were fighting, but I didn't get it right. People leave and it's not your fault, it's nothing you've done." She put her hand on his chest, over his heart, wishing she could fix him. "If I had left, it wouldn't have had anything to do with you. It would've been my failing, not yours."

He said, "You made me want to come out of the black box. I didn't know if I could, I'd gotten so comfortable in there. I have very kind friends, and they put up with a lot from me and didn't challenge it, they just took me for what I was. Rose is one of them."

"Whereas I..." Maybe she didn't like where this was going after all.

"You didn't know. What you were dealing with. I didn't have a history with you. I wanted one."

They had something in common. She was realizing it for the first time, and that was pretty amazing. Also pretty blind, pretty stupid. He called the thing they had in common—which, when you cleared everything away and got down to it, was fear—a form of psychopathology, whereas she'd always called it Anna. Just her way.

"I have to feed the bird," he said. "Every two or three hours—"

"I know, but first—"

"Right, you want to know *why*. And I can't say. It's a mystery. Maybe I thought you could use someone like me. The first day we met, you were so..."

"Bitchy?"

"Prickly. Covering up a hurt. Maybe I recognized you. Or maybe it was just time for me to come around," he theorized, "maybe—"

"Maybe I had nothing at all to do with it. Right place, right time. I could've been anybody. I could've been Cathy Doran." But she had to laugh: it was so obvious that she was saying these things so he would disagree with her.

He cleared his throat. "Things I love about Anna." He held up one finger. "Hair."

She swatted him.

"These aren't in order. Really nice hair."

"I hate my hair. It's like a bird's nest—that's probably why you like it, you see it as habitat."

He put his hands in her hair, and of course then she didn't hate it so much, and he never got around to finishing his list. Or feeding his

Forster's tern, not for quite a while. For a recent victim of smoke inhalation, she had a lot of stamina.

Much later, they went outside with Cork for a walk, and wound up sitting at the end of the dock in the crisp moonshine, listening to the sounds of water and cicadas and rustling leaves. The *Wind Rose* bobbed in the gentle river current, silver light from the moon gleaming on its white-painted spars. In its metaphorical shadow, it was impossible, at last, for Mason not to talk about Theo. Anna had been wanting that intimacy with him for a long time, even when they were barely speaking and she had the smallest right to it. What an openhearted gesture, to share your unglamorous grief with another person, to let someone see all your pain and anguish because of a grievous loss. She didn't take the honor lightly. And not that she was any kind of a substitute, no human quid pro quo, but at least she had something besides sympathy to give him back now, something more substantial than words. Mason, ever generous, seemed grateful for the gift.

22

Warm chocolate and hazelnut, oh, what a luscious smell. Rose stuck a toothpick in the center of the first of her four soufflés. Perfect, still a little runny in the center, and shallow fissures were snaking across the top as the rich cake began its classic fall. Sometimes everything went right. People would marvel over these, and she would smile with modest pride. To those who didn't already know—not too many in this crowd—she wouldn't confide that one of the easiest things in the world to make was a soufflé.

These had cooled enough to refrigerate. "Billy, I'm leaving the whipped cream garnish to you. Use a hot knife when you cut them, and don't forget, more chopped hazelnuts on top of each serving. Ten servings to a soufflé, I'm thinking."

"Okay, Chef." Billy Sanchez stopped slicing blanched asparagus spears long enough to grin at her. "Feels good to be back at work, doesn't it?"

"It feels wonderful." Automatically she checked his neat piles of shaved Parmesan and chopped mint, his bowl of beaten eggs. Billy was making asparagus frittatas for an appetizer. "Easy on the pepper," she cautioned. A joke—Billy had once served pureed jalapeños to Dwayne at family meal and told him it was olive paste.

Billy's station was near the new half-door to the dining room. Beside it, Rose saw that Anna had tacked on the wall a new list of rules for servers, the last thing they'd see before going out on the floor.

1. Never leave the dining room empty-handed.
2. Never say no to a customer. Say, "If we've got the ingredients, you can have anything you want."
3. Compliments to the chef should be delivered immediately. Complaints—handle on your own.
4. Don't run, people think there's a fire.
5. Don't laugh, people think you're laughing at them.
6. Whoever asks for the check first gets it.
7. If business is slow and you want it to pick up,
   a. Sit down to eat.
   b. Light up a cigarette.
8. Smile! Smile! Smile!

Somebody had added a ninth rule in ballpoint pen at the bottom. It couldn't be anyone but Vonnie.

9. Don't bother counting your tips. It all evens out in the end.

The argument at the big stove was rising in volume and getting harder to ignore. Rose wanted to stay far, far away, but she also wanted to check on the polenta she was serving with braised pork and olive sauce in approximately—she checked the brand-new clock on the wall—ten minutes. The last thing she had to do was stir in the cheese and herbs, and timing was critical.

"Rose, come here and taste this," Carmen called over.

Trapped.

Billy kept his head down but he made a low, snorting sound, *skkkk*, in the back of his throat. Rose pretended stepping on his foot was an accident.

Hard to believe, but Carmen and Frankie were still fighting over minestrone. Cannellini or kidney beans, macaroni or ditalini, cabbage versus string beans versus peas. Passionate bickering over stock only or stock with water had gone on for days, *weeks*. What could they still have to disagree about?

"Taste," Carmen commanded, thrusting out a steaming spoon. Close beside her, Frankie stood with her fists on her hips, tense as a spring trap. They'd look wonderful together in a photograph, Rose thought, a splashy profile in a food magazine—big, round, and florid next to milk-pale and minute. *The Chefs of the Bella Sorella.*

Well, this was a no-win. She took a careful slurp of the thick soup and hummed, "Mmm," simultaneously equivocal and appreciative—years, it had taken her to perfect that tone. The soup was really delicious. But whose side would it behoove her to be on this time? She was getting too old for this.

"It's good, right?"

She regarded Carmen's stuck-out chin with caution and said yes.

"Doesn't need anything, right?"

"Need," she echoed thoughtfully. "Well, *need*, you know, that's so..."

"It doesn't need any basil pesto to finish it off," Carmen declared, laying her cards down all at once.

"Ah. What do you think?" Rose asked Frankie straight out—which she was allowed to do; Carmen was the chef and Frankie was the sous-chef, although Rose, who had conferred these titles herself, took every opportunity to avoid them.

"The pancetta wasn't my idea," Carmen got in before Frankie could answer. That was true; Carmen had been violently against the addition of Italian bacon on the grounds that real minestrone was meatless. Nonsense, Frankie argued, Lombardy minestrones always had pancetta, and besides, the whole point of minestrone was to put in whatever you liked, whatever was fresh and on hand, including meat. "Now she wants to add *pesto*," Carmen said, rolling her lips back in revulsion—as if to say, "Now she wants to add *maggots*." "But then it'll be too salty. *Troppo salato!*"

"No, it won't."

"Yes, it will."

"No, it won't. I don't *make* salty pesto."

"You can't *help* making salty pesto."

"Did you taste it?"

"Did you put parmigiana in it?"

"Yes."

"Well, then." Carmen folded her beefy arms. Case closed.

Frankie glared. She'd been moving a little closer with each heated exchange; if they were the same height, they'd be nose to nose now. As it was, they were nose to enormous bosom. Abruptly, she stepped back. "Okay."

Carmen blinked, then stalled out in confusion. "Okay?"

"You're right, it would be a little salty. I think it would give it some depth, some heft, but for some people's tastes it would be too salty."

Carmen set the spoon down distractedly. She looked at Rose. So did Frankie. She was as surprised as they were; she was used to refereeing disagreements, not blessing unions. "How about some lemon juice?" she tried. "At the very end."

"Lemon juice," they repeated. They looked at each other with suspicion.

"Okay with me," Carmen conceded.

"Freshness," Frankie said. "A little acidic goose."

"Finish it off."

"Kick it up a note."

"Give it some bite."

The rehab of the burned-out kitchen included bright white walls and more intense lighting, a handsome wood slat floor, gleaming new stainless steel appliances and equipment. In addition, a lot of things weren't where they used to be. Changes to floor patterns and the placement of work stations made moving around easier, faster, and more logical. For example, the reach-in refrigerator wasn't below the chef's station anymore, it was *beside* it. Result: Carmen and Frankie didn't have to bend their knees and lean over three or four hundred times a day to prepare or finish off plates of food. Rose liked to think their new spirit of cooperation and compromise sprang from the fundamental nobility of their natures, but if it came from aesthetics or ergonomics, that was fine, too, or feng shui for all she cared. Dwayne had a new three-tub pot sink, and it had turned him into a new man.

"Time to start plating," she decided after another glance at the clock. The menu was simple—luckily, because there weren't many of them to serve it. Vince was working drinks and Anna was passing hors d'oeuvres; everybody else was having a good time, and that was as it should be. They were on schedule, though. Billy's frittatas were done, the polenta was perfect. Grilled fennel gratin would be an experiment; same with Carmen's rosemary grissini. Rose was spooning olive sauce over plates of pork and polenta as fast as Frankie could pass them to her when Anna slammed in through the door, carrying a couple of empty trays. She looked harassed but beautiful, Rose thought—not that she was prejudiced. She thought of Anna's phone call last night, to ask what she was wearing. Her dark red dress, Rose had answered; "I don't know if you've seen it or not, it's got—" "Hah," Anna interrupted, "I knew it! I wanted to wear *my* dark red dress." Rose had laughed and told her to go ahead and wear it—but no, she'd chosen a long, heather-gray skirt and a low-cut red sweater, and high-heeled boots she planned to take off later for dancing. *I must have looked like that in my thirties*, Rose thought, with a mellow rue. *I wish I'd known it. I'd have had a better time.*

"The crostini and mussels went like hotcakes," Anna announced to the kitchen at large. "They will absolutely work great for tapas."

"What about the eggplant fritters?" Frankie asked, slicing pork into serving pieces at the speed of light.

"Good, but not as good. But they know we've got a feast coming, so they're saving themselves. How are we doing here?"

"We're good," Rose said, drying her hands at the sink. "Unless you think we should put everything on the bar..."

A chorus of *No*'s—they'd been through this, and she always lost. Majority had ruled that the guests should come into the kitchen to pick up their own plates.

"Okay, then," Anna said, "are we ready?"

"No!" Carmen, Frankie, and Billy finished what they were doing and began to strip out of aprons and tunics and shuck off their clogs, out of their work clothes and into their finery. Frankie finished last. She blushed when Anna and Billy whistled. "Oh, Jeez, cut it out, it's just a skirt. Would you get lives?"

"*Now* are we ready?"

"Ready!"

Anna held the door for Rose and clapped her hands to quiet the revelers in the dining room so Rose could announce, "Dinner is served."

They'd made a big U of the dining room, the long banquette on one side, connecting tables on the other two. The space in the middle would be for dancing, later. This dinner was special, like a formal family meal, except mixed in with the kitchen and waitstaff were some of the Bella Sorella's oldest and best customers, favored guests invited to celebrate the imminent reopening. "Good PR," Anna called it, a clever way to grab the loyalty and goodwill of the old-timers, get them invested in the new place early on. Maybe so, but Rose thought of it more as a gathering of old friends. After the meal and before dessert, she stood up to say so.

"I'll keep this short," she began after the tinkling of silverware on glasses stopped and the room quieted. "Thank you—thank you all for coming—it's wonderful to look out and see the faces of so many of my friends, those of you it's been my pleasure to employ, and those it's been my pleasure to serve for—well, too many years to say, and if I did it would make us all feel ancient. Thank you for coming, thank you for helping us celebrate the fact that we survived. It could never have happened without you, and I have to say thanks in particular to those of you who put in so many long hours, long, *unpaid* hours, helping with the hard, dirty work of cleanup, which we thought would never end. But it did, and now, thanks to you, we're not only going to make it, we're going to come back better than ever. Yes! Look around, just look at our beautiful new restaurant. And smell—did you ever think that smoke smell would go away? And if this fabulous dinner Carmen and Frankie and Billy made for us tonight as a run-through, a sort of dress rehearsal for Tuesday—to make sure everything in our brand new kitchen actually works—if this meal is any indication of things to come, doesn't it make you even *more* confident that we're going to be a fine success? Yes. So let's say thanks to our chefs by toasting them—and I drink to you, all my friends, my family. I love you all. *Salute*."

Other people got up to say grateful, flattering things—Anna, Vonnie, Roxanne, who owned the jewelry store across the street, old Mr. Kern, a retired florist who hadn't missed a Friday night at the Bella Sorella in twenty years. Rose was the recipient of so many toasts, she began to feel like the bride at a wedding reception. Her chocolate hazelnut soufflés were a gratifying triumph. Over coffee—from the brand-new cappuccino machine, a complicated miracle of gleaming copper and stainless steel, big as a pipe organ and almost as expensive—the old game of renaming the restaurant started up again. It didn't seem to faze anybody that the time for a new name had obviously passed—they were opening in four days as the Bella Sorella. But Rose listened to Bella Rosa, Casa Rosa, Mama Rosa, Zia Rosa—Il Giardiniere, Giardiniere di Fiori, Giardiniere di Rosas—and she gave them all her thoughtful, considering look even though nobody believed in it anymore. "She hates everything," Dwayne sulked. Frankie said, "Why don't you just call it

Rose and Anna's Restaurant?" Anna laughed, but Rose patted her chin with her fingers, thoughtful.

Vince and Frankie had argued for days over what kind of music to play after dinner. He'd wanted a classic oldies band, she'd wanted a hip-hop group. The Honey Lickers played rhythm and blues, and were supposed to be a compromise. If that was a compromise, Frankie said, she was Dr. Dre. Beyond the fact that Frankie didn't care for the band, Rose had no idea what that meant.

"Check that out," Carmen said, pointing with a glass of wine at Vince and Frankie on the dance floor. "Look how stiff she is. Like she's never slow-danced in her life."

Rose had to agree. It was easier to see Frankie jumping up and down in a mosh pit than plodding around in Vince's arms to a dreamy Anita Baker love song. "Doesn't she look pretty, though?" She had on a billowy white poet blouse tucked into a tiered skirt of bright, flouncy colors, feminine and bohemian, not Frankie's usual style at all. She wore hoop earrings, too, and a gay fuschia scarf tied around her bald head. She was barefooted. She looked like a gypsy.

But when the dance ended, she looked relieved. She dropped Vince's arms as if she couldn't get away fast enough and padded over to Rose's and Carmen's table for a drink. "Hey," she greeted them, pouring ice water into a glass and drinking it down without stopping. It was hot and she was sweating—before Vince, she'd danced with everybody else—but she kept her pretty scarf on. She had a *little* bit of vanity, Rose was glad to see. "Hey, Carmen," she said, "you wanna dance?"

"Yeah, right." Under the snort and the sarcasm, though, she looked tickled. "So what's the deal with you and Vince?"

"Me and who?" She fanned herself by pulling her blouse away from her chest and fluttering it.

"Come on. You guys an item or what?"

"Jeez, Carmen. No. Shit, no, we're not an *item*. For one thing, one of like a hundred things, he's too young for me. I like an older guy."

"How's that been working out for you?"

Frankie's hard eyes bored into Carmen, gauging if that was a shot. No, she decided, and shrugged. "Hey, Vince is okay. In fact, I just said I'd go out with him, you want the latest. One time, like an experiment, a one-time shot, very unlikely it'll work out."

"Oh, Frankie," Rose said, patting her heart. "You big romantic fool."

The party got louder, crazier. Vince opened another case of Rubesco di Torgiano. "Told you we should've had a cash bar," he whispered to Rose, half serious. It was a good thing they had no neighbors to complain about noise, good thing Carmen wasn't upstairs trying to sleep. In fact, she was out on the dance floor, two-stepping with Dwayne. Check *that* out, Rose thought, spellbound.

The band took a break, and during the interlude of relative quiet Luca approached the microphone on the makeshift stage and asked for silence. He looked small but handsome, Rose thought, more dressed up than anyone else tonight in a black suit, spit-shined black shoes, and matching matinee idol hair. "*Scusi, scusi. Prego*, my friends. *Scusi*. Attention, please. Hey! *Zitto!*"

Quiet.

"*Grazie*. I have announcement, very special to say. Tonight, is even more for celebration than our grand reopening—tonight is *miracolo*, miracle, because—guess what—Fontaine, who you love so much, is consent to be married to me! *Si*, a miracle—Fontaine, *cara*, come, be with me here—"

Oh no. Rose forced a smile and began to clap with the others, but Anna caught her eye and the message passed between them: *Oh no*.

Blonde and radiant, and tiny again in a sheer blue slip dress, Fontaine walked across the floor to the surprised applause, holding her new baby in her arms. Behind the shy smile, Rose thought she looked stunned, as if Luca's announcement still shocked her, too. Gracie, she'd named the baby; she had Fontaine's silky fair hair and delicate features, and nothing of Eddie, everyone had been glad to see, at least not at four weeks.

Luca put his arm around Fontaine's waist and drew her close, beaming down at the sleeping infant. "I am so lucky," he said into the microphone. "Now I have not only Bella Sorella, which I love so much, but also sweet new *bella famiglia*, my wife, my own little baby." He drew an enormous white handkerchief out of the pocket of his black coat and wiped his face. No one laughed or teased him, not even Jasper, not even Dwayne. "Today is best day of all days. Today I'm in love with my life again. Thank you, everybody, *grazie di tutta la sua gentilezza*. I am so happy. So happy."

Maybe it would work. *Un miracolo*. Only half of all marriages lasted anyway, under the best of circumstances—wasn't that the statistic? Oh, but poor Luca, Rose thought, watching him shake hands with his pals from the kitchen, suffer their pounding fists on his slight shoulders, blush under their coarse ribbing. By his lights he was saving Fontaine, and he got a beautiful *bambina* in the bargain. Ready-made family. Fontaine would feel lucky at first, as if she'd been rescued, but what then? She was a child herself—Luca was almost twice her age. Not to mention that she'd never shown any interest in a man like him before, a gentle, nurturing, sweet-tempered mensch of a man. How could this possibly work? And what damage would it do when it unraveled?

She ought to dance, wake herself up from the blue mood she'd fallen into. But Rose stayed where she was, feeling like a duenna, turning down partners with a laugh or a joke. Anna winked at her over Mason's shoulder, and she admired how neatly they danced together, how passionate and controlled, caught up tight in each other's arms. Theo had loved to dance. He'd loved to hold her close and twirl her around, pluck her off her feet like a girl. He was graceful, too, for such a bear of a man. She missed him beyond speaking.

Oh, she didn't want to sink into melancholy, she didn't want to think about Paul or Theo or the inevitability of loss while the band played "Let's Stay Together." But she thought, *Maybe this isn't my world any longer.* Maybe it was time to relinquish it to the young. She'd had her turn. Maybe the best she would ever have was memories. She felt brittle, as if her bones were drying out.

"Rose, could you hold her for a minute? Just for this one song? Luca says we have to dance." Very gently, Fontaine laid the baby on Rose's knees.

Gracie's steel-blue eyes were wide open. They locked on Rose's when she leaned over and murmured, "Hello, baby," stroking the thin, see-through pink of her delicate ear. "Hello, beautiful girl." Gracie blinked back an intent greeting. Who could be sad or distant or ironical with a month-old baby in her arms? Life was for being alive, being with people you loved already or might love someday. Eat, dance, laugh. Warm, squirmy life was right here, Gracie's little bow mouth still pursing on her mama's phantom breast. Rose put her lips on the baby's satiny temple and let herself be comforted.

The Honey Lickers played their last song, the guests began to trickle away. Rose quashed a halfhearted staff movement to clean up the mess in the kitchen tonight. "No, no, tomorrow's soon enough," she insisted, although it broke her cardinal rule against leaving cleanup for the morning. "But that's an open invitation to vermin," Vonnie reminded her—"that's what you always say, Rose, you know you do." Yes, but this was a special occasion, and besides, a hostess couldn't very well ask her honored, dressed-up guests to stay late, put on their aprons, and clean up after themselves.

She said good night to her friends, her employees, one by one. Carmen had gone up already, complaining her feet were killing her. Rose intended to be the last out and lock up after herself, so she was surprised, after a final trip back from the kitchen, to find Anna sitting by herself at the bar, waving good night to the last guests, a wobbly Tony and Suzanne.

"I called them a cab," she told Rose. She turned in her stool and patted the one next to it invitingly. "Sit for a minute?"

She sat, and couldn't help admiring the new floor in the soft light over the bar. It was faux tiles, bright squares of clay, yellow, and pale blue, painted over the old pine boards. Water damage from the fire had ruined the old carpet, to Anna's delight; she'd wanted to strip the floors bare throughout the restaurant, no rugs at all, and Rose had wanted pretty new carpet everywhere. This was their compromise: cheerful, painted floor around the bar and at the host's podium, beautiful new peach-colored carpet in the dining room. They both won.

"Where's Mason?" Rose asked.

"Oh, he went home, he has to get up early tomorrow. He's going to Canada."

"*Canada.*"

"Yeah, didn't he tell you? Some place in Saskatchewan called Last Mountain Lake. He's taking pictures of cranes."

"Heavens."

"I know. It's like he's making up for lost time."

"All those hours he missed flying on airplanes," Rose joked, although it wasn't really a laughing matter. Mason had had a setback a couple of weeks ago—out of the blue, he couldn't walk into a lecture hall for a long-planned talk and slide show on marsh birds of the Chesapeake. It wasn't public speaking, it was *being inside* that had panicked him, simply being in a place he couldn't legitimately get out of for an indefinite length of time. Strangely enough, though, the next day he'd breezed through a scheduled appearance for the local Audubon chapter, and that had also involved being inside, being captured—the same circumstance as the night before, but this time without incident. It was the unpredictability of his attacks, he said, that gave them their power.

"Do you think he'll be all right?" Rose wasn't sure if she meant in Canada or in general.

"Yes," Anna said, "I do. Eventually. Because he's getting more and more philosophical about it, which means less and less ashamed. He says when the embarrassment dies, so does the fear. He wanted me to go with him," she added, smiling. "Not to save him or anything, just for fun."

"You *should* go. Why don't you?"

"Oh, too much to do, plus I'd miss the reopening—he's not coming back till Wednesday." That reminded her of something. She got up and went behind the bar, began poking around in the back-lit pyramid of liquors and liqueurs, searching for something.

"But you'd have gone with him if the timing had been better? To Last Mountain Lake? You wouldn't have been bored?"

"I know, it's pathetic. If I wanted to see him at all, I'd have to stand in a wet, cold blind all day, handing him telephoto lenses."

"But you'd've gone anyway?"

"What can I tell you." She made a face. "We're at that stage."

Rose felt a stab of pleasure for her; sympathetic excitement. She might be getting old, but thank God she could still enjoy her loved ones' romantic prosperity. "Do you think it will work?" And she could ask questions like that now, and Anna would answer, shyly—still getting used to telling secrets again—but without the slightest sign that she thought they were too personal or none of Rose's business. A sea change.

"Well, I guess that depends on what you mean by work."

"I guess I mean *last*."

"Oh, Rose. I don't know. I want it to—but I always want it to, and it never has before. I'm afraid to hope."

"But where does that get you? You should never be afraid to hope. I say that at the risk of sounding pompous."

"That's nice, but tell me, does that optimism spread as far as Fontaine and Luca?"

Rose groaned. "I don't know why I didn't see that coming." She put her elbow on the bar and her cheek on her hand.

"What, you don't think they'll live happily ever after?"

"Oh, dear lord. I hope they live happily through the honeymoon."

"Really. Now, see, I think they've got a shot. She's young, he's sensible. She's sweet, he's adorable. And the baby's an angel. What's not to work?"

Rose smiled. Anna was only disagreeing with her, she suspected, because she liked the novelty of reversing their optimist-pessimist roles. "I hope and pray," Rose said fervently, "that you're right and I'm wrong."

"Ah, here it is. Look what I got. I hid it so Vince couldn't find it."

"Why?" It was a bottle of Jacopo Poli, beautiful, the frosted miniature globe a work of art.

"Because it's just for us. To toast." She slipped two brandy snifters from the new overhead brass rack—the old wooden one was too smoke-blackened to save. "Want an ice cube? I'm having an ice cube, I don't care. How can you drink this stuff at room temperature?"

"I thought you hated grappa."

"I'm coming around. It's an acquired taste and I'm acquiring it." She filled two glasses and handed one to Rose. "Okay, well." She was self-conscious all of a sudden. "To the new Bella Sorella. Better than ever. To the grand reopening. And—to us."

"To us."

They sipped the crisp, intense brandy, hummed over it, held their glasses to the light, talked about wholesale prices, and what Vince had said about ice-cold grappas replacing neat vodkas as a new, fashionable drink with young people. Then Rose said, "Speaking of being afraid to hope. I used to be. For this."

"What?"

"You and me, sitting here together, toasting an enterprise. Not only without antagonism, but with . . ." She paused, searching for a word that wouldn't scare Anna to death.

"Yeah," she said, before she could find it. She came around to the front again, pushing her stool aside with her stockinged foot and leaning against the polished wood bar. Their forearms touched. "Me, too. I never pictured this, to tell you the truth. I might've wanted it, but I'd never have hoped for it. I'd've thought the odds were bad, and I hate losing." She leaned over to put her nose close to a bowl of scentless chrysanthemums, a leftover party decoration. "Rose?" She swirled the ice cube in her glass and took another small sip of grappa. "Thanks."

"For what?"

"For letting me come home."

She laughed. "*Letting* you."

"Thank you for not giving up a long time ago. Even though I gave you plenty of good reasons."

"Oh no."

"You could've written me off a hundred times. Nobody around here would've blamed you."

That was sweet, but Rose didn't want apologies. "Don't be so hard on yourself."

"Don't be so nice to me. I haven't forgotten anything you said. That night at my house. You said a lot of true things."

It seemed so long ago. "All I regret," Rose said, sighing, "is the time we wasted. I'm getting very miserly about time." She liked the look of their side-by-side images in the mirror. Without her glasses, she could only see two dark-haired, narrow-faced women with big black eyes. One young, one old. "I've thought of the new name for the restaurant," she said.

"You what?" Anna stopped staring back in the mirror and faced her. "No, you haven't. This close to the reopening? Rose, we don't have time! Oh, you're kidding. Aren't you?"

"I know, it's absurd, the timing couldn't possibly be worse. But I can't help it, it just came to me tonight. What it has to be, what it absolutely has to be."

"*What?*"

"But," she said hastily, "if you don't like it, that's fine—just because I thought of it doesn't mean we have to use it."

"Right, okay—*what*?"

Then she didn't want to say it out loud. Superstitious or something. She reached for a pencil on the bar and wrote it on a cocktail napkin. ROSEANNA.

What did Anna do? She laughed. With surprise at first, surprise and delight, but then her laughter went low and knowing, as if at an old joke she knew well but still loved. A laugh of recognition.

Funny, Rose thought, that's just how she'd felt when the name came to her—as though it wasn't new at all. As though it had been there all the time.

"Well?" she said when Anna's laughter finally sighed to a stop. The suspense was gone, but she still wanted to hear the verdict.

Anna used the napkin to blot her eyes. "It's perfect. And it's so obvious."

"It's so obvious. But I couldn't have thought of it any sooner."

"It wouldn't have been perfect any sooner."

It had to grow into itself. *They'd* had to grow into it. Germinate, ripen, and flower, Rose thought. She was feeling a little drunk.

"Roseanna. Roseanna," Anna said, experimenting. "Wow, it's sexy. It's Italian, it's very womanly. It's sophisticated, but it's also sort of... homey. Isn't it? Warm. Roseanna will take care of you."

"It doesn't leave anything out." That was the thing.

"And just think, Rose, you'll get free drinks for life. Is it the Roseanna Restaurant? Café?"

"It's just Roseanna."

"Yes. It's just Roseanna. Let's toast."

They touched glasses again. "Roseanna," they said, and drank to themselves.